The GUARDIAN

Other Books by
GERALD N. LUND

The

GUARDIAN

A NOVEL

GERALD N. LUND

DESERET
BOOK

SALT LAKE CITY, UTAH

Library of Congress Cataloging-in-Publication Data

Lund, Gerald N., author.
  The guardian / Gerald N. Lund.
     pages   cm
  Summary: Thirteen-year-old Carruthers "Danni" McAllister receives an enchanted pouch as a birthday gift from her grandfather, which she must use to save her family from the deadly extortionist known as "El Cobra," who is holding her family for a $20 million ransom.
  ISBN 978-1-60907-246-9 (hardbound : alk. paper)
  1. Kidnapping—Fiction.   2. Magic—Fiction.   3. World War, 1939–1945—France—Fiction.   I. Title.
  PS3562.U485G83 2012
  813'.54—dc23   2012034549

Printed in the United States of America
Worzalla Publishing Co, Stevens Point, WI

10   9   8   7   6   5   4   3   2   1

To Jewell G. and M. Evelyn Lund,
whose love of books left their posterity with a legacy
which continues to bless, enliven, and enrich the
generations who followed

PROLOGUE

In the Rhine Valley
Near the border between France and Germany
Friday, October 13, 1871

She felt their presence long before she could see them. And what she felt was so dark and so horrible it sent shudders through her body. She knew what they were after, and she knew what they would do to get it. Though her lungs were on fire and her legs were ready to give out on her, she took her daughter's hand in hers and pulled her gently forward.

"Only a little further, *ma chérie*," she whispered. "Then you will be safe."

Though confused by the events of the last half hour, the girl still had the presence of mind to notice that her mother had said, "*You* will be safe," not "*We* will be safe."

"No, Mama, don't leave me."

Faintly on the morning air, they heard the baying of dogs.

Holding tightly to her daughter's hand, the mother broke into a stumbling run, plunging into the welcoming thickness of the forest ahead of them.

When they reached the top of the low ridge five minutes later, they stopped to catch their breath. They stayed within the deep shadows of the trees, but from their vantage point, they could see the whole sweep of the narrow valley below. At the far end was a cluster of homes surrounding the white steeple of the village church. Most of the homes had roofs of red tile, but here and there, a few were covered with thatch. Square patches of emerald-green vineyards were enclosed by meadowlands speckled with milk cows and stacked with round bales of hay. Farther on, forested hillsides were already splashed with the brilliant colors of autumn.

Below them to the left, about a kilometer away, they could see their own little homestead. The outbuildings crowding the thatched house looked like piglets nuzzling up to their mother for breakfast. The smoke from the breakfast fire rose in a nearly vertical line against the deep blue of the sky. It was a picture of beauty and serenity.

Except for the dark figures swarming around the house. There were half a dozen of them. Several carried rifles. Others held back hunting dogs that were straining at their leashes.

Two men burst out of the house, dragging a figure between them.

"Papa!" the girl gasped. She buried her face in her mother's shoulder and began to cry.

Her mother held her daughter close, keeping her from seeing the torch arc upward, flipping over and over until it landed on the roof. Moments later flames began to spread through the thatch, sending up billowing black smoke.

Reaching out, the woman took her daughter by the shoulders and shook her gently. "Angelique! You must be strong, *ma chérie.*" Her grip tightened. "Your father would want you to be strong."

Sniffing back the tears, she nodded.

The mother watched as the men formed up and started along the path that led in their direction. She could make out the dark form of a man lying on the ground near the front of the burning house. The mother kept her daughter turned to face her. "Listen to me carefully, child. We're going to split up now and—"

"No, Mama!"

She shook her gently. "You must do as I say. Continue on this trail. In about two kilometers you will come to a village. Go around it. Do not go through it. Let no one see you."

"The men will hurt you, Mama. They think you are a *sorcière,* an *enchanteresse.*"

"Angelique!" Her voice was sharp with urgency. "There is no time. I will lead the men deeper into the mountains, but once they realize you are not with me, they will come for you. It is you they seek. You are the one with the gift. You must be far away by then."

The girl started to cry again, but the urgency of their situation left no time for comfort. "At the bottom of the hill, you will come to a small creek. Walk in the water for as long as you can. The creek will lead you to a river. When you come to the river, turn north. Soon you will come to a bridge. Cross into France and follow the signs for Strasbourg. Before you reach the city, you will see a narrow road between two vineyards. Watch for the sign for Le Petit Château."

Finally the girl realized that nothing she could say or do would deflect her mother from trying to save her life. "Yes, Mama," she whispered.

"Follow the sign. Before you reach the village, you will see the château off to your left. Go there. Ask for Monsieur Alexandre Chevalier. When you find him, tell him your name and the names of your parents."

"But, Mama, our name is Chevalier."

The baying of the hounds was growing louder. "Alexandre Chevalier is your grandfather. You have not seen him since you were a little baby, but you will be safe with him."

"But, Mama—"

"Shush, *ma chérie*. Now, give me your coat so the dogs will follow me."

The girl hesitated, then she removed her coat and handed it to her mother.

"Hurry," she said. "Hurry as fast as you can. That will keep you warm." She turned toward the valley. The dogs had the scent now, and their masters had turned them loose. They were coming at a full run and would enter the forest in moments.

Mother and daughter hugged tightly for a few moments, then the mother pushed Angelique away from the embrace. From beneath her coat, she withdrew a cloth pouch.

Surprised, the girl gave her a strange look. She had seen her mother and father take the pouch from a locked chest beneath their bed once or twice, but she had never seen it up close. She only knew it was something they both treasured, though they never spoke of it in her presence.

It was a square piece of cloth, about the width of her mother's hand. Seeing it in the morning light, she realized it was actually one long, rectangular piece of heavy cloth. The fabric was of coarse weave, light brown, plain, and folded in thirds. The first two folds had been stitched together to form a pocket, and the final third folded over in a flap that covered the entire front of the pouch. A hand-carved wooden button kept the pouch closed.

A lighter band of fabric ran across the width of the flap, just above the button, and was stitched in place with dark thread, leaving a short fringe above and below. Across the band, a faint design had been embroidered with a thread that matched the fabric. A braided rope handle formed a loop long enough to go over the shoulder. The fabric was worn in spots and looked quite old.

"Take this," her mother said, thrusting it at her.

Angelique took it. "But it's Papa's, Mama." She ran one hand over the flap and the hidden design. "What is this here?"

"There's no time for that." Her mother shook her gently. "The pouch is yours now. Your father planned to give this to you tonight, when we celebrated your thirteenth birthday. I'm sorry. We could have explained so much more if there had been time. Guard it well, Angelique. Never let it out of your sight. The men are after this, as well as you."

"Is there money in it?" She could already tell there was nothing bulky inside the bag.

"Its value does not depend on what it carries, but who carries it."

"But it is only an old pouch," her daughter said. But even as she spoke, she put the strap over her shoulder and held the pouch tightly to her chest.

"Go quickly, my child. Do not stop. Do not even look back. *Que Dieu te garde.* Go with God."

Without another word, she turned away. Dragging Angelique's coat on the ground behind her, she broke into a trot, turning onto a narrow path that moved higher up the ridgeline.

Angelique watched for a moment, tears streaming down her face, sure that her heart would break even as she stood there. Then she turned and started running.

She knew that this day, her thirteenth birthday, which had started out so wonderfully, would be the last day she would ever see her mother or her father again.

———————

Angelique did more than just give a wide berth to the first village she came to. Anytime she saw someone in the distance, either ahead of her or behind, she slipped off the road into the trees, or hid in nearby bushes. Sometimes, to her surprise, she sensed when someone was coming before she either saw or heard them. She recognized how odd that was, but in her urgency did not think much about it. Though the sun had warmed her body, her feet were still like blocks of ice from walking in the creek for nearly an hour.

Her feet were sore; hunger twisted her stomach. Her family had been cooking breakfast when they heard the men coming and she and her mother had fled. She wanted desperately to sit down and rest for a time, maybe beg a loaf of bread and some cheese from some kindly farmer's wife, but the fear she had seen in her mother's eyes drove her on.

Finally, an hour after crossing the river, her step slowed. Vineyards lined both sides of the road as far as she could see. She could make out a small wooden sign up ahead on a post. Looking around to make sure she was alone, she increased her pace.

A huge sense of relief swept over her when she drew close enough to read the sign. There were three words—Le Petit Château—and an arrow pointing left. She had no sooner turned off the road when a man stepped out of the vineyard about fifty meters ahead of her. She stopped, unconsciously holding the pouch tightly against her body, her heart hammering in her chest. She glanced over her shoulder, poised for flight.

"Bonjour," the man called. He raised a hand in greeting, but came no closer.

"Hello," Angelique answered after a moment. He was far enough away that he was not directly threatening to her, yet she didn't want to keep going and have to pass him.

"Are you the one I am supposed to meet?" the man called. His voice was rich and kind. It was hard to tell at this distance, but he looked like he might have gray hair and a beard. His clothes were those of a farmer, not someone of importance.

"Pardon?"

"I know," he said, laughing softly. "It sounds strange, but about a quarter of an hour ago, I had a strong impression that I needed to come here to the Strasbourg road, that there was someone I was supposed to meet here."

That took her aback. But she was still suspicious; her mother's warning had been very specific. "What is your name, monsieur?" she finally called.

"Alexandre Chevalier. And yours, mademoiselle?"

For a moment, she didn't believe her ears. Could this really be? Then, as a great rush of relief washed over her, she said, "I am Angelique Chevalier. I believe I am your granddaughter."

———————

Le Petit Château, France
Friday, June 7, 1940

It was one of those early summer days that make the world seem glorious. Everywhere the eye turned, the scenery was splashed with a thousand shades of green. Birds flitted from tree to tree. The soft hum of bees was everywhere. The sky was such a brilliant blue that it seemed it might overwhelm the earth.

The château itself, barely large enough to warrant the name, was surrounded by meadows on three sides. Today, Pierre LaRoche, master of the manor, was in the largest of the meadows, cutting the first crop of meadow hay. Watching him swing his scythe back and forth with effortless grace, one might have wondered why a healthy man in his early thirties was not in the French army, fighting for his country. But from a distance, one could not see his twisted leg, crippled when he was seven years old by a bull's swinging horn. That injury, and a farm deferment, kept him home with his little family. His wife recognized it for the blessing it was; he harbored a nagging sense of guilt that he was doing nothing for his country.

But on this day, the war was coming to them. Though his rhythmic movements never stopped, he kept looking up, searching the azure-blue expanse and cocking his head to better hear the distant rumble of thunder. Thunder on a day when there were no storms in the sky.

He stopped, stretching his back for a moment, then looked around for his son. Jean-Henri was by the stone wall separating the meadow from the vineyard. Immersed in some game of his own making, the small boy had a stick and was tracing the patterns of the stone masonry.

"Jean-Henri?"

The boy turned. *"Oui, Papa?"*

"Stay on this side of the wall."

"Oui, Papa." He went back to his tracing.

Pierre LaRoche was the fifth generation of his family to work this land. His third great-grandfather on his mother's side, Alexandre Chevalier, had come to this beautiful little valley, purchased ten hectares from the village elders, and started construction of a small château made from a stone quarry on the property. The village elders were so impressed at having their own local château, they renamed the village Le Petit Château.

During the last hundred and fifty years, the château had expanded a little, and the amount of property had doubled. Being near the Rhine River, a natural boundary between Germany and France, meant that the area went back and forth between the two nations, but that made little difference to the villagers. For them, life did not change much.

Until now.

Nine months ago, Adolph Hitler had sent the German army

across the border into Poland and put a new word into the vocabulary of war—*Blitzkrieg*—the lightning war. Bypassing traditional fortifications and racing ahead with tanks, artillery, and supporting infantry, he invaded Finland, Denmark, and Norway in quick succession, leaving Europe reeling. And just a month ago, the Nazi Panzer divisions rolled into the low countries of Belgium, Luxembourg, and Holland. The German eye was on a much bigger prize—France. Holland surrendered in five days, Belgium in eighteen. France was still holding on, but four days ago, word had come that Paris had been bombed and French forces were in retreat everywhere. There was already talk of surrender.

Yesterday, the war took on a new reality for the citizens of the Rhine Valley. The Panzer divisions simply bypassed the vaunted Maginot Line—a string of forts, bunkers, and tank traps along the Rhine—then turned south to encircle the rest of France.

Pierre glanced to the northeast. The rumbling sound seemed to intensify. A frown creased his forehead, bringing a shadow to his dark eyes. What did all this mean for little villages such as his? Would they become German, or remain French? For centuries the citizens of the area had adapted to their different masters, and much of the population spoke both languages. But the stories coming out of the war zones were alarming. If only half were true, this was going to be a different kind of occupation, and even the smallest villages might be in for terrible times.

He sighed gloomily, checked on Jean-Henri once more, then lifted his scythe again.

About quarter of an hour later, Pierre again stopped his work. The artillery was silent, but from the north there was a deeper sound. *Crump! Crump!* Moments later he thought he felt the ground tremble beneath his feet. Bombs! Big bombs. War was approaching, and it was coming fast.

His ear caught another sound. It was faint, and for a moment he thought it was only the hum of the bees. He glanced around. Jean-Henri was about fifty meters away, sitting by the well near the château. He was poking at something with his stick, totally engrossed.

Looking up and around, Pierre tried to focus on the sound. It was more distinct and quickly growing louder. Then he saw it. An airplane was moving across the sky, north to south, no more than a kilometer or two away. He peered at it, squinting against the light. The silhouette was easily recognizable—thin fuselage, glass canopy, inverted gull-wings, and two landing gear struts with wheels attached to the undercarriage. It was a Junker JU 87, better known by its nickname Stuka—an abbreviation of the German word for dive bomber. Though the war had been on less than a year, the Stukas had become one of the most feared and hated weapons of the German war machine.

Now Pierre understood the deeper explosions. It was the Stukas going after individual targets with deadly accuracy. As he watched, the airplane banked right and started coming straight at him. He dropped the scythe in horror and spun around. "Jean-Henri! Run! Hide!"

As he turned back, he was startled by how rapidly the plane was growing in size. He could see the blur of the propeller and the sunlight glinting off the canopy. The sound of the engine was growing louder every second. It was a beautiful sight in one way, and for a moment he was mesmerized by it.

"Pierre!"

The shout from his wife jerked him around. She had come out the front door of the château. Her face was upturned, and she held one hand up to shade her eyes. To his surprise, he saw that she had the pouch clutched to her chest.

"Get down, Monique!" He waved his arms like a madman. He was gratified to see her leap off the porch and crouch down behind the stone steps. At the same moment, he saw Jean-Henri scamper be-hind the well, which was also made of heavy stone masonry.

He broke into a lunging, awkward run, still shouting and waving his arms. As he ran, he looked over his shoulder. The plane was huge now, and coming at him with breathtaking speed. It was about two hundred meters above him, but coming in a shallow dive. He saw yellow flashes from each wing. Instantly the hammering of machine guns followed, almost swallowed up in the roar of the engine.

He flung himself to one side. Rolling three or four times, barely aware of the roughness of the ground, he looked up in time to see two lines of geysers—mud, dirt, and grass spouting upward—coming di-rectly at him. The sound of the heavy caliber bullets hitting the earth was like the vicious snapping of some horrible monster, but the noise was so rapid it almost blended into one continuous blast of sound.

Throwing his hands over his head, he buried his face in the grass as the bullets passed by him on the left and right, missing him by two or three meters on either side. As they ripped past him, he leaped up, looking around frantically for his wife and son. But he had no sooner started to get up when some giant's hand swatted him from behind.

He flew four or five feet through the air, then landed hard and rolled over and over. He ended face up, staring dazedly at the empty sky. His ears rang; it was like he had suddenly been wrapped in a cocoon.

Where was he? What had just hit him? He turned his head. Directly to his right, a dark shape was climbing almost straight up, rapidly diminishing in size. It took him another second or two to realize that the Stuka had pulled out of its dive just as it had passed over Pierre. It was probably no more than fifteen or twenty meters above him, and moving at close to five hundred kilometers per hour. The blast of its wind stream had knocked him rolling.

Trying to get to his feet, Pierre only made it to his good knee. Everything seemed to be spinning around him. He was confused and disoriented. Finally, he regained sufficient presence of mind to re-member his wife and son. He raised his head, looking toward the château. There was no sign of his wife. That was good. He registered that the twin tracks of ripped up earth did not lead toward the house, but went straight across the meadow. That was good too.

Impressions were coming faster now. He glanced up. The Stuka was a black speck high in the sky, but as he watched, it gracefully arched over and started another dive, this one nearly vertical. He gaped in horror. Again he tried to get up, and this time he managed to get fully to his feet. He swayed back and forth, looking around wildly.

What he saw sent a chill through him colder than the coldest of winter blasts. Directly ahead of him, about forty meters away, Jean-Henri was coming out from behind the well. He was facing away from Pierre. His head was tipped back, moving slowly from side to side as he scanned the sky. For a moment, Pierre wondered if his son had been injured somehow. Then it hit him. He was looking for the Stuka.

"No!" he cried and broke into a hobbling run.

Jean-Henri didn't hear him. His total focus was on the sky, and he was moving out into the meadow where the trees wouldn't block his view.

"Run, Jean-Henri!" It was a primal scream, but even as he shouted it out, he knew the boy couldn't hear him.

One of the unique things about the Stuka dive bomber was that its designers had included a siren in the craft to add to its psychological effect on anyone on the ground. As the plane's speed increased, the siren came on, and it sounded like the scream of a wounded banshee.

No! A dive that steep meant the pilot was going to bomb them.

Yelling, shouting, sobbing, Pierre stumbled and went down. Scrambling up again, he pushed himself harder. But he knew with a horrifying reality that he would not reach his son in time.

He stopped and cupped his hands. "Run, Jean-Henri! Run!"

Why wasn't he running? Why was he standing there, looking up at the aircraft coming straight at him? Pierre wanted to close his eyes. He wanted to drop to his knees and pray. He wanted to leap across the entire distance and knock his son out of the way.

Somewhere in the back of his mind, he realized that Monique was screaming too. Out of the corner of his eye, he saw her running, her dress billowing, her long dark hair flying out behind her. She had the pouch in both hands as she ran, holding it high, as if to ward off the black shape hurtling toward them.

And then, to Pierre's utter astonishment, Jean-Henri did the unthinkable. With the Stuka coming straight at him in a black blur, he raised one hand and waved at the pilot.

Pierre raced forward, his eyes fixed on the bottom of the fuselage, watching for the long dark shape of the bomb to break free and start its own peculiar scream as it fell toward the ground.

But the guns never fired. Nothing dropped from the plane. About three hundred meters up and a hundred meters out ahead of their son, the plane suddenly pulled out of its dive, flashing over their heads so fast they momentarily lost sight of it.

Gasping, Pierre whirled around.

As the Stuka pulled away, rapidly disappearing into the blue sky, it waggled its wings. Once. Twice. Then a third time.

The pilot was waving back!

Half an hour later, Pierre still had not returned to cutting hay. He sat on the steps, shoulder to shoulder with his wife, their hands tightly clasped. Jean-Henri was playing a few feet away. He had two small plastic airplanes, a gift from his grandmother. One was in each hand as they dove at each other in a mock dogfight.

"Enchantement," Monique said finally, half under her breath. The old pouch was in her lap, and she stroked the embroidery with one hand.

"What did you say?"

She turned. "Don't you remember what your mother said on the day of his christening?"

"I do, but I have never believed in enchantments or protective spells. That was just her way of giving him a grandmother's blessing."

She gave him a sidelong look, but said nothing. She looked down at her lap. She traced the embroidered letters on the flap with one finger. *"Le Gardien,"* she murmured, not looking at him.

"It *was* a little miracle," he said, "I grant you that. But that doesn't mean it was some kind of magic. It's more likely that when the pilot saw Jean-Henri waving to him, he was reminded of his own son—or brother, or nephew—and pulled up just in time."

She was watching her son. "If that is what you wish to believe, then believe it."

"But you don't." It wasn't a question.

"I know what my eyes saw."

"You are a dreamer, my love," Pierre said. He leaned over to kiss her.

Just before their lips touched, she pulled back and smiled. *"Enchantement,"* she said again. Then she kissed him back, squeezing his hand all the tighter.

PART ONE

Danni

CHAPTER 1

Hanksville, Utah
Friday, June 13, 2008

This is the personal journal of Carruthers Monique McAllister.

But if any of you guys ever call me Carruthers, KAPOW! You'll be wearing a black eye for the rest of your life. Just wanted to make that clear.

Actually, everyone calls me Danni.

I know. It makes no sense at all, but I'll explain in a minute.

Today is Friday the 13th. And today is my 13th birthday! How cool is that?

But my birthday party isn't until tomorrow. ⁀" I really, really wanted to have it today, but there's no way Mom would let me have a party on Friday the 13th. She said we can't tempt the fates. When I asked her what that meant, she just shook her head. But she wouldn't budge. My birthday party is tomorrow. CRAZY!!!

Don't get me wrong. I think Mom is way cool. But she has friggatriskaidekaphobia. That means she's scared of Friday the 13th. I found that on Google. Grandpère says they must

17

have invented Google just for me because I'm always asking questions and want to know everything. He's right. I love
Google!!

Grandpère doesn't believe in this whole bad luck thing
and went ahead and gave me my present today. It was this
journal. Mom was all right with that as long as I waited until
tomorrow to actually start writing in it. I didn't say anything,
which she took to mean I agreed. Too bad for her.

At dinner, when Mom wasn't looking, Grandpère slipped me
his pocket flashlight and a couple of extra batteries. So that
explains why right now I'm writing under the covers in my bed.
Glad he included extra batteries, 'cause I've got a lot to say.

Okay, let me tell you about Grandpère. He's my grandfather (Mom's dad), and he has lived with us since my
grandmother died of a stroke five years ago. His name is
Jean-Henri LaRoche. It's French. Oh, and BTW, it's not
pronounced Jeen Henry, like we'd say it in English. It's Zhahn
Ahn-ree. But we all call him Grandpère. (You say Grahn from
the back of your throat, like you are going to spit. BTW, I
think Grandpère is a waaay cooler name than Grandpa.)

As I said, my full name is Carruthers Monique McAllister.
I was named after my mother and my great-grandmother,
Grandpère's mother. My mom's full name is Angelique
Carruthers LaRoche McAllister. (It's easy to fall asleep be-
fore you get through saying that. Ha-ha.) The other side
of Mom's line comes from Ireland, and their last name was
Carruthers, so that became her middle name.

When I was born, Mom decided she wanted me to represent both the Irish and French sides of our heritage, and
thus my name. But why, oh why, did she decide to make
my first name Carruthers? Ugh! Sometimes Mom can be seriously weird. Not in a bad way. But seriously! I mean, really?
Carruthers? It totally sounds like an Irish pub. Not cool!

Fortunately, Dad solved the problem. When I was little, Dad always used to sing me Irish songs to get me to sleep. His favorite was "Danny Boy." He sang it to me almost every night. And one night, when I was three, when he finished, I sat up in bed, pointed to myself, and said, "I Danny Boy." From that point on, I've always been Danni to my dad. He changed the "y" to an "i" so it looked more feminine (and so Mom didn't freak). Even now, he keeps reminding her "Danni" is as Irish as "Carruthers."

Dad only calls me Carruthers when I'm in trouble. Mom never calls me anything <u>but</u> Carruthers.

So anyway, I'm Danni McAllister. I'm thirteen years old (as of today). I have my mom's dark hair, but Dad's green eyes and some freckles. Dad calls them leprechaun kisses, and Ricky thinks they're cute. That helps.

Oh, who's Ricky? Ricky is Ricardo Manuel Luis Ramirez, my best friend—but only his dad calls him <u>Ricardo</u>. We didn't start out being friends though. We hated each other in elementary school. When I was in the fourth grade, Ricky—who was in the fifth grade—found out my name was Carruthers. He thought that was so hilarious he started telling everybody about it one day in the school cafeteria. When I gave him and two of his buddies bloody noses, he went back to calling me Danni. And so did everyone else. ⌣

Our middle school is in Bicknell, which is about sixty miles from Hanksville. Since his house is the second bus stop from mine, we sit together every day. I have a lot of other good friends, but none of them are as good a friend as Ricky.

Anyway, back to me. I am exactly five feet three inches tall. I hope I'm still growing, but Grandpère thinks this is it. My favorite food is peanut butter pizza. (Just kidding!) It's actually cheese enchiladas and fried ice cream. My favorite color is light purple (lavender, my mom calls it), and my favorite hobbies are reading, hiking, camping, and riding four-wheelers. I love taking our ATVs up into the Henry Mountains near our home to search for old Spanish gold mines. Sweet!

I live on a small ranch on the north side of Hanksville, Utah. We have a few head of cattle and grow some of our own hay. It's the greatest place on earth to live. There are national parks and monuments all over the place down here. And Lake Powell. We have jet skis and a houseboat we share with another family. I <u>love</u> Lake Powell. It's the greatest.

As I said, my mother's name is Angelique. (That's pronounced Ahn-zhel-eek, not Angel-leak.) I think it's an amazing name. Especially for her. She is very beautiful, with long black hair and gray eyes. She speaks fluent French because when she was growing up, Grandpère and Grandmère spoke French in their home. She was raised in Boulder, Colorado, where Grandpère taught French literature at the University of Colorado.

Mom loves beautiful things, and often dreams about living someplace like Paris or London. I tell her she ought to be a fashion model. She just says, "Oh, you!" but I can tell she likes it when I say it.

———

"Carruthers?"

I jumped like a snake had been dropped down the back of my shirt. I turned off the flashlight, slammed my journal shut and stuck it under the pillow, then threw back the covers just as Mom opened the door.

"Are you all right? I thought I heard someone talking in here."

I gulped. I always talk to myself when I write. "Umm . . . no, Mom, I'm all right. Really. I can't sleep." I gave her a big smile, the kind which always gets me out of trouble.

She came in and sat down on my bed. Absently, she reached across and pushed one strand of hair away from my face. "Do you hate me for making you wait until tomorrow for your party?"

"No." Disappointed, yes, but I could never hate my mom. "It's all right." I squeezed her hand. "Really, it's okay. But why won't you and Cody come camping with us tomorrow?"

She laughed softly. "Because my idea of roughing it is having to adjust the air conditioning unit in a hotel room by hand. Maybe next time."

Yeah, right. Not in my lifetime.

She stood. "Daddy called awhile ago. He was in Price. He said he'll be home around eleven."

I glanced at the clock: 10:41. "Did he get my new cowboy boots?"

"He didn't say, but I'm sure he did."

"Tell him to come in and see me, even if I'm asleep."

She smiled down at me. "I won't have to."

Getting to her feet, she bent down and kissed me on the forehead. "Happy birthday, Danni."

My eyes opened wide. *Danni?* Did my mother just call me Danni? Then I saw the smile behind her eyes. This was her way of saying she was sorry about the party. I raised half up, threw my arms around her, and gave her a hard squeeze. "I love you, Mom."

"And I love you too, Carruthers. More than you can ever know."

I laughed. I guess one Danni was all she had in her. She blew me a kiss, moved back to the door, and reached up to turn off the lights. She dropped her hand. "I'll leave this on," she said. "May as well write in your journal at your desk and save Grandpère's batteries for when you really need them."

"I . . . umm . . . my journal?"

She laughed aloud. "I may be superstitious, but I'm not blind. You can write until your dad comes home, then it's off to bed. Promise?"

"Promise," I said. As she closed the door, I threw the covers back and climbed out of bed.

———◆———

Okay, so that was so totally cool. Mom just called me Danni. That may be the first time ever.

I've already told you a little about Grandpère. He was in born in France. He is very tall—over six feet—and wears a little French goatee. It's cute. His hair is black too, but starting to turn gray around his ears. He always wears a French beret when he goes out. Since everyone around here wears cowboy hats—well, except for one or two—some people have taken to calling him Grand<u>beret</u> instead of Grandpère.

After World War II, Grandpère's family came to America and settled in Boston. That's where he met the Carruthers family and my grandmother. (BTW, when Grandmère died, that was the saddest I have ever seen my grandfather.)

I have only one sibling, my little brother, Cody. He's ten, has red hair, and ten tons of freckles. All my friends think he's wickedly adorable. Not me. My dad's first job after getting his doctor's degree was in Cody, Wyoming, so Mom named him for the city. I keep telling Code (that's what I call him) that he's lucky they weren't living in Albuquerque. Or Butte, Montana (ha-ha).

After Cody was born, Mom couldn't have any more kids. Cody and I fight sometimes, but not as much as we used to. He's way smart and helps me on the computer sometimes. And he loves math. (I tell him that's because Mom dropped him on his head when he was a baby.) He's a funny kid. And fun, too. And he's got a smile that makes me laugh even when I'm so mad at him I could spit. But for a kid—and especially a boy—he's okay.

My dad—or <u>Papa</u>, as they say in French—is the funnest

and best dad anywhere in the world. He's amazing! He and I are really close and do everything together. His name is Lucas McAllister. Guess what his nickname is? Not Luke. Everyone calls him Mack, just like they do his father, Grandpa Mack. Except Mom never calls him Mack or Luke. She always calls him Lucas. She thinks Lucas and Angelique sound musical together.

Dad grew up in Butte, Montana. Grandpa Mack was a mining engineer at the copper mine there, but they lived on a small ranch outside of town. That's how my dad became a cowboy. He went to college in Colorado and Michigan, and now he's a mining engineer consultant. BTW, I was born in Michigan while Dad was getting his—

Hey! Dad's truck just turned in to our lane. Gotta go!

CHAPTER 2

"Hey, Danni!"

I looked up. It was just after ten the next morning. The battered old Ford F-150 pickup was just pulling into the front yard. Charlie Ramirez, Ricky's dad, was driving. Ricky was beside him in the cab. He was waving as they pulled up.

I slapped a couple of strips of tape on the last of the crepe paper and left the rest for Mom to fix. It was her thing anyway, not mine.

Ricky jumped out of the truck, holding his backpack and sleeping bag in one hand and a present wrapped in light purple paper in the other. "Thanks, Dad," he said.

"Yeah, thanks for letting Ricky go camping with us, Mr. Ramirez," I called. I really meant it. I never thought he would let Ricky be gone for two whole days. Ricky's mother had left them some time back, so he had a lot of responsibility tending his two younger sisters and helping with the family's small farm.

Charlie Ramirez gave me a quick nod; he wasn't much for

long conversations. He looked at Ricky. "Ricardo, you help Mr. McAllister. And mind your manners."

"Yes, Papa."

With a wave, Ricky's dad drove off again.

When I turned to Ricky, he had a grin as wide as the state of Utah. He looked a little goofy, actually. But that was all right. I'm guessing I did too, because I was ready to jump up and down. Ricky was at my birthday party *and*—unbelievably—was going camping with us.

"Our stuff's over there by the truck," I said, motioning toward the barn. "Dad doesn't want us to pack it in until he's here."

Still grinning, Ricky trotted over and tossed his stuff on the pile. In a minute he was back, still carrying the present. He stuck it out at me like he was eager to get it over with. "Happy day-after-your-birthday, Danni."

I slugged him. "Chill! You don't have to tell everyone that." I took it. "But thanks for remembering."

"Remembering what?"

"That lavender's my favorite color."

"It is?"

I slugged him again, only this time harder. He just laughed.

He turned and called out to where Mom and Dad were blowing up balloons and Grandpère was putting candles in the birthday cake Mom had ordered special from Mrs. Oliver in town. "Hi, Mr. and Mrs. McAllister. Hi, Mr. LaRoche."

They waved.

Squinting in the bright sunshine, we surveyed the yard. Spread out beneath the large cottonwood tree in front of the house were several decorated tables. One was filled with presents, one had the cake on it, and all of them had balloons and crepe paper decorations.

"This all your idea?" he asked as I set down the lavender-wrapped present on the table. "Thought you said it wasn't going to be anything special."

"This is my *Mom's* idea of not anything special. She even bought party hats for everyone. *Hello!* You'd think I was six or something. Fortunately, Dad and Grandpère vetoed that idea."

"Your Mom's funny sometimes." Seeing the look on my face, he added quickly, "But she's cool, too."

"Yeah, in a really strange sort of way." I picked up the scissors and tape, and motioned for him to move to the next table with me.

Rick was still watching my parents. "Everyone thinks your mom and dad are great, you know. They're so different," he said, wistfully, almost talking to himself. "It's great that they love each other so much."

I watched Ricky out of the corner of my eye, sensing what was behind that statement. Ricky's dad is Hispanic—his grandparents were from Guatemala—but his mother was pure California girl. He got his dark black hair and deep brown eyes from his father, but his fairer skin and facial features from her. (All my girlfriends think he looks like a really young Antonio Banderas.)

I'm not sure how his parents ended up in Utah—Ricky's never said—but I know his mother hated it here. A year or so ago, she called Mr. Ramirez and their children together one night and announced she was leaving. Ricky said his dad was so shocked that all he could think of to say was, "But what about the kids?" With Ricky and his two sisters standing right there listening, her answer was, "If we go to court, it will be to decide who *has* to take them, not who *gets* to keep them."

Ricky doesn't talk about it anymore—he refuses to say anything bad about his mother—but rumor in town is that Hanksville and the isolation out here wasn't the only reason she left. They say she was ashamed to be married to a Hispanic.

As far as I know, the family's never heard from her since she left.

So I wasn't surprised that he'd watch Mom and Dad and feel a little envious.

He was giving me a strange look and I wasn't sure why. "What?"

"Some people in town say that one morning we'll wake up and your family will just be gone."

I jerked up. "Who said that?"

"Sheesh, Danni. It wasn't me. Don't take my head off."

"Well, it's not true."

"Uh . . . well, the story is, your mother only agreed to come here because your dad was trying to get a start as a mining consultant. She said she'd stay no more than five years."

"Yeah, and that was eight years ago."

"So it's not true?"

I began to sense what was behind all this. "It is true. When my parents first came to Hanksville to look at the land that was for sale, Mom kept saying, 'No! No! No!' She's from Boulder, Colorado—a university town renowned for its quality of life, its culture, education, and art. The greater metropolitan area of Boulder holds about a quarter of a million people." I made my voice sound like I was reading off a brochure.

Ricky laughed. "Heck," he drawled, "we've got twenty-seven hundred people in our county alone. That's a little over one person per square mile. Bet Boulder can't match that."

Laughing, I pulled a face. "I think that was part of the problem. But she knew how much Dad wanted to do this, so she agreed to stay."

"What happened to change her mind?"

"She got to know the people. And there are so many beautiful places around here for her to paint. Oh, she'd still love to be in a big city somewhere, but now she says she wants Cody and me to finish school here. She agrees with Dad that this is a great place to raise kids."

I could see the relief in his eyes, and it touched me to think he'd been worrying about us—me—moving away. He turned away, a little embarrassed. We were quiet for a time, both of us watching my parents.

When Dad thought Mom wasn't looking, he snitched some frosting off the cake. She caught him at it and slapped his hand. His answer to that was to put some frosting on her mouth, then kiss her.

"You don't know how lucky you are, Danni," Rick said quietly.

I turned in surprise. "Yes, I do," I said. Then, embarrassed that my eyes were suddenly burning, I jumped up. "Let's get this over with and get out of here."

"I'm for that," he said with a grin. "Except for the cake. Don't rush the cake part."

I slugged him again.

"Ow! How come girls get to hit boys, but boys can't hit back?"

"'Cause that's the proper order of the universe."

To prove it, I gave him the scissors and tape and told him to finish up with the decorations while I got something from the house.

I watched him walk away from me, thinking about how strange it was that we were such good friends. We have nothing in common except for our dark hair and slender builds; we look enough alike that we could be brother and sister. Actually, in the details, he comes out much better than I do.

But we really are different. I'm brash and opinionated; he thinks everything through carefully. I'm bossy; he's easy to get along with. I love to read and learn things; he loves to work with his hands, take things apart and fix them. I'm a motormouth; he's quiet. Except when we're not around other people. Then he talks a lot. Like seriously, he goes on and on forever. And, though you'd never know it, he's a terrible tease.

My friends keep giving me a bad time about Ricky being my boyfriend. He' not. He's just my best friend who just happens to be a boy. If he was my boyfriend that would ruin everything.

CHAPTER 3

"Happy birthday, dear Danni. Happy birthday to you."

As the singing stopped, everyone started clapping and hollering.

"Blow out the candles," Tanner Kingston called out.

"Yeah. Show us how many boyfriends you have," Marti Benson added.

Then Lisa Cole just had to do it. "There's only *one* boyfriend. Right, Ricky?"

I glared at her, then shot a quick glance at Ricky. His ears were bright red, and he was pretending he hadn't heard. Lisa's my second best friend, but she can be such a pain sometimes. If she keeps saying stuff like that, I might have to send her to the bottom of my list. Maybe off it completely.

Bending down, I took a quick breath, then blasted all thirteen candles out with a single puff. *So there, Miss Lisa Smarty Pants.* I glanced at Ricky again. He was visibly relieved.

Then someone gasped and people started hollering again. I fell back a little. One of the candles was on fire again. How had I missed that one?

"Danni's got a boyfriend! Danni's got—"

I blew out the candle again before anyone else could join in with Lisa. Then to be absolutely sure, I licked my thumb and forefinger and pinched out the wick, pretending it was Lisa's nose.

I saw Grandpère watching me, his eyes twinkling with that mischievous look he sometimes got. So that was it. It was Grandpère. "It's one of those trick candles that you can't blow out," I explained to everyone. "Right, Grandpère?"

He shrugged.

And at that precise moment, the stupid candle burst into flame again. I jumped and gave a little yelp. Everybody thought that was hilarious. They were clapping and yelling and stomping their feet. Before Lisa could start in again, I jumped up, ripped the candle off the cake, and dunked it in the nearest glass of punch. There was a momentary sizzle and a wisp of smoke. Not wanting to take any chances, I held it there for another moment.

"Ah," Grandpère said soberly, "that should do it."

To my surprise, Mom stepped forward to stand between me and Grandpère. "Stop it, Dad," she hissed, really angry at him. Then, turning around, she forced a bright smile and clapped her hands once. "Okay, everyone. Find a chair. Before we have cake and ice cream, Carruthers is going to open her presents."

As everyone scrambled for seats, I glanced at Grandpère. He smiled, gave a little bow, and snapped his finger. I was still holding the candle in the punch, and to my utter astonishment, the wick burst into flame again. I pulled it out. It was still burning brightly. I ducked it into the punch a second time, but it kept right on burning, making a gurgling sound and little smoke bubbles in the punch.

I looked at the others, but they were already moving away. Except for Ricky. He had come up right beside me and was staring at the smoking cup of punch with eyes bigger than a couple of paper plates.

I turned back to Grandpère. "How did you—"

He could look so innocent at times. At other times he was like a little boy caught putting a frog in his sister's bed. Right now, his expression was a combination of both. He gave me a sad little smile, did another little bow, then blew me a kiss. The very instant he did so, the candle sizzled and went out. And this time, it stayed out.

The presents were nice, but predictable. Grandma and Grandpa Mack sent a new sweater and skirt. Lisa and three of my other friends went in together on a buckskin vest, which I loved. Ricky got me a new hat to go with it. (I guess they told him what they were doing.) Cody got me the table game Hilarium.

When Mom handed me her present, I knew immediately what it was, and suppressed a groan. From the size and shape of the box, which was wrapped in purple paper, I knew right away that it was a new dress. And she'd probably thrown in a couple of training bras too. Great! In front of everybody. Ricky leaned forward so he could see better, which wasn't helping. Pretending to fumble a little as I tried to open it, I lowered the box to my lap, hoping maybe I could ditch the bras under my chair without anyone seeing.

However, to my surprise, inside was another box; and in that one was another box, and then another. And then my jaw dropped. I squealed so loud it probably startled the cattle out in the pasture. It was a new cell phone. I couldn't believe it. Mom and I had been fighting for the last three months over whether I was old enough to have my own cell phone, and she hadn't budged an inch.

I leaped up and threw my arms around her. "Thank you, Mom. Thank you, thank you."

"You're welcome," she said. Then she pulled me closer. "Had you scared, didn't I?" she whispered. "You thought it was a new dress."

I laughed right out loud, then hugged her tighter. "You're the greatest, Mom. I love you so much."

"And I love you, Carruthers." Eyes dancing with anticipation, Mom placed her hands on my shoulders and turned me around. "I think it's your father's turn now."

Dad was at the other end of the table, but to my surprise, he held nothing in his hands. His expression was apologetic, almost sorrowful. I felt a sinking feeling. Where were my cowboy boots?

"Danni, I . . ." He looked away. "Those boots you wanted were sold out. I'm so sorry."

I managed a smile of sorts. "That's all right, Dad. You tried."

"I can either give you the money, and we can look for them the next time we go up to Salt Lake City, or"—he reached behind the table for something—"you can have this instead."

For a split second, my brain wouldn't register what my eyes were seeing. Then I gave another shriek. I dashed around the table to where he stood, holding out a rifle in both hands.

"Is that mine?" I cried. I was vaguely aware of the oohs and aahs sounding all around me. "Is that really mine?"

"Yep. It's a Winchester—"

I cut him off. "I know, I know. A Winchester lever-action, repeating rifle. It's a copy of the original Winchester Model 1873, the gun that won the West." I caressed the stock, loving its cool smoothness. I turned and sighted down the barrel at the barn. "Oh, Dad. Thank you so much. I love it."

Mom joined us and laid a hand on my shoulder. "Carruthers, you know how I feel about guns. But I also know that when you're out camping or with the cattle, there are rattlesnakes and coyotes and other things that can be a problem. So I told your father I wouldn't object. But you have to promise me that you'll be very, very careful. I never want you shooting it around the house or anywhere near town. Or going hunting just to kill things."

"Yes, Mom."

"Anytime it's in the house, it stays locked in the gun cupboard. And you never bring it into the house when it's loaded. And—"

"Geez, Mom, all right. I get it."

I was instantly sorry as I saw her face fall. Then I felt the rifle jerked from my hands. I turned to see my father, just inches away from my face.

"You want to reconsider what you just said there, Danni?" he said in a low voice. My dad rarely got angry, and mostly it was when Cody and I were sassy to Mom, and this was one of those times.

"I . . . I'm sorry, Mom."

"That's not an apology, Danni," he said. "That's closer to an insult. Your mother didn't say one thing that I don't fully agree with, so let's try that again."

Face flaming, keenly aware of everyone's eyes on me, I went over to her. "I'm really sorry, Mom. You're right. I'll do everything exactly as you said. And I appreciate you letting me have it." I meant it this time.

For a long moment, she looked into my eyes, searching. Then she smiled. "Good. Then happy birthday."

Dad returned the rifle to me. He brought out a leather case for it, and everything was all right again. "Grandpère's gathered up a whole garbage sack of empty pop cans," he said, "and I've got two cartons of shells in the truck. We'll stop along the way somewhere and let you and Ricky do some target shooting."

———

It took another hour before everyone left and we had things cleaned up and put away. While Ricky and I loaded our personal gear into the truck, Dad and Grandpère saw Mom and Cody off for Salt Lake. Mom was going shopping and had promised to take Cody to two movies if he would go with her instead of with us.

By the time Dad and Grandpère joined us, Ricky and I had made us a comfortable spot on a couple of sleeping bags in the back of the truck. We would ride there until we left the highway, then we'd get inside the cab to avoid eating dust the rest of the way.

"Where are we going, Grandpère?" Last night, I had asked Dad that question, but all he would say was that Grandpère had planned the whole trip and I would have to ask him.

"Our main destination is called Horseshoe Canyon," he said, "but we'll make other stops along the way."

"It's part of Canyonlands National Park," Dad added, "but it's a detached area to the northwest of the park. It's pretty remote."

"Good. I like remote. And what's there?"

"If I were to tell you," Grandpère answered, "that would spoil the surprise."

"Have you been there before, Mr. LaRoche?" Ricky asked.

"Nope." He winked at me. "But Danni's not the only one who loves Google."

⬤

We turned off the highway about twelve miles north of Hanksville, and Ricky and I got into the truck. Then we headed east, kicking up billowing clouds of red dust as we went. We made slower time on the gravel road, of course, but after half an hour, Dad let the truck roll to a stop. Ricky and I were playing a game on my new cell phone. We looked up in surprise, because Dad had told us we'd be at least an hour before we reached the canyon. There was a long sand dune off to our right, but nothing else in sight.

"Why are we stopping?" I asked.

Dad turned around. "Do you want to learn how to shoot that rifle or not?"

I shot up so fast I cracked my knee on the seat in front of me. *"Serious?"*

———— ◆ ————

The next hour was one of the best ever. Dad had brought along his old Marlin bolt-action .22 so Ricky could shoot something too. Grandpère lined up the cans along the sand dune, and, after ten minutes of safety instruction and some pointers on shooting, we went at it.

It really grated my cheese that it took me almost a full magazine of shells before I hit my first can. And all the while, Rick was popping them off like they were the size of a barrel. It was all I could do to restrain myself from reminding him that this was my birthday, not his. The brat!

But after an hour, I could hit eight out of ten consistently, which helped wipe the smirk from Ricky's face.

We tried shooting some cans while they were in the air, which only proved that Hollywood and reality are miles apart. The movies make it look so easy, but even Dad could only hit a can about half the time. And he's good.

In fact, that was my final humiliation. As we were ready to pack up, Dad asked if he could try my rifle. When I handed it to him, he filled the magazine to the full—seventeen shots. Then he stepped out ahead of us, and surveyed our shooting range. By now, the cans were scattered everywhere. Didn't matter. Jacking shells into the chamber as fast as he could pump the lever, he hit seventeen cans in a row, sending them skittering across the ground.

As we started off again, I made myself two promises. One, by the end of the summer, I would be a better shot than Ricky. Two, by that same time, I would duplicate that feat of Dad's, preferably with Ricky there to see it.

About twenty minutes later, as we were bouncing along a particularly bad stretch of washboard road, Grandpère suddenly pointed to the right. "There it is," he said. "Turn here, Mack."

Startled, my dad slammed on the brakes and slid to a halt. Off to our right, another dirt road headed south. There were no signposts. "Uh . . . Grandpère," Dad said, "the turnoff to Horseshoe Canyon *is* to the right, but not for at least another five miles or so. We're not there yet."

"I know. But first we go here."

Dad glanced back at Ricky and me.

I leaned forward over the seat. "What's down there, Grandpère?"

"The Cottrell Cabin."

"Ah," my father said.

Ricky and I exchanged looks. "The Cottrell Cabin?" I asked. "What's that?"

Grandpère turned around. "You probably know it by its other name—Robbers Roost."

"Oh," Ricky said. "Yeah, I know about that. That's where Butch Cassidy and the Sundance Kid hung out with their gang after they robbed banks or held up trains."

"Exactly right," Grandpère said. "Well done, Rick."

I scowled at him. What was this? A "Let's show Danni how much better I am than she is" contest? Had he forgotten this was *my* birthday party? I decided to show him I was above such petty attempts to show off. "What's there, Grandpère?"

"Not much. Just the remains of the old cabin."

"You're the boss, Grandpère," Dad said as he put the truck in gear and we started rolling again.

When I thought Grandpère wasn't looking, I caught Ricky's eyes and mouthed, "Boring!" But when I turned back, Grandpère was staring at me, and it was clear he was disappointed.

"Danni," he said, "in this life, there are no uninteresting things, only uninterested people."

Face flaming, I started to mumble an apology, but then suddenly a strange, eerie feeling came over me. My skin started to crawl. I jerked around, expecting to see someone coming up behind us. But there was nothing. Yet the feeling only deepened. For a moment, I wondered if we were in some kind of danger.

"I don't want to go," I blurted.

Dad hit the brakes, and we came to a stop. He turned around. "Why not?"

"Something's wrong. I don't want to go there."

Grandpère turned around fully to look at me. "What are you feeling, Danni?"

A little shiver ran up and down my back. "I don't know. Something spooky all of a sudden, and it's creeping me out. It has something to do that cabin."

For a long moment, Grandpère peered into my eyes, then he slowly nodded. "Okay, Mack. I've learned what I wanted to know. Let's skip Robbers Roost and head for Horseshoe Canyon."

CHAPTER 4

On the rim of Horseshoe Canyon, San Rafael Desert
Saturday, June 14, 2008

It is 7:35 P.M. We're setting up camp near the trailhead to Horseshoe Canyon, which is our destination tomorrow. I'm writing in my journal now because Dad says that since it's my birthday, I don't have to help. We're about a million miles from nowhere. We haven't seen another vehicle or person since we turned off the highway. The only thing out here that isn't a natural part of this barren, empty landscape is one of those dark brown, smelly National Park Service toilets, and a small wooden sign confirming that we were now in the Horseshoe Canyon Unit of Canyonlands National Park. That's it. No trees, no shade, no water. No nothing. You bring what you need, or you do without. Sweet!

I don't have a lot of time because Grandpère says there's no overnight camping in Horseshoe Canyon, so we have to leave early tomorrow so we can get in and out in one day.

It's been a fun day. My birthday party was good, and the shooting practice was awesome. But one weird thing happened. After we finished shooting, Grandpère wanted to go to this place called Robbers Roost, but as soon as we turned off the road, I had this awful feeling that something was wrong. Weird, right? I'm getting as bad as Mom, I guess. Later, I asked Ricky if he had felt anything, but he said no. But the minute we turned around and left, the feeling was gone again. So I—

"May I join you, *ma chérie?*"

I looked up in surprise. I had been concentrating so intently on my writing that I hadn't even heard Grandpère come up beside me. Without waiting for my answer, he sat down on the sleeping bag. I looked around. Dad and Ricky were by the truck, talking about something.

"Is supper ready, Grandpère?"

"Not for a few more minutes." He looked at my journal and smiled. "So you've started writing in it already."

"Actually last night." I grinned. "Under the covers. Mom caught me at it."

"Yeah, she told me. Said I was a corrupting influence on you."

"She's always known that, Grandpère."

"You're right about that. Good thing she loves me."

"You look tired, Grandpère."

"*Oui.* I am feeling my age."

"You're not old, Grandpère," I said gallantly. "You're only seventy-four."

He laughed softly as he touched my shoulder, pulling me closer.

Scooting a little on the bag, I slipped my arm through his. "Thank you for all this, Grandpère. It's been the best birthday ever."

He leaned back on his elbows and closed his eyes. I watched him for a moment, studying the lines of his face, the neatness of his goatee, the wrinkles around his mouth and eyes. There might be sixty years' difference in our ages, but I felt closer to him than I did to any of my friends. Even Ricky. Crazy—but totally cool as far as I was concerned.

"Grandpère?"

His eyes opened.

"Why did you want to take us to Robbers Roost anyway? If it's important, we can stop there on the way home tomorrow."

He sat up again, turning to face me more squarely. "A question first. What do you think it was that you were feeling out there?"

"Umm . . ." I chewed on my lower lip for a moment, something I always did when I was thinking hard. "I'm not sure. But I didn't like it."

What he said next caught me off guard, because it seemed like he'd forgotten his question. "Hollywood, with their usual gift for playing loose with the truth, glorified Butch Cassidy and the Sundance Kid. They turned them into these fun-loving guys who never hurt people if they could help it. But that isn't true, Danni. The men that came out here to hide were vicious outlaws and cold-blooded killers."

His expression was suddenly far away. "One of the realities of life, Danni, is that there is evil in the world—evil men, evil women, evil influences. To think otherwise would be to leave ourselves vulnerable."

I still wasn't sure what he was trying to say, and he evidently saw that in my eyes.

"I wanted to see if you would feel anything out there." A slow, almost sad, smile followed. "But I didn't expect you to while we were still miles away."

"That's why you wanted to go there?" I blurted in dismay. "To see if it spooked me?"

"Danni, yesterday you turned thirteen years old. In the Old

Country, that means you are no longer a child. You are a young woman. It is time that you begin preparing for that."

I liked the idea that I was no longer a little girl, but Grandpère's words were still bugging me. "Did you want to take me there specifically to see if I felt something?"

"I wanted to go there to see if you have the gift, Danni."

I rocked back a little. "The gift? What gift?" I suddenly felt like I had ants crawling over my skin again.

"I believe that what you sensed today was a lingering presence of the evil that once was here." He leaned closer, peering into my eyes. "Not everyone can feel that, Danni. Especially not from such a distance."

The ants were joined by goose bumps on my arms. But strangely, it wasn't an unpleasant feeling, like before. It was more of a tingle of excitement, a thrill of wonder.

"It is a gift, Carruthers, and you must learn to trust those feelings when they come."

I looked up, surprised. He never called me Carruthers. "Did you feel it too, Grandpère?" I finally asked.

He nodded. "Not nearly as clearly as you did, but, yes, I felt it too." He reached out and gently touched my cheek with the back of his hand. "Don't ever dismiss such feelings as meaningless. Give heed to them, and they will be a protection to you in your life."

I wasn't sure what to say. Or how to respond.

"Remember the rattlesnake?" he asked softly.

It took me a moment to remember. I hadn't thought of it for a long time. Two or three years ago, our family was coming home from a camping trip after celebrating my birthday. As we pulled up in front of the house and got out of the car, I stopped dead in my tracks. "We can't go in, Daddy," I said. "Something's wrong."

At first, he laughed it off, but Grandpère took it seriously. Me and Mom and Code stayed outside while they went inside to look. Someone—probably me—had left the back door open a crack. Inside the house, under Cody's bed, they found a four-foot-long rattlesnake.

"Are you saying . . . ?" I stopped, not sure how to ask my question. But just then, Dad and Ricky came back to join us.

"Hey, you two," Dad said. "Dinner's almost ready. Let's eat."

"I'm famished," I cried. I started to get up, but he shook his head, glancing at the journal. "No, today we serve you. Go ahead and finish writing. We'll be just a few more minutes."

———

I have to quit now. Supper will be ready in a few minutes. Just had a long conversation with Grandpère. Much to think about. Some of it leaves me feeling uneasy. But what I thought was weird before makes more sense now. Can't explain now. Will try to write later.

But one good thing. I am thirteen years old as of yesterday, so I am no longer a child. I am a young woman. And I have a gift. No, not a gift—THE gift!!! (I wonder what it is.)

———

With supper done and cleaned up, we sat around the fire for a while, talking and laughing. Dad has a whole string of what me and Cody call "daddy jokes" which, for some reason, he feels compelled to drag out whenever he gets around a campfire. Mom calls them "groaners." They are so dumb that you can't help laughing at them, even as you groan.

"Did you hear about the man whose sister gave birth to twins—a boy and a girl?" Dad began. "She asked her brother to name them, so he called them Denise . . . and Denephew."

Ricky didn't help, because he thought that was hilarious. His laughter only encouraged Dad. "Did you hear what happened to the cat that crossed the desert on Christmas day?"

I groaned. How many times had I heard that one? Rick, trying to smother his laughter, said, "No. What?"

"He got Sandy Claws." Dad was trying to keep a straight face, but he couldn't. He was like a little kid telling knock-knock jokes. Once he got started, he never ended. He was actually snorting as he laughed. "One more. A man and his wife were visiting Hawaii. On the beach, they noticed an older gentleman who looked like a native. The man went up to him. 'Excuse me,' he said. 'I was wondering if you could tell us the correct way to pronounce the name of your state. Is it Hawaii, or Havaii?' 'Havaii,' the man said without hesitation. 'Thank you,' the tourist said. 'You're velcome,' came the reply."

"Please, Dad," I cried, making a gagging motion with my finger. "No more. I can't stand it." But Rick was holding his stomach he was laughing so hard. I gave him a hard poke. "Come on," I said. "It wasn't *that* funny."

Grandpère stood up. "I think you just passed my limit too," he drawled. He yawned. "I think it's time to turn in. We've got a long day tomorrow. The Grand Gallery is about three hours in, and it will be hot by afternoon, so we'll want to get an early start."

"You're not going to tell us what the Grand Gallery is, are you?" I asked.

He smiled. "Discovery is one of the greatest joys of the human mind."

I had expected nothing less.

"Okay," Dad said. "Let's turn in. Danni, you want first shot at the toilet?"

My face flamed. "I'm in no hurry," I lied. I was actually getting pretty desperate. It had been a long time since our last stop. "Ricky can go first."

To my surprise, Ricky dropped to one knee, bowed low, and then did one of those little rolling motions with his hand, like people do when they're greeting royalty. "You first, m'lady," he said gallantly.

"Chill it, Ramirez," I sniffed haughtily. Royalty indeed. But my body was shouting at me to stop being an idiot. So I stuck my nose in the air and proceeded toward the small brown building, walking with as much dignity as possible under the circumstances.

CHAPTER 5

Horseshoe Canyon, Canyonlands National Park
Sunday, June 15, 2008

We left the trailhead just after sunup and descended about eight hundred feet into Horseshoe Canyon. There, the canyon was pretty wide, but as we moved south, going deeper into the canyon, things improved. Great red cliffs began to close in on us, towering above us like fifty- or sixty-story buildings.

When we came around a bend in the wash, the canyon straightened out for a stretch about the length of a football field. And there it was, the biggest and longest set of rock art I had ever seen. This had to be the Grand Gallery. For almost the entire length of the right side of the cliff, the whole rock face had sheared off millennia ago, leaving what looked like a gigantic, nearly smooth "white board" on which the ancients had come to paint.

As we gazed in hushed amazement, Grandpère spoke. "I would suggest we explore what is before us individually and at our own pace. Afterward, we can get together and discuss it as you wish." He immediately set off, waiting neither for an answer nor compliance.

———

I chose to walk swiftly along the whole length of the Grand Gallery, not waiting for the others. I wanted to get an overview of the place before trying to take in the details. At first, I took out my cell phone and snapped a couple of pictures, but as I moved along the Gallery's length, photography was quickly forgotten and I shoved my phone back in my pocket.

Our family loved to find Native American rock art sites—and there were hundreds of them in our area. But the vastness of this collection was unlike anything I had ever seen, not only in size but in scale. As I walked the length of the cliff face, I counted nearly sixty humanlike figures, most of which were bigger than life, seven or eight feet tall. One monster high up on the wall had to be twenty or twenty-five feet tall. And the "canvas" itself was immense, at least two hundred feet long and forty or fifty feet high, ten times bigger than anything I had ever seen before.

When I started to retrace my steps, I paused to study each figure and the surrounding details. Most of the images were of strange, humanoid creatures. Strange because most had no legs or arms. The bodies were shaped like long, narrow bottles—kind of like gigantic test tubes—with a head perched on the top. Others had—

"Tell me what you're feeling right now." Grandpère spoke behind me, making me jump. I had been so engrossed in the art, I hadn't heard him come up behind me.

I turned around. "What?"

"Are you feeling anything here, Danni?"

I considered that for a second or two, focusing inward. "A sense of awe," I finally said. "Even reverence. It's amazing."

That seemed to please him. "Maybe that's why the Ancient Ones chose this place. It's like painting a great cathedral, or the Sistine Chapel."

"Yeah," I said. "That's it. It's like it's a temple."

He smiled, then he moved off again.

As I continued on, I was intrigued by his question. Some of the humanlike figures looked strange, almost like aliens. Or mummies. That was actually a better word. They looked like mummies wrapped for burial. That would explain why they didn't have any arms or feet.

I was surprised to realize that even looking at a bunch of mummies, I felt uplifted and inspired. It was so different than what I had felt yesterday when we spoke of Robbers Roost.

Moving on, my eyes flicked back and forth. There were strange-looking creatures. A few of the heads had eyes and mouths, but some faces were blank. Some heads had horns; others had rabbit-like ears. I even saw one creature that looked like it had an antenna sticking out of its head. Amused, I wondered if he was some early form of an iPod or MP3 player.

Scattered among these "humans" were various animals—snakes, birds, rabbits, small dogs, and what looked like antelope or mountain sheep. I laughed out loud at one drawing of three animal figures. Two looked like antelope with stick heads and long straight horns. The other looked like a goat, or maybe a sheep. But all the bodies were large and fat, way out of proportion to their heads and horns. They looked like round barrels with stick legs. But that wasn't what made me laugh. Directly in front of the largest of the animals was one of the "bottle men," only he was tiny, not even half as tall as the sheep. He was holding a bow with an arrow notched in the string, pointing it directly at the sheep's head.

"Hey, little guy," I murmured, "if you manage to kill that thing, just how do you plan to get it home to the wife and kids?" I took out my phone and snapped a picture of him. As I did so, a thought popped into my mind: *They were people, just like you.* But of course they were. Why then the odd thought?

I studied the little man, wondering if this was a self-portrait. And then I understood. He was no different than my dad—out trying to put food on the table for his family. And I bet he loved his wife, and played with his kids, and maybe sang them to sleep at night. Even though these ancient ones were thought to have lived two thousand years ago, they were very much like us.

Looking around, I saw Grandpère a few dozen feet away. I cupped my hand and called softly. "Grandpère?"

He immediately came over to me. Hearing me, Ricky came over too.

"Yes?" Grandpère said. "Do you have a question?"

"I do," I said. "Why do you think the figures look so strange?"

"Perhaps they only look strange to us."

"I think they look like aliens from outer space," Ricky said.

"I think they look like mummies," I said.

Grandpère was thoughtful. "Some people believe we've had aliens come to earth and that ancient people thought they were gods. Do you believe that?"

We both shook our heads. "No way," Ricky said. "Too far out."

"So why would they paint mummies on the walls, do you think?"

I had already asked myself that question. "Maybe this was an old burial ground."

"In a riverbed? Not likely. Think about *who* the mummies represent more than *what* they represent."

That drew a blank from both of us.

"Let me ask you another question. Each Memorial Day we put flowers on Grandmère's grave—why do we do that?"

"To remember her," I said.

"And why did we put a gravestone over where she's buried?"

"So you know where she is," Rick said.

I looked up again, a thought stirring. "So if these are mummies, then maybe they represent their ancestors. And this is their memorial to them."

Very serious, Grandpère turned to face us. "Danni, when Grandmère died, do you remember what you said at the viewing, as you stood by her casket and looked at her body? You were nine at the time."

"I said, 'This isn't Grandmère. Where did Grandmère go?'"

"And what did I say?"

"You said she went to heaven. So she could look down on us and watch over us."

He looked up at the wall and the figures painted there. "Maybe these people also believed that the ones they loved didn't really die either, that only their bodies did."

Ricky's mouth was a big O. "They painted them up here on the wall so they could look down on them too, right?"

Grandpère smiled, clearly pleased. "We don't know for sure, but I like that idea."

CHAPTER 6

We had lunch in the shade of the cliff, near where we would re-join the path that led back to the truck. We found a place where the sand was soft and not too rocky. We talked a little about what we had seen and the feelings we had, but mostly we were content to sit together in the profound quiet of the canyon.

When we finished eating, Dad suggested we take a quick nap before we headed back. We cleaned up any trash we had dropped and stretched out.

———

I woke a half an hour later when Ricky sat up and stretched. I also sat up.

"Sorry," he whispered. "Didn't mean to wake you."

"No apologies," Dad said, sitting up as well. "It's probably time we started back." He looked at Grandpère. "Are you ready?"

Grandpère was already sitting up, and I couldn't see any sand on his shirt. Had he even laid down? "Would we have time for one more thing?" he asked. Then he grinned. "Well, actually, two more things?"

"Of course," Dad replied.

As Grandpère leaned forward, I was amazed at his energy and determination. If he was tired from a short night in a sleeping bag and three and a half miles of hiking, it didn't show.

"I'd like to share another story with you, if I may." He reached up and stroked his beard, as was his habit when he was thinking deeply. "This story happened in Bluejohn Canyon, which is only a few miles up canyon from where we are right now. It is the story of a man named Aron Ralston."

I didn't recognize the name, and moved closer to Grandpère.

"Aron Ralston was an avid outdoorsman, mountain climber, and mountain biker. Late in April, 2003, Aron came to Utah to do some mountain biking and desert rock climbing. The place he chose was Bluejohn Canyon, a very narrow slot canyon with several vertical drops.

"Sometimes we grow overconfident in our own abilities—especially when we are experienced and think we are wise—and we forget to use common sense. That's what Aron did. He came alone. He brought only sufficient supplies for one day. And . . ." He paused, then finished softly. "And he did not tell anyone where he was going.

"He parked his truck at the Horseshoe Canyon trailhead—just as we did—and biked to the top of Bluejohn Canyon. His plan was to rappel down the canyon, hike back out to his truck, then drive around to the top of Bluejohn and retrieve his bike. Because he planned to be back that same night, he wore only a T-shirt, shorts, and hiking shoes. He had no jacket or extra clothing. In his backpack were two burritos, less than a quart of water, a small first-aid kit, a video and digital camera, and some rock climbing gear."

Though I wondered why Grandpère had chosen this place and

time to tell us this story, I was quickly becoming engrossed in his words.

"At first all went well, and Aron was exhilarated by the challenging climb. But about sixty feet from the bottom, he had to descend a narrow vertical shaft. As he worked his way down, he came to a place where rocks from above blocked the way. Known as chock blocks, one large one was nearly round and was tightly wedged between the narrow canyon walls. The only way to continue was to go over it."

"I remember this story," Dad murmured.

Grandpère nodded in acknowledgment and went on. "Using his climbing gear, he got on top of the rock, but as he was going down the other side, the boulder suddenly shifted under his weight, dropping another foot or two. As he threw out his right hand to catch himself, the boulder crashed down on his forearm and hand, not only crushing them instantly, but pinning him between the rock and the canyon wall."

You know how sometimes when someone shows you a cut, or when someone tells you about a bad injury they had, you feel this sudden spurt of adrenaline and you feel sick to your stomach? Well, that was what I felt at that moment. I had to look away.

Grandpère continued in a low voice. "The pain was horrific, of course, and he nearly fainted from the shock. However, he managed to assess his situation and tried to free himself. He tried moving the boulder with his body. It wouldn't budge. He used his small pocketknife to try to chip the stone away from his hand. The rock was too hard. He used his climbing ropes to try to move the stone even a little. It still wouldn't budge."

"Did he die there?" I asked, the queasiness in my stomach growing more pronounced.

Grandpère shook his head. "With deepening despair, he realized just how grim his situation was, and how foolish he had been to come without being better prepared, and especially without telling anyone where he was going. Bluejohn Canyon was so remote and such a difficult hike, he knew the chances of someone coming along and finding him were slim to none. And he knew there would be no search party, because no one knew where he was. And thus started what became a six-day ordeal."

"Six days?" I cried. The thought made my stomach churn.

"Oui." Grandpère looked up canyon, as if he was seeing all of this in his mind. "As the ordeal continued, his situation deteriorated quickly. He ran out of food and water. He began to have hallucinations. The pain would come and go in terrible waves. He was hot by day and cold by night.

"I would have been praying nonstop," Ricky whispered.

"He did some of that too," Grandpère said, nodding. "By the fifth day, accepting the inevitable, Aron videotaped a farewell message to his family, hoping someday someone would find him and the camera. Then he scratched his name, birth date, and the next day's date—the day he assumed he would die—in the softer rock of the canyon wall. He also scratched in RIP—rest in peace—like they put on gravestones."

Moments before, I had wanted Grandpère to stop, but now I was hanging on his every word. I had to know how the story ended.

"When he awakened on the morning of the sixth day, Aron prepared himself to die, almost welcoming the prospect because it would end his ordeal." Grandpère's head came up, and his eyes moved around our little circle. "Then something quite remarkable happened. Aron would later call it an epiphany, a vision of sorts. He saw a man he knew was himself walking down the canyon, then stepping into a sunlit living room. A three-year-old boy in a red polo shirt came running toward him. Somehow he knew that this was his son. When he bent down to scoop him up, he saw that the man's right arm had a prosthetic hand. He lifted the boy with his left hand and swung him up on his shoulder.

They were laughing together, and the man danced and twirled the boy around, steadying him with his good arm and stump.

"In an instant, the vision was gone. But Aron knew this was not just more delirium, and that knowledge gave him the courage to act. He had to live. If that vision was going to become a reality, then he had to survive. And he decided that the only way to free himself would be to amputate his lower arm and hand."

"No!"

I wasn't sure if it was me who cried out or Ricky.

"If he didn't, he would die," Grandpère said. "And then came another revelation. In his mind, he suddenly saw what he had to do to cut through the bones of his arm. Remember, he had only a dull pocketknife. He saw that if he twisted his body in a certain way it would create enough torque to cleanly snap first one bone, then the other. Which he did. Desperately fighting to stay conscious through the waves of agony, he then amputated his arm just above the wrist and freed himself."

"I remember when the story made the news," Dad said after a minute or two, his voice hushed. "I didn't realize it took place so close to where we were."

"Don't stop, Grandpère," I cried. "Did he make it?"

He nodded. "Actually, the end of our story occurred not far from where we are sitting right now." Grandpère took a quick breath. "Once he was free, Aron administered first-aid to his arm, then managed to rappel down the remaining sixty-foot drop using only one hand—an incredible feat considering his physical state. Then he started hiking the eight miles out to his truck. He was weak, exhausted, dehydrated, and in shock, but he hiked with surprising energy and vigor.

"A short time after passing through the Grand Gallery, he saw a family from Holland ahead of him, hiking back toward the trailhead. He called to them and asked for their help. That quickly led to his rescue."

With a twinkle in his eye, he looked at the three of us. "Any other questions?"

"What about the little boy?" I cried.

"Ah, yes. What about the little boy?" He leaned back. "A few years later, Aron married, and he and his wife now have a little boy with blonde hair, whose name is Leo. Aron, who was an engineer by profession, helped design a prosthetic hand for himself. It is a hand which he can also use when he's mountain climbing, which he still does on a regular basis."

"Wow!" Ricky breathed. "That's incredible."

"So," Grandpère said after a few moments, "are there lessons we learn from this story?"

"Yes," Ricky and I said together.

"What?"

We looked at each other, and I motioned for him to go first.

"Don't go out alone without telling someone where you are?"

"Yes. How many times do you think Aron wished he could have made that decision over?"

"Hundreds," I said.

"Indeed. What else?"

He looked at me, but I knew he was looking for more than the obvious, and I could tell Ricky had another answer. So again I deferred.

"Like you said," Ricky started, "even if we're really good at something, we can get overconfident and do dumb things."

That was true, and I realized that was a tendency I had to watch in myself. I prided myself on being independent, and I insisted on doing things my way, even if Dad or Mom warned me I might get into difficulty. But something else was stirring in my mind. And it had to do with Leo, Aron's little boy.

I raised a hand. Grandpère nodded at me. "I think Aron learned that there are things which were even more important than dying."

"Go on."

"Why not show him getting rescued, or in the hospital afterward? That would have given him hope. Or why not just show him how to break his bones so he would know how to cut off his arm? Why show him his little boy first?"

No one spoke. I wasn't ready to answer. I was still working through the implications of my question in my mind. Then Dad cleared his throat, and Grandpère nodded in his direction.

"Aron had lost the will to live. He had given up, remember? But seeing his future son restored his will to live. It was that vision that gave him the courage to break his arm and then amputate it."

"Exactement!" Grandpère exclaimed softly, using the French without realizing it. "After hearing Aron's story, someone wrote of his experience: *'There is no force on earth more powerful than the will to live.'* When he heard that, Aron added five more words: *'Except the will to love.'* He also said on many occasions that he believed there are higher powers around us that we do not recognize, and that sometimes we are able to call upon them for help."

As I watched Grandpère, I marveled. I thought we had come out here just to camp and have a good time. Now I saw that Grandpère had a few other things in mind. I wondered how long had he been planning to share this story with me on my thirteenth birthday. And why? Knowing Grandpère, he'd leave it up to me to figure it out. So I asked him a simpler question.

"What is his book called? I want to read it when we get home."

"Between a Rock and a Hard Place," Grandpère replied. "I recently bought my own copy. You are welcome to read that."

We all sat in silence, deeply moved by the power of the human spirit.

Then Grandpère stood up. "One more thing," he said with an apologetic smile, "and then we can go."

CHAPTER 7

Grandpère knelt beside his backpack and unzipped one of the pockets. When he stood again, he was holding a small, flat package wrapped in lavender paper with a crushed purple bow. "Carruthers Monique McAllister, would you come forward, please?"

Surprised, since he had already given me the journal, I did so. He turned me around so I was facing Dad and Ricky. "When I turned thirteen, my father, Pierre LaRoche—your great-grandfather—took me on a special camping trip too. There, deep in the forests of Maine, he gave me a present. And he told me that on his thirteenth birthday his grandmother had taken him into the mountains and given him that same present—a present she had received from her father and mother."

"Really?"

"We know for sure this item has been in our family at least a hundred and fifty years, and we think much longer than that. My great-great-grandmother on my mother's side, Angelique Chevalier, wrote about the day she received this gift from her mother on her thirteenth birthday. That was in 1871. She said it looked old at the time, but unfortunately, she wasn't able to learn more about this gift from her parents."

A present that was at least a hundred and fifty years old? Double sweet! I had visions of a priceless necklace, or some other family heirloom, and now I would be the one to receive it.

"So this gift doesn't necessarily pass from father to son?" Dad asked.

"No, there is no set pattern, either in the one who gives it or the one who receives it. It may even skip a generation if there is no child worthy to become the caretaker of the gift."

I looked up at him. "Can I open it, Grandpère?"

He extended the package to me. "Of course, my child."

His words were said with such solemnity that the urge to snatch the box from him and rip it open was instantly gone. I was no longer a child, but a young woman, and therefore, I could no longer act like a child. I carefully took the package from him, bowed my head, and said, "Thank you, Grandpère." I stood on my tiptoes and kissed him on the cheek, feeling his day-old stubble and smelling the trail dust on his goatee. "Thank you so much."

Even as I did so, however, I realized that what I was holding in my hands was not some piece of jewelry, or even something heavy or bulky. Beneath the wrapping paper, the gift was soft and pliable, and weighed very little. Keen disappointment washed over me. It felt like a sweater, or maybe a blouse of some kind. It was definitely something made of cloth. An old sweater? Hardly what one longed for.

Trying hard not to let my face show what I was feeling, I slid my fingers beneath the tape. I opened the paper and let it drop to the ground, staring at what lay in my hands. It wasn't a sweater. It wasn't clothing of any kind. It was just a piece of heavy brown cloth, about nine inches square. I stared at it for several seconds, not sure if this was another of Grandpère's little jokes or not.

I guess he sensed my puzzlement because he gave me a nudge. "Turn it over," he suggested.

I did so, and saw that it was a medium-sized purse, made from a single piece of cloth which had been doubled over on itself three times. The first two squares were stitched together to create a pouch. The last square was folded over in a flap that covered the whole front of the pouch.

To my surprise, the flap was not plain like the rest of the pouch. A band of lighter-colored fabric ran horizontally across the flap. The flap was fastened with a wooden button that had obviously been carved by hand. There was a long braided rope handle folded across the front of the pouch. Both the rope and the button were worn smooth, and the fabric also looked quite old. It was different, no question about that. But I was managing to curb my enthusiasm. *Whoopee! An old worn-out fabric purse.*

Grandpère laughed, startling me. "You are containing your disappointment much better than I did when I got it, Danni. I thought for sure I was getting a dagger with a jewel-encrusted handle, or some priceless coat of arms—something totally awesome, as you would say. When I saw what it was—or rather, what it wasn't—I think I pouted for a week."

"Danni," my father warned. "What do you say to your grandfather?"

I hugged him tightly. I wasn't mad, just disappointed. Then I realized that Grandpère was in his seventies, and I was just three days into being a teenager. It was not a surprise that we valued different things. "Thank you, Grandpère. I will treasure it always."

"I doubt that," he said, still chuckling. "But that will come soon enough."

I bent my head and examined the gift more closely. I saw something I hadn't seen before. Across the lighter band of material on the flap, an intricate design had been embroidered in silk thread that matched the color of the fabric exactly.

But then something else caught my eye. There were four smaller images on the flap, also embroidered, all identical to one another, in each corner. They were placed diagonally so that each one pointed inward.

I leaned in. These images were much smaller, not even an inch long. I recognized what they were immediately. I had seen the image—the symbol—many times. It consisted of three parts. A central shaft, narrow at the bottom, but expanding gracefully out into an elongated diamond shape, like the blade of a two-edged sword. On either side of the shaft were two more delicate shapes. Thin at the bottom, they swelled outward, but then curled over and drooped downward like the petals of a flower. At the bottom, the three elements were bound together with a thick band.

"It's a fleur-de-lis," I exclaimed. I looked at Dad and Ricky. "Each one of them is a fleur-de-lis."

Grandpère smiled. "Very good, Danni. Very good." Then he cleared his throat as though embarrassed. "Though *flur-de-leese* is the American pronunciation of the word. The proper pronunciation is *flur-de-lee.*"

"What's a fleur-de-lis?" Ricky asked.

Proud that I could answer, I said, "It's French for the 'lily flower,' or 'flower of the lily.' It represents a lily, or what we call an iris. These here are stylized representation of the flower. It's a very popular symbol in France." I looked up at Grandpère. "Wasn't it also a symbol of the French monarchy?"

"*Oui.* Indeed it was. And many other European royal houses. The fleur-de-lis can be found on countless shields and coat-of-arms."

"Really," Rick said, peering at them closely. "I've seen it before, but I didn't know what it was."

I turned back to Grandpère. "Are they on there because the pouch comes from France?"

"Perhaps. But the fleur-de-lis has many different connotations. It can represent royalty, purity, beauty, integrity, honor." He looked down at the pouch. "Many times the central part of the fleur-de-lis is softer and more curved, like the lily petal it represents. But notice that these look more like spear points. That's because sometimes the fleur-de-lis was attached to a long shaft to form a spear. The end was made of steel and sharpened to a deadly point. Often, such spears were used by royal guards as they stood watch outside the palace or at the city gates. So the fleur-de-lis is also a powerful symbol of protection or guardianship."

"I remember," I said eagerly. "You once showed Cody and me a picture of one of the guards at Versailles. We thought that was so cool we made our own spears with broomsticks and foil fleur-de-lises on the end of them."

Grandpère laughed softly. "I'd forgotten that." He nudged me a little. "Though the plural of fleur-de-lis is *fleurs*-de-lis, not fleur-de-leeses."

I could tell he was teasing, so I ignored that. I held out the pouch so Dad and Ricky could look at it more closely.

Ricky took it with an almost reverential awe. "This is seriously awesome," he said, almost in a whisper. "And it's how old?"

"At least a hundred and fifty years," I said.

"Probably more like two hundred, near as we can determine," Grandpère added.

"Wow! Two hundred years. Crazy!" I shook my head in wonder.

Dad laid a hand on my shoulder. "This is a very special and wonderful gift, Danni."

"I know." I turned back to Grandpère and gave him a hug.

He kissed me on the top of the head, then held me at arm's

length. "So are you going to just look at the outside of it all day? Or are you going to see what's inside?"

That surprised me. I had already felt the pouch with my hands, and I could tell there was nothing in it. But, eager to show my appreciation, I took it back from Ricky and undid the button. I lifted the flap and looked inside. Nothing! The bag was absolutely empty. I even ran my hand around inside it, but there was nothing there. I laughed. At him and at myself. "Good one, Grandpère. You got me on that one."

With that same solemnity he said, "Remember the candle from yesterday, my dear?"

My head snapped up.

"Never assume the fire is out, just because it is not burning."

It took a second or two for that to sink in. "It *was* you," I cried. I noticed Ricky's head had come up too.

It was like Grandpère hadn't heard me. "And don't assume that something is empty, just because there's nothing there."

Not sure if he was still teasing me, I dutifully looked again, this time opening the pouch to the sunlight and peering inside. As soon as I did so, I yelped in surprise. There was a pocket on the back interior of the pouch. And to my total surprise—more like shock, actually—there was a single sheet of paper inside, about the size of a 5 x 7 picture. How could I have missed that before?

Feeling a tingling sensation sweep through my body, I stared at the paper.

I heard Grandpère chuckle, then felt him nudge my arm. "It's all right to take it out," he said.

So I did. When my fingers touched it, I realized it was more than just a piece of paper. It was heavier, like card stock. As I pulled it out, I also saw that it was not pure white but a light beige. I turned it over and saw that the front of it was filled with lines of elegant, hand-lettered script. I read them quickly, then marveling, turned around and held the card up for Dad and Ricky to see.

"What does it say?" Dad asked, leaning forward.

Stepping back, I slipped my arm around Grandpère's waist. "It's titled *The Four Remembers of Life.*" I felt Grandpère's hand on my shoulder as I read the lines out loud.

"Number one: Remember, you are unique.

"Number two: Remember, there is purpose to your life.

"Number three: Remember, you are free to choose what you are and what you become.

"And number four: Remember, you are not alone."

We all stood in silence for a moment or two. Suddenly and surprisingly, I felt a tightness in my throat. I carefully slipped the paper back into the pouch and buttoned the flap. Then I looked up at Grandpère. To my even greater surprise, his eyes were filled with tears.

"Happy birthday, *ma chérie*," he said huskily. Then he kissed me on both cheeks in the French way.

I couldn't have answered him if I wanted to, so I just threw my arms around him and held him as tightly as I could. We stood there, at the bottom of Horseshoe Canyon, at least fifty miles from the nearest sign of any habitation, with two men looking on. And we had a good cry together.

PART TWO

Guardian

CHAPTER 8

Hanksville, Utah
Thursday, August 21, 2008

It's hot! ☹

I mean <u>seriously</u> hot. Even for Hanksville. When I came out of the house, it was like stepping into a blast furnace. I almost turned right around and went back inside and stayed in my bedroom. But Cody and his buds are playing Wii football in the family room. With Mom gone to Grand Junction to some interior decorator's show, and Dad in the mountains with a client, there's no one to make them shut up—certainly not me—and I couldn't stand it anymore. I checked the thermometer Dad keeps on the back of the garage—112 degrees! And that's on the shady side of the garage.

I'm down here by the river in my special place. Last year I found this place about a quarter of a mile from our house. There's this little clearing in a thick patch of willows and brush, with one large cottonwood tree nearby. By cutting back some of the brush, Dad helped me make a path, and he brought down the small wooden bench from the basement. There's plenty of shade, and the temperature is always about ten degrees cooler here. Best of all, no one can see me from the house or the lane, so it's my own little private place. Which I need right now.

School starts next Monday. I'm glad in a way. Except for our camping trip to Horseshoe Canyon in June, it's been a long summer. <u>Boring!</u> Ricky works all the time with Dad now, so I don't see him very much. And my other friends are driving me crazy.

Explanation. Last night, I had a sleepover with four of my friends—Lisa, Angie, Megan, and Brianne. I don't know what came over me when I had the idea—boredom, I guess— but Mom agreed that I could have it at our house because it's the last weekend before school starts. We had a lot of fun at first—we ordered pizza, and Dad fixed us root beer floats. Then we played games and watched a movie.

But as usual, when we finally went to bed, we started talking instead. I always feel like a third thumb when that happens. The other girls talk mostly about clothes and boys, and who's hot, and who's dating who, and who's making out, and who just had their first kiss. UGH!!! I mostly listened, hoping that Lisa or Angie wouldn't start talking about Ricky and me.

But they did, of course. Stupid little comments, snicker- ing to each other when they thought I wasn't looking. Teasing me about blushing whenever they talked about him. Blah blah blah.

I finally got so ticked off that I told them that first, Ricky and me were just friends and that there was noth- ing romantic about our relationship at all. (More sniggers and stupid giggles. Geez Louise!—that's my Dad's saying—you'd think they were a pack of three-year-olds.) Second, I told them that no matter what our relationship was, it was none of their business anyway.

Well, that shut them up, all right. But it also kind of threw a wet blanket on the party too. They all clammed up, and Lisa and Angie especially went into this huge freeze-out mode.

I guess to get even, Angie started in on the pouch.

See, when we got back home from our camping trip in June, I had Dad put up a nail in the wall next to my dressing mirror. I hung the pouch there, flap side out, where I would see it every day. I don't have any other pictures or stuff up in my room, but I was really proud of Grandpère's gift. And what he said that day—about the Four Remembers of Life—was kind of special too.

But I hadn't thought about the fact that my friends hadn't been in my bedroom for a long time. And I hadn't said anything about the pouch to anyone but my family and Ricky. So when everyone came into my bedroom, they started peppering me with questions about what it was and about the Four Remembers of Life, which Mom had framed and hung on the other side of my mirror. I tried to explain, but it sounded pretty lame. Dumb, actually, to be honest. And I guess I have to admit I was embarrassed by it. So I shut up and changed the subject.

I guess Angie sensed how important the pouch and the Four Remembers were to me, so she started in. Oh, she was all polite and smiley, and she pretended like she was interested. But I knew better.

Megan: "Will you be taking it to school with you?"

Angie (snotty): "That would make for an interesting fashion statement."

Lisa: "So, did your Grandfather write those remembers just for you? I mean, did he think you especially needed them or something?"

Angie (stupid smile): "Yeah, but I wouldn't think he'd have to remind you that you're unique." (Translation: Unique—meaning "different," "odd," "strange," "peculiar," "geeky," "weird.")

Talk about catty! I started a slow burn, but vowed I

wouldn't let them get to me. What hurt the most was when Brianne, who had seemed uncomfortable with all of this up to that point, said—I'm sure with the best of intentions— "You really are unique, Danni. Your grandfather got that right."

She meant well, and I appreciated it, but the look on the others' faces said it all. It was all I could do not to cry then all I could do not to tell them all to go home right then. Fortunately, after that nobody said very much and eventually we all went to sleep. This morning, nobody said much at breakfast either, and they all left as quickly as possible. Even Mom noticed it and asked me what was wrong.

I started to explain what had happened, but she cut me off. She was late leaving for Grand Junction, and she said we'd have to talk about it tonight.

I shut the journal, sticking my pen in my pocket. I didn't feel like writing anymore. I felt rotten enough without putting it on paper. I leaned back, closing my eyes. After a few minutes, I reached down and picked up the pouch from the bench beside me. I placed it on my lap, faceup, and smoothed it out with my hand.

I wasn't sure why I'd brought it with me. Grandpère had given me a pretty serious charge to always make sure it was safe, so I usually took it with me whenever I left the house for very long. But I didn't consider this leaving the house. I guess I was worried a little that Cody and his friends might go into my room. I could picture them playing catch with it or making fun of it. Whatever the reason, I had grabbed it and brought it with me.

I sighed. I could feel the heat seeping into my body, and I relaxed a little. I let my mind go back to that day two months ago in Horseshoe Canyon. Twice since then I had gone to Grandpère and tried to get him to tell me more about the pouch. What was it supposed to do? How did it work? Was there something I was supposed to be doing with it? Was it related to "the gift"? That kind of stuff. Both times he had gotten a mysterious little smile on his face and shook his head. "Some things you must discover for yourself" was all he would say. No surprise.

I wasn't sure what to make of it anymore. Nothing strange or mysterious had happened since I had gotten it. I had even taken it to bed with me a couple of times. I would lay there for a long time, holding it close to my chest. I don't know what I was expecting—tingling sensations? A vision, maybe? Some grand burst of enlightenment? Angelic choirs singing an anthem? But nothing happened. Except that I felt really stupid.

A few days after we were back from that camping trip, Mom told me a story about when Grandpère was six years old. One day a dive bomber came. When the pilot saw Grandpère's father out in the field, he shot at him and nearly killed him. But Grandpère, instead of being scared, was so fascinated that he walked right out in the open and started to wave. The plane dove at him, but he just kept waving. And finally, the pilot waved back.

Mom told me that Grandpère's mother—Monique LaRoche, my great-grandmother and my namesake—said that the pouch had protected him. Now wouldn't that be nice? Only one problem: It wasn't happening for me.

A few weeks ago I was showing off a little for Ricky on the four-wheeler and it flipped over, throwing me off. I banged up my knee and scraped a bunch of skin off my arm. So no protection there. And Cody and I nearly stepped on a rattlesnake out in the pasture a couple of days ago. Scared the heck out of me. I had the pouch with me that day, too. If it could turn a German pilot away, why didn't it warn me about the snake?

I sighed again. It was a sound of weariness, frustration, discouragement. I reached out my hand and traced the patterns of the four fleurs-de-lis as I had done so many times before. Cody had told me that if I didn't stop doing that, I'd wear it out and I wouldn't have anything to give to my kid on his thirteenth birthday. But maybe he's just jealous that I got it and he didn't.

The sunlight filtering through the foliage above me dappled the pouch, making it look like there were two different colors of yarn in the embroidery. I liked the effect, and leaned a little closer to examine it once again. The other embroidery on the pouch, so delicately done as to be almost invisible, was what I loved most about my pouch.

My fingers moved slowly across the letters. That day in the canyon, I hadn't realized that was what they were, but now I recognized them for what they were—individual letters in an elegant French script that spelled out two words. But those two words still puzzled me a little.

Finally, laying the pouch aside, I leaned back and closed my eyes again, trying to push everything out of my mind, at least for a little while.

CHAPTER 9

"Hey!"

When Ricky spoke, I jumped so fast I nearly fell off the bench. I leaped up, brushing at the back of my hair, turning my head so he wouldn't see me blinking the sleep out of my eyes. "Hey, yourself. Umm . . . What are you doing here? I thought you were taking care of your sisters."

"I was. Dad got home early. I was coming in to get a few things at the grocery store. Cody said you were over here in your private place, so I thought I'd say hi before I headed home."

"Hi," I murmured. What a nice thing to happen. Perfect timing on his part. I sat down again, picking up my journal and the pouch and setting them aside.

"Whatcha doin'?" He sat next to me on the bench.

"Writing in my journal. Just thinking." I pulled a face. "Wallowing in a really good case of the 'poor me's.'"

His eyebrows came up. "What's wrong?"

"Nothing. Just feeling a little down. Probably just the heat."

"I'll buy that. Even up in the pines it was ninety-something." He peered more closely. "This wouldn't have anything to do with your sleepover last night, would it? Cody said it went bad."

"I don't want to talk about it," I snapped.

His hands came up, warding me off. "Whoa. Okay. New topic." He smiled and reached in his pocket. "Here."

He held out a magnifying glass.

"What's that?"

"A magnifying glass."

"I can see that," I said in disgust. "What's it for?"

"Your grandpa told me to bring it out here for you. Didn't you ask for it?"

I started to shake my head, then jerked upright. "Was that all he said?"

"Yeah. Just, 'Give this to Danni. She may need it.'" He grinned. "What are you doing? Frying ants like we used to do when we were little?"

"I never did that—you did." Why in the world had Grandpère thought I needed a magnifying glass? I took the glass from Ricky, an idea forming in my head. "Here. I want to show you something."

I lifted the pouch and put it on his lap. "You have never had a chance to hold the pouch before, to really look at it. So here's your chance."

He gave me a puzzled look, then did as I asked. "What am I supposed to be seeing?" His fingers moved across the flap. "There are the four whatchamacallits."

"Fleurs-de-lis."

"Yeah, those things." His fingers moved down. "Hey, is this lettering? I didn't see that before."

"Neither did I. Not until later." I scooted closer, pushing against his shoulder, and handed him the magnifying glass. "Look at the first

74

one. It looks like a capital L, right? And the next one is definitely an E. That spells *le* in French, which is the masculine form of 'the.'"

"Oh." He barely heard me. He was concentrating hard. He bent over the pouch. "G. A. R. D." He read the letters of the second word, moving the glass slowly. "I. There's another E. And finally . . . uh, an N." He lowered the magnifying glass.

I said the phrase aloud in my best French accent: "Le GARDY-en."

"The garden?" Ricky wondered. "Why would someone name a purse 'The Garden'? That's weird."

I smiled sweetly at him. "Since I asked Grandpère the same question, I think I'll let him answer that."

⎯⎯◆⎯⎯

"No," Grandpère said, "it doesn't mean garden."

"Is it similar to an English word?" Ricky asked.

He smiled. "I think with a little searching you could answer that on your own."

"Gardening," Cody blurted.

His buddies had gone, and he was in the thick of it with us.

"No, it has nothing to do with the garden or gardening." Grandpère turned back to me and Ricky. "I'll bet it wouldn't take a lot to find the answer on Google."

"Grandpère," I cried. "We worked hard on this. Won't you help us?"

"Can I give them a hint?" Dad asked.

Grandpère gave a quick nod.

Dad took the pouch, turning it so it faced me and Ricky. Then he tapped the fleur-de-lis in the upper right-hand corner. "It has something to do with these, actually."

"Flower," Cody shouted out.

I gave him my best withering look. "That would have to do with gardens too."

"Oh."

"Royalty?" Ricky guessed. No response.

"Remember when we were in Horseshoe Canyon?" Dad asked. "Grandpère named several things the fleur-de-lis can represent. But there was one in particular you were quite excited about, Danni."

"Guards!" Ricky blurted. "Does it mean guards?"

Grandpère gave him a slow smile. "Close, but not close enough."

Ricky and Cody fired off several more words: *Soldiers. Sentries. Keepers. Spears.* Cody even threw in "National Guard." Grandpère watched them calmly through it all, shaking his head. I sat back, thoroughly enjoying the show. Finally, he took pity on them.

"Mack is right. This is actually a title, and it has to do with the fleurs-de-lis. What do you call a person who serves as a guard?"

And then it clicked. "Guardian," Ricky sang out.

At last the smile was full. "That is correct. *Le Gardien* means 'The Guardian' in English."

CHAPTER 10

"Hi, love."

I looked up from my journal. "Oh. Hi, Mom. What are you still doing up?"

"Can't sleep when your dad's gone."

"What time is he supposed to be back?"

"He said a little after midnight."

I glanced at the clock: 11:17.

"And why are *you* still up? Last day of school leave you too excited to sleep?"

"Right," I said, making a face. "All we did was sign yearbooks. We didn't even go to class. It was basically all over by one o'clock, but somebody forgot to tell the bus drivers, so they didn't come until three."

"And that's what you're writing in your journal?" She was openly skeptical.

She had me. Except for the last hour, it had been a really fun day. "It was okay. I'm just catching up." I hesitated for a moment, then added, "Wanna talk?"

"Sure. Two insomniac females—we may as well make the best of it."

As she shut the door behind her, I closed my journal, stood up, and went to the bed. I stretched out, patting the other side of it. "Girl talk?" I teased.

Laughing, she lay down beside me, letting her dark hair spread out across the pillow. "Sure you can stand it?"

I scooted closer to her, turning on my side so we were facing each other. "I'll try. But if I start to hyperventilate, promise me you'll stop. Okay?"

She shook her head in mock despair. "Oh, Carruthers. Where did you come from?"

"Dad says I'm pure you. Sorry, Mom, it's all your fault."

She laughed. "Yeah, right. Like I ever wore cowboy boots when I was your age. Or rode horses. Or slept out in the open in a moldy sleeping bag. Or ate mac and cheese with hot dogs."

"Or went into a tailspin if your mother asked you to put on a dress."

"Exactly right." She reached out and briefly touched my cheek. "It'll serve you right if you get a little girl who's all frills and lace and dolls and dress-up."

"Never happen," I said.

"Oh, yes it will, and you'll love it."

I knew she was probably right, but I wasn't about to openly admit it. After all, I had an image to maintain.

"So, how does it feel to know that your middle school days are over?"

"Like I just had a pardon from the governor."

Her laugh was a merry tinkle. "Go on. It wasn't that bad. Come fall, you'll be a lowly little freshman ninth grader at the high school. No more big woman on campus."

"If I wasn't graduating, me and Cody would be in the same school next year. That would be seriously mental."

More serious now, she took my hand. "I'm really proud of you, Carruthers. Straight A's."

"Thank you."

"No problem," she murmured, smiling.

"Ha!" I cried.

Her eyes opened wider in surprise. "Ha what?"

"You just said, 'No problem.'"

"And that's a problem?"

"Don't you remember that twenty minute lecture you and Dad gave me a few weeks ago?" I launched into a gruff voice, trying to sound as pompous as Dad had. "What is it with you teenagers nowadays? The proper answer to 'Thank you' is 'You're welcome,' not 'No problem.'"

She looked startled for a moment, then went on the offensive. "It wasn't a twenty minute lecture; it took about ten seconds." She smiled triumphantly. "To which you had no answer, I might add."

There was a flash of headlights on the ceiling for a second or two, and we both raised up our heads to listen. But there was no sounds of a vehicle in the lane. Probably someone just turning around out on the highway.

"Anyway," she said as we settled back down again, "your father and I are very pleased that you take your studies seriously."

"Thank you," I said primly.

"You're welcome." She laughed.

It was a warm moment between us, and so I decided that even though it was late, it might be a good time to bring up something I had been thinking about for several days now. "Mom? Can I talk to you about something?"

She propped herself up on one elbow. "Of course. What is it?"

Well, I . . ." I took a deep breath. "Promise you'll hear me out before you shut me down, okay?"

Her eyes narrowed slightly, but she nodded. "Okay."

Another deep breath. I had been practicing this speech for two days now, but suddenly I felt like my mind had been erased and never reprogrammed.

"It can't be that bad," she said. Then she frowned. "Is it?"

"No, it's nothing bad. It's . . . I think it's good actually."

"Good for me or good for you?"

When I had no answer to that, she sat up, crossing her legs and facing me directly. "Okay, let's hear it. I'm ready."

"Uh . . . do you remember how earlier this month I left my backpack on the bus on a Friday afternoon? And I couldn't get it back until Monday?"

"Yes, and it had the pouch in it."

"Exactly. I felt horrible. Grandpère never said anything, but I knew he was disappointed in me. When he gave the pouch to me last year, I promised I'd always be careful with it and always take good care of it."

"But it turned out all right." She laughed softly. "Even if someone had taken it, that thing is so old, it looks like something from the Salvation Army store. No one would take it."

"Yeah, right. So . . . umm . . . I was wondering like . . . I mean . . ."

"My goodness, Carruthers. Just spit it out. What is it?"

"What if I *didn't* take the pouch to school every day next year?" As she started to react, I rushed on. "I mean, for school activities, like football games or a dance or something, then I would, but not every day. Not just for school."

"But, Carruthers, you know—"

"I wouldn't just leave it lying around. I could get a little chest, or maybe Dad could put a lock on my closet door. Then I could leave it home and it would be safe."

"No, Carruthers!"

"Mom, listen to me. High school is different. There'll be a bigger

80

chance of having it get lost or someone taking it." Or making me feel even more like Miss Number-One Ditz of Wayne County.

"No, Carruthers," she said more strongly now. "We already discussed this once. I want that pouch with you every day. That's non-negotiable."

"*Mom!* You promised to hear me out."

Her mouth opened, and then she clamped it shut again. "Go on." But her eyes said it all. The discussion was over in her mind. And that made me mad.

"You don't know what it's like, Mom. Even though I keep it in my backpack and never take it out, all the kids know about it. It's like I'm the freak of the eighth grade. I mean, who else in the entire United States of America carries around an empty, two-hundred-year-old purse? They tease me about it all the time. It's . . . it's just weird."

"Is that why you left it on the bus?"

"No! But thanks for thinking I'd do that."

"Let me ask you something, all right?"

I sighed. Here came the counterattack. "Yeah, yeah. Go ahead."

"If your friends thought wearing a seat belt—or a life jacket when you're on the jet skis—was stupid or childish, and they teased you about it, would you stop wearing them?"

"Of course not. But it's not the same thing. Those are meant to protect you."

Mom's eyebrow raised slowly.

Whoops. Wrong thing to say. "Okay, I know that's how you see the pouch, but that's just it. It's not—"

"It's called the Guardian, Carruthers. I didn't give it that name. Neither did your father or your grandfather. It's had that title for a long, long time. Someone gave it that name for a reason. It can protect you every bit as much as seat belts or life jackets can—just like it protected Grandpère when that plane came at him."

"He says that was just a stroke of good luck."

"Yeah, and his mother said it was the pouch that saved him." She tossed her head in exasperation. "Why would you want to leave something like that at home?"

"Because I'm not in any danger at school, Mom. It's the same thing every day. Boring. Dull. Safe."

"Do you remember Columbine High School in Colorado?"

I should have known that was coming. "I was four, Mom. No, I don't remember. But you've told me about it enough times. Even if something like that did happen here, do you think the pouch is going to stop a bullet? Come on, Mom. Get real. I'm not talking about throwing the pouch away. I . . . I just don't want to take it every day. It's the biggest joke in school."

"Well, I worry about you," she said as she stood up from the bed. "*Every day*. And knowing you have the pouch with you has been a great comfort to me."

I shook my head. I knew I had lost. It was like trying to convince her to let me have a birthday party on my actual birthday—I was never going to win that fight.

I had saved my best shot for last, hoping I wouldn't have to use it, but I had no other choice.

"About two months ago, someone started the rumor that I kept food in my pouch. Since we're not allowed to have food in the classrooms, I started leaving my pouch in my locker. Greg Kelly somehow got in there, and he filled the pouch with Twinkies. Then he put it in my backpack without me knowing about it. In algebra, he told Mr. Arnold that I was sneaking food into class."

Mom frowned. "What happened?"

"Everyone thought it was hilarious, of course. Except Mr. Arnold. I ended up in the principal's office. And now everyone calls me Twinkie McCallister. I even had people sign my yearbook that way."

"Why didn't you tell me? I know the Kellys. I'll call his mother."

"Oh, goodie. I'm sure that will help."

"Sarcasm does not become you, Carruthers. And the answer is still no."

"Please, Mom! Please!"

She stopped as she reached the door. Without turning around she said, "I'll talk to your father about it, but if he asks me what I think, you know what my answer will be." She opened the door. "I'm sorry, Carruthers. Good night."

Before she could close it, I was off the bed and to her side. "Will you at least do one thing for me, then?"

"What?" she asked suspiciously.

"My birthday is on Saturday this year. You said I could take some of my friends to Provo to the Seven Peaks water park. But if I do it on a Friday or a Monday, Ricky and some of the others won't be able to come because they work. If I promise to take the pouch, will you please, please, let me celebrate my birthday *on* my birthday? Just once? I'll even wear the pouch in the pool if you want." I tried to lighten the mood. "Along with my life jacket *and* a seat belt."

Mom didn't say anything. I thought I had gone too far, because from her face, I could tell she was either very hurt or very near to throwing me on the bed and spanking my bottom. Either way, I didn't expect an answer.

I started to turn away, but she surprised me. "You always did have a gift for slipping the blade between the ribs, Carruthers. But be careful. The tongue that bites others can bite you too." She gave me a fleeting, humorless smile. "But, yes. I agree. You can have your birthday party on your birthday. Good night."

She closed the door, leaving me standing alone with my mouth open in surprise.

CHAPTER 11

I stopped at the end of the basement hallway and listened for a moment at the door to Grandpère's apartment. Then I knocked softly. "Mom says we're leaving for church in about half an hour," I called.

"You can come in, Danni," he sang out. "Door's open."

I walked in, then stopped. I expected him to be getting ready for church, but he was already in a white shirt and tie and was sitting on the couch in the small alcove he used for his office. He had a book on his lap.

"Whatcha reading, Grandpère?"

"Whatcha? Is that French or English?"

I stuck out my tongue at him. "What are you reading, Grandpa?" I emphasized each word slowly and distinctly.

"Ah," he said as moved over and I sat down beside him. He closed the book, marking his place with his finger, and showed me the cover: *The Decline and Fall of the Roman Empire*. The book was about four inches thick, and I noted that his finger held a place about two thirds of the way through.

"Oh," I cried, "can I read that when you're finished? I've heard it's a marvelous book."

His look made me laugh.

Leaning forward, he found a bookmark on the table beside him, inserted it in the book, then set it down. Only then did he look at me. *"Petite maligne,"* he said disdainfully.

I snuggled up against him. "What does that mean?"

"Smart mouth," he growled.

"Yep," I agreed cheerfully. "That's me. Just ask your daughter."

"You two fighting again?"

"Not since the last day of school. We're kind of in Mexican stand-off mode right now."

He grunted, but said nothing. Then he put his arm around my shoulder. "Tell me about your party yesterday."

I nudged him with my elbow. "Why didn't you come? We had loads of fun."

"I seriously considered it."

"Why didn't you, then?"

He sighed and scratched his goatee. "Well, I decided that if I put on a swimming suit and sat by the pool, it would simply be too much competition for all the other guys."

"Yeah," I retorted, trying not to laugh. "Besides, you would have had to furnish sunglasses for everyone so they wouldn't be blinded by those white legs of yours." Grandpère absolutely refused to wear shorts of any kind, even in the hottest part of the summer.

"You're in high cheek today, aren't you?" he said.

"Cheeky is my middle name," I shot right back at him.

He just laughed. "So it was fun?"

"Yes. It was a great birthday."

"Girl-boy ratio?" he asked with a straight face.

I counted quickly. "Three to one—girls to boys. That's counting Cody."

"Ah, no wonder Ricky had that silly grin pasted on his face when I saw him at the Chevron station last night. It was like he had been in hog heaven all day."

"Did he say that?" I retorted, knowing Grandpère was trying to goad me into a reaction.

Mom's voice floated downstairs. "Carruthers, will you make sure Grandpère's ready?"

Cupping my hands, I shouted back. "We're both ready. We're waiting on the rest of you."

She answered something unintelligible, so I assumed she heard me. I glanced at the clock on Grandpère's fireplace mantel. It was only 8:20, and we didn't have to leave until 8:40. "Grandpère? Can I discuss something with you?" Any lightness was gone from my face.

"Uh-oh," he murmured. "Incoming artillery."

I slapped his arm. "Stop it. I just want to ask you a question."

"*A* question?" he exclaimed. "I'll bet it's more like forty, knowing you."

"Okay, so forty questions."

"This wouldn't happen to be about the conversation you and your mother had a couple of weeks ago, would it?"

"No," I shot right back. "Well, not directly."

He chuckled. "You could have a promising career in politics. Go ahead, Danni. Fire away."

There was no hesitation like I had felt with Mom the other night. I knew I could be totally open with Grandpère and that meant a lot to me.

"Do you think the Guardian pouch is enchanted, like your mother said it was?"

"Oh my, yes."

That rocked me back. "You do? Before you said you didn't."

"Yes, but your mother let you go to Seven Peaks yesterday, which was the thirteenth day of the month. When I heard that, I assumed you and the pouch had put some kind of spell on her."

"Oh, Grandpère! I'm serious."

"All right. Go ahead. Ask me a question."

"I just did."

"Ask me a question I can answer."

My shoulders lifted and fell. Sometimes he could be so maddening. "Okay. What's the pouch supposed to do for me?"

"*Do* for you? You talk like it's alive. Like it's a person or something. Why would you think that?"

"Uh . . . I dunno. You made it sound like . . ." I stopped, not sure how to complete that sentence.

"You've had the pouch for a year now. Have you ever seen it do something for you? Like clean your room, or help you with your homework? Go to the store to get milk?"

"Come on, Grandpère," I exclaimed. "I'm really serious."

"So am I. Has it ever done any magic?" His eyes twinkled momentarily. "Other than enchanting your mother?"

I ignored that. "She thinks that because it's called *Le Gardien* that somehow I have to have it with me every single moment of every single day. I feel like I'm being smothered."

"And you told her that?"

"Yeah, kind of. Not in those exact words, but—" I jumped up and started pacing, too agitated to sit still anymore. "I looked up the synonyms for *guardian* on Google the other day: Protector. Caretaker. Keeper, as in zoo keeper. Custodian. Escort. Defender. One who safeguards something or someone."

He nodded thoughtfully, but said nothing.

"Mom makes me feel like I'm three years old again. Like I can't step out the door without someone hovering over me. I'm fourteen, Grandpère. I don't need a caretaker. I don't need an escort or a body-guard or a keeper. Why can't she see that?"

"Maybe because you sometimes give her cause for worry."

I didn't want to go there. "Do *you* think I need to take the pouch to school every day?"

"No."

I stopped pacing. "Really?"

"When I gave you the pouch, I charged you to take good care of it, to keep it safe. That involves as much an attitude about it as it does behavior."

I winced, thinking of when I had to tell him that I had left it on the bus.

"We're talking about more than just putting it in a safe place. I never said you had to always have it right with you. But you are the keeper of the pouch. I was for many years, but that responsibility has passed to you now."

"So what exactly does that mean?"

He had a faraway look in his eye. "I would never leave it alone in the house if there wasn't going to be anyone home for longer than an hour or two." He paused. "Actually, I put it in a drawer until I was seventeen, and I only took it out every few months."

"Really?"

"Yes. But that's not a recommendation. My father was disap-pointed that I didn't take it seriously enough. And the reason I took it out when I did was because there came I time when I desperately wished I had had it with me."

"Really? What happened?"

"That's a story for another time."

I wanted to push him on that, but he continued before I could.

"Danni, the biggest thing about being the keeper of the pouch is how you view your responsibility. If you're casual about it, then even keeping the pouch with you every minute of every day won't be enough."

Ouch!

"But if you take it seriously, then I think you can use your best judgment about what is required. If another responsible person is at home, I think you'd be all right to leave it here."

"So will you tell Mom all that?" I cried eagerly.

He slowly shook his head.

"Why not?" I wailed. "She'll listen to you."

"First, because she already knows all of this. Second, because I'm not going to be enlisted in the battle with your mother on either side. You two need to work it out."

"But she won't listen to me, Grandpère."

"Strange. That was exactly what she said about you."

I made a sound of high frustration. "Why does she think I need a nanny?"

"A nanny?"

"Yeah, that's what it feels like. Like I'm taking a nanny to school with me every day."

"Interesting choice of words."

"What do you mean?"

"Unfortunately, television and the movies have turned the concept of a nanny into empty silliness, almost like they're a big joke. But in my day, being a nanny was an honorable and important occupation."

"You're kidding me, right?"

He pressed his lips together and a warning flashed in his eyes. "I had a good friend in graduate school who was from England. His family was part of the British nobility—very rich, very upper-class. He talked about his nanny all the time. She was there when he and his brother were born. She lived in the mansion with them; she was with them virtually every day of their lives. He told me once that when he was little, he sometimes hated her because she was always correcting him or making him do things he didn't want to do. But he also said that by the time he was ready to leave for college, he felt closer to his nanny than he did to his own mother. Whenever he had a problem, he would confide in her and ask her counsel before he talked to his parents."

"Okay, so I used the wrong word. But that doesn't change—"

"Danni," he cut in, "you asked me a question. Do you want the answer or not?"

My face was flaming. "Sorry, Grandpère." I sat back down beside him. "Go on."

"In ancient Greece, the families of the very wealthy often had a manservant who had the responsibility for the children, in much the same way as a nanny did in England. The Greek word for those men, which roughly translated into English, is *schoolmaster, teacher,* or *tutor.* But no English word really captures the full essence of what a tutor was. The same is true in French, for that matter. *Gardien* is the closest word in French."

"Oh," I said softly. The image of the ornate letters so cleverly embroidered into the pouch came to my mind.

He faced me. "The responsibility of the tutor was much more than just educating the child. He was charged to protect them physically, intellectually, and morally. His task was to bring the children to full maturity and prepare them to become responsible adults and contributing citizens of society."

"And that's what the pouch is supposed to do for me?"

"The pouch can do no more than you will let it do. But I would hope that eventually you'll come to see it as a gift rather than an obligation, as a blessing rather than a burden."

"I understand, Grandpère. Sorry for being such a brat." But inside, I was thinking that, tutor or not, *Gardien* or not, I didn't need a nanny right now. And I wasn't going to become the laughing stock of Wayne County High School next year either.

To my surprise, Grandpère reached over and patted my hand. "I'll take it up with your mother," he said. "I'll talk with her."

"Really?" I cried. I threw my arms around him. "Thank you, Grandpère. Thank you."

He lifted a finger and pointed it at me. "I'm not promising anything. Your mother feels very strongly about this too for reasons that perhaps she will some day explain to you."

I gave him a sharp look. "Like what?"

He brushed it aside. "You're fourteen, Danni. You are moving rapidly toward becoming a mature and responsible young woman. But there are still things you can learn. And your mother is still the best one who can teach them to you."

"I know, I know."

"Remember that old parable about the oak and the willow?"

I thought for a moment, then shook my head. "No, I don't."

"When the wind blows strong, the willow bends. When the wind blows strong, the oak breaks because it will not bend." He smiled, getting to his feet. "Unfortunately, you're both French and Irish so you've got a lot of oak in your nature." He pulled me to my feet and gave me a quick hug. "We'd better get upstairs."

As we left his apartment and started for the stairs, I stopped. "Grandpère?"

"Oui?"

"Do you think there could be other pouches out there, other *Gardiens?*"

His lips pursed momentarily. "I have no idea. I wouldn't be surprised, though. Maybe not actual pouches, but I believe there is

something that helps us from time to time, a higher power that that
intervenes in our behalf."

"Like what?"

"Like seeing your unborn son as you are preparing to die, and
then finding the will to amputate your arm so you can live to see him
some day. Like maybe having an ancestor who watches over us and is
allowed to intervene in our behalf from time to time."

"But those aren't the same as having a nanny," I suggested.

He laughed. "Oh, Danni. Like I said, there's a lot of oak inside of
you, girl. A lot of oak."

I laughed back. "And I wonder where I get that from."

———◆———

That night, after everyone was asleep, I laid awake in my bed,
my cheek resting against *Le Gardien*. Over and over, I thought about
Grandpère's words. Over and over, I remembered my heated conversation with Mom. And over and over, I thought about walking into
high school on the first day of school with the pouch in my backpack.

And finally, I came to a decision. I got up, went to my dressing
table, and hung the pouch back on its nail. I sighed, tired of it all.
I wasn't going to put it away in a drawer like Grandpère had done,
but neither was I going to carry it around like some fabric crutch I
couldn't do without.

Maybe when I was seventeen or eighteen I'd take it down again.
But until then, it was going to just hang around and wait for me to
grow up. That's just the way it was going to be for now.

PART THREE

Rhodium

CHAPTER 12

Monday, June 13, 2011

Happy birthday to me! Today, I turn sixteen years old. Oh, and FYI, that's SWEET sixteen, and never been kissed. Ooh. TMI. WTMI.

Once again I'm not having a birthday party on my birthday. But this year, it's not because of Mom. Since agreeing to let me have my fourteenth birthday party on my _actual_ birthday, she's kind of loosened up on the whole bad luck thing. No, this time it was Dad's fault, but I'm not complaining.

Dad and Grandpère have some mining clients coming in from Canada next weekend to look at a mine. Dad said we have to go up and check things out today, birthday or no birthday. So we're leaving later today and going up in the mountains for two days. That's cool with me. Way cool.

But before we do that, something else happens first. Ta-dah! Dad's taking me to Price to get my driver's license. Yep, that's right. Keep your kids off the sidewalk, folks—after today I'm driving on my own. No more learner's permit. No more having to have an adult in the car with me. SWEET!!!!

Mom and Cody aren't coming with us today. No big surprise. Since we're going into the high country and will be covering some pretty rugged terrain on the ATVs, Mom didn't want Code to go. Dad agreed. So she and Code are going to Denver with Beth Armitage, Mom's best friend. Mom's taking several of her latest paintings to a gallery over there. Cody's all bummed out and mad, but Mom promised to take him to that big aquarium in Denver, so he'll be okay.

Mom did her part for my birthday last week. In addition to throwing me a party on Saturday, on Friday she took me shopping in Salt Lake. Guess what I got? That's right, ladies and gentlemen. I am now the proud owner of a new iPhone. WITH INTERNET ACCESS! About time. I was the only kid in the whole Intermountain West with a clunky old dinosaur of a phone and no Internet access. (I have to pay the $30 monthly fee for data access, but it's worth it.)

I gotta go. Dad and I are leaving early for Price so we can be the first ones at the driver's license place. Then we'll come back here, pick up the four-wheelers, Grandpère, and Rick, and then head for the Henry Mountains. Yep. That's right. Rick's going with us, which is no small miracle. I was sure his dad would say no when Dad asked if Rick could go with us. But Rick's been working part time for Dad since March—not just here on the ranch, but helping with the mining stuff too. When Dad told Charlie we were going up to check out some claims for a client and needed Rick's help, Charlie reluctantly said yes. (I'm doing a little dance right now.)

Oh yeah. And if you're one of those that Lisa and Angie have been telling that Rick and I are into big-time making out now, let me set the record straight. Not true. Absolutely not true. He hasn't even held my hand yet. Which is fine by me. Really. Well, I wouldn't fight him if he did, but that's not the point. The point is that we're just friends. Making out with him would be seriously weird.

Well, enough of that. Gotta get going.

━━━━◆━━━━

Five minutes later, as I was spreading out the stuff I was going to take with me on the bed, there was a soft knock on my door.

"You awake, lazy bones?" It was Cody.

"Ha! I've been up for an hour." Or maybe half that. "Come in."

Cody isn't a morning person, so to see him fully dressed with his hair combed at this hour was a bit of a shock. I glanced at the clock on my dresser: 5:49. Stifling a yawn, I said, "I thought you and Mom were leaving way early."

Suddenly Mom was standing behind him. "We are. We're here to say good-bye." She came in and gave me a hug. "Have a great birthday today, Carruthers."

"I will. It's already been the best ever. Thanks again for my phone, Mom. It's great."

"You know," Cody said with a pouty look on his face, "Mom and Dad are spoiling you rotten. A phone. Camping. Riding ATVs."

"No kidding!" I said brightly. "It's about time."

"This only happens on your sixteenth birthday, you know," Mom said. "Next year it's bread and water." She shook her finger at me. "And no helium balloons or party hats either."

That made me laugh out loud. "Promise?"

As she smiled, she glanced toward the window. "Dad said to make sure you were awake. He's out loading the four-wheelers on the trailer."

"I'm getting there."

"Nuh-uh," Cody said. "You're still in your pajamas. And your hair looks like something a cat spit up."

As I yelped in protest, Mom chided him. "Be nice, Cody. Even if it's true, you don't say things like that out loud."

"Mom!" I cried.

Cody grinned at me. "If I were you, I'd wear a hat today. A really big hat."

"Thanks, Code. Just what a girl needs to hear." But I was smiling. I had already seen myself in the mirror and knew I was in for a lot of work. But that was Cody. He never thought about what he was going to say first, he just let it all come out. I reached up and fluffed my hair a little. "I thought I'd leave it like this for my driver's license picture."

Mom laughed too. "You know what they say, Carruthers. If you really look like your driver's license picture, you're too sick to drive. I suggest you take a brush to it."

"Or the hay rake," Cody said. He jumped clear as I swung at him.

Grinning, he waved. "Bye, Danni." He thumped down the stairs.

"Breakfast's on the stove," Mom said, moving toward the door. "Just heat it up, okay? Dad's already eaten."

"No problem. Good luck with the gallery."

"Thanks." A frown momentarily creased her forehead. "Carruthers, I want you to be especially careful driving your four-wheeler today. Okay?"

"Sure."

Her eyes were suddenly grave. "I mean it, Carruthers. You're going to take the pouch with you, right?"

"Right."

"Promise?" Her voice was earnest.

"I promise." I looked at her more closely. "What is it, Mom? What's the matter?"

Her frown deepened, and for a moment I thought she was going to say more, but then she shook her head and forced a smile. "It's nothing. I just want you to promise me you'll be careful. Okay?" She kissed me on the forehead, tipping her head up a little to do so. When she stepped back, she sighed. "It's probably a little too much—how do you say it?—friggatriskaidekaphobia?"

My mouth dropped open a little. I had never told her about that word, yet she had pronounced it perfectly and without hesitation.

She gave me another quick hug, this one tighter than before. "Love you," she murmured.

"Love you too," I said, hugging her back. "You're the best."

She laughed. "Not when it comes to camping, but fortunately your dad and grandfather make up for that." She headed for the door. "See you tomorrow night."

"Kay. Have fun in Denver."

As she shut the door behind her, I went to the dressing table and picked up my pen.

> Well, that was strange. Mom was . . . I'm not sure what she was.
>
> Memo to self: Ask Grandpère why Mom feels so strongly about the number 13. And who told her about friggatriskaidekaphobia?

I decided to put my hair in a French braid; that seemed like the best way to tame it. Glancing at myself in the mirror, I decided that Cody's advice had some merit. I did need a hat. I opened the drawer and found my Zions National Park cap I'd bought last summer. Checking myself one last time, I pulled the braid through the hole in the back of the hat. Then I wet my fingers, smoothed down one last strand of hair that had a mind of its own, and pronounced myself acceptable.

Just then I heard Dad's voice float through my open window. "Danni, ten minutes."

"Be right there," I called back before I closed the window. Moving quickly now—I was hungry and wanted to grab breakfast—I turned to my bed, stuffed my journal and a heavy hoodie into my bag, and zipped it up. I looked around the room one last time.

"Uh-oh!" I grunted as my eyes fell on the pouch hanging next to my mirror. "I'd better not leave you behind." It had been less than ten minutes since I gave Mom my solemn promise, and I'd already forgotten it.

I walked over to where the pouch hung from its nail. I leaned close and blew softly on it. I felt the old familiar stab of guilt as dust rose from it in a small cloud. "Poor Nanny," I murmured. "Always so patient, even when I neglect you."

I'd had the pouch for three years now. As I ran my fingers over the four embroidered fleurs-de-lis, my mind slipped back across those years and across the fifty miles that separated me and Horseshoe Canyon. That day, not far from the Grand Gallery, came back to me in quick snatches of vivid memories—me standing in front of Grandpère, busting my buttons when he told me I was no longer a child but a young woman now, feeling a thrill of excitement when he solemnly said, "You are now the keeper of the pouch."

And now three years later, it hung on my wall, often forgotten, typically neglected, usually not even noticed. I didn't really feel like I'd broken my promise to Grandpère. I took my responsibility seriously and I never left the pouch out where it might get lost or stolen. And if no one was going to be home, I would always take it with me. But lately I'd been leaving it hanging on my wall next to the Four Remembers more often.

I remembered how I used to think the pouch might have been enchanted or magical somehow. But I knew better now. It was just an old, worn-out pouch. I knew it was part of my heritage and a tie between me and my past ancestors, and there had even been days when I was not ashamed of it. Those were the days I took it to high school with me—to Mom's shock.

I never took it out of my backpack or showed it to anyone, of course, because by then, I already knew none of my friends would understand.

The day after I had that long talk with Grandpère about nannies and tutors and guardians, I told Rick about what he'd said. We were with some friends having burgers at Blondie's, but I guess someone at the next table overheard our conversation, because after that, anytime anyone from school saw me, they'd say "Hey, Danni, how's your nanny?" or "Hi, Danni. Hi, Nanny." Then they'd laugh as if that was most hilarious thing they'd ever heard. But, as Grandpère pointed out, juvenile minds think just about anything is hilarious.

Some of the boys even made up a song about it. I tried to explain to them that the pouch actually had a name—*Le Gardien,* or the Guardian, in English—but that was a mistake. They just made it part of the song.

> *Danni and Nanny and the Guardian Pouch,*
> *Sitting together on a big leather couch.*
> *Danni needs Nanny, but Nanny's a pouch.*
> *No wonder Danni is a big fat grouch.*

Even after two years, just thinking about the song made me wince. Only someone with the maturity level of SpongeBob SquarePants would find that funny. All it did was make me resent the pouch more.

Since then, I started thinking of it as "The Nanny Pouch." But after a while, it wasn't like an insult anymore. For me it was more like a pet name you'd give to something you're fond of, like a cat or a horse or something. *Le Gardien* felt too stiff and ponderous; not a good name for the nanny, which I had also started to think of as a *him*.

Just then my cell phone exploded with noise. I gave a little squeal, whirling around before I remembered I'd chosen "Zombie Rock" as my new ringtone. Heart pounding, I took it out of my pocket and swiped the slide bar with my thumb.

Seeing who it was on the caller ID, I let it ring three more times. Then covering my mouth and faking a gruff voice, I punched the button. "Carruthers McAllister's Answering Service. At the beep, please leave your name, number, and many wonderful compliments." Pause. "Beep!"

"Hi, Danni."

Even though he only said two words, I instantly knew something was wrong. "Mornin', Rick." I held my breath, afraid I already knew what was coming.

"Happy sixteenth birthday."

"Thanks. What's up?"

"Uh . . . is your dad there? I tried his cell phone, but he didn't answer."

"It's probably down on the kitchen table." I paused, but he didn't respond. "He's out by the barn loading up. I can go get him if you need me to." I drew in a quick breath. "Is something wrong, Rick?"

Another long silence, then a soft sigh.

"You can't go today, can you?"

An even longer pause, then, "Nope."

"But your dad promised."

"Danni, I—"

"Did you tell him that we're not just playing, that Dad and Grandpère are doing some work for a client, and that you'll be helping them?"

"I did, but—"

"It's your job, Rick. Doesn't he understand that?"

He broke in sharply. "Danni, Dad got me a full-time job at the mine."

"The coal mine? No!"

"I start the day after tomorrow."

I felt like a fist had slammed me square in the stomach. I hunched over, closing my eyes. "No, Rick. You can't."

Several people in Hanksville worked in the coal mine up in the hills. Dad had done some consulting work for the mine about three years ago, and one day he took me down inside the mine with him. Once we got off the lift and walked into the tunnel, I nearly went bonkers. I kept having this awful sensation that the ceiling was pressing down on me, and that the walls were closing in from both sides. I was so sure I was going to be crushed that Dad had to take me back out again. Even now, the thought of being down there in total darkness with thousands of feet of rock and dirt over my head made me nauseated.

Rick laughed, but it was forced. "You're such a squirrel, Danni. I'll tell Dad that you said I can't do it. I'm sure he'll change his mind."

"I didn't mean that, Rick. I just—Why? Why now?"

"We learned yesterday that Mom's lawyer got the court to double the alimony Dad owes her every month."

"What? No! That's not fair."

"Come on, Danni, you know the score. That's how life is sometimes."

I sank down slowly in one of the chairs and closed my eyes. "I know," I whispered. "I'm sorry."

"One more thing, Danni. I won't be going back to school this fall either."

CHAPTER 13

"Please, Dad."

I was fighting hard not to cry. I've never been a weeper, so whenever I do cry, Dad knows it's important. And the way it was going right now, I could see I might need tears as a last resort. And they wouldn't be fake if they did come. "I have to go with you."

"I'm sorry, Danni. Talking to Mr. Ramirez about this is going to be hard enough without having someone else there. Especially you."

"I have to go with you," I said, barely able to get the words out. "I promise I won't say a word. Please, Daddy. Please!"

It wasn't planned, but suddenly my eyes were burning, and I knew they would be glistening in the morning sunlight.

He finally nodded. "All right." Suddenly his finger was just an inch from my nose. "But not a word, Danni. You have to give me your word on this."

"Anything, Dad. I promise."

"And you're not to get out of the truck."

"But, Dad! I have to—" I clamped my mouth shut when his head came around slowly and I saw his look. "All right. I promise."

"Even if I end up going in the house to talk, you're not to get out of the truck for any reason."

"What if you have a heart attack right in the middle of everything? Could I come help you then?"

He shook his head without even a trace of a smile. "I'll make one exception."

"Wonderful. What is it?"

"If Charlie invites you to join us, then it's okay."

"Dad! There's more of a chance of a meteor striking Hanksville than of Mr. Ramirez asking me to listen in."

"I know. Deal or no deal?"

"Deal," I finally said. "You have my word." I said it with great solemnity. In our family, giving your word was like writing out a contract and having it notarized in blood.

"All right." For a moment, he didn't move, then he frowned. "What about your driver's license?"

I'd forgotten all about it. "This is more important. I'll get it when we get back."

"Good," he said. "I agree. Go tell Grandpère where we're going. Tell him it'll be after noon before we're back."

Noon? It wasn't even seven yet, and Rick's house was just a couple miles down the road. I'd never heard Rick's father utter more than half a dozen words at any one time, so if Dad was thinking this was going to take hours to work out, he was in for a surprise. But I said nothing and went into the house to find Grandpère.

———

When we blew past the turnoff to Rick's house, I thought Dad had missed it. He hadn't said a word since leaving home.

"Uh . . . Dad? We just passed Rick's."

He didn't even turn to look at me. "We're going to Bicknell first."

"Bicknell?" I cried. That was fifty-eight miles away. "But—"

Once again he shot me a look that cut off any further conversation. I vowed I would not speak again until spoken to.

That proved to be another hour. In Bicknell, Dad dropped me off at the local café, gave me some money to buy some breakfast—I hadn't eaten anything after Rick's call—then disappeared for an hour. By the time he pulled up again, I'd met up with a couple of kids I knew from school. Dad waved hello to them, but as I got in the truck, all he said to me was, "You all right?"

When I nodded, he looked at his watch. "It's almost eight thirty. We could make Richfield in another hour."

"Richfield?" Before I could say anything else, he was already pulling onto the highway headed west. "Why Richfield?" It was another hour west of Bicknell and in the opposite direction from Hanksville.

"There's a driver's license office in Richfield."

I was dumbfounded. I had just assumed I'd have to wait for another day.

"It's only another hour from here. And Price is two hours from Hanksville. So it's about sixes either way."

"What about Mr. Ramirez?"

"Rick told me his father worked the midnight shift at the mine last night. He usually sleeps until about noon, so we can't see him before then anyway." He let off the gas. "But if you don't want to get your license today, we can go back to the house and count cobwebs in the garage."

"Give me at least one full second to think about that," I said with a grin. "Can I drive?"

"Why not?"

It was 12:25 when we reached the turnoff to the Ramirez house. Dad spoke for the first time in nearly an hour. "Pull over, Danni. I need to be driving when we go in."

I did so, and we changed places. As Dad started up again, I rolled down my side window. He shot me a look.

"I think we need some fresh air," I said quickly.

"All right, but remember our deal."

"I do, Dad. And I know you're right. You need to talk to him alone. I just hope you're close enough so I can hear." When he nodded, I asked, "What are you going to say, Dad?"

But I wasn't sure he'd heard me.

To my everlasting joy, when we turned into Rick's yard, Charlie Ramirez was in front of his garage, working under the hood of his pickup truck.

"Good," Dad said, looking around quickly at the empty yard. "Rick's not here."

He parked about ten yards away. I crossed my fingers—on both hands actually—hoping against hope Mr. Ramirez wouldn't invite Dad into the house. As I watched Dad walk toward him, I wondered what the chances were that Dad could change Charlie's mind. About one in twenty-two gazillion, I decided.

On the way here, I'd said something to that effect, and Dad gave me a funny look. "Sometimes, we make assumptions about people that aren't correct," he said.

I asked him what he meant by that, but didn't answer me.

Dad waved at Mr. Ramirez. "Hey, Charlie," he said, extending his hand as he reached him.

Mr. Ramirez took a shop rag out of his pocket and quickly wiped his hands, then shook Dad's hand. "Hello, Mack." There was a momentary pause. "Suspect you're here about my boy."

"Suspect you're right," Dad said easily, "but I'm not here to call you out on it."

"Ain't nothing to say," Charlie said. "Don't like it myself, but sometimes the boxes you get shoved into don't come with a whole lot of choices, so I won't be changing my mind."

"Trying to change your mind would be saying that I think you're wrong. Not so. What you're doing for your family is nothing I wouldn't do myself under the circumstances."

I couldn't help but stare. Dad was agreeing with him? I groaned inwardly.

"Actually," Dad said after a moment, "I'd like to talk about a possible alternative that maybe throws another option into that box you're in."

Mr. Ramirez visibly tensed. "Don't need no charity, Mack."

"I'm not here selling charity, Charlie. You've got a problem. I've got a problem. I think we might be able to solve both of them at the same time."

Wary, but clearly interested, Charlie finally nodded. "Go on."

"I don't need to tell you that Rick's the best hired help I've ever had. He's a hard worker, thoroughly dependable. I'll bet he saved me more than his entire wages last month just fixing up equipment and getting that old tractor running again. When it comes to mechanics, he's got a gift, Charlie. Add in the fact that he can run circles around me on a computer, and I think you can appreciate why I don't want to lose him as an employee."

It was so simple, and so absolutely brilliant. I nearly shouted with joy.

"I understand," Mr. Ramirez said. "Ricardo is a good boy, but we need him earning a man's salary."

Dad nodded thoughtfully. "What are you going to do with the

girls if both you and Rick end up working the same shift at the mine?"

It had been rough on the Ramirez kids ever since their mother left; Raye was eight now; Kaylynn was eleven.

"The mine foreman has already agreed to let him and me work opposite shifts, so one of us will always be home. Come fall, my sister and her two kids from Moab are gonna move in with us. She's going through a bit of rough spot right now too."

"Good of you to watch out for her." Dad took a quick breath. "What if I wasn't paying Rick a boy's wages? What then?"

I saw Mr. Ramirez's jaw set, but Dad rushed on before he could object. "Maybe Rick's already told you this, but I've acquired three new clients in my consulting business this last month. Suddenly I've got more work than my father-in-law and I can handle. I was going to talk to you about this once we got back from this camping trip, but let's do it now." His head came up a little as he met Mr. Ramirez's gaze. "I want to hire Rick full time for the summer."

Mr. Ramirez reared back, instantly skeptical, but Dad continued. "I'm paying fifty cents an hour better than what they're paying starters at the mine."

He swung around, eyes spitting fire. "I said we don't need no—"

"I'm not just talking about ranch work. Rick is picking up this mining stuff about as quick as anyone I've ever seen, and he's totally taken over all my computer work—especially my spreadsheets. Right now, he's working on updating my website. I've got no choice, Charlie. I need a full-time man. If it's not Rick, I'll have to find someone else. And I can't spend half the summer training someone new."

He stopped, giving Mr. Ramirez a chance to digest all that. As for me, I was soaring. This was perfect. I held my breath as Rick's father stared out across the desert land to the south.

"I'm telling you straight, Charlie. There's no charity here. I'm willing to pay Rick a premium wage because he's my first choice. He's bright, he's dependable, and he can work flexible hours."

I had to duck my head so Charlie wouldn't see me grinning like a silly fool. Then came the bucket of cold water.

"And what happens come fall when school starts again?"

Dad nodded. "Rick told me he wasn't going back to school his senior year. I'm guessing you don't like that idea any better than he does."

"I don't. But you do what you have to do."

"I totally agree. But maybe there's another way to do it." Dad glanced in my direction. "Danni and I went over to Richfield to get her driver's license this morning. Stopped at Bicknell on the way. While I was there, I slipped over and talked to LaVere Gladden, the high school principal."

I sat up again. So that's where Dad had gone after he'd left me at the café.

"Go on," Mr. Ramirez said, his face darkening. I could see the conversation was close to ending.

"I told him I was thinking about hiring Rick on as an apprentice. The school has work-release programs and vocational classes where the students can get high school credit. After I explained what Rick would be doing for me—learning the mining trade, doing web design, managing my computer files—Mr. Gladden said he was sure he could get approval from the school district to give Rick work-release credit for his time. Which means that if Rick goes to school for three hours in the morning and works for me afternoons and evenings, he can still graduate with the rest of his class. Still get his high school diploma."

"But—"

"Policy doesn't allow me to hire him full time while he's in school, but I can give him up to six hours a day. I know that's not the same as he'll be making at the mine by then, but I gotta tell you, Charlie, by the time he's worked all this year, and next summer, he'll be making more with me than he can at the mine. And what's more, with that kind of experience, he should be able to get a full tuition scholarship to any mining or engineering school in the West."

"You really think so?"

And in that moment, I knew Dad had won. The hope and pride in Charlie's voice as he asked that simple question said it all.

Dad nodded. "He's that good, Charlie. And you know me well enough to know I'm not just blowing smoke here. He's got what it takes to write his own ticket and make you real proud. And I'd be honored to have some small part in making that possible."

To my surprise, I found myself suddenly crying. Not just for Rick. I loved my father more at that moment than anytime I could remember.

Through my tears, I saw Mr. Ramirez's Adam's apple bob a couple of times. He turned away. For almost a full minute he stared out across the alfalfa field behind the house, his fist clenching and unclenching as he tried to get his emotions in check.

To my surprise, when he turned back, he was smiling. It wasn't much, but he was smiling. "And I suppose a condition for making this offer is that Ricardo goes with your family on that camping trip today?"

Dad managed to look surprised. "Only if you can spare him. But it's not just a camping trip; we're actually headed for the high country to do some work for one of our clients. Rick would be working about four hours a day with us, same as now."

Mr. Ramirez shook his head, but it was in surrender, not further combat. "Ricardo's down at the hardware store getting parts for our washing machine. You could stop by and tell him."

I was already reaching for my cell phone, but Dad's next words cut me off. "No, Charlie, I think that should come from you. Our departure time's pretty fluid. Just have him come by when he's ready."

"All right, I'll call him right now."

Dad wasn't quite done. "You know, if he can bring that old 4Runner you gave him, we could use the extra space for our gear. I'd pay him mileage."

Mr. Ramirez shook his head, but I could tell underneath the stoic expression, he was inwardly amused. "Would you leave a man no pride?" he asked softly.

Dad laughed. "Well, if you're going to be all hard-nosed about it, I guess there's nothing I can do."

They shook hands then, both of them perfectly at ease with each other. To my surprise, as Dad started for our truck, Mr. Ramirez followed. He came right up to my window. "Did you get all that, Danni?"

I about choked. I thought I was being so cool about everything. "Yes," I mumbled, my face getting warm. "Thank you, Mr. Ramirez. Thank you so much."

His eyes searched mine for a long moment. Then he nodded, satisfied by what he saw, I guess. "If it were any other friend, the answer would be no." He looked at Dad. "This is a fine daughter you have, Mack. She's been good for my Ricardo."

"And he's been good for me, Mr. Ramirez," I said, a lump in my throat again. And this time, it wasn't because Rick was going with us today, or because he wouldn't be dropping out of school in the fall. It was because I was suddenly wondering how I had ever thought that Mr. Ramirez was a little bit scary.

CHAPTER 14

The Henry Mountains begin about twelve miles south of Hanksville, and then run basically parallel with Utah Highway 95 about thirty miles, almost all the way down to Lake Powell. Our plan was to turn off the highway about fifteen miles south of town and head straight west into the high country.

Dad and Grandpère were in the lead, pulling the trailer. Rick and I were in his 1990 Toyota 4Runner. It looked like a beat up, old junky car, but Rick had fixed it up so it ran like a Mercedes. We had the back filled with our personal gear, while the camping gear and everything else was either in Dad's truck or on the trailer with the four-wheelers.

I was still filled with wonder over what had happened that morning. And Rick? Well, he was trying to hide it, but I knew him well enough to know he was wavering between a state of shock and euphoria. I could only imagine what it all meant for him: a full-time job, not having to work in the coal mine, being able to stay in school, the possibility of a university degree. He was trying to be casual about it, but it was so phony, I kept laughing right out loud at him.

"What are you thinking?" Rick asked me out of the blue after about five minutes of silence.

I started a little. No way could I tell him the truth. So I went to what I had been thinking about a few minutes earlier. "I was thinking about three years ago—about you and Dad and Grandpère and me heading out on a trip, just like now."

"Yeah. We had a great time, didn't we? You barely thirteen; me an old man at fourteen."

I laughed and socked him gently on the shoulder. "We thought we were really something, didn't we?"

"We were. Standing in the Grand Gallery, looking up at all those paintings. That was when your grandfather gave you the pouch—"

I jerked forward. "Oh no!"

"What?"

"I left Nanny home."

He gave me a funny look. "Say what?"

"Nanny, the pouch. I was getting ready to put it in my duffel bag when you called this morning. After that, I never thought of it again." I slapped my forehead. "I'm sorry, Rick, but we've got to back."

The look Rick gave me said a lot, but he himself said nothing. Probably in his mind, I was getting all worked up over an old pouch hanging on my wall. I grabbed my cell phone and hit Dad's speed-dial number, praying that he wasn't out of cell phone range already.

Dad picked up immediately. "Hi. What's up?"

"I forgot to get the pouch."

Silence.

"Dad?"

"We're already running late, Danni."

"I know that, Dad," I said, "but I promised Mom. She specifically asked me to bring it on this trip."

"I locked the house, Danni, and we haven't had a burglary in Hanksville for as long as I can remember. It'll be okay."

He was right. It was no big deal. Except to me. I was tempted for a moment, but then I remembered the look in Mom's eyes. "I promised, Dad. And besides, it's been three years now since Grandpère gave me the Four Remembers, and I was going to give him a report on them tonight. I really want the pouch with me when I do that."

I heard him sigh and say something to Grandpère. I listened intently, but couldn't make out the words. If Grandpère said not to worry about it, then I'd let it go.

"Danni?"

"Yes, Dad?"

"How far behind us are you?"

"We're only about seven or eight miles out of Hanksville."

"Okay. We're almost to the turnoff. You go back and get it. We'll leave the trucks at the Lonesome Beaver Campground, on the north side of Bull Mountain, and take the four-wheelers in from there. We'll start unloading them and wait for you there."

"Thanks, Dad. We'll hurry."

Rick was already slowing down and looking for a place wide enough to turn around.

———

Once we were back on the road and headed south again—the pouch on the seat beside me—I took out my phone and called Dad. It went straight to voice mail. No surprise. Coverage out here was sparse at best, and heading into the mountains would cinch that for sure.

I glanced at the speedometer. The needle was steady as a rock right at sixty-five. I looked at Rick. He sat straight in his seat, eyes fixed on the road ahead, both hands on the wheel.

"Did you know that almost all speedometers register a few miles an hour faster than you're actually going, especially at higher speeds?"

His eyes never left the road. "And your point is?"

"You're really not doing sixty-five. You're doing closer to sixty."

There was no reply. And the needle never moved.

"Come on, Rick. This stretch is so desolate, we're lucky to see a highway patrolman once a decade. Besides, they always give you a five-mile-per-hour cushion. You could do seventy-five and not be in trouble."

"The speed limit is sixty-five," he grunted, sounding as if he were talking to one of his little sisters. And we kept on at the same exact speed.

"We've still got a long way to go before we make camp tonight."

"And whose fault is that?"

"Forget it," I snapped, turning to stare out the window. I was miffed and wanted him to know it. But knowing Rick, he was probably just amused that I couldn't budge him.

Growling deep in my throat, I took out my phone. I turned it on, then swiped at the screen until I found the icon for the camera. I was still learning all of the phone's features and hadn't done much with the camera yet. I wanted some pictures of our trip so I decided to practice a little.

Turning in my seat, I snapped one of Rick. "I'll call that 'The Old Slowpoke.'"

"Considering how long we've been friends," he said dryly, "I think the least you could do is call it 'The Great and Handsome Old Slowpoke.'"

Argh! He was so maddening. I couldn't even tease him into a reaction.

Up ahead, I saw three or four range cattle just off the road. I brought the window down quickly and, ignoring the rush of wind, leaned out and snapped three pictures in quick succession. The first one was blurry, but the other two weren't too bad. I held up the phone, and Rick actually glanced at the screen.

"They're moving faster than you are," I said.

When he didn't answer, I sighed deeply to let him know of my exasperation. Up ahead there was a speed limit sign showing sixty-five miles per hour. I leaned forward and shot it through the windshield as it whipped past. All I expected to see was a white blur, but to my surprise the sign was exactly framed and the clarity was perfect. Then my jaw dropped. It wasn't a six and a five. It was a *seven* and a five.

"Ha!" I cried, sticking my phone out. "Look at that, cowboy. The speed limit is seventy-five here, so get the lead out."

Rick snatched the phone out of my hand. "What?" He held it right in front of his nose. "That can't be. I just looked at the sign. It said sixty-five. It's only seventy-five on the freeways. How'd you do that?"

"How did *I* do it? What? You think the camera is lying? Oh, sure. I took a picture, then in ten seconds, I edited the photo and changed it to seventy-five miles per hour. Or maybe I got up early this morning and said to myself, 'Ole Slowpoke's gonna need some help getting us down the road.' So I went out, bought a new sign, got a shovel, and—"

"All right, all right," he exclaimed. "I get it, Danni." He shot me a glance, and I felt the truck accelerate. He was smiling, but it was a little strained. "Sometimes tangling with you is like dealing with a front-end loader."

"Sorry," I murmured. "And thanks."

He said nothing. To my joy, the needle didn't stop until it was hovering close to eighty miles per hour. "Way to go, Ramirez," I cried. "I take back everything I ever said about you."

"Whatever," he said. But he was still smiling.

———

Two or three minutes later, we were in the bottom of one of those endless dips in the highway where it passes through one of the many dry washes. Just as we started up again, cresting the hill from the opposite direction and coming fast, we saw a white car—a white car with a rack of red and blue lights on top.

Rick instantly let off the gas, but it was too late. The lights came on, and the cop car was already slowing as we whipped past it.

"Crud!" Rick muttered and shot me a dirty look.

I turned in time to see a cloud of blue smoke burst from the tires as the cop car did an amazing one hundred eighty degree turn. Milliseconds later, it was in full pursuit. No need. Rick was already pulling off to the side of the road.

Rick warned me to let him do the talking, and I kept my mouth shut as the trooper asked for his driver's license and registration. But when she said she was going to cite him for doing seventy-eight miles an hour in a sixty-five zone, I timidly raised my hand.

She stopped. "You have something to say, miss?"

"I do, Officer Blake," I said, reading her name off her tag. "As we were driving just a minute ago, I was taking pictures with my cell phone."

"Yes? So?"

I held up my phone. "I just happened to take a picture of the speed limit sign, and—"

I could see that I had lost her about halfway through that sentence. So I leaned over, holding it out for her to see.

Her double take was classic, just like in the movies. She leaned in, and grabbed the phone out of my hand. "Where were you when you took this?"

"Just a few miles back."

There was a flash of anger. "This isn't funny, young lady. You can do whatever you want to doctor your photos, but you're interfering with the duties of an officer of the law."

"She took it a couple of minutes ago," Rick said. "I watched her."

"Ma'am," I said in my most timid voice, "look at the scenery behind the sign. It's the same as where we are."

She squinted first at me, then at the picture. When she stepped back, she touched Rick on the shoulder. "Mr. Ramirez, you come with me." She jabbed a finger in my direction. "You! Stay here. And by the way, Miss McAllister, I know your father. If you're playing some kind of joke on me, he'll hear about it by sundown."

"I'm not, ma'am. I swear."

Officer Blake and Rick climbed into the patrol car and drove off; they were gone less than ten minutes. When they returned, no one got out for a minute or two. I moved the side view mirror so I could watch the car without turning around. Finally, the passenger door opened and Rick got out. He bent down, said something through the rolled-down window, then smiled and waved. As he stepped back, she swung the car around and roared away, headed north again.

Taking his time, Rick came around to his side and opened the door.

"Well?" I burst out. "What happened?"

He gave me back my phone. "She apologized for pulling us over."

I grabbed his arm. "Really?"

"She's headed back to the office to find out who changed the speed limit without telling the road officers about it. She's pretty ticked, actually."

———— •— ————

119

We drove for a while in silence, both lost in our thoughts. I was still working it through in my mind. I had looked at the sign just before I snapped the picture, and I was almost positive it had said sixty-five. Rick said he had done the same thing. But now?

I picked up my phone again and turned it on. As the screen lit up, I gave a low cry and dropped it, as if it were hot.

Jerking around, Rick looked at me. "What's wrong?"

My breath was coming in short, quick gulps. An eerie feeling was coursing through my body. I held up the phone, turning it so he could see for himself that the picture on my phone was of a speed limit sign filled with a big 65.

For almost a full minute, he said nothing. Then his eyes finally met mine. "What's going on, Danni?" he asked in a hoarse whisper.

I tried to be jaunty so he wouldn't see my real feelings. "I'm not sure. But I sure hope Officer Blake doesn't check that sign again as she goes by."

Another five minutes passed. "You can't tell Dad," I said. "He'll ground me for the entire summer if he knew I encouraged you to speed."

Rick stared straight ahead, his brow furrowed and his mouth in a pinched line. Finally, he looked at me. "If I came back with a speeding ticket after getting one just two weeks ago, I think Dad might change his mind about everything we agreed to this morning."

I drew in a breath sharply. "No, Rick. He'd be mad at you, but he wants you to go to school. He wouldn't give all that up just to punish you."

"You don't understand, Danni. Of course he's happy about what happened today, but he's big on us accepting the consequences for our choices. And there's something else. Ever since my grandparents came here from Guatemala, he's felt like he's had to battle for everything we have. He's proud of that—that he's never taken a handout, that everything we have now is because of what he's done."

"But—"

"He's grateful for what your dad did this morning, but it was one of the hardest things he's ever done, to acknowledge that he needed help from someone else. And if that means no more to me than this?" He shook his head and looked away.

I stared at him. I didn't know what to say. I felt suddenly sick. "Rick?"

"What?"

"The next time I'm being a stupid twit, just stuff a sock in my mouth, okay?"

He gave me a low chuckle. "It would have to be one of mine. I don't think yours would be big enough to make a difference."

"Hey!" I cried, lifting my fist to slug him. Then I let it drop. He was right. I turned my head and stared out the window.

"Danni? Whatever you did, and however you did it, thank you for making it right."

"I didn't do anything, Rick. It just changed." I dropped my voice to a whisper. "Did we just imagine it?"

"No. Officer Blake and I went back to that sign. We walked right up to it. It read seventy-five miles an hour. She even felt it to make sure something wasn't pasted over it."

"But how is that possible?"

"It's not. Except that it happened."

CHAPTER 15

It was nearly sundown before Dad, who was in the lead, raised a hand and let his four-wheeler roll to a stop. We were about eight thousand feet up on the northwest flank of Mount Pennell, the second-highest peak in the Henry Mountains. For the last mile we'd been in heavy timber, following a faint two-track road that was barely visible in the waning light.

With the sun behind the hills to the west, the air temperature had quickly dropped, and despite it being mid-June, we were wearing sweatshirts and gloves and seeing our breath.

As we stiffly climbed off the machines, I looked around. We had come out of the trees into a relatively level area at the base of a steep hillside. It was a small clearing, but obviously not a natural one. There were numerous old tree stumps all around us. Somebody had done some logging up here, but a long time ago.

I felt a nudge on my arm. When I turned, Rick was pointing up the hill. About a hundred feet above us was a lighter splash of color on the mountainside, clearly visible among the scattered trees and brush. It was narrow at the top and fanned out at the bottom.

"Dad? Is that a mine?"

Looking up, he smiled. "No, Danni, it's not *a* mine. It's *our* mine. We're calling it the Danny Boy Mine."

"Really?" I squealed.

His grin spread across his face. "That doesn't mean it's yours, but Grandpère and I both like the name."

I squealed again and hurled myself at him, nearly knocking him over. "Oh, Dad! Can we go in it?"

"Not tonight," he said. "We've got to set up camp before it's totally dark. And I'd like some supper."

"And we need to hear Danni tell us about the Four Remembers," Rick added.

I scowled at him.

"Don't give me that look," he said. "That's why we went back for the pouch."

———

We sat around the campfire, huddled in close to take advantage of the warmth, sometimes talking quietly, sometimes just enjoying the silence.

"Look," Rick said, pointing toward the eastern sky. As our eyes lifted, we saw a flash of brilliant white light streak across the sky. With the moon not up yet and no city lights whatsoever, we had been seeing shooting stars all evening. This one was the biggest, the brightest, and the longest so far.

As it disappeared, Grandpère said, "That one's in a real hurry,"

I gave him a funny look. "What do you mean?"

"My father always used to say that a shooting star was an angel on his way down from heaven to help someone on earth."

"Ah." I liked that image. "It was kind of headed east," I suggested. "Maybe it's Grandmère on her way to make sure Cody and Mom are all right over in Denver."

"Oh no," Grandpère drawled. "That was much too slow for Grandmère."

We all laughed and then fell silent, searching the skies above us. The view was breathtaking. Like a thousand million diamonds flung across space. The Milky Way painted its luminous path across the whole breadth of the sky, looking very much like someone had indeed spilled a bottle of milk across the celestial realms.

After a while, Grandpère cleared his throat. "Since she has not yet volunteered, I'd like to see by a show of hands how many are waiting to hear that report on the Four Remembers from the keeper of the pouch."

Three hands shot up.

I sighed, then nodded. It was a good time, and the setting was perfect—crisp, fresh air, a crackling fire, a breathtaking panorama over our heads, and the best company in the world. And part of me really wanted to do it. Well, at least some of it. Reaching for the pouch, willing Nanny to give me some help, I got slowly to my feet. "Okay, but I'm only going to talk about one Remember tonight. Maybe two."

They nodded and settled back to listen. I took a deep breath, held it while I quickly collected my thoughts, then began. "I'm going to start with something that will, at first, seem totally unrelated to any of the Four Remembers, but just bear with me for a little bit. Okay?"

More nods. I could feel my heart thumping in my throat, but this was a pretty friendly audience. Even if I stumbled a bit, I wasn't going to get stoned. "Dad, do you remember the first time you read me the nursery rhyme of Humpty Dumpty?"

His face was blank. "How long ago was that?"

"I was probably four or five. But I remember making you read it again and again as I looked at the pictures. I can still see them in my mind. The first one was of this huge egg with a boy's face and dressed in boy's clothes, sitting on a wall. Then there was a picture of him falling, and finally he was on the ground, all broken to pieces."

"I do remember. When I read the part about all the king's horses and all the king's men not being able to put Humpty back together again, you were quite annoyed. 'Why didn't they just take him to the hospital?' you wanted to know."

"Yeah. And I also asked why he was an egg. Who ever saw an egg wearing clothes? I thought that was the dumbest thing I'd ever heard."

He chuckled. "You were really quite put out. You said it was a stupid story and that you didn't like it one bit."

I laughed softly as I remembered how upset I had been. "Do you remember what you said next?"

"I told you it was only a stupid story if you thought it was a story about an egg."

"That's right. Which didn't help, by the way. Not then, anyway. But now I realize it's not a story about an egg, it's a story about life."

I turned to face Rick directly. "Just this afternoon, I learned for myself that what may seem like trivial, unimportant choices can have enormous consequences." *Like goading someone into going five miles per hour faster than they were supposed to.* "My being stupid nearly unraveled all the good that Dad did this morning."

Dad and Grandpère exchanged puzzled glasses. I didn't explain further.

I faced Grandpère. "When you told us the story of Aron Ralston, you said something that has stuck with me ever since. You said that Aron didn't tell anyone where he was going because he was only going to be gone for one day. Then you said, 'How many times do you think Aron wished he could have made that decision over?' That was all you said, but I couldn't get that question out of my head. He must have kicked himself so many times for being so foolish. He had knocked the egg off the wall. But deeply regretting it didn't do one thing to make things better."

My voice was soft as I quoted from the nursery rhyme. "'And all the king's horses, and all the king's men, couldn't put Humpty together again.'" I took a breath. "Remember number three says, 'Remember, you are free to choose what you are and what you become.' But I want to change it just a little: 'I am free to choose who I am and what I will be, but I am not always free to choose the consequences of my choices.'"

"Very well put," Grandpère murmured.

"I realized today that it's not just what we *want* that matters. We have to want the consequences of what we want too. If we don't, we'd better not do it. I learned today that our choices—even if they're made with good intentions—can end up getting things broken. Toys. Cars. Our hearts. Our lives. Other people's hearts and lives. If we forget that, then, like Aron Ralston, we can find ourselves between a rock and a hard place." I let out a huge sigh of relief. "That's it. That's what I've learned."

I snapped my fingers. "Oh, one other thing. I read something in a book a few months ago, and I liked it so much, it now is on my mirror where I can see it every day. It is three simple words: 'Decisions determine destiny.'"

"A profound thought," Grandpère said.

I looked directly at Rick. "I'm so sorry for what happened today, Rick. It was incredibly stupid of me."

"I know," he said with a wry smile. Then he sobered. "But in this case, you *did* put things back together again. Don't ask me how you did it, but it turned out all right."

Grandpère was giving us both searching looks. "Is there something you two would like to share with Mack and me?"

"No!" we both blurted out simultaneously. We smiled at each other, then I turned back to face the others.

"Well, it's getting late," I said. "I think that's enough for tonight."

"Oh no," Grandpère said, "you said maybe you would talk about two Remembers. I'm going to hold you to it." He peered at me. "How about Remember number one: you are unique."

I jerked forward in surprise. That was the one I had been worrying about the most all day. That was the one I had determined to leave to last, hoping we'd never get around to it.

"Yes, Danni," Dad said softly. "I'd like to hear about that too."

I decided to play it funny, keep it light, keep 'em laughing. "Ah, yes," I said, smiling ruefully, "*You are unique.* But of course we are unique. And that has got to keep God and His angels busy. No two people are exactly alike. In all the world, and throughout all of history, there is not a single other person who is exactly like Carruthers Monique McAllister." I did a little bow. "Hold the applause, please. Also, sighs of relief are not allowed."

Rick sniggered. Dad smiled. But Grandpère just bored into me with those deep gray eyes of his. After a moment, he said, "Go on, Danni."

So much for the keeping-it-light approach. I decided the second-best option was speed. Talk as fast as possible and don't take questions. Without realizing it, I was clinging to Nanny like he was a life preserver.

I sighed again, only with more pain. "Actually, I love knowing that in all the world there is no one exactly like me—not now, not ever before, and not ever again. That's so weird in a way, and yet, strangely enough, I'm okay with that. I find it seriously creepy to think there might be a clone of me out there, getting into trouble, causing the people she cares about to do stupid things, making her mother wonder why doing girl things is not part of her nature."

Rick stirred. "Getting mad if someone does anything better than she does."

I shot him a dirty look. I realized my palms were sweating, and I rubbed them on my jeans. "You're just chapped that I can shoot better than you now."

"In your dreams," he said right back.

Grandpère leaned in closer. "You're stalling, Danni."

To my surprise, I suddenly wanted to say it. Wanted to let it all spill out. I looked at Rick. "You can't be here for this."

He gaped at me, then, face flaming red in the firelight, he started to get up.

"Oh, sit down," I snapped. "But you have to plug your ears."

Totally bewildered, he sank back down. For a moment, I was afraid he might actually cover his ears, but, gratefully, he didn't. I could see that he could see that I was just being me. I turned my back on him and spoke only to Grandpère and Dad.

"My name is Danni McAllister. And I *am* unique. But unique isn't all it's cracked up to be. Unique is another way of saying you're weird, which is another word for odd, strange, peculiar."

"Danni . . ." Dad began. But he stopped and shook his head.

"I present the following evidence in support my argument. I have my mother's long dark hair and large eyes, but very little of her natural beauty, grace, or charm. I—"

"Hold it," Dad exclaimed. "Everyone says you look just like your mother. You have a natural beauty of your own, Danni."

I held up a hand. "Please. No comments until I'm finished. I have my father's green eyes and freckles, but, unlike his eyes, which are always so kind and patient, mine are more like weapons. I glare at people, or scowl at them. Dad says my freckles are leprechaun kisses.

128

Maybe so, but before summer is over, mine will look more like I had my cheeks tattooed. My head is too big, and my ears stick out. In fifth grade, Jamie Fredricks, the most annoying boy I've ever known, said I reminded him of one those little Mexican Chihuahua dogs."

"No way, Danni," Rick said from behind me. I ignored him.

"And it's not just him. Everyone tells me I'm different. They mean it as a compliment, I guess, but I know what's really behind it. I *am* different. I'm stubborn, pigheaded, always rushing into things without thinking. Mom keeps trying to teach me how to be graceful and gracious. So far, it hasn't taken. She thinks I resist her because I'm a natural tomboy, but down deep, it's because I know I can never be like her. That's why I fight her about wearing dresses and ribbons and . . ."

I was shocked at how painful it was to hear me actually put my feelings into words.

"They just make me look all the more gawky and geeky. So I put on this big front about being independent and not caring about girl things."

That was enough. It hurt too much. "So yes," I concluded, "I am unique. I just wish I weren't quite *so* unique."

"All in agreement?" Dad said very quietly. I didn't look up, but I could see that no one raised a hand.

Except Grandpère.

"Thanks, Grandpère." And I really meant it, though it hurt like fury to see his hand in the air. But at least someone was being honest with me.

"*Ma chérie,* I have some bad news for you." There was a twinkle in his eye, but his face was completely grave. "One of the reasons you feel inferior is because you are."

My head snapped up.

"Well, you are. In some ways. And the reason you feel inadequate is because you are. And the reason you feel like you're not perfect is because you're not. Not in any way."

"Thanks, Grandpère," I said with a bitter laugh. "I needed that."

"None of us are," he went on gently. "And what you are feeling is what we all feel in some way or another at some time or another. We all do stupid things. We all make mistakes. We all get caught up in ourselves, and say things or do things that we regret."

"Amen," Rick murmured.

"Right on," Dad agreed.

"And the further bad news is," Grandpère continued, "I'm in my seventies, and I still have feelings of forever falling short. That's just life, my dear child."

To my surprise, he got up, came over, and put his arms around me.

Tears came to my eyes, but I didn't fight them. I threw my arms around him. "Thank you, Grandpère," I whispered. "Thank you for not saying how lovely and smart and wonderful I am and all that other kind of stuff."

"Oh, Danni," he whispered, bending down to kiss the top of my head, "I say that all the time."

"You do?"

His voice was suddenly husky. "Yes. With my eyes and with my heart."

He was right. I saw that in his eyes all the time, and it always warmed my soul. I hugged him back. "Thank you. I love you so much, Grandpère."

"*Oui,*" was all he managed to say in reply.

CHAPTER 16

Mt. Pennell, Henry Mountains
Tuesday, June 14, 2011

I was the last one up the next morning. As I gradually pried my eyes open, the first thing I saw was Dad's empty sleeping bag. Then I realized what had awakened me—the smell of wood smoke and frying bacon. Definitely one of the world's finest aromas. I rolled out of my bag and started putting on my hiking boots. I didn't even get my first stocking on before I grabbed my parka and put it on. It was cold!

When I came down from the trees a few minutes later, fully dressed and with my morning makeup on—yeah, right!—I saw Rick coming toward the fire from the opposite direction, carrying an armful of dead wood. Grandpère was getting a jug of orange juice out of the cooler.

Dad was crumbling bacon into a frying pan full of scrambled eggs. "Ready in about one minute. Grab your plates."

I loved this part of camping the very most. Breakfast around a campfire. No established campground. No picnic tables or fire pits. A hearty appetite sharpened by the mountain air. And no one else around but us. As I heaped my plate full and took one of the cups of juice, Rick shook his head in amazement.

"Hungry?" he asked with a sardonic smile.

"Don't push it, Ramirez," I growled. "We've got a lot of work to do today."

"I wasn't pushing, just asking."

As we settled in to eat, Rick looked at my dad. "Mr. McAllister? Is this one of the lost Spanish gold mines?"

He chuckled. "No, Rick. And by the way, now that you're a full-time employee, you can call me Mack."

"Yes, Mr. McAllister," he said evenly. I smiled. Rick told me once that his dad didn't like him calling adults by their first names. He didn't think it showed enough respect.

"This was one of the Wolverton mines," Dad explained.

"Oh," we both said. Down in Hanksville, near the Bureau of Land Management office, was the old Wolverton mill. The huge old mill, with a waterwheel at least twenty feet tall, had originally been built up in the mountains by a man named Wolverton back in the late 1800s. He'd come out from back East to look for lost Spanish gold mines. Some years ago, the BLM disassembled the old mill and moved it down to Hanksville.

"He filed the first claim on it," Dad continued. "When things didn't pan out for him, he sold most of his properties. It's had several owners since then."

"Cool!" This mine was over a hundred years old.

But Rick wasn't about to be deflected. "Do *you* think there are lost Spanish mines up here?"

"Nope."

"But you said—" He was clearly disappointed. And a bit bewildered. So was I, to be honest.

Grandpère chuckled. "Letting everyone think we're up here looking for lost Spanish gold is Mack's way of keeping people from asking too many questions about what we're really doing."

Dad nodded. "And you two are not to change their way of think-ing. Part of this job is keeping things to ourselves." His eyes moved from mine to Rick's. "In fact, what we do today, especially, stays with the four of us. Well, five of us. Mom knows all about this, of course. But not Cody. And you're not to tell him, Danni. Agreed?"

For some reason, that warning set my hackles prickling. Not that I was hurt by what he said, but because I suddenly had a faint feeling of . . . I wasn't even sure what to call it. It was like there was some kind of presence nearby.

I looked around, searching the trees and the hillside above us. Was there someone out there? Or something? I saw nothing, but still felt goose bumps pop out up and down my arms.

Come on, Danni. Now you're starting to sound like your mother.

Even as I chided myself, the feeling started to go away. It was probably all the talk about lost Spanish gold mines, I decided. Or—I had another thought—maybe this was part of the gift Grandpère said I had. Maybe I was feeling the presence of some of those early Spanish explorers. Maybe even Wolverton himself. That was seriously creepy.

"Something wrong, Danni?" Dad asked, watching me closely.

For a moment, I considered telling him the truth. But the feeling was fading quickly. "No," I said finally. "Just looking for wildlife."

Rick's focus was still on topic. "So are we looking for gold?" he asked.

"Nope," Dad said. "Already found that." Then, at Rick's look, he grinned. "It's only a few thousand dollars worth. In another of Wolverton's mines. But the vein ran out after just a few feet."

"So what *are* we looking for, Dad?"

He leaned back, a mysterious smile tugging at the corners of his mouth. "What do you two know about rhodium?"

"Rhodium?" Rick asked.

"You mean rodeos?" I said at the same time.

"No, rhodium. R-H-O-D-I-U-M. Rhodium."

Rick and I exchanged glances, but he was as blank as I was. For which I was grateful. It really fried my bacon when he knew the answers and I didn't.

Dad turned to Grandpère. "Tell these kids about rhodium, Jean-Henri."

"Gladly," he replied. "Rhodium is a precious metal belonging to the platinum group of metals. It is silver-white in color and is usually found only in connection with nickel and platinum. It gets its name from the Greek word *rhodon,* or rose, because sometimes it produces salts that are rose colored. It is very rare. In fact, it is a hundred times more rare than gold."

Rick and I leaned forward, our eyes wide.

"Really?" Rick said in awe.

"It is called one of the 'noble' metals because it is resistant to corrosion and oxidation. In fact, even when you heat rhodium to extremely high temperatures it doesn't oxidize."

"Oh," I said, trying to sound impressed.

He rubbed at the bridge of his nose, and I could tell he was fully into what Mom called his "professor mode."

"Aren't you going to ask me why it matters if rhodium doesn't oxidize at extreme temperatures?"

"Why does it matter that rhodium doesn't oxidize at extreme temperatures?" Rick said.

I was surprised to see that he had taken a pocket notebook out and was writing as fast as he could.

"Because then you can use it in the manufacture of things that produce very high temperatures, like spark plugs, industrial furnaces, and especially in automotive catalytic converters."

"That sounds enormously exciting," I volunteered.

"Manufacturers think so," Dad replied. "And they're among the few who can afford to buy rhodium."

I perked up. Maybe this stuff wasn't as boring as I thought. "So it's worth a lot?"

Dad bowed in Grandpère's direction with a grin. "On that question, I defer to my esteemed colleague, Professor Jean-Henri LaRoche."

"Thank you, Doctor McAllister," Grandpère said, returning the grin. "Currently, rhodium is selling for just about double the price of gold, and about a hundred times more than the price of silver."

"Oh, my gosh!" Rick blurted. "Really?"

"When I checked the other day," Grandpère went on, "rhodium was selling for a little more than three thousand dollars per troy ounce."

Rick was writing furiously. "About how big would an ounce of rhodium be?" he asked.

"About the size of a sugar cube. However, back in two thousand eight, the world suffered a temporary shortage of rhodium. Before it leveled out again, rhodium was selling for ten thousand dollars an ounce."

I whistled. Ten thousand bucks for a sugar cube? That was serious money. Suddenly I had another thought. "Is this a rhodium mine, Dad?"

He shook his head. "There's no such thing as a rhodium mine. Almost all rhodium is produced as a byproduct of nickel or platinum mining."

My face fell. "Oh."

His smile turned impish and sly. "But it would be nice to be the first exception to that rule, don't you think?"

My head snapped up. Dad's grin totally split his face.

"There are hard hats with lamps on them in the blue duffel bag. Grandpère, would you grab those burlap sacks? Rick, get our camping shovels. And Danni, there's a small mining pick on the back of my four-wheeler. Will you get it?"

CHAPTER 17

When we reached the mine shaft, we switched on the lamps attached to our hardhats and fell in behind Dad. As we moved toward the opening, I could see there had been activity up here recently. Fresh rock, footprints, some trash from the mine in a pile to one side. I made them stop while I took a few pictures on my camera phone. I wanted to remember everything about this trip.

As we entered the actual mine shaft, which was low enough that we had to duck our heads, my anxiety shot off like a rocket. Memories of that day I went into the coal mine with Dad suddenly came rushing back.

I was comforted to see a whole row of screw jacks lining both sides of the tunnels. They were placed at regular intervals beneath existing crossbeams, and in a couple of places, new crossbeams had been put in place to shore up the ceiling. My anxiety began to melt away. I should have known Dad wouldn't work in dangerous conditions.

"Did you do all this, Dad?" I called.

"Me and Grandpère," he said. "There's still more to do, but we'll only do that if we find what we're looking for." He looked at Rick. "Now you can see why I want to hire you full time. We've still got a lot of work to do."

Rick nodded, only half listening. He was examining one of the jacks more closely, fascinated. "How much weight can these bear, Mr. McAllister?"

"About twenty-five tons each."

He ran his hand along the metal. "Sweet!" he murmured.

We moved about a hundred or a hundred and fifty feet into the shaft. The light from the entrance was only a faint glow, and we had to use our headlamps to see. Slowing my step, I directed my light on the walls. There were still some places covered with what looked like a hundred years of dust and grime, but there were also fresh pick marks in a couple of other places where larger, circular patches had been cut away. Evidence of someone looking for something valuable.

About another hundred feet in, Dad slowed, then crouched down, directing his light on the left wall of the tunnel. "This is it. Come on up."

Gathering around him, we peered at the wall. A patch of rock about six feet square and a foot or two deep had been hewn out of the wall with picks. Piles of rubble lay on the ground. Dad stepped back so we could see better. Grandpère moved in alongside us, leaning over to get a better look. I guessed he hadn't seen this either.

"See anything unusual?" Dad asked.

I squinted, moving my light across the wall. Lots of pick marks. A couple of deeper gouges. Most of the rock was the same deep gray color, almost black. Rick and I saw it at the same instant. He reached out before I could and touched a thin, irregular line of rock that was lighter in color than the surrounding wall. It had a dull, silver-gray metallic look to it, somewhat like lead.

"This looks like a vein," Rick said, running his finger along it.

"Not a vein," I cried. "A whole seam." My voice echoed up and down the tunnel. "Is it silver, Dad?"

"No. That's what Wolverton thought too. Silver, or lead. He took samples down to the assayer and had them tested, but when the assayer told him it wasn't either silver or lead, but some unknown metal with no value, he gave up. He closed the mine and put it up for sale a few weeks later."

I jerked around, gaping at him. "Is this rhodium?"

Dad grinned like a kid on Christmas morning. In answer, he took out a folded sheet of paper from his pocket. "Gather around please."

We moved in, focusing the beams of our lamps on the paper.

"This is a report from the assayer's office in Salt Lake City. I received this a few days ago by registered mail," Dad said.

I shivered, and not just from the cool air inside the mine. I was so excited I thought I was going to jump out of my skin.

Pulling the paper closer, he began to read. "'To McAllister Mining Consultants. Attention: Lucas D. McAllister. Dear Mr. McAllister: In regards to the sample of powdered ore you submitted on May third of this year, we provide the following analysis. Sample Number One, Danny Boy Mine, Shaft Number One. The powder sample was loaded in a holder for analysis. It was examined using an X-ray diffractometer using Cu K-alpha radiation—' Blah, blah, blah—lots of scientific jargon." He looked up, winked at me, then continued reading, more slowly.

"'Results and Discussion: Patterns for the ore sample show this powder contains significant amounts of the element rhodium (symbol Rh; atomic number 45). Approximately 28 percent of the sample submitted is nearly pure rhodium.'"

He looked up, a triumphant smile across his face. "'Special Note: Because the results of this analysis run contrary to known characteristics of rhodium, along with the fact that no known rhodium deposits have been found in this particular area of North America, we took the liberty of running a second, independent evaluation of the samples submitted. This confirmed all aspects of the previous evaluation. With best regards,' Etc."

Grandpère let out a long breath. "Twenty-eight percent," he said in awe. "Oh my!"

Dad folded up the paper and returned it to his pocket. His face was grave, but I could see the excitement dancing in his eyes. "What do you say we get to work and fill those sacks? I'd like to take about a hundred pounds down with us. We've got some people who are very anxious to see this."

———————

It was nearly four o'clock by the time we had filled our four bags, eaten a cold meal, and started to pack up the campsite. We were tired, but still going strong on the excitement of what we had found. Dad and Grandpère strapped the ore sacks to the backs of their four-wheelers. Rick and I took our camping gear.

As we secured the last bungee cords on the machines, Grandpère laid a hand on Dad's shoulder. "All along I thought this whole idea was half crazy and that we were just having some fun up here, Mack, but now . . ." He cleared his throat quickly, "I'm really proud of you."

"You're part of this too, Grandpère. It's not just me." He turned to Rick and me. "And you are too. Now you see why we have to keep this strictly between us. We talk to no one, not until after we get this confirmed and make doubly sure our claims are properly registered. Word gets out, and we'll have people crawling all over this mountain."

"How much do you think what we have here is worth, Mr. McAllister?" Rick asked.

"What do you think, Grandpère? I'd say we have a little more than a hundred pounds of ore. But there's a lot more overburden in this stuff than in the sample I gave the assayer's office. Do you think we could get five kilos of good metal out of this?"

"Well," he mused, "that would be about eleven pounds, or about ten percent. I think we can do a little better than that. Maybe ten kilos."

"So how much would that be worth?" I asked.

To my surprise, Rick had his notebook out and a pencil in hand again. He looked at Dad. "How much is a troy ounce compared to a regular ounce?"

"Slightly more, but not enough to worry about now. Calculate it based on sixteen ounces to a pound." I could see that he was pleased with Rick's eagerness.

"So"—he was scribbling as he thought out loud—"a kilo is 2.2 pounds, or about . . . um . . . let's see. Sixteen plus sixteen, plus about three more ounces, would be thirty-five ounces per kilo." He looked up. "Right?"

"Right so far," Grandpère responded, grinning.

He was still scribbling and talking to himself. "If we have ten kilos, that's three hundred fifty ounces. At three thousand dollars an ounce, we have . . . um . . ." He stopped, leaned in closer, checking his math. When he looked up again, his jaw was slack. "That's one million, fifty thousand dollars worth of rhodium, Mr. McAllister."

"Shut up!" I cried.

Grandpère jerked around. "What did you say?"

Dad laughed. "It's all right, Grandpère. That's just the teenage way of saying, 'You gotta be kidding.'"

A million dollars? For a half a day's work with picks and shovels? I couldn't believe it. I leaned heavily against the nearest four-wheeler. We all stared at each other, stunned.

Dad finally turned to me, his face completely sober. "Let's get one thing straight right now, young lady," he said. "You're not going to get a birthday present like this every year."

I feigned a pout. "Really?" Then I grabbed my cell phone. "Then I have to have at least one picture of my million-dollar birthday."

CHAPTER 18

By the time we were off the mountain and back at the campground where we had left the trucks, it was almost eight thirty. As we got off the machines and stretched, Dad turned to Rick. "We can get this, Rick. Why don't you take off and surprise your dad by being home early? And tell him thanks again for letting you come."

"I . . ." He glanced at his watch, and then at me.

I nodded. "I'll stay here and help. It would be a real nice thing, Rick. Let him know how grateful we are."

"You sure?"

"I'm sure," Dad said. "And knowing how hard it is for Danni to cross that line between death and the resurrection each morning, let's not start work until about ten tomorrow."

Rick ignored my cry of protest. "Okay. And thanks again for everything, Mr. McAllister." He grinned. "I've never made a million dollars in one day before."

"Neither have I," my dad answered with a laugh.

I walked Rick to the truck and watched as he threw his sleeping bag and backpack in the rear of the 4Runner. "See ya tomorrow, Danni."

I briefly touched his arm. "I'm so glad you got to be here for all this, Rick."

He nodded as he opened the door and climbed in behind the wheel. But he didn't close the door. He looked at me kind of funny.

"What?"

"What you said to Grandpère last night . . ."

"Yeah, what about it?"

"For a kid with freckles and an attitude, you did all right."

"Hey!" I said, thrown totally off-balance by the praise in his eyes. The only way to cope with that was to make light of it. "It's only the middle of June. You think I've got freckles now, wait until August. And keep calling me freckle-face, and you'll see what an attitude really is. And besides, who are you calling a kid? I'm sixteen now, and have a driver's license, and—"

He cut in quickly. "Chill, Danni. I mean it. I thought what you said was real special. It was for me anyway."

I didn't know what to say, so I just mumbled "Thanks, Rick. See ya tomorrow," and stepped back.

He looked like he wanted to say something else, then changed his mind. He shut the door, started the engine, and waved as he pulled away.

—•—

It took us more than an hour to get everything loaded and another forty-five minutes to get back to the highway and turn north back toward town. The clock on the dashboard showed 10:27.

"Dad?" I spoke in a low voice because Grandpère was snoring softly in the backseat.

"Yes?"

"What are you going to do with all that money?"

He didn't hesitate, which told me he'd been thinking about it already. "Actually, we're going to sell the mine."

"*What?* No, Dad."

"We faxed the original assay results to a company that mines nickel up in Manitoba, Canada. They've made us an offer. They're coming down this weekend to see it for themselves. Unless there's some unforeseen hitch, we'll close on the sale next week."

"But why, Dad? If it's worth this much?"

"In the first place, it takes a lot of money to get a mine producing, Danni, and they've got it. Besides, neither Grandpère nor I are interested in running a mine. We like finding them."

"How much did you sell it for?" I was pretty hurt. Name a mine after me, then sell it off without even asking.

"The final, agreed-upon price, is . . ." A slow smile played around the corners of his mouth. "No, I think I'd better not say until it's a done deal. Wouldn't want you to get your hopes up."

"So are we going to be rich?" I didn't wait for his answer. "If Rick's right, and we make a million dollars for every hundred pounds of ore, we're going to be really rich. Right?"

A passing car illuminated his face for a moment. "Would you like that?"

"To be rich? Uh . . . I'm not sure."

"Why not?"

"Will being rich change how we live?"

"Well, for one thing, you could buy your own car."

"Wicked!"

"When you turn twenty-six."

"Dad! I'm serious."

"So am I. But you have to wait your turn. First thing I'm going to do is buy a bright red Ferrari F430."

"Go on!" That was Dad's dream car, but imagining him driving up to our little country store in a car worth a quarter of a million dollars seemed a bit out of touch.

"What if we built a new house out on that nob that overlooks the river?"

"Nuh-uh. Everyone in town would think we're getting all snooty and stuff."

"Good." He reached over and took my hand. "We live pretty good, don't you think? I mean, sure, we'd get Mom that new refrigerator she's been wanting, and recarpet the family room where you and Cody spilled red punch. Maybe put in that sunporch Mom's been talking about so she can have her own studio."

"Do we still owe money on the ranch?"

"Yes, about sixty grand, so we'd pay that off. Maybe travel some, I expect. Take Mom and Grandpère and the rest of us to France again."

"I would like that," Grandpère said, sitting up behind us, surprising us both.

"Me too," I said. "How about Rome while we're over there? Italy has the most handsome men in the world."

"I beg your pardon," Grandpère said.

"Next to France," I hastily added.

This was fun. I didn't want to be super rich, like the people I saw on TV, but being a little rich sounded kinda nice.

"Or," Dad said seriously, "what if we created a trust fund to help other kids, like we helped Rick?"

That thought set me back. "You mean give them money?"

"Not directly. I'm not sure that would be wise. But suppose we set up a foundation that could help find them jobs, teach them a trade or a skill, find scholarship money for them so they can go to college, make sure they graduate from high school."

"That would be seriously cool, Dad. I mean, seriously!"

Grandpère leaned forward and nudged me. "Think about the second Remember: There is purpose to your life. Mack's idea would give some real purpose to our lives." He smiled. "I mean . . . umm . . . we're like talking some real serious purpose here."

It was a pretty good imitation of a ditzy teenager. Like me. Laughing, I reached back and took his hand. "You're seriously cool yourself, Grandpère."

Turning back to Dad I asked, "Could I be part of that too, Dad?"

"What do you think, Grandpère? Have we got a place for Danni?"

"Well, after this trip," he said, his voice sober, "it's obvious you and I need someone who can translate Teen Speak. You know, kind of help us old guys bridge the generation gap. You up for that?"

"What do you think?" I answered gleefully.

I woke with a start, clawing the air, trying to pull myself out of a blackness that seemed to have a thousand hands grasping at me and pulling me down. I guess I was yelling too because next thing I knew, Dad's hand was on my shoulder, shaking me. "Danni! Wake up. It's all right. You're okay."

My head was swinging back and forth, my breath was coming in rapid, shallow gasps, and I'm sure my eyes were bugged out like I was a crazy lady. All around me was darkness, and I wasn't sure where I was. Then I saw a light coming toward us. Quickly it become two lights, and a car flashed by us in the night, and I remembered we were in Dad's truck.

"Breathe deeply," Dad said in a soothing voice. He gently rubbed the back of my neck as he spoke. I did, and immediately things started to settle down.

I felt Grandpère's hands on my shoulders. "You all right, *ma chérie?*" he asked.

A deep sigh escaped my lips. "Yes . . . I . . . I think so."

"Bad dream?"

"No, I . . . umm. . . . I'm not sure. I felt like I was drowning or something." Instantly, the panic was back, surging up like a monstrous wave. My heart was pounding. My mouth was dry. My hands were trembling. And what was really, really weird was that I suddenly wanted more than anything in the world to hold the pouch in my hands. I slid away from Dad far enough to reach into the side pocket of the door. The minute my fingers closed on the fabric, I felt a huge relief. It was like the fear was being pushed back, letting the calm return.

"It's okay now," I said. "I'm all right." I took another deep breath, releasing it slowly. I looked out into the night. "Where are we?"

Dad pointed out the windshield. "Those are the lights of Hanksville off in the distance. We're about five miles from home."

I looked at the clock: 11:57.

He patted my knee. "It's been a long two days. I think you're just very tired."

"I am, but this trip has been so great, Dad. Thank you so much for—"

I stopped dead, my flesh crawling again. Chills raced up and down my spine, and for a moment I couldn't speak. I began to shiver violently. "Dad, stop the truck! Something's wrong."

He gaped at me for a second, then immediately let off the gas and put his foot on the brake. We coasted to a stop on the side of the road. "What's the matter, Danni? Are you sick?"

I was, but not in the way he meant. I was sick with fear. I had a major case of the creepy-crawlies.

"What is it, Danni?" Grandpère said, gripping my shoulder. "What are you feeling?"

How could I describe it? It was awful. It was making me light-headed and nauseated. "It's like that day you said we were going to Robbers Roost. Like there's something evil nearby." I stopped, focusing inward. "No, that's only part of it. It's . . . It's like something bad is going to happen."

"Are you sure it's not just the dream coming back?" Dad asked.

"No," Grandpère said. "She's right. I feel it too."

That didn't help. "What is it?" I cried. The feelings were coming so fast I could hardly define them. "I feel it has to do with the mine." I grabbed Dad's arm. "No, wait!" My heart hammered so loudly in my ears I could barely hear myself. My fingers dug into his arm. "Dad! Mom and Cody are in danger. We have to find them," I blurted out. Where had those words come from?

Stunned, Dad gaped at me. He exchanged a look with Grandpère.

"Mack, is your pistol still in the glove compartment?" Grandpère asked. That was the last thing I expected to hear.

Dad nodded. "Get it for him, Danni." He lifted his phone even as he spoke. "I'll call Angelique. Make sure everything is okay."

"No," I cried, surprising myself.

"Why not?" Grandpère exclaimed.

"I . . . I don't know. I just know that we shouldn't call them."

Dad and Grandpère exchanged another look, then Grandpère said, "Go, Mack. We've got to go now."

Dad popped the truck in gear and roared off, peppering the trailer with gravel from beneath the back wheels.

Grandpère touched my shoulder. His voice was low and filled with urgency. "Danni, listen to me. No matter what happens, don't let go of the pouch. Do you understand? Don't let go of the pouch."

PART FOUR

El Cobra

CHAPTER 19

"Yes, Grandpère," I whispered. Then, turning to Dad, I said, "Hurry, Daddy. Hurry."

As we turned off the highway into our lane, I grabbed Dad's arm again. "Turn off your lights, Dad. And slow down." He gave me a strange look, but did as I asked.

"What is it, Danni?" Grandpère asked.

"Someone's there. At the house." We were about a quarter of a mile away, but I could feel that uneasy feeling growing stronger.

"Who?" Dad demanded.

"I . . . I'm not sure. Someone. Mom and Cody are very frightened." I blinked. How did I know all of that?

Dad slowed the truck to a crawl, but the tires of the pickup and trailer still crunched loudly on the gravel. He turned off the engine and let the truck roll to a stop near the barn. He punched the overhead switch so that the interior light wouldn't come on when we opened the doors.

My fists were clenched as I held the pouch to my chest. *Please, let them be all right.*

The area around the house was quiet. Mom's SUV was parked in the driveway, not in the garage, but it looked like every light in the house was on.

"They should be asleep by now," Grandpère said in low voice. "Weren't they supposed to be back from Denver by seven or eight?"

"Yes," Dad said. "I told them we would be late and not to wait up." Taking the pistol from me, he got out of the truck.

"Which duffel bag has the rifles?" Grandpère asked as Dad started strapping on his weapon.

"One of those on the bottom," he said. "But there's no time to look for them now. Danni, let Grandpère out. You stay here."

"Dad, no. I—"

His look cut off any protest. In moments, both he and Grandpère were running in a low crouch, staying in the grass so as to not make any noise. When they reached the house, Dad tried to look in the windows, but all the blinds were closed. Motioning to Grandpère, they tiptoed onto the porch. Dad hesitated for a brief second, then he burst through the door, pistol drawn, Grandpère on his heels. A moment later, the door slammed behind them, and then there was silence.

I waited for a long time—maybe all of ten seconds—and then I was out of the truck, carefully shutting the door behind me. As I started for the house, the living room drapes pulled back enough to show the dark shape of someone's head looking out. I almost shouted and waved, a rush of relief sweeping over me, but then the drapes closed again. I stopped, fully expecting Dad or Grandpère to open the door and call for me. But there was only silence.

Though I sorely wanted to find my rifle, I pushed the thought aside. It wasn't easily accessible. And there was no time. I had to find out what was going on inside the house. I pulled out my cell phone, preparing to call 911, then I remembered I had taken so many pictures up at the mine, my battery had died. And in the rush to get ready, I had left the charger at home.

Shoving the phone back in my pocket, I angled toward the barn. The equipment shed kept me out of view of the house, and I headed around back. Clinging to the pouch like it was a life preserver, I made it to the corner of the house. I stopped and listened intently for a few moments, then peeked carefully around the corner to see if anyone was there. The back porch light was on, providing some visibility. I saw two large, boxy Hummers parked by the gazebo. Both were black and gleamed in the light from the yard lamp. I drew back. Not good. My mouth was dry, my heart was pounding, and my legs felt weak.

After a moment, I risked another look. There was no one in sight. If there were someone in those Hummers, there was no way to know it. Not from where I was, anyway. I would have to risk it. Keeping low, I started along the back of the house. *Oh, please let there be a window I can see through.*

No such luck. My anxiety was crackling like a Fourth of July fireworks show. With ten acres of alfalfa in front of the house, and the first of the barren hillsides rising behind it, no one was close enough to see into our house so usually we left the blinds up, even at night, but now they were all closed.

I heard a noise behind me and started to whirl. A pair of powerful arms grabbed me from behind and lifted me off my feet. I screamed. One hand wearing a surgical glove clamped over my mouth. A voice growled in my ear. It was harsh and raspy, almost like gravel being shaken in a can. He spoke in Spanish, but though I was in my second year of Spanish at school, the only word I caught was *señorita.*

That was all right. I didn't need a translator to know I was in trouble. I immediately forced myself to go totally limp. It was a trick

Dad taught me when he and I used to wrestle. My arms were already folded across my chest because I was holding the pouch. So instead of struggling, I surrendered, letting my body relax. In response, the man's grip relaxed too. Then I thrust my arms outward, hard, breaking his grip, and I dropped like a rock.

It worked. I was free. I took off like a shot as he yelled at me. My legs were pumping like pistons, and I felt a thrill of exultation. A second figure stepped out from between the Hummers. He wore a ski mask, green doctor's scrubs, and surgical gloves. The holster around his waist was empty, because he had the pistol and its silencer pointed directly at my head.

I slid to a stop, hands shooting skyward, one gripping the pouch. "Don't shoot," I cried.

The first man came pounding up and grabbed me from behind again. The one from the Hummer came right up into my face. "El Cobra said not to hurt you. Don't tempt me," he hissed in English with a hint of a Spanish accent.

He barked something in Spanish at my captor. The other man let go and came around to face me. To my surprise, he was only an inch or two taller than I was, and he had a lot of weight on him. Mom might have called him "pleasingly plump." A better phrase from my Spanish class popped into my head: El Gordo. The fat one.

I saw he wore the same kind of scrubs, gloves, and ski mask as the second man. Only El Gordo also carried an assault rifle with a silencer slung over his shoulder. The combination was so bizarre, the scrubs and surgical gloves so totally out of context with the ski mask and the rifle, that it turned my blood cold.

The guy from the Hummer took his place behind me. He was the opposite of Gordo. He was tall and muscular, built like a weight lifter. He wore a pair of heavy Doc Martens; the yellow stitching easily identifiable even in the dim light. He took the pouch from me, checked it quickly to ensure it was empty, then hung it over my shoulder. Then he grabbed my arms and yanked on them hard. I moment later, I felt the cold steel of handcuffs close around my wrists and heard a metallic click.

He leaned in. I could feel the hotness of his breath on my neck as whispered into my ear. "All right, *señorita*, let's go."

CHAPTER 20

"We found this one sneaking around the back, El Cobra," the guy wearing the Doc Martens said in English as he and Gordo led me into the family room. My whole family was there. Dad and Mom were on the love seat. Mom was crying, and her eyes were puffy and red.

Directly in front of them, a man in green scrubs stood with a pistol pointing at them. He wasn't as tall as Doc, but he clearly had been pumping a lot of iron too. His scrub top strained against the muscles of his chest and biceps. Aside from his powerful build, there was a commanding presence about him, and I noticed that everyone kept their eyes on him.

Grandpère and Cody were seated on the couch across from Mom and Dad. Grandpère was inscrutable—calm, unruffled, almost regal. He held Cody's hand. Cody looked pale, but his head was up, and his eyes were defiant as he glared at our captors. He was mad, and suddenly I wanted to hug him and tell him how proud I was of him. Grandpère's eyes never left me, and I had the feeling he was trying to tell me something.

The man they called El Cobra started talking to my captors in Spanish, so I looked around the room quickly. There were three other men, all dressed exactly the same. In the light, they looked like six aliens with their green-clad bodies, ghostly white hands, and black heads with hollow eyes. Each one had an assault rifle with a silencer too. One man stood guard at the front door. Another, noticeably shorter than the others, stood behind Grandpère and Cody. A third stood back near the window where he could see everyone.

My eyes went back to the person standing behind Grandpère. Not a man, I thought. A woman. She was the shortest of them all, and slight of build. And curvy, though her scrubs hung on her like a sack. Interesting.

Ironically, everything else in the room seemed perfectly normal. The house had not been ransacked. There weren't bullet holes in the wall or any signs of struggle. The men must have come in some time after Mom and Cody got home. Or, more likely, they were already here, waiting.

I suddenly realized there was another oddity in all this. My mind was not numb with panic. It was past midnight, and I was tired. Yet my mind was firing like it was on full throttle. Not only were all these details registering with perfect clarity, but I was making connections, putting things together. Perhaps it was one of the effects of the adrenaline rush that had been coursing through my body since that moment I woke up screaming.

"She has a cell phone," El Cobra said in English. "Find it."

He had a slight accent—maybe Spanish, but I wasn't sure. Whatever it was, his English was excellent. I was trying to absorb as much detail as possible so I could tell the police later. Were they members of a Mexican drug cartel? Stories of isolated ranchers being brutally murdered along the Arizona border came to mind, and my panic meter shot up sharply. What was the cartel doing this far north? And why us?

My thoughts were cut off as Doc stepped forward and started his search. My cell phone was in my jacket pocket. He found it immediately, but that didn't stop him from completing a pat down, his hands lingering a half a second longer than was necessary. Everything about the guy gave me the shivers. I couldn't see his face behind his ski mask, of course, but I was confident he was ugly. Everything about him felt ugly.

Then he grabbed my arm, fingers pressing hard into my flesh, and steered me toward the couch. "Move it!" he barked.

"Ow!" I cried. "You're hurting me."

He turned me around so I was facing him, then gave me a shove backward. I crashed down on the couch, nearly hitting Grandpère. The cuffs dug deeply into my wrists, and I yelled in pain.

"Stop it!" Mom shouted, leaping to her feet. El Cobra stepped in front of her, but she knocked him aside with one shoulder and went after Doc like a heat-seeking missile. "Take those cuffs off of her!" she yelled, sticking her face right up to his ski mask.

Doc started to raise his pistol, but if Mom saw it, she gave it no mind. She spun around to face El Cobra. "If you hurt my children, you'll get nothing from us. Nothing! Do you hear me?"

We were all stunned by her ferocity. One moment she was in tears; two seconds later she was a mama lion going for the jugular. I could see that Dad was even more shocked than El Cobra was.

Doc came up behind her and jammed the muzzle of his pistol against her back.

She knocked it away with her elbow, not even turning around to see what it was. "Now!" she shouted at El Cobra. "Take her cuffs off."

El Cobra eyed her for a long moment, then nodded at Doc. "She's right. We're not here to hurt anyone. Take off the cuffs."

It was like a huge collective sigh exploded from us all as Doc pulled me to my feet. A moment later, the cuffs were off, and Mom and I were in each other's arms. She was still breathing hard, and I could feel her chest rising and falling. She brushed her hand against my cheek. "Are you okay?" she whispered.

"I am now," I said, my voice tinged with awe.

"This is a mistake," Doc snarled. "The girl's a hellcat. She nearly got away outside."

"Then watch her," the boss said. "If she tries to get away, she's yours." El Cobra looked directly at me, stabbing the air with one finger. "You hear that, Danny Boy? And he's not the only one who would love to get his hands on you, so behave yourself. *¿Comprendes?*"

It felt like an icy draft swept across my bare flesh. I knew he meant what he said, and that was frightening enough. But what really turned me cold was having him call me Danny Boy. Anyone in town could have told him my nickname was Danni, but no one except Dad ever called me Danny Boy. If he knew that, then he knew a lot about my family, and that was truly frightening.

My chin came up, and I managed to meet the marble black eyes that peered out at me from beneath his mask, even though I was shaking like a leaf in a hurricane.

Doc tossed El Cobra my cell phone, who dropped it into an open duffel bag at his feet. As he did so, I caught a glimpse of the butt of Dad's pistol and wondered if they had disarmed him without a fight. Then I saw El Cobra staring at me. I felt another flutter of fear.

"What's that?" he asked.

For a moment, I didn't know what he meant. Then I saw he was looking at the pouch. I pulled it off my shoulder and held it out before Doc could grab it. "It's an old pouch I carry around for good luck. There's nothing in it."

"She's right, El Cobra," Doc said. "I checked. It's empty."

El Cobra snapped his fingers, and Doc took the pouch from me and tossed it to him. He caught it with one hand. Sticking his pistol in his belt, he patted the pouch briefly, then looked inside. Finally, he looked up at me. "Why do you carry an old, useless purse?" Before I could answer, he nodded. "Ah, *sí*. This is the purse your grandfather gave you for your birthday. The nanny pouch, no?"

I winced, feeling Grandpère's eyes boring into me. My mind was frantically working. Whoever El Cobra's source was, it had to be someone from Hanksville, someone anxious to pass on the town joke—Danni and Nanny. Which meant this wasn't a random home invasion.

"Well, *señorita,* have you nothing to say? Why do you carry around an old, useless purse?"

"It belonged to my great-grandmother," I answered. "It has been in our family for many generations. It has great sentimental value, nothing more."

"I see. Perhaps I shall keep it then, to make sure you give us no further problems."

"No!" I couldn't help myself. "It means nothing to you. Please give it back."

I could sense those glittering black eyes taking my measure. I forced myself to meet his stare. After a moment, he suddenly flipped the pouch in my direction, like he was throwing a Frisbee. My hand shot out and grabbed it.

He laughed, a cold, mirthless bark. "Hear me well, *chiquita.* You will do as I say or else I will personally stuff that purse down your throat. *¿Comprendes?*"

Chiquita. Little girl. A term of endearment for one's girlfriend. I felt physically sick. *"Sí."* I turned my face away and found myself looking directly into Grandpère's eyes. The disappointment in them was evident, and after a moment, I had to turn my gaze elsewhere because they only made me feel worse.

CHAPTER 21

With me put in my place, El Cobra called a war council. He moved to one side, keeping Mom and Dad clearly in his sights, and began talking to Doc and the woman. Their voices were low enough I couldn't tell if they were speaking in Spanish or English. They seemed to argue about something, then finally come to some agreement.

El Cobra came back and sat on the coffee table directly in front of Mom and Dad. His pistol waved nonchalantly in front of their noses. The others returned to their places. Mom was subdued again, staring at her hands. Her fingers interlocked and twisted together as though she was in pain.

"Okay, then," he began. "Here's the deal, Mr. Lucas McAllister." He cocked his head. "May I call you Luke?"

Dad shrugged. "No one calls me Luke. It's Mack, Lucas, or Mr. McAllister."

"Okay, Luke. Here's the deal. And, by the way, I will not be repeating myself, so listen carefully. We have no desire to hurt you or your family. We're here to negotiate a simple business deal. When we're done, you'll never see us again."

He leaned forward, looking directly at Dad. "It's important for you to believe that, Luke, so you don't complicate matters. You have a beautiful family, and you can make sure nothing happens to them simply by cooperating with us. There is no way you can identify us, and when this is all over, we will simply disappear, and it will all be over."

"What is it you want?"

"If you try anything, such as thinking that you can contact the police, your family will be the ones to simply disappear, and none of you will ever be seen again. Do you understand me?"

Dad's head bobbed briefly. "What is it you want?" he asked again.

"Twenty million dollars."

I gasped. So did Grandpère. The blood drained from Mom's face. Dad nearly choked. Then he shocked everyone by laughing in the man's face. "I don't have that kind of money."

"Oh, really?"

"We have about three thousand dollars in our checking account and twenty-three thousand in savings, but—"

"We know exactly how much money is in all of your accounts, Luke, but thank you for being cooperative. That is what I'm talking about."

Something was wrong. El Cobra seemed to know everything about us—my nickname, what I called the pouch, how much money we had in the bank, when we would be home. If he knew so much, why ask for such an outrageous fortune when he knew we didn't have it?

He reached down and fumbled in the bag at his feet for a moment. When he straightened, he held a sheet of paper, folded in half. My head came up with a snap. I remembered the impression that had come to me shortly after I awoke from my nightmare. *This is about the mine.*

He unfolded the paper, feigning puzzlement. "Let's see," he mused. "What have we here?"

He held it up in front of Dad's face. Shock flashed across his face, then Dad's shoulders slumped, and hope drained out of him like water down a rain pipe. Courteous as an English butler, El Cobra turned and held up the paper for Grandpère, Cody, and me to see. I heard Grandpère's sharp intake of breath. But I was not surprised. It was the report from the assayer's office, a duplicate of what Dad had showed us this morning. So that answered one question. The report had named the mine: Danny Boy, Shaft One. That's how he knew my nickname.

When El Cobra spoke again, any trace of amusement was gone. His voice was cold, hard, and menacing. "Luke, we know about your offer from the Canadians. When I first learned they were paying you a cool twenty million dollars, I thought somebody had been out in the Canadian cold for too long."

Twenty million dollars? No wonder Dad hadn't wanted to tell me the amount.

Seeing my expression, El Cobra laughed aloud. "So little Danny Boy didn't know how much her mine was worth. I don't blame you for not telling her, Luke. In a town like Hanksville, such news would spread like wildfire." He bent over, his face just inches from my dad's. "And when I learned what rhodium brings in per ounce," he said, "well, all I can say is, 'Excelente, señor. Muy bien.' So tell me, Luke. How much do you think those four sacks of ore you brought back are worth?"

I felt a little jolt. He knew about the ore? Was that what I had felt this morning at breakfast? Had there been someone up there in the trees watching us?

Dad considered his question, then said, "We won't know until we—"

The man moved so quickly that Dad didn't even have a chance to flinch. In one instant, El Cobra had jammed the muzzle of his pistol into Dad's cheekbone. Mom screamed. I yelled. Cody gasped. Grandpère leaped to his feet.

Instantly Gordo, Doc, and the others were in our faces, waving their weapons. Grandpère fell back heavily onto the couch. It had all happened so fast. No wonder they called him El Cobra.

"Let me ask that again, Luke," he said, his voice tight. "How much rhodium did you bring down with you? I know you haven't had it assayed yet, but give me a ballpark guess."

Though my heart was pounding and my breath had caught in my throat, once again my brain registered a piece of trivia. This guy used American slang like a native. He had lived in the United States a long time, perhaps most of his life. Maybe he wasn't Hispanic at all.

To his everlasting credit, Dad lifted his head slowly, even though it must have pushed the pistol into his flesh even more. "The sample we had assayed was carefully chosen. This is pretty much raw ore."

The pistol was withdrawn. "Go on."

"We have a vein about twenty-five feet long. It looks promising, but in the mining business, how much good ore is in a vein is always a crap shoot. A vein can run for as much as a mile, or it can peter out after a few feet. After an independent investigation, and after receiving a copy of the same report you have there, the new owners are betting there's a lot more than twenty million dollars worth of rhodium in the mine. And they're probably right."

"Then why sell it?"

"I'm not interested in running a mine. Also, there'll be a huge capital investment to get it running. Plus there's always a chance the

US Forest Service won't approve any kind of mining operation up there, let alone a big one."

To my surprise, Grandpère spoke up. "If I may, sir, I have a pen and a small notebook in my shirt pocket. We are thinking the ratio of rhodium to ore is about ten percent. I could quickly figure how much rhodium those four sacks would yield if we are correct."

"Check his pockets," El Cobra snapped to Doc.

He leaned over and roughly yanked a pocket notebook and pen from Grandpère's shirt front.

"You're the LaRoche part of the McAllister and LaRoche partnership, aren't you, old man?" El Cobra asked.

"Yes."

"Make it fast."

Doc handed Grandpère the pen and notebook. As Grandpère began to write rapidly, I wondered what he was up to. Ricky had already done the calculations. Was he stalling for time? But why?

Dad spoke, pulling my attention back to him. "If you let my family go, I'll sign the mine over to you. It could be worth a lot more than twenty million."

El Cobra offered a hard, mirthless laugh. "Oh, you'd love that, wouldn't you? Us registering the mine in our names. Coming up to work it every day. Getting cozy with the local sheriff." He turned to Grandpère. "Come on, Gramps. What's it worth?"

Grandpère held up one finger, continuing to write with his other hand. Finally he tore out a sheet and held it up. Doc snatched it from him. He looked at it and did a double take. He walked over to his leader and handed the paper to him.

El Cobra looked at it, and his eyes perceptibly widened. "One million dollars?" he cried. "In four sacks of ore?"

Grandpère nodded. He lowered his hands. "*If* we're right about there being ten percent rhodium. That's only a guess. Right now, all we have are four bags of rock."

El Cobra let loose with a string of Spanish words, talking to his henchmen. There was considerable elation among them. The shortest one, the one right behind Grandpère, said something and confirmed my earlier guess that she was a woman.

She must have sensed I was watching her, because she turned to face me. What I saw startled me. The light was fully on her face, and though she was hooded like the others, I saw startling light green eyes through the eye holes. I hadn't expected that, and I had to reexamine my assumptions. Maybe this wasn't a Hispanic gang after all, just a gang with Hispanics in it. I actually felt relieved in some small way. The Mexican drug cartels had a reputation for ruthless brutality and merciless elimination of their enemies. These were hardly regular churchgoers, but maybe they weren't cold-blooded murderers either.

Just then I felt a touch on my leg. I looked over. Grandpère was motioning with his eyes for me to look down. I did and saw that he held the notebook down low and close to his body, but turned so it was facing me. The page was filled with big, bold letters.

WHEN I STAND UP TAKE CODY AND THE POUCH AND HIDE IN YOUR OLD FORT. TRUST ME!

I nodded. My body felt like a coiled spring. I was ready to do anything to release the tension.

Grandpère didn't look at me as he leaned forward. "So what is your plan, *Monsieur* El Cobra?" As he spoke, he casually closed the notebook and put it back into his shirt pocket.

"It's simple," El Cobra said. He looked at Dad. "The closing on the sale of the mine is Tuesday morning, right?"

Dad nodded. "Yes. Nine o'clock at a bank in Salt Lake City."

"When everything is properly executed, your Canadian friends will transfer twenty million dollars into your company's account. Everyone will shake hands and congratulate each other. You and the old man will then return to your car, where I will be waiting. We will drive to a secure location not far away, where my *compadres* will be waiting with your wife and children."

Mom gasped, her eyes widening in shock. Cody gave a low cry beside me. But from Dad's expression, I could tell he had already seen that one coming. He merely nodded.

"We will then transfer your twenty million dollars into an account in the Cayman Islands. We will leave you securely locked in a room, and make our departure. Just before our plane takes off for an international destination, I will call the Salt Lake City police department, and tell them where you can be found, and you shall be free within the hour."

"What guarantee do we have that you will keep your word?" Dad asked.

"None," he said easily. "Except for this. As I said, you cannot identify any of us. You will have no idea where we have gone, but I can assure you that it will be to a country which does not have an extradition treaty with America. Finally, remember this. For a twenty million dollar theft, there will be a vigorous but short-lived manhunt. For the murder or the disappearance of an entire family, that manhunt will go on forever. Do you agree?"

Dad didn't respond either way. "So what happens between now and then?"

"You and Grandpa will stay here, going about your daily business, acting normal in every way. You will tell people that your wife decided to take the children to Montana to see their grandparents there. But they will actually be much closer at hand than that. I assure you they will be perfectly comfortable and well-cared for. Once each day, at a time of our choosing, you will be allowed to talk to them."

Mom buried her face in her hands. Dad moved closer and took her in his arms. "It's all right, Angelique. It's all right." He stroked her hair.

"If you do exactly as I say, we'll let you keep the four sacks of ore. If Pops here is right, you can come out of this with a little over a million dollars. That should motivate you not to be difficult. But if you cross me, you'll have nothing. Not even your life. *¿Está claro?* Is that clear enough for you?"

I believed him. And I think Dad did too, because he said. "Yes, I understand."

At that moment, Grandpère gave my leg a hard knock with his knee. Then he stood up. "Well, I don't," he shouted. He started toward El Cobra, fists clenched. "This is an outrage! What right do you have to—"

Instantly, the others sprang into action, moving in to cut him off, rifles jerking up and pointing at his chest. Grandpère pushed right into them, jaw tight, head jutted forward. Gordo lifted his rifle and slammed it into Grandpère's back. He went sprawling.

Mom screamed and was at his side in an instant. The other members of the gang closed in around them both, weapons ready.

My heart was pounding so hard I thought I might faint, but the instant I saw that all the attention was focused on Grandpère, I leaped up, grabbing Cody's hand. I yanked him to his feet and headed for the back of the house, half dragging him behind me.

CHAPTER 22

We shot out of the family room and into the hall, took three running leaps to the left, and burst out the back door into the night.

"No, Danni!" Cody cried, trying to pull away.

I gripped his hand tighter and raced toward the back of the garage.

In gratitude for Mom's willingness to move to Hanksville, Dad promised her that once his consulting business was up and running, we would add a major addition to the house. A year later, we added a new two-car garage and converted the old garage into a new kitchen, family room, and dining room. Dad's original intent was to turn the space above the garage into an office, and so he had installed a door and an outside set of stairs. But by the time the garage was done, Dad had ended up converting a downstairs bedroom into his office. We used the attic only for storage now.

Behind me, I could hear shouts and what sounded like furniture crashing. I had to get around the side of the house and up those stairs before anyone came outside. If they didn't see us immediately, they'd have to stop and figure out which way we had gone.

"Run, Cody! Run!"

He finally stopped fighting me, and we rounded the side of the garage a couple of seconds before we heard the back door slam open with a loud crack. More shouts. Rapid Spanish. A woman cursing bitterly in English.

I gave Cody a shove. "Up the stairs," I hissed. "Don't make any noise." Not waiting for him to comply, I ducked under the stairs, reached my fingers into the crack between the cement and the bottom stair, and retrieved Dad's key. Moments later I was beside Cody, fumbling frantically to get the door unlocked. We ducked inside, closed the door softly, and I locked it behind us.

Just in time. Through the window I saw a figure come running around the house and pull up at the sight of the stairs. He looked at the darkened doorway above him, then took the stairs three at a time. I pushed Cody down, and we dropped out of sight.

The man grabbed the doorknob, rattling it noisily. A flashlight beam lit up the attic, sweeping back and forth. He rattled the door again and then turned and ran back down the stairs. "Nothing up here," he cried.

"Quick," I said in an urgent whisper. "Into the fort."

"I can't see," Cody said, his voice high-pitched and frightened.

"We can't turn on the lights. Here, take my hand." Holding my other hand out in front of me, I carefully made my way toward what we affectionately called "Fort McAllister."

Once it became clear Dad wasn't going to be building an office up here, Cody and I petitioned for permission to build a playhouse. We used leftover plywood, wooden boxes, sheets of cardboard, old blankets, and anything else we could scrounge up, creating a space about twenty feet square, which butted up beneath the steeply pitched roof.

It had been Cody's idea to make it into a fort. We had battlements, tube cannons, a flag that Mom helped us design, and a mixed

population of "civilians"—Barbie dolls and Harry Potter characters—
guarded by G.I. Joe action figures. We were the envy of all our friends,
and the other kids begged us to let them play up here.

I had outgrown the fort four or five years ago and hadn't been up
here since. I had to cover my nose to stop from sneezing as we kicked
up dust, even moving as slowly as we were.

Below us pandemonium reigned, and it was rapidly increasing
in volume. The only thing that gave me any comfort was the fact
that I kept hearing El Cobra shouting, "No shooting. I don't want
them hurt." That and Grandpère's words in my mind: *TRUST ME.*
Moments later, Cody and I were huddled together in the fort, two
old, musty blankets pulled over us.

We could hear them hunting for us. Sometimes, the voices drew
nearer, and we held our breath. Other times they moved away. I could
tell they were searching out near the barn and the equipment shed.
We jumped when the garage doors rumbled beneath us, but a moment later, the woman called out something in Spanish, and her footsteps left again.

Just as I was beginning to dare hope that we might get away, I
heard Doc's voice.

"Where do these stairs go?" he demanded.

To my utter shock, Grandpère answered. "To the attic. We use it
for storage, but the kids have a playhouse up there."

No, Grandpère! We're up here. You told us to come here. I heard
footsteps on the stairs, and I immediately understood what was going
on. If Dad and Grandpère didn't cooperate . . . I didn't finish that
thought in my mind.

"It's locked," another voice said.

"I have a key," Dad said after a moment's hesitation.

"I'm scared, Danni." Cody's voice was soft, almost a squeak.

I felt for the pouch, suddenly wanting to have it in my hand. I pulled it close to my chest with one hand, then gripped Cody's hand with the other and squeezed tightly. "We'll be all right, Code. We'll be all right."

Inside my mind, there was a maniacal laugh. *You have at least six armed people looking for you. They hold your mother, father, and grandfather captive. They're demanding twenty million dollars in ransom. Tell me, Danni—what part of that makes you feel like everything is all right?*

A moment later, we heard the door open and footsteps enter. We heard a click as someone flipped the light switch. Nothing happened.

Click. Click. Click.

Dad spoke. "The light's not working. Must have tripped a circuit breaker in that last thunderstorm."

I felt Cody's hand squirming in mine and realized I was holding him so tightly I was hurting him. *Let it be the woman. Please, if someone has to find us, don't let it be Doc.*

El Cobra spoke. "Give me your flashlight." A gleam of light appeared beneath the blanket. "All right, *señor* Luke. Call your kids out. Now."

CHAPTER 23

Knowing it was over, I reached for the blanket and started to pull it back. But at that instant, I felt a white-hot stab of pain in my chest. No. Not pain. More like an electric shock. And while it jolted me hard, it was not altogether unpleasant. It shot through my chest at the exact spot where I held the pouch against my shirt. Stunned, I realized that the pouch was hot. And not just from body heat. It was actually hot to my touch.

"Danni. Cody. If you're in here, come out now." Dad's voice was quiet.

"Danni?" It was Mom this time. "It's over. Show yourselves."

The footsteps moved closer. Talk about a jumble of emotions and thoughts! One part of me was terrified, but in my mind, I was still thinking clearly. Maybe not calmly, but clearly. I felt Cody move beside me.

DON'T MOVE! STAY WHERE RIGHT WHERE YOU ARE!

The words came into my mind with piercing surety. My hand shot out and grabbed Cody's elbow. I yanked him back down. "Stay down!" I said, pressing my mouth against his ear.

Footsteps were all around us. "Where is this playhouse of theirs?" El Cobra asked.

"There, in the corner," Grandpère said.

The flashlight beam swept back and forth, probing the darkness. They were almost to us. I could hear the sound of their breathing. My heart was banging so hard I was sure it would give us away.

LET GO OF THE BLANKET!

Again, the abruptness of the thought startled me. It wasn't a voice I heard, or even a voice inside my head. It was just a feeling, a powerful feeling of clarity and sureness. I leaned over, putting my mouth to Cody's ear again. "Let go of the blanket, Code." I released my own iron grip on the wool fabric.

"And what have we here?" a voice said gruffly.

We both jumped as the blanket was ripped away and tossed aside. I threw my hand in front of my face as the brilliant light was shown directly into my eyes. Then it moved to Cody's face. I could see the outline of several dark figures standing behind the light.

I tensed, half expecting a blow, but to my astonishment, the light beam moved past Cody and probed the length of the attic. "So much for that idea," Doc muttered. "Where else might they be?"

"Uh . . ." Dad was looking directly at us, his eyes like saucers. "This is their fort. Uh . . . I thought this is where they'd be." The beam turned and caught him and Mom in the light. Both of them were staring at us, their mouths agape in astonishment.

I was pretty much in shock myself. Doc had been no more than six inches from my face. I could even smell the cigarettes on his breath. He had looked straight into my eyes. I thought I had seen a flash of something, but then it was gone. And he had backed off, shaking his head in disgust. I had never known such stark terror before. Now I was equally filled with amazement and wonder.

The light flashed across us again without stopping. "Well, they're not here," El Cobra snapped. He turned to Dad. "Is there another way into or out of this the attic?"

Dad glanced at us again, his eyes filled with warning. Then he turned to El Cobra. "Uh . . . yes. Down at the far end, there's an access hatch through the garage."

As they started away, El Cobra moving out in front with the light, Mom stepped back, moving directly in front of us, blocking us from view.

Suddenly El Cobra stopped, muttering something in Spanish.

"What?" Gordo said.

"Look at the floor, idiot." That was Doc. The flashlight beam pierced the darkness of the attic.

I couldn't help myself. I had to see what was going on. I leaned forward just enough that I could see past Mom's legs to where the light was probing farther into the attic. A thick layer of dust covered the floor. There were no footprints down the rest of the attic, and fortunately, they couldn't see where we had come in because their own footprints had trampled ours out.

"They haven't been in here. Which means they're somewhere outside." I could tell from Doc's voice that he was seething.

"So why aren't all of you outside looking for them?" El Cobra snapped. They moved away, heading toward the door.

I shrank back as they passed, holding my breath. Mom waited until the men had passed her, then stretched out her hand toward us. I reached up and touched it. Her fingers clasped around mine for a brief second, and then she let go and followed after the men. No one so much as glanced in our direction. A moment later, we were in total darkness again.

For at least fifteen minutes we sat there mostly in silence. Occasionally, we'd lean over and whisper in each other's ears, but mostly we just listened to the sounds of the search going on outside. After everyone had finally left the attic, I was shaking so hard I had to lay the pouch on my lap and sit on my hands to get them under control. What had just happened? How could this be? I could have poked Doc in the eye had I chosen to, and he wouldn't have even blinked. It was like we were . . .

Now, with the time to think about it, I finally finished that sentence. It was like we were invisible. I shook my head at the sheer impossibility of that, then picked up the pouch and laid it against my cheek. It was still warm, but not hot any longer. Thoughts coursed through my head in a bewildering tumble. I thought of a birthday candle that wouldn't go out. Of a speed limit sign that toggled back and forth between 65 and 75 miles an hour. Of a sudden, horrible premonition of danger.

And what about that jolt of power I'd felt? Had that come from the pouch? My mouth fell open. Was that what had made us invisible?

"No way!" I said out loud.

To my surprise, Cody burst into tears beside me. I pulled him into my arms. His sobs were like great shudders racking his body. "It's all right, Code," I said over and over, rubbing his back.

I felt awful. Here I was, trying to figure out what was going on, and I hadn't given a second thought to what Cody must be feeling. In the last hour, he'd seen armed men take over his house, and his entire family had been held at gunpoint and threatened with abduction and possible death. As if that weren't enough, I had dragged him off without warning, and we had come within a cat's whisker of being caught.

Had he even comprehended yet what had just happened to us?

I could feel him pulling out of my embrace a little. He was sniffling more than crying, and his body was only trembling a little. I put both hands on his shoulders and turned him so he faced me in the darkness. "I'm sorry, Cody. I shouldn't have dragged you into this. But—"

"How come they didn't see us, Danni?" he cried.

"Shhh!" I said, putting a finger to his lips.

He reached up and took my hand away. "They couldn't see us, Danni," he whispered. "It was like we were invisible."

"I know."

"But how—?" He stopped. "We've got to call the police."

"No," I cried. "We do that and those men will hurt Mom and Dad. Or Grandpère." I could feel tears hovering just below the surface. I pulled Cody close. My hand ran across the pouch as I tried to think of what I could say to comfort him. There wasn't much, but there was one thing. "Cody, something just saved us. And so we have to save Mom and Dad and Grandpère now. Do you understand?"

"But how, Danni? What saved us?"

"I don't know, Code," I said, my voice curt with frustration at all his questions. "We'll have to figure that out later." My mind was off and running again, and instead of fighting it, I let it have its head. "We'll go out through the garage," I said. "They will have looked there by now, so they'll be gone."

"But what if they see us?"

"Code, listen to me. They can't see us. We know that now. We'll be all right."

"What are we going to do?" he wailed.

"I don't know yet, but we're not alone, Code. We're being helped. We'll go to Dad's truck. I want to get my rifle. Maybe we can drive away if they're not looking. After that, we can decide, okay?"

"Can I go with you?" he asked. His voice held such pleading that tears instantly came to my eyes.

"Oh, Code, I won't leave you. Not ever. Let's give it another five minutes. See what they do. Then we'll make our move."

"I'm scared, Danni."

"So am I, Code, but remember, we're not alone. We can do this."

CHAPTER 24

We waited another ten minutes just to be sure, then felt our way across the attic and to the access hatch for the garage. We could hear Mom and Dad and Grandpère still occasionally shouting our names, but the sound was sporadic now. It wasn't hard to find the hatch in the dark because there was light coming through the cracks around the edges of the hatch. Not good. That meant the garage lights were on.

After listening for a moment, I carefully lifted the hatch cover a crack, hoping I could see enough to tell if anyone was guarding the garage. I jumped as I heard three soft pops in quick succession. One by one the bulbs in each light fixture exploded, and the garage went dark.

We shrank back, expecting someone to start yelling. It didn't happen. *Maybe the garage doors are shut,* I thought, *and no one can see that the lights just went out.* Whatever it was, we couldn't wait around to see what developed. I removed the cover completely. "Okay, Code. Down you go. Get under Dad's workbench until we can see what's going on."

The pitch-black of the attic was replaced with the soft glow of moonlight coming through the side window. With that, we could see the ladder mounted to the wall that provided access to the attic. Cody scooted through the hole and down the ladder. I followed right behind him. Once my feet hit the concrete, I groped my way to the bench as quietly as I could. I felt Cody touch my leg and then dropped down beside him.

"What now?" he whispered.

"I'm going to peek out the side door. If the coast's clear, we're heading for the truck." Not waiting for his answer, I moved. When I opened the door a crack, it was like turning on a light. The moon was nearly full and shining directly on the door. I opened it another inch, peeking through the crack, listening intently. From my angle I could see the front of our house. The moonlight was bright enough that I could see two figures standing on the front porch—one tall, one much shorter. Probably El Cobra and the woman, but I couldn't be sure. I couldn't see anyone else.

I started to turn toward Cody to signal him to come, but as I did, I saw a dark shape coming toward me. Just as it registered that it was Cody, a cold hand grabbed me by the arm. My reaction was instantaneous and instinctive. I gave a low cry, fell back, and swung my right arm in a horizontal arc. I connected with something hard.

"Ow!" Cody cried.

"Shh!" I hissed, then reached for him and pulled him to me. "Don't sneak up on me like that, Code. You scared the heck out of me."

"Well, you about took off my ear."

"Okay, okay. I'm sorry." I turned back to the door. "There are two people on the porch. Unfortunately, the minute we step out, we'll be in bright moonlight and clearly visible." I reached for the pouch and brought it around in front of me, holding it up for him to see. I grinned. "Except for the fact that we happen to be invisible right now."

His mouth turned down. "Are you sure?"

"It worked before. Come on, let's go." As an afterthought, I said, "Hold my hand." I hoped that would increase his courage a little.

Opening the door wide enough for us to pass through, I peered back and forth.

GO! GO NOW!

I jumped as the voice inside my head sounded again. And though there was no audible sound, I felt like it was shouting at me. I clutched Cody's hand with mine, and hung on to the pouch with the other. "Here we go."

NOW!

We shot out of the garage, staying on the sidewalk that paralleled it; our footsteps were barely audible. When we reached the front corner of the garage, I turned sharply left and headed for the equipment shed that was about thirty yards away. So far so good. No shouts. No gunshots. It was working.

The thought had barely formed when a dark figure stepped out from behind Mom's SUV. He was tall and angular. Doc! I stopped immediately and felt Cody crash into me. Pulling him with me, I shrank back against the garage doors.

"I see you," Doc cried. His words were followed immediately by the soft pop of a silenced pistol. A bullet tore into the wood about two feet over our heads. "Hold it right there."

"He can't see us," I whispered in Cody's ear. "Stay with me." But as I started to move along the door, another shot popped. The second bullet hit no more than a foot in front of my nose, sending splinters of wood against my face hard enough to sting.

"I said," he snarled, "don't move. The next one will take your knee out."

I straightened, holding up both hands.

"I thought you said he couldn't see us," Cody said under his breath, raising his hands as well.

I let go of the pouch in disgust. "That's what I thought too."

They put Cody and me on the couch between Mom and Dad this time. Grandpère sat on the recliner closest to me. A bruise was starting to show on his right cheek. El Cobra and Doc were in deep conversation in Spanish, but in low voices. El Cobra kept glancing over at me.

I was still reeling from shock. In the attic, my face had been caught squarely in the beam of a flashlight—a large flashlight—that was just inches from my face, and no one had seen me. This time, though he had been at least twenty feet away, and there was only moonlight, Doc had seen me instantly. I was bewildered, confused, almost dazed. The voice had shouted at me to run, just like before. Had I chosen to run the wrong way? Why had the pouch been so insistent that we go now? Or was it even the pouch? Was it because I decided to play Super Chick for my little brother? Maybe it was all just sheer exhaustion. The clock on the wall showed that it was past one thirty. I had been awake for almost twenty-one hours.

I felt a burst of irritation. *Come on, Nanny,* I felt like shouting. *If you can't help us, at least don't make things worse.*

Nothing.

I leaned over slightly. "Grandpère?" I whispered. "Are you all right?"

El Cobra spun around. "You! Danny Boy! Keep your mouth shut."

"I'm all right," Grandpère said softly. His next words shocked me. "And so are you."

The boss left the others and stalked over to us. The rest of the group formed a half circle around us. All the weapons were up and fully ready. El Cobra stopped in front of me, his eyes spitting fire through the holes in the ski mask. "I was hoping we could keep this simple and uncomplicated," he said in a tight voice, "but it seems like that's not going to be the case." His hand shot out and grabbed me by the chin, jerking my head up to look at him.

"Ow!" I cried. His fingers felt like blacksmith's pincers on my jaw. "Let me go."

He did, flinging my head roughly to one side. "You nearly got your parents killed, young lady. Is that what you want?"

"No." I kept my head up and forced myself to meet his gaze without flinching. I couldn't show fear. Strange as it seemed, amidst the rage, I sensed a touch of admiration from him.

"Where were you?" he suddenly asked.

"In the attic. You passed right by us."

He looked at Doc. "I told you so."

His henchman said nothing, but I sensed that underneath the quiet, he was seething. Two dumb hick kids had made him look like a fool.

El Cobra and Doc locked eyes for several seconds, then the woman stepped up between them. "We've been here too long. We've got to get out of here."

To my surprise, she had a British accent to match her blue eyes. Or maybe she was Australian. And she sounded young, at least ten years younger than El Cobra.

Thankfully, her words galvanized him into action. "Right." He pointed at Doc and started barking commands. "Eileen and I will take the wife and kids with us. We'll use their SUV. Get the keys out of her purse. Luke and Grandpa will go in the first Hummer with you and Juan Carlos. The rest of you will bring up the rear in the second Hummer."

He swung back to Doc. "Put cuffs on all of them."

Doc cleared his throat. "I thought we were leaving Dad and the old man here."

"That was before. Everybody goes with us now until we get things sorted out."

He turned to the woman. "You and Lew pull McAllister's truck behind the barn where it can't be seen. Anyone comes by, things need to look normal."

Gordo raised a hand. "But, *Jefe*, I thought—"

I knew that word. It meant boss, chief, the man in charge. Not a surprise. By this time there was no question who was the boss.

"You aren't being paid to think, Lew," El Cobra snapped. "Tomorrow we'll have our local contact leave a notice with the post office to hold their mail for a couple of weeks. We'll have him spread the word in town that the other grandpa's sick, and the family has gone to Montana to see him."

He swung around and planted himself squarely in front of my dad. "As for you, Luke, I want you to call your buyers and tell them the closing is happening this Friday."

"I'm sorry," Dad said, his voice even and calm. "They are the ones who set the schedule. They're flying into Moab on Saturday afternoon. If they're on time, the plan was to take them up to the mine site that evening, then take them into it on Sunday. That wasn't our preference, but they said that's the only time that works for them."

"So why close on Tuesday if you finish on Sunday?"

"We probably will finish on Sunday, but we can't be sure if they'll want to spend more time at the mine. And once they're satisfied, we still have to travel to Salt Lake. They're the buyers," he said simply. "We meet their schedule."

"He's lying," the woman exclaimed.

Grandpère spoke up. "If your sources are as good as you think they are, you already know all this."

Dad went on quickly. "We start making sudden requests for changes in what we've set up, and it could rattle them." His head came up. "But you have my word that my father-in-law and I will cooperate fully. We won't put our family at risk."

El Cobra glared at Mom. "You better hope he does, *señora*,

because if something goes wrong, you and your kids will be fish food."

She ignored him.

As for me, his threats made little impression. I was exhausted. Mentally. Physically. Emotionally. I felt like my arms and legs weighed a hundred pounds each and that my mind—which had been working at warp speed before—was rapidly becoming hard concrete.

I felt a touch on my arm. Mom had reached across Cody to take my hand and hold it tightly. To my surprise, the tears were gone. She was still pale and obviously shaken, but there was no longer the dazed look in her eyes. I could see anger smoldering there instead.

"Are you all right?" she asked in a low voice.

"No touching," one of the unnamed men barked. Heavy accent. Another Hispanic. He stepped up quickly and jabbed Mom with the muzzle of his rifle.

She pulled back, but continued to look at me.

"I'm fine," I said.

As the man stepped back, she looked me squarely in the eye and mouthed, *Don't give up.* Then she turned back to Dad as if nothing had happened.

I was flabbergasted. I shifted my weight, trying to get more comfortable, and bumped against Cody. I winced. Something heavy and sharp jabbed into my ribs. As I shifted my body again, I realized that whatever it was, it was in the pouch. I still had the strap over my shoulder, and I wondered if the pouch had bunched up when I sat back down, because it was a hard lump, and it was hurting me.

I reached around with my right hand, then stopped as I saw that the man who had jabbed Mom was watching me closely. I dropped my hand again, then pretended to wiggle my body into a more comfortable position. As I lifted my head, I saw that he wasn't the only one looking at me. El Cobra's gaze was fixed on me as well.

"What's the matter, *chiquita?*" he asked, coming toward me.

I went rigid, which only made me all the more conscious that there was something hard and heavy in the pouch. "Nothing," I said. But Grandpère's words came into my mind, as though he were speaking them aloud: *"Never assume the fire is out, just because it is not burning. And don't assume that something is empty, just because there's nothing there."*

Suddenly, a tingling sensation coursed through my body again, and I was filled with wonder. The fear was gone, and I felt perfectly calm.

El Cobra stood over me, watching me closely. Then his hands shot out, and he grabbed me by both elbows and pulled me to my feet. He yanked the strap over my head and the pouch off my shoulder. He hefted it once, then again. "What the—?"

The others moved in closer to see what was going on.

"What have you got in here?" he asked me.

I shrugged. "I have no idea." It was the truth.

He jerked forward, his face close to mine. "You little hellcat," he screamed. "Don't lie to me." He whirled to Doc, raging now. "I thought I told you to search her."

"I did," Doc shot back.

El Cobra nearly tore off the button as he yanked the flap open and reached inside. His body went rigid. He looked at Doc again. "You searched her, and you didn't find this?" He withdrew his hand, and everyone in the room gasped. He held a gun that looked identical to Dad's.

El Cobra lifted the pistol closer to his face and began examining it more carefully. To my astonishment, he suddenly burst out laughing. In seconds, it was a full-throated roar. We all stared at him like he'd gone mad. Still laughing, he held it up for all of us to see. "It's a toy," he cried. "A replica. A child's plaything."

He turned the pistol so he could look down the barrel, shook his head, then flipped it around for us to see. "Look. The barrel doesn't even have a hole in it."

It was clearly a cheap plastic imitation. It didn't even deserve being called a replica.

He turned back to me. "What are you up to, *chiquita*?" he said, his voice low and menacing.

"I didn't know it was there, I swear. Your guy searched me, and the pouch was empty."

With a snort of disgust, he tossed the pouch and the pistol on the coffee table.

BLAM! As the gun hit the wood surface and bounced, it blasted off a round. The bullet plowed into the ceiling above our heads, and plaster rained down. The pistol skittered across the table and crashed to the floor. BLAM! BLAM! BLAM! On semiautomatic mode, the blasts came in rapid succession. Bullets were flying everywhere. A picture on the wall shattered. The vase that Dad had bought Mom in Paris exploded in a spray of porcelain. The lamp in the corner disintegrated.

BLAM! BLAM! Everyone was screaming and diving for cover. El Cobra dove behind the couch and knocked Dad over. Doc flung himself down and behind across the floor, hands over his head.

And then, through all the noise and the tumult and the chaos, that inner feeling that was as powerful as a shouted command came again.

RUN, DANNI! RUN!

The pistol continued to fire as I reached down and grabbed the pouch. I yanked Cody out of his chair, and before anyone could react, we plunged out of the door into the night.

PART FIVE

Flight

CHAPTER 25

There's nothing like naked fear to give wings to your feet.

Cody and I flew out the door, leaped off the porch, and started across the front yard. Inside, the pistol was still firing, not rapidly, but steadily. Enough to keep them down, I hoped. We were fully exposed by both the yard light and the moonlight as we ran. If anyone looked out the window they'd see where we were going. I desperately hoped that until the pistol stopped blasting away, that thought wouldn't occur to anyone else. Pulling on Cody's hand, I turned left, away from the cone of light thrown out by the yard light.

"No, Danni," Cody cried, jerking his hand free. "This way."

"Not the barn!" I grabbed for him, but missed. "That's the first place they'll look."

"I have a place," he called back over his shoulder.

Ready to throttle him, I darted after him. Was it better to stay with him and get caught, or to have at least one of us remain free? It only took half a second to answer that, so I put on a burst of speed and caught up to him as we neared the barn. I threw one arm around his neck and dragged him to a stop. "We have to get out of the light. We can hide down near the river. The barn's the first place they'll look."

He clawed at my arm, pulling it away from his neck, and took off again. "Follow me, Danni."

I was stunned. This was not like Cody. Then I realized that inside the house the shooting had stopped. I could hear voices yelling and screaming. And there I stood, like some stupid statue in the full glow of the light.

I instinctively clutched at the pouch, seeing if it felt warm, praying that it would take out the yard light like it had the garage lights. Nothing. *Le Gardien* was definitely falling down on his job.

I turned and ran, my feet pounding across the gravel. As Cody disappeared through a side door into the barn, I heard the front door slam open.

"There they are!" someone shouted. It sounded like Doc. "Stop or I'll shoot."

I didn't think he was bluffing, but I was running on pure adrenaline, and nothing was going to stop me before I got inside. There were three soft plops, and I heard the bullets slam into the barn just left of the door.

"¡Estúpido!" El Cobra shouted. Then followed a string of Spanish which, loosely translated, was, "If you hurt those kids, I'll feed you to the sharks for lunch." I say loosely because he included a few more colorful words. As I thought that, I realized with a start that I could understand his Spanish almost perfectly.

The three shots eliminated any further hesitation on my part. I hurtled through the door into the darkness of the barn. As I slammed the door behind me, total darkness enveloped me. I instantly pulled up short. Even though I couldn't see a thing, I still felt safe. At least for the moment. The smell of hay, horse manure, and oats was something I knew well. We kept our horses stabled here in bad weather, but in the summer they were out in the pasture.

"I'm over here," Cody hissed. I heard a soft scuffling sound, then he grabbed my hand and started pulling me. "This way."

We didn't need to see. We both knew this barn as well as we knew our house. We moved down the central aisle, past the four horse stalls, past the tack room with its saddles and bridles and the pungent smell of leather.

Cody stopped as we neared the east end of the barn where we stored the bales of hay that would feed our stock through the winter. The smell of dried alfalfa was strong. The stacks weren't as high as they would be later, because we had only brought in the first crop of alfalfa, but they were still tall enough to almost fill this end of the barn, ascending in steps from the floor up to the loft, which was directly above us.

"Hold it," Cody said, pulling me to a stop. He let go of my hand and moved a few steps away. I could hear him fumbling among the buckets, boxes, and other stuff in a small alcove next to the last stall. Then, "Got it." Instantly, there was light. Not much, but enough. Cody held a pocket-sized Mag flashlight. Outside, men were shouting, and I heard the crunch of feet on gravel. We had to get out of sight and fast. I wasn't about to make the mistake of counting on invisibility a second time.

"Come on," Cody cried, clambering up the levels of hay bales like a squirrel jumping from tree limb to tree limb. I followed, not exactly sure how this was going to help. Did he think they wouldn't look on top of the hay? Then to my amazement, he stopped. Holding the flashlight in his mouth, he grabbed the twine of one of the bales and heaved it to one side.

I started to protest, but clamped my mouth shut when I saw that he had just uncovered a hole at his feet.

"Quick," Cody said. "Inside." Not waiting for me, he dived into the opening.

I was still standing there gaping when I heard the side door crash open.

"Get down!" Cody hissed, grabbing my foot. At the same moment, he turned out the light.

I went into the hole after him headfirst. I expected to fall on him, but he was already out of my way.

"Help me pull the cover back in place," he whispered.

Reaching up, I grabbed the twine, and together we tugged the bale back in place. When it was laid across the hole, it completely covered it. As we finished, Cody turned the flashlight back on, covering it with his hand in order to keep the light dim. He flashed it around. I was dumbstruck. There was a whole cave down here, maybe ten feet by ten feet, with the walls, floors, and ceiling made of hay bales. It wasn't one large open space but two narrow corridors on either side, with "pillars" made of bales which held up the "roof."

Cody turned the small beam on one corner, revealing overturned cardboard apple boxes which formed a low table. On them were bottles of water and old ice cream buckets filled with bags of Cheetos, granola bars, and candy bars. At my look, Cody grinned. "Remember the Boy Scout motto? Always be prepared."

"With all that food, what about mice?" My eyes searched the corners and cracks for any sign of movement.

"We put d-Con all around the cave. No mice. Welcome to Fort Cody."

"Maybe we should make you the Guardian," I murmured gratefully.

"What does that mean?"

"Never mind." We heard the barn door open. "Turn off the light," I hissed.

We huddled close together, listening to the sounds of our pursuers entering the barn, El Cobra's steady stream of Spanish urging them on. Or so I assumed. With a start, I realized that just as quickly as it had come, my gift of interpretation was gone. *What gives?* I shook off the question. Anything that might have to do with the pouch was becoming more confusing with every passing minute.

"Please don't hurt them." Mom's voice was clearly frightened, but it didn't sound like she was crying, as near as I could tell. "They're just frightened children."

"*Señora,* they're going to be a lot more than that if you don't call them back."

A tiny flash of light hit my eyes, and I instinctively jerked back. The men had those powerful flashlights out and were sweeping the lights back and forth.

"Don't worry," Cody said softly. "Me and Jordie left two narrow cracks in the front wall as peepholes so we can see what's going on in the barn. But they're too narrow to allow anyone to see inside, especially from a distance."

Jordie was Cody's best bud. His parents ran a small garage in Hanksville. As if that mattered at the moment.

Dad spoke up. "There's a light switch over there. May I turn it on?"

Someone grunted, and a moment later small shafts of light dimly penetrated our little cubbyhole. "Does Dad know about this place?" I whispered.

"Yes, but Mom doesn't." He touched my shoulder then crawled up to one of the cracks.

I followed and pressed my eye to the other crack. *Bless you, Cody McAllister and Jordan Woods.*

Our peepholes—or peep slits—looked straight down the length of the barn. I counted quickly. I could see seven people, counting

Mom, Dad, and Grandpère. I assumed the rest of them were looking for us and were out of our line of sight.

Dad cupped a hand to his mouth and shouted, "Danni! Cody! If you're in here, come out now."

"They won't hurt you," Mom added. "But you have to show yourselves."

Cody stirred. Thinking he was going to obey, I grabbed his arm. He shook it off and glared at me. "I'm not going anywhere," he hissed. "No way."

"Sorry," I murmured. Realizing that it was his quick thinking that had saved us, I touched his cheek briefly. "Thank you, Code. This is perfect." Then I had another thought. "What if they stand on top of us?"

"It won't collapse," he said proudly. "Me and Jordie made sure of that."

I turned back to our peephole. It's funny how much a quarter-inch crack can reveal if things are far enough away from it. We could see the whole main aisle of the barn and most of the people in it. They were milling around, waiting for direction.

Grandpère's voice sounded next. "Danni, if you're in here, you need to do what's best for your parents. We don't want anyone getting hurt."

What's best for your parents. I thought it was interesting that he phrased it that way. What was best for Mom and Dad was for us not to get caught. El Cobra might be raging, but he wouldn't hurt Dad or Grandpère because they had to be at the closing, and he wouldn't hurt Mom because that would take away his leverage with Dad.

Once again I marveled at how clearly I was thinking. "Grandpère's telling us not to come out," I told Cody.

"I know," he said.

El Cobra issued more directions, and then they all started

moving, spreading out, coming slowly toward us, checking the stalls as they came. A bucket crashed as Doc gave it a vicious kick. Someone knocked over a sawhorse with a saddle on it and it crashed to the floor.

"Is there a back door to this place?" That was from El Cobra.

"Not a back door," Grandpère said. "Another side door on the right, up there near the hay."

"See if it's open," El Cobra barked.

Even as someone moved across our line of vision, Doc growled, "They're in here. I can feel it."

Maybe he could, and maybe he couldn't, but thanks to Cody and Jordie, he wasn't going to find us. I was absolutely sure of that.

They searched for five minutes, stomping around in the loft above our heads, slamming things around, muttering nasty things to each other. Hay rained down on us when two of them climbed the stack to make sure we weren't hiding on the top. They walked right over the top of us, but the roof never budged.

And all the time El Cobra raged. He sent three of his men outside to look for us. He threatened Mom. He threatened Dad. They kept pleading with us to come out. But I could tell neither one of them really meant it.

When the three men returned, El Cobra's rage turned into a cold fury. He called everyone to gather around him. Even through the crack, I could see that they were getting nervous. They had to be panicking. What if we got away? What if we were even now calling the police?

El Cobra wasn't the only one who was upset. The woman came up to him; she only reached about to the top of his chest. "*¡Vámonos! ¡Vámonos!*" I caught something about *la policía*. Then she switched to English. "We have to go." She stood on her toes and shoved her face next to El Cobra's.

He stared right back at her, but she didn't budge. Then, without warning, El Cobra swung around and threw a punch at my dad.

He never saw it coming and the blow caught him square on the jaw. He crashed back heavily against the wood planking of the nearest stall, then crumpled into a heap in the straw.

Mom screamed, darted past El Cobra, and fell to her knees beside Dad. Grandpère started moving forward too. This time it was Doc who reacted. He clubbed Grandpère from behind with a clenched fist, sending him to his knees. "Stay where you are!" he shouted.

Muttering under his breath, El Cobra pulled out his pistol and strode over to Dad. He aimed the muzzle at Dad's head. No one moved. I drew in a sharp breath and closed my eyes.

Nothing happened. When I opened my eyes again, El Cobra had stepped back. But I could see his chest rising and falling. The others stood motionless, not daring to risk calling his wrath down on them. He stood still for nearly thirty seconds, and then he began to speak rapidly, but in perfect control. And he spoke in English.

"Forget the kids. We have to get out of here. Eileen, you get the keys to the SUV. And while you're in the house, straighten things up as best you can." He reached in another pocket. "Here's the girl's cell phone. There's a charger in the kitchen. Leave them on the table where she'll find them. Then lock the door behind you in case someone comes."

As she started away, he called after her. "And bring that purse to me."

She slowed, looking back. "You want that old purse?"

"Yes. And bring the vehicle back here when you're done. No lights."

As she went out, El Cobra turned back to Dad. "Where are the keys to your truck?"

Dad reached in his pocket and handed them over without hesitation.

El Cobra tossed them to one of the others. "Move his truck and the ATVs around back where they can't be seen from the road." He turned to Gordo and one of the others. "Get the Hummers up here too. No lights."

"But, *Jefe,* do you think it is wise to leave one of us here? What if the kids called—"

The pistol whipped up so fast that I barely saw it before I heard the soft pop of the silencer. Gordo let out a cry and jumped to one side. Whether that was what saved him or the fact that Cobra deliberately missed him wasn't clear, but Gordo got the message. He broke into a waddling run after the woman. The other men hurried out as well.

In another instant, El Cobra returned to loom over Dad. He grabbed him by the shirt and hauled him to his feet. "Let's go." He jabbed him in the ribs with the pistol. "I'll burn this place to the ground with you and your family in it if you even think about resisting."

"I understand," Dad said.

"No," El Cobra screamed. "You don't understand, *señor* Luke. No more problems. *Nada.* None. *¿Comprendes?*"

Grandpère got back to his feet, wincing with pain. "Why do you assume that we can control everything? Mr. and Mrs. McAllister didn't tell the children to run. We didn't put that pistol in the pouch."

He swung around, the pistol coming up and pointing at Grandpère's head. "You are starting to really annoy me, Grandpa."

To my astonishment, Grandpère straightened to his full height and snapped right back at him. "Then maybe you'd better take something for your nerves, *Monsieur* El Cobra. Your little operation is unraveling at the seams. Those kids are panicked. They could be on their way to town right now to call for help."

"He's right, *Jefe*," Doc said. "We've been here for nearly six hours now. If they did go for help, then—"

"They've not gone anywhere," he hissed. "They're still here somewhere."

For a long moment, El Cobra teetered between rage and rationality, then he finally lowered the gun and stepped back. He turned in our direction, surveying the expanse of the barn. "If you can hear me, *chiquita*, listen up, and listen good. If we see a police car of any kind, or an aircraft circling over our heads, or anyone snooping around, I'll feed your Mom and Dad to the fish. And then I'll come looking for you and your little brother. Do you hear me, little one?"

I heard him. I turned away from the peephole and sat back against the hay, feeling sick to my stomach. A moment later, we heard the truck start up outside, then drive around so it was parallel to the barn, but on the side away from the road. The door slammed, the barn lights went out, and we heard the door close. And finally we were alone.

CHAPTER 26

Cody and I lay perfectly still for the next several minutes, listening intently to what was going on outside the barn. We could hear the soft murmur of voices but could not catch any of the words. Car doors opened and shut. We heard the two Hummers come from around the back of the house. Moments later, a third vehicle approached—Mom's car. More doors. More voices. Finally, three vehicles drove away, one following after another.

"They're leaving," Cody whispered into my ear.

"Shh!" I hissed, grabbing his arm to silence him. I strained forward, focused intently on the sounds of the receding vehicles. They were fading fast, but suddenly the sound abruptly diminished. "That's got to be Gordo," I said to Cody. "Sounds like one vehicle stopped out by the equipment shed." That was a guess, of course. My ears weren't that good, but my sense of danger was pinging like a submarine's sonar. "Let's go up in the loft. We can see better from there."

"What if they left someone in here with us?" he said, his voice strained.

That brought me up short. I had watched them go out and was pretty sure I had accounted for all of them, but I sure didn't want to be wrong. The feel of danger was still strong, but not like it was close by. "Let's give it another five minutes."

———

"What time is it?" I asked after what felt like an hour and a half.

A soft glow came on beside me. Cody's wristwatch had a black neoprene band that not only told you what time it was, but also had a stopwatch, alarm clock, calendar, compass, altimeter, toaster, blender, and garbage disposal all in one. The light went out again. "It's three twenty." He paused. "That's a.m. by the way."

"Yeah. Thanks for reminding me." I leaned forward, peering through the crack between bales at the darkness of the barn. We hadn't heard a single sound. "Okay. I'm pretty sure there's no one else in here. Help me get the top off, real quiet-like, then I'll check for sure. If we're okay, I want to go up in the loft and look around."

We moved the bale with hardly a whisper of sound. Moving carefully, I stuck my head up and listened intently. There was nothing. The moonlight filtered through several cracks in the wooden walls, filling the barn with a faint, soft light. It wasn't much, but after the total darkness of the fort, it was enough to see quite a bit. I let my eyes sweep the interior, watching closely for any movement. I focused on what I was feeling, and I found nothing there, either. Finally, I sighed. "It's okay. We're alone."

He wiggled up beside me. "I'll be back in a minute."

"No. You stay here."

"No, Danni. I'm going with you."

"It's better that—" Then I changed my mind. "Okay, but leave the hole open. If we hear someone coming, we're back inside your cave like a couple of rabbits."

"Okay."

"I think it's all right if you turn on the flashlight. Just keep it mostly covered, and don't shine it directly on the walls or windows. They might see the light through the cracks."

"Right." The flashlight came on but then it disappeared again as he dropped back into the hole.

"What are you doing?"

"Just a minute." A moment later he appeared, handing the flashlight to me. "Okay. Let's go." He had something cradled in his arm, but I couldn't tell what it was.

I kept the flashlight mostly covered by my hand, lighting the way as we made our way off the haystack and over to the ladder which led up into the loft. "You always keep a flashlight hidden in the barn?" I asked him as he started to climb.

He looked down and grinned. "Yeah. Why?"

"Good job." I touched his ankle. "I'm glad you didn't listen to me, Code. If you had, they would have caught us for sure."

"So you're saying I was right and you were wrong?" Even in the darkness, the smugness was evident in his voice.

"I suppose so."

"Wish Mom and Dad were here to hear you say that." He laughed, then scampered up the ladder, using only one hand. He held something in front of him, and I heard the soft rustle of a plastic sack.

The barn loft covered the eastern quarter of the barn. We used it mostly to store the grain we purchased for our stock. It had two large double doors with a block and tackle for hauling things. From there, I figured we could see if we still had Gordo for company.

We did. In the full moonlight, we could clearly see one of the Hummers parked behind the equipment shed.

"I can see one man," Cody said. "Do you think they left two?"

"No. Remember when El Cobra told Lew to stay behind, he said he was going to send some help. How long it will take for them to get here we don't know. But that means we've got to get out of here as soon as possible."

But where to go? We couldn't just strike out blindly. Discouraged, I dropped down on a bag of grain. But as the despair began to rise, I reminded myself that we were free. We had done it. We had gotten away a second time. And that was so remarkable I decided we could take five more minutes to recover our balance before starting to move.

Something cold touched my arm. I gave a low cry and whirled around.

"Geez, Danni. It's just a bottle of water," Cody said. "Aren't we the jumpy one?"

I took it, then a moment later felt something pressed into my hand.

"Hope you like Kit-Kats," he said.

I didn't much, but right then a piece of Styrofoam would have been welcome. I opened the bottle and took a long drink, then ripped the paper off the bar. "You're a pretty handy guy to have around, you know that?"

It was hard to see his expression in the moonlight, but he seemed very serious. "Wish Mom and Dad were here to hear you say *that*," he drawled again.

I started to laugh, then went instantly serious. "Me too, Code. Me too." After a few moments, I turned to Cody. "How long ago did you build the fort?" I asked.

"About two weeks, when we were bringing in the first crop of hay."

"Where did you get the idea to do it?"

He didn't answer. I peered at him more closely in the faint light. His head was down, and I could see he was fidgeting a little. "Cody?" I prodded. "Is there something I should know?"

"Promise you won't go all crazy on me?" he mumbled.

"What did you do?"

"Uh . . . Remember that day you and Mom went to Moab?"

"Yeah. What about it?"

"Well, me and Jordie were playing wizards and warlocks out here in the barn while Dad and the others were bringing in the hay. I was the wizard. And . . . um . . . so like, I kinda got this idea. Since Mom thinks the pouch is enchanted, I thought it might be fun to pretend we were casting evil spells on our enemies."

I shot him a hard look. "You took the pouch from my room?"

"Only for an hour. I put it back."

"It was still wrong," I cried. "It's not a toy."

"I know," he said meekly.

I bit back my desire to read him the riot act and asked another question. "So what does playing wizard and the pouch have to do with the fort?"

"Well, while we were playing, suddenly I got this idea to build a castle to protect us from the evil necromancer."

I burst out with a giggle. "Necromancer? Do you guys really talk like that?"

He sniffed loftily. "Do you want to hear this or not?"

"Yes, go on."

"So anyway, the idea caught us off guard, but we both thought it would be cool. So, with Dad's permission, we started stacking a few bales on top of each other, but all we managed to do was build a very wobbly wall. While we were working, I put the pouch over my shoulder, so we wouldn't step on it or something. And then it just came to me. I saw it all in my head. I suddenly knew how to build a real fort—one that no one could find. And so we did."

"Are you saying the pouch told you to do that?"

"Not then. Now I am."

I got a rash of goose bumps. Could that be possible? Cody was a pretty resourceful kid, but in building this fort he had outdone himself. Could it be that the pouch gave him the idea? Like in the last hour or so when my brain knew exactly what to do. I shook my head. That was a pretty heavy concept.

Frustrated, I dropped my head in my hands and massaged my temples. After a few moments, I picked up the pouch and laid it on my lap. *Did you do that?* I ran my finger along the nine letters that formed the pouch's name. *Are you the inspiration behind this fort of his? Come on, Nanny, spit it out.*

I instantly regretted the thought. And it wasn't just because I knew Grandpère found that nickname offensive. Considering all that had happened recently—from the speed limit sign changing, to the toy pistol blasting off bullets, to being temporarily invisible—to refer to the pouch as Nanny seemed like a mockery, almost a sacrilege. Maybe *Le Gardien* wasn't as bad a name as I thought it was. It sure seemed to fit tonight.

"Danni?"

"Yes?"

"Were we really invisible tonight?"

After a moment I shook my head. "No, Code. Dad and Mom could both see us, and I think Grandpère could, too. It was just that—" I took a deep breath. "Somehow, the others had their eyes blinded to our presence."

"Yeah. That big guy was so close to me I could smell his breath. Pee-yoo! It was awful. When he stuck his face up close and looked right into my eyes, I thought I was going to pee my pants."

I giggled. "Me too."

"Tell me about the gun. How did you do that?"

I reached out and laid a hand on his arm. "Code, I know you have a hundred questions, and so do I. But right now I don't have a lot of answers, and we can't sit around here talking about it. We've got to get out of here."

He was quiet for several moments, and I thought I had hurt his feelings. But then, in that slow drawl he used because he knew it drove me bonkers, he said, "So, are you saying you don't know?"

I couldn't help it. I burst out laughing. He started to giggle too. In moments we were laughing together on the floor, hands clamped over our mouths, so we wouldn't make too much noise. It felt good to laugh, and when it finally subsided, we lay there together, shoulders touching, enjoying the chance to relax for a moment.

Cody reached out and took the pouch from me. He hefted it, then ran his hand across the flap. "It's warm."

"It's a warm night."

"No, it's really warm."

Surprised, I took it back. He was right. It was definitely warmer than when I took it off my shoulder. Remembering that it had been almost hot before, I had a sudden idea. Maybe this was part of how it worked. I also remembered how sometimes, when I was holding it, thoughts came into my mind. I clutched it to my chest and immediately felt the warmth penetrate my shirt. I held it close for almost a full minute.

"Cody?"

"Yes, Danni?"

"We've got to get out of here now. We've got to find Mom and Dad and Grandpère."

He rocked back. "But how?"

"Stay here. Watch old Gordo out there. If he starts coming, call me."

"Where are you going?"

"Not far. I need to get some things from Dad's truck." I took a quick breath. "And a couple of things from the house."

CHAPTER 27

I was in and out of the house quickly, using the back door and keeping the barn between me and Gordo. The primary thing I was after was my phone. El Cobra had wanted me know that he was leaving it and the charger on the counter. Why? Because it was his way to let me keep in touch with my family. I guess it said something that he thought I would figure that out on my own. It was like we were playing a game of cat and mouse. I didn't turn the phone on, of course. First, because it needed charging, and second, because I didn't want him to know I had it yet.

Since they had locked the house, I had to go in through the window. I hoped he had also left the "toy pistol" behind, but wasn't surprised when it was gone. I thought about grabbing some food from the fridge—one Kit-Kat wasn't doing the job—but the sense of urgency I was feeling about getting out of there changed my mind. I turned off the lights and exited the way I came in.

On the way back to the barn, I stopped at the truck and climbed up in the back. With a little effort, I found Dad's rifle, two boxes of shells, and my overnight bag. I also grabbed a few other essentials: two sleeping bags, our water jug, a pair of binoculars, and what was left of our food. Then, in a low crouch, I headed for the trailer. I lowered the side ramp, careful not to let it drop. Then I unhooked the rear ATV and rolled it off the trailer. Fortunately, when they brought Dad's truck and the ATVs around behind the barn, they were no longer on gravel and the four-wheeler came down with very little noise. I lashed our stuff on the back, took a quick peek around the barn to make sure Gordo was still in place, then went inside.

Things were coming together in my mind, except for one primary obstacle: Cody. Though we were brother and sister and raised by the same parents, Cody's mind and my mind worked very differently. Cody's mind was very precise, very mathematical. He once told me that the reason he's so good at math is because he breaks the problem down into smaller parts, then works on those one at a time. When he's done, the problem is solved.

Me? My mind is more like a ping-pong game. My thoughts bounce off one another in rapid succession, first one direction, then another. And if I'm not careful, sometimes they flash right past me. And right now, my mind was playing ping-pong at breakneck speed. An idea was forming. It felt good, but I already knew Cody wasn't going to like it.

When I climbed back up the ladder into the loft, Cody didn't need the moonlight to see what I was carrying. I heard his sharp intake of breath.

"Where did you get that?" he cried in dismay.

"Shh!" I leaned Dad's rifle against a bag of grain. "From Dad's truck." I took the pouch from my shoulder and took out two boxes of shells. I set one down, then opened the other and started to load the rifle.

He gaped at me. "Are you going to shoot that guy?"

"No," I said. "But we need something to make him listen." I was only half concentrating, my mind already wrestling with the problem of going up against an assault rifle. After a moment, I saw that Cody kept glancing up at me, his eyes wide. "What?" I asked.

"Did the pouch make these boxes of shells?" he asked in awe.

"No, silly. They were in Dad's duffel bag with the rifle."

"Oh." He seemed disappointed.

"We can't just hang out here 'til they give up, Code. The longer Mom and Dad are gone, the harder it's going to be for us to find them."

"You mean us *and* the police."

"No way. You heard what El Cobra said. We bring anyone else in and they'll shoot Mom and Dad."

"So *we* have to stop them—just you and me? That's crazy."

I didn't say anything. It was hard to disagree with that assessment. I put the last shell in the magazine, left the chamber empty, then made sure the rifle was on safety. Done, I set it aside. I turned to face Cody. "The first challenge is to get away, and that won't be easy because we need transportation. We either take the truck or one of the ATVs."

"You *are* crazy!" he blurted. "The minute you start either engine that guy will know we're here and come running."

"Yep! That's why we've got to do something about him first."

He threw his hands up. "We *have* to call the police, Danni. We *have* to."

"Shh! Keep your voice down." I knew shushing him would only upset him more, but I felt my irritation rising. I had enough on my mind without having to fight him. "Who would you have me call, Code? Deputy Carlson?" The Wayne County sheriff's office was in Bicknell, over fifty miles away, but Deputy Carlson was assigned to the eastern part of the county, and he and his wife rented a little house in Hanksville.

"Why not? We can slip out of here and go to his house. And . . . and he could call the Utah Highway Patrol for help, and . . . and they could come and arrest that guy out there."

"And what if that guy out there sees him coming and calls El Cobra and tells him we've called the cops? You can bet they left him a radio."

He looked away.

"Besides, you heard El Cobra say they've got a local contact in town. That's how they know so much about us. I know it's a long shot, but what if that contact just happens to be Deputy Carlson?" I reached out and touched his arm, pleading now. "We can't take any chances on that, Code."

"What about the FBI? Can't they help when it's a kidnapping case?"

I hadn't expected that. I hadn't even thought about the FBI, and it was an option that made a lot of sense. But even so, I shook my head. "Maybe later. We've got to get out of here first. And to do that, we've got to take the fat guy down."

"So you *are* going to shoot him."

"You've been watching too much TV, Code. Way too much."

In response to that, his jaw set, and he folded his arms and looked away, ignoring me.

I felt like yelling at him. Him and that precision mind. But then I suddenly knew that this wasn't going to work if we were fighting each other every step of the way. I took a deep breath and tried something else.

"Cody, do you remember when I came home from that camping trip on my thirteenth birthday? I told you all about it that night. Do you remember me telling you about that guy named Aron Ralston?"

"The guy that cut off his arm?"

"Yeah. And do you remember the lessons we learned from that story?"

"Never go camping alone in the desert without telling anyone where you are."

"Well, that too. But more important, we learned that we can never give up."

There was no answer. I nearly grabbed him, wanting to shake the answer out of him, but I knew he had to come to this conclusion himself if this was going to work. He pulled his legs up, hugging them tightly, and rested his head on his arms. I crossed my fingers. Finally, his head lifted. "All right, Danni. I'll do whatever you say."

Eyes burning, I threw my arms around him. "I love you, Code. You're the coolest bro ever."

"I know," he said, pushing me away. "Be sure you tell Mom and Dad that when this is over." He flashed me one of his silly grins. "So what do you want me to do?"

I felt a rush of gratitude. He was seriously cool. Taking his hand, I began to talk. Though his eyes got wider, he said nothing more until I finished.

———

I checked on Gordo again. For a moment I couldn't see him and panicked. Then I saw a tiny pinpoint of glowing red. He was smoking a cigarette, clearly convinced that we were long gone. All the better for us.

When we were down in the main part of the barn again, I looked around, going through it all again in my mind. Finally, I turned to Cody. "You ready?"

In the dim light of the moon, I saw him swallow quickly, but he nodded without hesitation. Gripping the rifle firmly, I moved over to the side door that opened toward the equipment shed; Cody was right behind me. "Okay, Code. I'll be right here. Once you see him start to move, you get back in here fast. You hear me?"

"Yeah." I thought I heard a tremble in his voice.

I touched his shoulder briefly. "Go."

He turned on the flashlight and stepped out the door.

I had positioned myself so that I could watch Gordo through the crack of the door. Though I couldn't see him, the red glow of his cigarette was clearly visible. For several moments, it didn't move. *Some sentry,* I thought. If El Cobra was here, he'd probably shoot him. If Gordo didn't look over here and see Cody, we were going to have to run over there and hit him with a baseball bat. But suddenly the cigarette arced away, and I saw his dark shape step away from the Hummer. He grabbed for something, stepping out into the moonlight. The assault rifle was still over one shoulder, but both hands were up to his eyes, looking through his own binoculars.

"Hey!" he shouted. "Hey, kid. Stop right there!" He broke into a hard run toward us.

"Now, Cody!" I hissed. "Hurry!"

That was unnecessary counsel. Cody flew through the door, and I slammed it shut behind him. He ran to the nearest stall, then stopped, turning to face the barn door, chest heaving. Just like we discussed.

I guess maybe I had been watching too many crime dramas on TV, because my first thought was to wait until Gordo stepped inside, then, in a gruff voice, command him to drop his weapon. Seeing how fast he was coming, though, I threw that idea out the window.

I heard his footsteps slow as he drew close. Through one of the cracks, I saw a momentary flash of light. Good. He had a flashlight, one of those with a high-powered beam. There was a whisper of sound, then the door slowly opened. A rifle barrel appeared, followed by Gordo himself. He stopped, letting the flashlight beam sweep across the barn's open space.

The light caught Cody. His hands shot up. His eyes were wide, his mouth twisted with fright. There was no faking that. "Don't shoot, mister," he cried.

"Don't move," Lew barked. Moving carefully, he took another three steps forward. And that's when I lifted the butt of Dad's rifle and smashed it against the back of his head. He dropped like a sack of beans, the assault rifle and his flashlight clattering to the floor.

I stepped back and leaned against the wall of the barn because my legs were suddenly shaking so badly I thought they were going to buckle under me.

Cody ran over, grinning like a fool. "Way to go, Danni! Way to go."

CHAPTER 28

Though I was visibly trembling and felt like I was going to puke, my mind was back in the mode where everything was coming at me with perfect clarity, but, oddly, it was mostly coming as correction, rather than inspiration.

For example, as soon as my legs stopped shaking, I dropped to one knee beside the body. I reached to remove the ski mask, but I had the strongest feeling to leave it alone. Then I realized why. If I revealed Gordo's face, then I could identify him. El Cobra had stressed that when this was over we would be safe because there was no way we could tell who they were. So instead, I pressed my fingers against his throat to feel for a pulse.

Good. There was a strong beat.

"Should I get some rope?" Cody whispered.

"Yeah." Then again, I got a nudge. "No, wait. Don't touch anything. Leave the rifle and his flashlight where they are. Don't even turn off the light. He needs to think we hit him and ran. When he wakes up, he'll contact his boss, and I want El Cobra to think we're panicked and running blind."

Then I remembered something else. El Cobra had promised to send help for Lew. "We've got to get out of here. Let's go." We sprinted for the other door and burst out into the night. I ran to the four-wheeler and climbed up, motioning for Cody to join me. But the sonar started pinging again. Danger. And close. Then came the voice.

WAIT!

I jerked around and looked into the barn, half expecting to see Gordo back on his feet with his rifle pointing at us, but he was still sprawled out and not moving.

"What is it?" Code asked in a hushed whisper.

"I'm not sure." And then I heard it, the soft sound of a vehicle out in the lane. I was off the four-wheeler and to the corner of the barn in about three jumps. From that vantage point, I could see the hundred-yard stretch of our lane that led out to the highway. My heart plummeted.

Coming up the lane, clearly visible in the bright moonlight, was a large pickup truck, probably a Ford F-350 or a Dodge Ram. Its lights were off, and it was moving slowly. My first thought—or hope—was that it was one of our neighbors passing by; the lane wasn't exclusively for our house—but instantly I knew that wasn't the case. A neighbor wouldn't be driving without lights.

There was a crackle of sound from inside the barn, and both Cody and I jumped. "Lew, where are you?" We both ran back to the door and peered inside. Gordo hadn't moved. But his radio crackled again.

"Lew, do you copy?" Out in the lane, we heard the truck roll to a stop.

"What do we do?" Cody asked, voice tight as a wire. "Do we answer him?"

"No." There was no way we could ever pass for Lew. I had the binoculars around my neck, so I grabbed them. Mentally I crossed my fingers. *Please, let it be only one man.*

"Lew, do you copy? Over."

I heard the sound of a door opening and saw a figure get out of the truck. To my dismay, a moment later, another man got out of the passenger's side. Both men were carrying rifles.

My stomach twisted. How like El Cobra. Never leave anything to chance. I suddenly wanted to sit down. My knees were turning into rubber again.

"Let's get out of here," Cody whispered urgently, poking my back. "There's two of them."

"We can't. They'll hear us the instant we start the four-wheeler."

And then my brain kicked into inspiration mode. "We need some kind of a diversion," I whispered.

"What kind of diversion?"

"I don't know."

"We've gotta hurry, Danni," he wailed. "They're gonna come looking for Lew."

"I know, I know," I said, feeling increasingly desperate. I was chewing on my lip like crazy. "What we need is something that will draw their attention away from us, but something loud enough to cover our escape."

I grabbed the rifle. It was the only thing I could think of. "Get on the four-wheeler. Wait until I open fire, then take the four-wheeler out through the pasture and wait for me up on the ridge. I'll try to keep them pinned down until—" But even as I spoke, that same sarcastic voice in my head mocked. *Come on, McAllister. This isn't the movies. And you're not some female super-chick who can best two really, really bad guys in a gunfight.* I shook my head. "They'll still hear the motor."

"Try the pouch."

I jerked up. "What?"

"Try Nanny," Cody said again. "Hold it close like you did before."

"Don't call it that." But I did as he said, groping for *Le Gardien* like it was a lifeline being thrown to a drowning person. As I grasped it, both of us jumped as a terrible shriek split the quiet of the night. The sound was coming from the lane. We both peered around the barn. Outside, headlights were flashing off and on. The truck's horn was honking. And there was a high-pitched shriek that went off and on, like a woman screaming. Someone—or something!—had triggered the vehicle's alarm system.

The second guy whirled around. "Turn it off!" he yelled at the driver.

The driver was already hurtling the fence and running hard toward the truck. He yanked the door open and jumped inside. Nothing changed. Everything in the truck was on full alarm mode. The second man turned and sprinted back the way he had come. "Turn it off! Turn it off!" he screamed.

I grabbed Cody's arm and pulled him after me. "Let's go!" We raced out the opposite door, vaulted up onto the four-wheeler, and I gave the key a hard twist. It kicked into life, but I kept it on idle. Keeping the lights off and the barn between us and the truck, we started away, praying that the shrieking wouldn't stop until we were up and over the hill.

Hanksville straddles the junction where Utah Highway 24 coming south from Green River turns west and continues on to Capitol Reef National Park. At that point, Utah 95 breaks off and heads south for Lake Powell and Blanding. Our little ranch was about half a mile north of town, near where the Fremont and Muddy Rivers join to form the Dirty Devil River. On all sides of town, dry, barren hills rose up and gave way to the San Rafael Desert.

We reached the top of the hill and looked back. We could still hear the truck's alarm blasting away and see the headlights flashing off and on. The two men were waving their arms and yelling at each other. In the moonlight, had the two guys looked in our direction, they could have easily seen us. But they didn't look. They were too engaged in trying to shut off the system before the whole town turned out to see what was going on.

"Made it," I breathed. I turned my head. "You okay?"

"Okay?" he cried. "Listen to that racket. This is great!"

"Hold on. I'm going to pick up speed and get us out of here."

"Where we going?"

"To Rick's house."

Cody gave a curt nod. "Good idea. Let's go."

As we drove away, passing out of sight of the road below, the shrieking stopped. No more honking. I was tempted to ram the throttle full forward, but resisted, moving slowly enough to keep the engine at a low hum, and the dust to a minimum.

On top of the bluffs was a whole maze of gravel roads. We drove our four-wheelers up here all the time, so I knew the roads well. The first faint light of dawn was visible, and as we passed the cemetery, I picked up speed. We headed southeast until we reached a road that angled back toward Highway 95, south of town. I turned off the four-wheeler's lights as we crossed the highway and entered the south end of Hanksville. Rick's family lived a little west of town, down near where the highway crossed the Fremont River. There was no way we could totally bypass town, so we made our way through it, moving slowly until we were past any houses.

I was still nervous. By now, the two new guys had surely found

Gordo and had reported in to El Cobra. I would have loved to hear that conversation! The sky was growing lighter fast. I didn't think El Cobra would know that Rick and I were friends, but after tonight, I wasn't ready to assume anything. Though Cody and I were dead tired, as we reached the west side of town, I pulled the ATV into a thick patch of brush and willows in the river bottom and turned off the engine. "We walk from here."

CHAPTER 29

West of Hanksville, Utah

We arrived at the Ramirezes' property line about twenty past four. The eastern horizon was pretty bright, but the ground was mostly still dark. We circled around and came in from around the back of the house. I had the binoculars and Dad's rifle, and we kept stopping every minute or so to check things out. By the time we reached the house, I was confident that we weren't under surveillance. Which meant that, for now at least, we were still a step or two ahead of El Cobra's men.

I had planned to awaken Rick by tossing some pebbles against his window, but as we reached his house, I saw his light was already on. I knew he was usually up early to do his chores, but I didn't think it was this early. I moved closer and knocked softly on the glass.

———◆———

I had barely started explaining to Rick what had happened since we had left him the previous night, when he held up his hand. "Wait." Before I could protest he was gone. A minute later he was back with his father—barefoot, in red shorts and a gray T-shirt, and with sleep in his eyes.

"What's going on, Ricardo?" Charlie asked. I saw his eyes flick to the rifle then back to me. He sat down across from me and Cody.

I looked at Rick. "Did you tell your father about what we found at the Danny Boy Mine yesterday?"

He shook his head, then looked quickly at his father. "Mr. McAllister asked us to keep it completely confidential."

"Then you did right," Mr. Ramirez said, waving off the apology.

I took a deep breath and began, starting with what we'd found yesterday in the mine. When I told him that we had brought down about a million dollars worth of rhodium ore in four bags, he merely nodded, but I could the shock on his face. At least it helped make the story of a twenty million dollar ransom a little more plausible.

The only thing I left out were the details about the pouch and how it aided our double escapes. I planned to explain about the pouch to Rick when things weren't quite so urgent, but I sensed that Charlie Ramirez was going to have a hard enough time taking in this story without adding enchantment to the mix.

By the time I finished, Charlie's mouth was set in a hard line. "These are not amateurs, Danni. They are dangerous men."

"Yes, I know."

"And you carrying a rifle is only going to make that worse."

"I'm not planning an attack," I said defensively. "But we need to protect ourselves."

Instantly, he softened. "Of course. You're right. You've had a rough night." He leaned forward, completely earnest. "But you have to call the police, Danni." He waved me off as I started to protest. "Listen to me. I know you're worried about your family, and rightly so, but the best thing you can do for them is to get help."

"That's what I said," Cody piped up.

"And what if their local man happens to be in the sheriff's office?" I retorted. "Or, more likely, what if someone in the department lets it slip that my family is being held hostage? You know how our little town is, Mr. Ramirez. Everyone knows everyone else's business."

He exhaled slowly, and I could see that he knew I was right. I went on quickly. "I agree that we must be careful, but—"

Rick broke in. "It's been over an hour since you left your place. You have to assume those men have found the one you call Gordo by now. And that they've told this Cobra guy everything too."

Cody raised a tentative hand. Mr. Ramirez nodded at him.

"If it's a kidnapping case, can't the FBI get involved?"

"I was thinking the same thing," Mr. Ramirez said. He turned to me. "What would you think of that? They're the best."

I was shaking my head before he finished. "Maybe, but not yet. I'm not trying to be difficult, Mr. Ramirez, but remember, El Cobra had a copy of the assayer's report. He has access to our bank accounts. He could have contacts anywhere."

"I understand," Mr. Ramirez said. He got up and began to pace back and forth. "Assay reports are confidential, but it would be an easy matter to bribe a clerk. Same with a bank employee." He waved that aside, as if the idea were irrelevant. He squatted down so he was looking directly into my eyes. "You know I think highly of your father, Danni. And the rest of your family too. I will do anything I can to help. But it's a mistake to think we can do this ourselves. For example, assuming they haven't flown your parents out somewhere in a plane—"

I cut in. "No, I specifically remember El Cobra saying it was not very far from here."

After a moment, he nodded. "That makes sense, but even if you assume they're within a two hundred mile radius of here, that's still about forty thousand square miles of empty desert you have to search. You can't possibly find them on your own."

"But I don't have to find them." I took the cell phone from my pocket. "I think this is why he left me my cell phone. He can contact me whenever he wants. And when he does, we'll agree to having Cody and me give ourselves up. Maybe we can have the FBI track us or something." I wrung my hands. "I don't know, Mr. Ramirez. I just know I can't assume the police will do everything perfectly."

He sighed, clearly troubled. "I understand. And that—"

Rick jumped to his feet. "Wait! He left you your cell phone?"

"Yeah. I think he knew this was the best way to—"

He swung around to his father. "Not good, Dad. It's possible that Danni's phone has been tampered with. Maybe even corrupted with Spyware. That could explain how they knew so much. With Spyware, you can monitor every conversation, every text message." He stopped, his face suddenly pale. "And they can track her location."

I felt like he had just pushed me off a cliff. "But—I haven't had it on. The batteries are all but dead."

"Doesn't matter." He held out his hand. "Give it to me."

Bewildered and feeling sick, I took out my phone and handed it to him.

He immediately slid off the back and removed the battery. "As long as the battery's in it, it can be traced."

I was having a difficult time breathing. Rick was pale. He looked at his father. "Dad, I think there's a very good chance that this guy could know where she is even as we speak."

CHAPTER 30

For what seemed like forever, no one moved. There wasn't a sound in the house. Mr. Ramirez sat down heavily. He dropped his head in his hands, then rubbed at his eyes.

"Dad?"

He waved him off. After no more than ten seconds, he jumped up, strode to the fireplace, and took down his rifle. Then he turned off the lights. "Rick, you and Cody get the girls. Leave them in their pajamas, but bring some clothes for them. Danni, there's a cooler on the back porch. Fill it with any food we don't have to cook. And get anything you can find to drink. Put it in my truck."

We sprang into action as Charlie quietly opened the front door and stepped out on the porch. We were ready in less than five minutes. Kaylynn and Raye, Rick's sisters, were still too sleepy to be anything but confused. It made me want to cry. What had I done to this family?

By then, Charlie was back inside, peering out the front window. As we assembled, he began talking quietly but rapidly. "No one is here yet, but we have to assume they're on their way, so we have to act fast."

"What do you want me to do?" Rick said. I was amazed at how calm he sounded.

"I'll drive your sisters to Moab and leave them with your Aunt Shauna. She will make sure they're safe."

"But—"

"In the meantime, you're going to take your 4Runner and find a safe place to hide until I can get in touch with you. It's going to take me several hours to get the girls settled and safe."

I tentatively raised my hand as another thought came. We had been gone for over an hour. Why weren't the bad guys already here if they knew where I was? Rick's dad nodded at me. "Yes?"

"The two new guys don't know how many ATVs were on the trailer. I'm not sure that Lew, the other guy, will notice that one is gone either, not after getting whacked in the head. If they don't notice that, then maybe they think we're still close by and are trying to find us before they call El Cobra and tell him the bad news."

"Let's hope so, but we can't depend on it. I think it's best to leave your four-wheeler where you hid it. At least for now." He turned. "Ricardo, head west toward Cainsville. Don't go back into Hanksville. Find a place along the river where you can't be seen but will still be in cell phone range." He glanced at his watch. "I'll call you before ten." He turned to me again. "Danni, how much ammunition do you have for the rifle?"

"Two boxes."

"Good girl." He handed Rick his rifle. "You take this."

"We've also got some food and water on the four-wheeler," I broke in.

"Good. Get it."

"What do you want us to do until you're back?" Rick asked.

"Just stay out of sight. We've got to keep them guessing about where Danni and Cody are. Remember, they're going to have to be careful too, because they don't know if you've called the police or not. They can't go through town knocking on doors."

He looked directly at me. "Do you want me to take Cody with us, Danni? He could stay in Moab where it's safe."

"No, Danni," Cody cried. "I want to be with you."

The question knocked me off balance. My first impulse was the same as Cody's, but then I asked myself how Mom and Dad would answer that. He would certainly be safer in Moab, but he would be frantic and worried. Without thinking about it, I reached out and touched the pouch. It was cool again, but as soon as my finger ran over the rough fabric, I had my answer.

"Thank you, Mr. Ramirez, but I think he'd better stay with me. At least for now."

"I agree. It was just a thought." To my surprise, he came over and laid a hand on my shoulder. "It's going to be all right, Danni. What you and Cody have done so far is amazing. Your Dad and Mom would be very proud."

"I . . . I hope so." Suddenly I wanted to hug him. It was such a relief to have someone to talk to, someone to help. It hit me again what my coming here meant to Rick's family. "I'm sorry I've put your family in danger, Mr. Ramirez. I'm really, really sorry."

"Two days ago, your dad reached out and rescued my boy. I'm glad for a chance to repay the favor." He gave my shoulder a quick squeeze, then went to his daughters. "Let's go, girls. Into the truck."

As he reached the door, I called out, "Mr. Ramirez?"

"Yes?"

"Muchas gracias."

His teeth flashed white against his olive skin. "You are most welcome, *señorita* Danni. *Lo siento mucho.* I'm very sorry about all this." He turned and disappeared out the door.

After a moment, Rick, Cody, and I slipped out the front door and hurried to Rick's truck. As he started the engine, I gave him a sharp look. "I have a question for you, Mr. Ricardo Ramirez."

"And what would that be?"

"Can you disable the tracking device on my phone so it doesn't work, even if the phone is on?"

"I'm not sure. I'd have to look it up in the user's guide."

"And where is that?"

"On your phone, silly," Cody responded.

"Oh." Then came another thought. He'd only had his iPhone about a month. "How do you know all this stuff?"

He grinned impishly. "All my girlfriends have iPhones, and they're always asking me to teach them how they work. So when I got mine, I already knew a lot about it."

For a moment, I didn't know what to say. Then I saw his face and slugged him hard on the shoulder. "You wish! I'm serious, though, how do you know all this? I'm still learning how my phone works."

"Ah," he said, "but I don't spend an hour every morning before the mirror getting myself beautiful for the world."

"Of course not," I snapped. "You'd need a lot more than an hour."

"Ooh, touchy, are we?" Laughing, he leaned out of my reach. As we pulled out of his yard and headed for where we'd left the ATV, I spoke again. "Thanks, Rick," I said in a soft voice.

"For what? Being a brat?"

"For making me laugh right now. It felt good."

"Yeah," Cody said. "Really good."

PART SIX

Spyware

CHAPTER 31

Highway 24, West of Hanksville, Utah
Wednesday, June 15, 2011

After getting our things from our four-wheeler, Rick followed a narrow track along the river that eventually led to the highway. The sun was still a quarter of an hour from rising, but it was full light, and I felt vulnerable.

At the highway, we waited for a moment to make sure no one was in sight, then pulled out and headed west. "Any suggestions on where we hole up until Dad calls?"

Barely stifling a yawn, I shook my head. "I don't care where it is, just get us there." The exhaustion had caught up with me, and I was fighting to keep my eyes open. Cody, who was stretched out on the backseat, said nothing, and I wondered if he was already asleep. He could do that. Drop off before he'd even finished saying good night.

Envious, I laid my head back and closed my eyes. Now if I could only shut off my brain as well. The Guardian—I had determined that was what I was going to call the pouch from now on—was beside me on the center console. I reached out and picked it up. I laid it on my lap and ran my hand across the fabric. It was cool to the touch. I focused inward.

What are you feeling right now?

Exhausted.

No, I mean inside.

Exhausted! Burned out. Worried sick. What else do you want to know?

You didn't say anything about having a sense of danger, or feeling the creepy-crawlies.

Oh.

My hand stopped moving across the fabric. The realization came as an enormous relief. I began to trace the *Le Gardien* letters with my fingertips—something I seemed to be doing quite a bit lately. Funny how quickly your mind can change. I had resented the concept of a guardian or a nanny for a long time. Now all that was gone. As my mind kept going over and over the events of the last few hours, I realized that we were being guarded. Not always in a way that made sense, but we were. In fact, I couldn't think of a better word for it.

The one puzzle piece that didn't fit was the speed limit sign. Why that? We weren't in danger then.

No, came the answer, *but you were about to blow away everything your dad had done for Rick. Why would you think the pouch would only bless you or your family? And that's not all. The speed limit sign let you know that there was much more to* Le Gardien *than a dusty old pouch hanging on your wall.*

Wow! The thought blew my mind. That *had* been a turning point for me. It really did help me accept all the other stuff that had happened last night without going crazy. In fact, I realized I was even starting to directly look to it for help.

That was quite a thought, but I was so tired I was having trouble getting my head around it. I looked at Rick. "Have you got a place picked out?"

"I think so."

"Great. Wake me when we get there."

———◆———

My next conscious awareness was of the raucous cawing of crows. I opened my eyes and saw dappled sunlight on the windshield in front of me. Above me was the foliage of a large cottonwood tree. It took me a moment to remember why I was sleeping on the seat of Rick's 4Runner. When I did, I also became aware of the soft sound of the engine running.

Raising my head, I looked around for Rick. He was nowhere in sight. I half turned and checked the backseat. Cody was sprawled out there, breathing deeply. Good.

Moving carefully, I grasped the passenger side door handle and eased the door open. As I slid out and stood up, my right leg nearly buckled. Instantly it started to tingle with what felt like a thousand tiny pinpricks. My leg had gone to sleep.

Breathing deeply, I glanced up at the sky. The sun was not quite a third of the way to its zenith, which meant it was probably 8:30 or 9:00. I reached for my cell phone to check the time, then remembered that Rick had taken the battery out of it. Probably closer to nine, I decided. The heat of the day was starting to seep into the air in spite of the deep shade.

Curious but wary, I started around the 4Runner, wondering why Rick had left the engine running. The windows were down, so it wasn't to keep us cool. As I came around the front of the truck, moving carefully, searching the trees, I saw him immediately. He sat beside the truck, his back against the front door, knees up. A black cord came out of the open window above his head and connected to his iPhone. He was working on it, concentrating hard. His father's rifle was propped up against the truck within easy reach.

"Hi," I said softly.

He jumped a little. "Oh! Hi. Didn't know you were awake."

"I'm not. This is just a front."

He grinned. "Don't think I've ever seen you that tired before."

Without thinking, I reached up and felt my hair. I groaned. Where was my overnight bag with my hairbrush? Oh, well. The Wicked Witch of the West rides again. Since there was nothing I could do to make it better, I asked, "What time is it?"

He glanced down at the phone. "Eight forty-eight." Another grin. "You slept over three hours. I checked on you a couple of times just to make sure you hadn't checked out on me."

I sat down beside him, looking over his shoulder at the phone screen. "Whatcha doin'?"

"Checking the Internet. Learning about Spyware." A frown pulled the corner of his mouth down. "I'm sorry to say, but I'm pretty sure you have it on your phone. Can I ask you some questions?"

"Sure."

"How long have you had your phone?"

"Let's see." I counted backward, using my fingers to keep track. "Mom and I bought it on our last day in Las Vegas. That would have been . . . umm . . . last week."

"So, a week ago today."

"No, today is Tuesday, and—oh, I guess it is tomorrow now, isn't it? Okay, so yeah, a week ago."

"And in those first few days, while you were learning how to use it, do you remember any of the following happening?" He read from the iPhone's screen. "Has the phone ever lit up by itself? I mean, other than when you got a call or a text message or some other notification?"

I blew out my breath, trying to remember. "Yeah, maybe a time or two."

"Have you ever heard funny background noises while you were talking? Not loud, but maybe a clicking sound, something like that."

I felt something twist in the pit of my stomach. "One night right after I got it, when you and I were talking, I asked you if you could hear a funny noise on your phone. Remember?"

He sighed. "I'd forgotten that. One more. Have you opened any e-mails on your phone, especially ones from someone you didn't know?"

"Of course. I'm always getting junk e-mail."

"But you opened them?"

"Some of them. Not all of them."

Looking glum, he set down his phone. "Spyware can be sent through an e-mail. When you open it, the program automatically downloads to your phone."

I drew my knees up, laid my arms across them, and rested my head on them. On top of everything else that had happened, this was a devastating blow. "But how could someone put something on my phone without me knowing about it?"

"It is actually ridiculously simple. Usually it's done by parents who want to monitor their kids' messages or phone conversations, or who want to know exactly where their kids are all the time. Once it's on the phone, there's no way to detect it. At least, not without special equipment." He reached out and touched my arm briefly. "I'm sorry, Danni, but I think El Cobra has been listening to every call you've made and read every text you've sent or received."

"And tracked my locations."

He nodded. "Yeah, sorry."

I said nothing. I was still trying to process what that meant. I felt betrayed. Violated. I was embarrassed, thinking about all the stupid things I shared on my phone. Learning that some Peeping Tom had been watching my house for the last week wouldn't have been much

233

more disturbing to me. But I knew Rick was right. The Spyware was how El Cobra knew so much about me. Like my nickname. Any time I called Dad and he saw it was me on his caller ID, he'd always answer the phone with, "Hey, Danny Boy." And that's how El Cobra knew where the mine was, and how he could send someone to watch us. And how he knew about the bags of ore—I had taken pictures of them.

I had to force my mind away from it. I felt physically sick. "What about your phone?"

"No, there's no way. I don't even have an e-mail account set up yet. One of the things on my to-do list."

"Are you sure?"

"We've been here for three hours now. If they could track my phone, we wouldn't be sitting here talking about it."

"Oh. Good point."

As my mind kept working, something else clicked. If my parents' phones were tapped, that answered a lot of other questions. El Cobra had probably listened in on all of Dad's conversations with the Canadian mining company and the assayer. Dad sometimes did his online banking using his iPhone. If El Cobra could read it when Dad entered his password, then he had complete access to Dad's account. He would also have known about Mom and Cody going to Denver and when they were returning and that they would be in the house alone.

In a way, that was all bad news, but it was also a relief. El Cobra wasn't some mysterious superspy. This was a much simpler explanation. And that meant that maybe he wasn't as formidable an enemy as I had conjured up in my mind. Which meant a great deal to me right now.

CHAPTER 32

I stood back as Rick explained Spyware to Cody. No surprise that Cody understood it immediately. He was pretty good on computers and techno stuff. He had even helped me figure out my cell phone several times. He had questions, but they sounded to me like they were pretty savvy. As I watched them, I felt a little twinge of envy. Their easy casualness together—in spite of the four-year difference in their age—the whole male-bonding thing—was something I wasn't quite sure I understood.

"Anyone hungry?" I said when it looked like they might go on for another day or two.

"Famished," Cody said.

"Amen," agreed Rick.

They both stood up, and I noticed Rick's Levis were damp up to his knees. His sneakers were soggy and quite muddy. "Where have you been?" I asked.

For a moment, he looked sheepish. "That was the next thing I was going to tell you."

"What?"

"I waded across the river and found a spot where I could watch the highway without anyone seeing me."

"What for?"

"Just curious."

"And?"

He sighed. "About an hour ago, two vehicles passed, moving real slow. Fifteen minutes later, they came back again, headed east this time."

"Was one of them a black Hummer?"

"You got it. The other was a dark maroon Ram 1500. Two guys in that one. Only one driving the Hummer."

I wanted to sit down again all of a sudden, but I didn't. If Rick hadn't figured out the tracking feature on my cell phone, we would have been sitting at his house when El Cobra's men drove up.

"Were they wearing ski masks?"

"No. But the one in the Hummer wore green scrubs, just like you said."

"Then what?" I asked.

"That's it. They haven't been back."

He looked away quickly. He was funny that way. When he had something unpleasant to say, he found it hard to look directly at me.

"What else?" I asked.

"They were driving real slow, like I said, so I got a good look at them." He paused. "I didn't recognize any of them."

That surprised me a little. "So what?"

"You said El Cobra told you he had a local contact. That would have to be someone in Hanksville, right?"

Ah. And if that were the case, Rick would have recognized him or her—or them—immediately. I was glad someone was thinking clearly. "Which means, there's probably someone else out watching our house."

"That's the way I figure it too."

I turned and kicked savagely at the truck's front tire. Now what? We were safe here, and probably would be as long as we didn't move. We were also totally useless to my family if we couldn't get out of here.

"What are we going to do?" Cody asked, coming over to take my hand.

And Rick—steady-as-a-rock Rick—said, "First, we're going to grab a bite to eat, then we're going to wait for Dad to call. And then"—he smiled, but it was tight and grim—"then, we're getting out of here."

Rick's cell phone rang a little before ten o'clock. He got up and started pacing back and forth as he talked. He kept his back to us so it was hard to hear him. Mostly he was just listening, and saying, *"Sí,"* or *"Sí, Papá."* When he clicked off, he put the phone away then turned to Cody and me. Concern was heavy on his face. "My Dad's in Moab and my sisters are with my aunt. But he needs to get them some groceries and things before he starts back."

"How long?"

"About another hour before he's on the road again." Quick breath. "He wants to know if you've reconsidered calling the police."

"No!"

"That's what I told him, but he said to ask you to really think about it carefully. We can call him if you change your mind."

"I'm not going to change my mind, Rick. And if that bothers you, then thanks for your help and we'll see you later."

Cody jerked around. "Danni!"

Rick rocked back a little.

I regretted it the moment the words left my mouth. "I'm sorry, Rick. I didn't mean it."

"I know," he murmured, but I could tell he was still hurt.

"Really. I don't know what we would be doing if it weren't for you."

"She's kinda this way when she first wakes up," Cody explained, giving me a dirty look. "Dad says it's best to stay a mile or two clear of her for the first hour or two."

I spun around, but he laughed and danced away before I could pop him.

"It's true," he sang. "Grandpère says that sometimes you have to throw her raw meat to get her in a good mood."

Rick managed to hold his face to a stupid smirk. "Then let's get some breakfast in her."

"Are you comedians through now?" I said. Then, realizing the only way to stop their teasing was to bring things back to the issue at hand, I asked, "We can't just sit here all day doing nothing. What are we going to do?"

"Once it's dark, we could get away without them seeing us," Cody suggested.

Rick shook his head. "That won't be for another twelve hours. We can't wait that long."

"Well, well," I said, still irked by the raw meat comment. "Finally something productive from the more masculine half of this partnership."

"Two thirds, actually," Cody said, still in an impish mood.

"Say what?"

"There are two males and one female. It's not half, it's—"

"I get it, Code. Thanks for the math lesson."

Rick wasn't smiling anymore. He was watching me closely. "I

know you've been through a lot, Danni, but sarcasm doesn't become you," he said softly.

One of my gifts, according to Dad, is zippy—even stinging— comebacks. Dad hadn't meant it as a compliment. One of those comebacks came to me right now: *And sitting around making stupid jokes about me doesn't become you either, Ramirez.* But I bit it back and made myself swallow it. It didn't go down easy, but it did go down. Finally, I asked, "So what do we do?"

"Dad wants us to get out of here. Take the back roads until we're clear of Hanksville, then head for Salt Lake."

"Salt Lake?" I cried. "El Cobra's not taking my family to Salt Lake. Why Salt Lake?"

"I'll tell you, if you promise not to take my head off. It's just an idea that I discussed with Dad. He totally agrees. I've been thinking about it all morning while you were sleeping."

"Okay, I'm listening."

"Are you really?" he asked. He was smiling as he said it, but I could see it was a mild rebuke. Probably deserved, but certainly not appreciated.

"What's in Salt Lake City?" I asked.

"The Federal Bureau of Investigation."

"Great!" Cody exclaimed. "Can we eat something before we take off?"

CHAPTER 33

If you had asked me what it would take for Rick to change my mind, I would have said nothing. Once my mind is made up, I rarely change it. That's the Irish side of my nature. But for all my feisty, in-your-face attitude, I was deeply frightened. Most of that was about the safety of Mom, Dad, and Grandpère. It was like having a huge black cloud hovering over me. But I was also scared to death that I was going to mess things up, do something stupid that would only make things worse. Like getting Cody hurt. Or triggering El Cobra's wrath. I wasn't even sure I was right about my obsession not to involve the police. I was scared, and that's the straight of it.

But when Rick mentioned the FBI, I didn't stop to think. I shot to my feet and cried, "No! No! No! How many times do I have to say it? I will not take a chance on having someone betray us. No police. And that's final."

Rick said nothing, his face expressionless. After almost a minute, when it was clear he was going to wait me out, I sat down again. He went on like nothing had happened. "Danni, I know you're tired, and this is a highly emotional thing for you, but—"

I shot him a look hot enough to blister steel. "If you tell me to stop acting like a girl and to be more rational—meaning, think like *you*—I'm going to grab Dad's rifle and shoot you in the foot."

He rocked back, shocked. "Where did that come from?"

"Oh, I know what you and Cody are up to."

"Really? And what would that be?"

"You're convinced I'm wrong, so you'll help me come to my senses. Bring me back into the light. Why don't you just say it? 'Stop being an idiot, and do what *we* know is best for you.'" I had to stop. I was livid, my hands shaking with emotion.

He slowly got to his feet. The look on his face told me I had just crossed a line with him that I had never crossed before. Rick didn't have much of a temper, but now he looked like a volcano in its initial stages of eruption. His eyes were hooded, his jaw set in stone. Finally, he got his emotions under control and shook his head. "I'm not telling you to stop acting like a girl. I'm telling you to stop acting like Lisa Cole."

I was already regretting my outburst. I had to stop letting my tongue take over for my brain. But Lisa Cole? That only infuriated me even more. "El Cobra doesn't have *your* family, Rick. So you don't get to decide what I should or shouldn't do."

For one brief instant, he was stunned. And instantly I was sorry. Really sorry. "I . . . Rick, I didn't mean that. I—" I felt awful. If I were him, I would have turned around right then and gone home. Got in the 4Runner and left. Told Danni McAllister to take a flying leap. But he didn't do any of those things. What he did do totally knocked me back on my heels.

"If you think yelling at me will stop me from saying what you need to hear, then you don't know me. Stop freaking out like some airheaded, ditzy sixteen-year-old kid, Danni." He threw his hands up. "I mean, come on!"

"I *am* a sixteen-year-old kid," I fired back, "in case you've forgotten."

"No, you're not. That's what frustrates me so much. Remember what your grandfather said? You're not a kid anymore. You're a young woman. Don't you get it? What you have done in the last few hours is stunning, Danni. Absolutely brilliant."

"But—"

"So why all of a sudden are you acting like this? It's stupid, Danni."

"Oh," I said hotly, "because I disagree with you and Cody, now I'm stupid?"

"This has nothing to do with me. It's stupid because you haven't even thought this through with that amazing brain of yours. When you can tell me you've done that, that's when I'll shut up. Tell me why you won't call the FBI. Tell me what's worrying you. But don't just go off like a rocket and start yelling at everybody."

His voice softened, pleading. "You're one of the smartest people I know, Danni. And we need that from you right now, not some emotional meltdown because you're tired."

Though I was still seething inside, his words gave me pause. I took a deep breath, then another. Somehow I managed a smile. "Wow! Did you just pay me a compliment?"

My bad. Apparently, humor is not the proper response when the volcano is about to erupt.

"It's not funny, Danni. You keep going on like this—full throttle—when you don't even know which direction you're going, and someone's going to get hurt. Or worse."

That hurt so intensely that for a moment, I couldn't breathe. His eyes were like flint. Cody looked like he was going to burst into tears.

It was more than I could take. Feeling my own tears surging up, I whirled and started to walk away.

"Danni," Cody cried, stricken. "Don't go. We'll do whatever you think is best."

I spun back around. "Don't you get it? I don't know what's best. I don't know what I'm doing. You're absolutely right, Rick. Full throttle, no direction—that's me."

He started to speak, but I held up my hands, cutting him off. "No more body blows, please. That's enough for one day. Just leave me alone." I turned my back on them and walked swiftly away.

"Danni?"

I didn't stop. I didn't look back.

"Remember, you *are* unique."

I whirled back again, crushed and beaten. "Stop it!"

"You are, Danni. Can't you see that? You're smart, funny, creative, a joy to be around, and—" Rick exhaled in exasperation. "And beautiful. And maddening and stubborn and . . . beautiful."

"Please," I whispered. "Don't."

"You're the most remarkable person I've ever known."

I clapped my hands over my ears and closed my eyes.

"And you need to remember that your life has a purpose, Danni," he said loudly. "And in this hour, that purpose is to save your family. You can't walk away from that."

"Yes, I can," I cried. "I have to. Don't you see, if I keep going the way I'm going, someone is going to get hurt. You said so yourself."

He started toward me, and when he spoke, his voice was gentle and soft. "No, Danni, you can't walk away. You really can't. It's not in your nature. And that's what makes you so unique. That's what makes you what you are. That's part of your gift, Danni."

Stop! I'm begging you. Please, stop! My only defense was to go back on the offense. "The Four Remembers? You're throwing the Four

Remembers in my face? You still don't see it, do you? That's the problem. I can't measure up to them. I never have." My voice caught in my throat. "Now please, please, just leave me alone. I'll get cleaned up and try to act like a real girl for a few minutes. Maybe even bawl my eyes out for a while. Then I'll come back and 'man up.' We'll go to Salt Lake and talk to the FBI and save the world and I'll do whatever else you tell me to do."

He came a few steps closer, taking me by the shoulders. I refused to look at him. He put his hand under my chin and lifted my head until our eyes met. "Remember," he said gravely, "you *are* free to choose." I tried to jerk away, but he held my head fast. "Sorry, but that's life. Can't you see that the choices you've been making these last few hours have already profoundly changed things? You and Cody are free. You've got El Cobra knocked on his butt. He's on the defensive. And you want to quit?" He smiled. "Come on, Danni. Surely you're not going to leave it to the male side of this equation to fix things, are you?"

He was so exasperating. How could he make me laugh when I felt so awful and when I was so mad at him? I tried to turn my head away from his penetrating gaze, though I suddenly realized I didn't really want to turn away. I wanted to step closer to it, be immersed in it, be wrapped safely inside it and be comforted.

His fingers caressed my cheek for a moment. "And shoot me if you will, but there is one more Remember."

My eyes met his. "You say it," I murmured.

"No, Danni, you say it."

My head came up, my shoulders squared. I looked at Cody, whose eyes were large and filled with worry, then I turned back to Rick. "We are not alone," I said, my voice clear and firm. And then, filled with wonder, I said it again. "*I* am not alone."

"No," he whispered. "No, you are not."

244

"And what about Aron Ralston?" Cody said, grinning that crooked grin of his. "What do we learn from him?"

I laughed again, brushing quickly at my eyes with the back of my hand. "It's not fair. Both of you ganging up on me like this." Cody just gave me that quirky look of his, so I said it. "Never give up."

He gave a huge sigh, then in a plaintive voice asked, "Okay, *now* can we get something to eat?"

I went to him and swept him up in huge hug. "Not until I do something with my hair so I don't scare the crows away."

"Your hair is fine, Danni," Rick said gallantly.

I gave him a look of enormous pity. "You need to learn something about the word 'fine,' Rick."

"What's that?"

"Telling a woman that she looks fine, or that everything's fine, doesn't cut it. It's the most meaningless word in the world. Got it?"

"Got it." He grinned. "Thank you, Miss McAllister, for that very *fine* counsel."

And just like that, things were right between us again.

CHAPTER 34

I was a bit irritated that both Rick and Cody fell asleep on me. I mean, I was doing between thirty-five and forty on gravel roads. There were stretches of washboard, occasional ruts, and plenty of bumps to keep me awake after only three hours of sleep, but they slept through it all.

After a quick lunch in our hiding place by the river, we mapped out a route that would take us to Green River without having to be on the main highway except for a mile or two. And it completely bypassed Hanksville. Now we were on the last leg of that journey with only about five or six miles left.

Of course, with all that time to think, I kept going over and over what had happened that morning. Rick's anger. My anger. His words. My words. Him saying I was beautiful. *Twice!* Me wanting him to say it again after I finally brushed my hair out. Him being totally clueless and not even commenting when I returned with it brushed out. But he had given me an approving look, then handed me the keys and asked me if I wanted to drive.

I sighed, knowing all of this was just my way of avoiding the hard questions. Over lunch, I had agreed to at least talk to the FBI. But I was having second thoughts about it, so I went over Rick's argument in my mind again.

Okay, I accepted that the chance that El Cobra had someone working for him in the FBI office in Salt Lake was extremely remote. But my counter to that was, what if the FBI *did* come in, and then botched it? The FBI were good, but they weren't flawless. I couldn't remember any specifics, but I was sure I had read about cases where the FBI had fouled up big-time.

I glanced at Rick, whose head lolled back and forth, chin on his chest. I didn't need to wake him up. I was pretty sure what he would say in answer to that: "Of course there's a chance they might make a mistake, but the chances of *us* making a mistake are a hundred times greater." And he was right on that too. I hated that he was so logical.

Next argument. The resources of the FBI were beyond anything we could muster. And with their huge computer databases, they might already have a line on this guy. Maybe he'd pulled this kind of extortion racket before. Maybe they could track him through their vehicles or something. There was no way to argue this point either. In spite of all my misgivings, I knew Rick and his dad were right. We had to do it.

So I turned my thoughts to another issue. Where was El Cobra keeping Mom and Dad? If we knew that, we would have a huge leg up on freeing them. I racked my brain, trying to remember exactly what El Cobra had said about where he was going to hide us until the closing of the sale took place. I came up with two things. He had said it was "not far away from here"—Hanksville—and he had said that we would be comfortable and well cared for while Dad and Grandpère closed the sale. That might have been a lie, but I didn't think so. So he wasn't going to throw them into some cellar or underground pit where no one would ever find them in a hundred million years. It sounded more like he was taking them to some kind of house or cabin. But where?

Moab? Blanding? Price? I shook my head. Somehow, I couldn't picture him choosing a place in a town. He would want an isolated location, like someone's mountain cabin. Down here, that narrowed things considerably. We had a lot of desert, but not an abundance of mountains. There were the La Sals, southeast of Moab, the Blue Mountains, west of Monticello, and the Henry Mountains, where we'd been yesterday. All of those mountains were within a hundred and fifty miles of Hanksville.

Then, like a bell going off, two words popped into my head: *fish food.* Twice, while he was warning me against going to the police, El Cobra had made reference to fish—feeding my parents to the fishes. It was an odd thing to say when you were in one of the largest deserts in North America.

Then I jerked up so fast that I twisted the wheel and the truck rocked sharply. Startled, Rick snapped awake, grabbing blindly for the armrest on the door. Behind us, I heard Cody cry out, and a moment later he was looking over the seat.

"Sorry. Didn't mean to wake you two up."

Cody rubbed at his eyes, looking out the windshield. "Where are we?"

I ignored that. "I know where they are, Cody."

"Who?"

"Mom and Dad. Grandpère. Who do you think?"

"You do?" Cody exclaimed. "Where?"

"Yeah, where?" Rick echoed.

"I'm almost positive they're at Lake Powell. Probably in a houseboat."

"How could you know that?" Rick asked.

I told them what El Cobra had said. "Think about it," I said. "They could have had a houseboat waiting at Bullfrog Marina, which is only fifty miles away from Hanksville. And Lake Powell has over two thousand miles of shoreline, more than the entire west coast of the United States. There are dozens of narrow side canyons where they could anchor a houseboat and never be disturbed." I had another thought. "And when they left our house this morning, we heard them turn south on the highway. That doesn't prove anything, but it *is* the direction they'd go to get to Lake Powell."

"That makes a lot of sense," Rick said, nodding. "But it's still a huge area to search."

"Not as much as all of Southeastern Utah."

I could see the respect in his eyes. "Now that's what I was talking about, Danni. Using that brain of yours."

"Go on," I said, pretending to be demure. "You're just saying that because it's true."

"I mean it, Danni."

"I know you do. If I thought you were blowing smoke to make up for what you said this morning, I would have smacked you a good one by now. So, thank you."

I was soaring. I didn't know how, but I *knew* I was right about where Mom and Dad were. I wasn't just sure—I *knew* it. Suddenly I was eager to talk to the FBI.

Rick looked around. "How far are we from Green River?"

"Five, maybe six miles."

"Good. We'll gas up there. And I'd like to find a place to buy some more ammunition for Dad's rifle."

"Agreed." I hesitated. "Rick?"

"Hmm?"

"We're never going to make it to Salt Lake before the FBI office closes."

"I know, but we can call them 24/7. If we tell them this is about a triple kidnaping, they'll meet with us whenever we get there."

"I know, but . . . umm . . . Don't laugh, okay?"

"At what?"

"At me."

"Why would I laugh at you?"

"Because I'd like to wait until tomorrow morning to see the FBI."

He turned squarely to face me. "Why, for heaven's sake?"

"Remember, you promised not to laugh."

"No, I didn't."

"Yes, you did. I saw it in your eyes."

"Why would you want to wait? Every moment is critical, it seems to me."

"Okay, number one, we're not going to get to Salt Lake until this evening. The office will be closed." I held up my hand quickly, cutting him off. "I know that we can call them 24/7, but it won't be their main guy we talk to. Second—yes, timing is critical, but will a few more hours be that critical? I mean, the whole exchange thing doesn't take place until next Tuesday—that's almost a week away. Number three, like you said, they're going to want to talk to us in person and not just on the telephone."

"Yeah, so?"

"So look at me. I haven't had a bath in three days. My hair's a wreck—fine, but a wreck." I couldn't resist that one. "And my clothes smell like the boys' locker room—"

"How do you know what the boys' locker room smells like?" Cody broke in.

I ignored him. "Finally, and most important, Cody and I have only had three hours of sleep in the last thirty or so hours. I'm surprised my brain is working at all. I think we need to be at our best when we talk to the FBI."

I could tell he wasn't doing cartwheels over my proposal, but he finally bobbed his head. "All right."

"Just like that? No fight?"

"The clothes and the hair are no big deal. I mean, they won't be to the FBI," he backpedaled instantly. "But I can see this is important to you."

I rolled my eyes. "Are you just being nice so I won't take your head off again?"

"No, really. I can see some wisdom in what you're saying. Once you've told them your story, they're going to want to take immediate action, and you need to be sharp for that."

"Good. Glad you agree. So, when we get to Salt Lake, we'll find a motel and get a couple of rooms. That will give your dad a chance to catch up to us too. We'll make sure the motel has laundry facilities and—"

"And a swimming pool," Cody chimed in.

"And a swimming pool," Rick agreed.

"Uh, Rick," I said, lifting my foot off the gas.

"Yeah?"

"Do you . . . umm . . . happen to have any money? Or . . . uh . . . like a credit card or something?"

From the look on his face, I could tell he hadn't thought of this either. He extracted his wallet from his pocket and checked. "Six bucks and some change. I don't own a credit card."

"Neither do I. And I don't have much cash either. My wallet's in the side pocket. Check it and see."

He found it and a moment later pulled out some bills. "Nine dollars and change. That won't even buy us enough gas to get to Salt Lake."

"Or even a park bench to sleep on." My good mood totally deflated. It said something about how wired we all were that the need for money hadn't occurred to any of us. Not even Charlie Ramirez, evidently.

"Your folks' bank in Green River," Rick said. "Maybe we could go to the bank and see if they would give you some cash."

"They won't, not without authorization from Mom or Dad."

Suddenly, Cody leaned over the seat between us. "What about the money in the pouch?"

I jerked around. "What money?"

He pointed. "Right there. In the pouch."

I looked down and nearly swerved off the road. I slammed on the brakes and pulled off to one side. Fortunately, we were on a deserted road, and no one was riding my tail. The pouch was on the seat between Rick and me. The flap was unbuttoned and partially open. Peeking out from beneath the fabric was a corner of something green. I snatched up the pouch and reached inside. Slowly I pulled out a rectangular brick of money. My jaw dropped. "Oh! My! Word!"

I held it out for Rick, my mind refusing to process what my eyes were seeing. I was pleased to see his mouth drop open too. He took the packet from me, holding it gingerly, as if it were hot or something. He started thumbing through the bills.

"Is that a hundred-dollar bill?" Cody cried.

"No," Rick said in awe. "It's *twenty* one-hundred-dollar bills."

"Two thousand dollars?" I whispered.

Still staring at me, he slid the packet back into the pouch. "What do you mean you don't have any money?" A slow smile stole across his face. "Looks to me like you're buying, McAllister."

CHAPTER 35

Green River, Utah, is just off Interstate 70, which is the main east-west arterial link crossing central Utah and heading for Denver. Named for the Green River, which comes out of Wyoming, it is about the only place to stop for gas between Grand Junction, Colorado, and Salina, Utah. That makes it a tiny island of civilization in the vastness of the San Rafael Desert. Emphasis on tiny.

I thought it unlikely that El Cobra's men would be watching Green River, but just to be sure, I borrowed Rick's baseball cap and had Cody lay down in the backseat so as not to be seen. We crossed over the interstate and pulled into the first gas station we saw.

Taking turns, we used the restroom while Rick filled the truck with gas. We bought three large drinks, a bag of nachos, three sandwiches, and a package of red licorice—the one essential requirement for any McAllister road trip. The clerk, a blonde girl about my age, raised one eyebrow when I held out a hundred-dollar bill. "Nothing smaller than that?"

"No, sorry."

Rick spoke up. "Don't forget the forty-six bucks worth of gas." He smiled warmly. Suddenly, I was totally forgotten as the clerk made change.

"Can you tell me where we can buy some ammunition?" he asked, oozing Latin charm.

She lit up like she'd just won *American Idol.* "Sure," she said, and she proceeded to describe in great detail where the hardware store was, even though it was just a few blocks up Main Street and you would have to have been blind to miss it.

I finally tugged on his arm. "Come on, Ricky," I said sweetly. "Mother's waiting for us at the restaurant."

I felt the clerk's eyes burning into the back of my head as I herded him out. "Since I'm buying," I said as we approached the 4Runner, "can I still drive?"

"Sure. I'm easily bribed."

———

We were mostly quiet as we ate. Just three miles out of Green River, we left I-70 and turned onto US Highway 6 headed north for Price. Rick had decided he wanted to stop there to see if we could find a store that could check my phone for Spyware.

Finishing the last of my sandwich, I washed it down with a Sprite Zero, then glanced at Rick. "Uh . . . Rick?"

He groaned softly. "Why is it you always start problem conversations with 'Uh . . . Rick'?"

"How do you know it's going to be a problem conversation?"

"Okay, I don't. Sorry. Go ahead."

I wrinkled my nose. "Uh . . . Rick. This might be one of those conversations."

I could see him mentally brace himself, but he was gentleman enough to give me a quick smile, sickly though it was. "Go ahead."

"Promise you won't get mad?"

He shook his head ruefully. "First, I can't laugh. Now, I can't get mad either?"

"Yeah, that's part of the downside to being a male. Promise?"

"Okay, I promise."

Taking a quick breath, I said, "Having laundry facilities isn't enough."

"What?"

"At the motel. We talked about finding a motel with laundry facilities. I'm saying that's not going to be enough."

"I'm not following."

"All I have with me are my camping clothes—these jeans, this old shirts, my beat-up tennis shoes."

"Wash them and they'll be fine," Rick said, wary, as though he could sense what was coming and didn't like it. "It isn't a fashion show, you know."

"Yeah," Cody spoke up from behind us. "What more do you need?"

What flaw in my mental reasoning had made me assume two men would be able to see beyond what I was saying to what I was suggesting? Gritting my teeth, I said, "I need something a little nicer than what I have. And now that we have some money—"

"Wait. Are you talking about going shopping?"

"I don't want the FBI to see me like this. They'll think I'm some kind of homeless person."

Rick's only response was a snigger.

"What?" I sniffed.

"*You* want to buy a new dress?"

"Who said anything about a dress? I'm thinking of maybe some capris, a couple of nice shirts." I smiled. "Maybe a swimming suit."

At his look, I got a little defensive. "And it's not just for tomorrow.

Who knows how long it will be before I get home for a change of clothes? I noticed you put some other things in your bag."

He chuckled softly. "You're really something, Danni. If you want to go shopping, just ask. You don't have to use the FBI to justify it."

"I'm not using—" I cut it off as I realized he had just said yes. That was all I needed. "Okay. Thank you. I'm not talking like a mall. Something easy, like Target, or maybe a Kohl's."

"No!" Cody burst out. "Not shopping. You'll be *forever*! I want to go swimming in the pool at the motel."

"Did you bring a swimsuit?" I asked innocently.

His countenance fell. "I didn't bring anything, remember?"

I grinned wickedly. He had taken the bait without ever seeing the trap. "They'll have boys' swimming suits at Kohl's too. And we can get you something a little nicer to wear tomorrow too."

"Uh . . ." Seeing he'd lost, he nodded. "If we stop and eat somewhere first. I mean real food, not just convenience store junk."

I nodded. Cody would pretty much sell his soul if the food was right.

"Deal?" I asked, looking at Rick.

"Deal," he agreed.

———

As we drove north, Cody chattered away with Rick for a bit, but after yawning two or three times, he laid down and promptly went back to sleep.

Rick waited a few minutes, then peered over the seat. When he turned back, he shot me a hard look. "All right, you wanna tell me what's going on?"

"What?" I asked, feigning innocence.

"You know what. Where did you get that cash?"

"Oh, that."

"Yes, *that*. Two thousand bucks! What's going on, Danni?"

I had been thinking all morning that sooner or later I was going to have to tell him about the pouch. But I knew how incredibly unbelievable it was going to sound. I was afraid he'd think that all the trauma of last night had scrambled my brain. I was dreading the conversation. But the time had come.

Up ahead, I saw a convertible black sports car with the top down, traveling in the same direction as we were. "Uh . . . Just a minute. Let me get around this car."

I was coming up fast on the car ahead of me, and I had to let off the gas. The driver of the BMW was a woman. Her arms were bare and very tan. Rich blonde hair styled in a pixie cut was half hidden beneath a pink baseball cap. From back here, I couldn't see her face, of course, but I could see enough of her in her side view mirror to guess that she was in her late thirties or early forties. She was everything I was not. Studied cuteness. Classic elegance. Flawless skin. I couldn't actually see that, but I was sure that was the case.

Even though my foot was no longer on the gas pedal, I still had to tap the breaks. I looked at the speedometer: sixty-one miles an hour. I rolled my eyes. The speed limit was sixty-five, but everyone always went at least seventy.

And she was barely doing sixty.

I guess I should have been grateful for the distraction. I was looking for a way to forestall Rick from asking questions about the pouch, and now I had my excuse. The challenge of getting around Miss Perfect took over in my mind.

We were on a straight, level stretch of road, but for as far as I could see, there was an unbroken line of traffic coming at us. I edged up a little closer, hoping that the much larger bulk of the SUV would catch her attention and get her to speed up a little. No such luck. I could see that she held a cell phone to her ear.

And then I noticed her bumper sticker.

YES, IT IS FAST. AND NO, YOU CAN'T DRIVE IT.

"You've got to be kidding," I murmured. "This is her definition of fast?" The irony was too rich to miss.

"Danni," Rick said slowly. "Don't do it."

"Don't do what?"

"There's a passing lane in about five miles. There's no way you're gonna get around her until then, so you may as well lighten up."

"You sound like my mother," I grumped. I glanced at the speedometer. "Look. She's down to under sixty now."

"Maybe that's her way of telling you to back off."

"Are you kidding? She doesn't even know I'm back here. I'll bet she's talking to her plastic surgeon, or setting up an appointment to have her nails done at the spa."

He shook his head, but I could see he was trying hard not to laugh. "The bumper sticker's a nice touch," he observed with a straight face.

I harrumphed. "What it should say is, 'Yes, it is fast. Zero to sixty in two days.'"

He laughed. "Oh, Danni. Does your Dad know about this side of you? This passion for—" He jerked forward, peering intently through the windshield. "What the—?"

"What?"

"Look at the bumper sticker."

I did so and let out a startled cry. Now the sticker read:

YES, IT IS FAST. ZERO TO SIXTY IN TWO DAYS.

I swiped at my eyes and read it again. And this time I gasped. Even as we watched, six additional words appeared, one letter at a time, as if they were being typed out by a computer.

PLEASE DO NOT DISTURB SLEEPING DRIVER.

"Did you see that?" Rick cried.

"Uh . . . see what?" My head was spinning like a top.

"The bumper sticker! It just changed." He stared at me. "It actually changed lettering. Look what it says now."

I was reeling too, but I wasn't about to let Rick know that. "Uh . . . I don't think so, Rick. I don't think they make rewritable bumper stickers."

I locked my gaze forward, not daring to look at him again. I also let off the gas a little, letting the 4Runner fall back until it was hard to read the sticker clearly. I glanced in the rearview mirror. There were two vehicles behind us, but they were still a quarter of a mile back. Good. I had enough to worry about without having someone tailgating me like I was tailgating the BMW.

I realized my heart was pounding, and my breath was rapid and shallow. What was happening? It was like the speed limit sign all over again. The Guardian was beside me on the seat, but I hadn't touched it. Was this coming from the pouch? And if so, why? It made no sense. Changing a bumper sticker? I had to admit, it was the perfect rewrite for the driver. But why?

Before I could sort it out in my head, Miss Pixie Perfect finished her phone call.

"Good," I murmured. "So let's pick up the speed a little, ma'am."

No such luck. She reached down to the seat beside her. I couldn't see what she was doing, but a moment later her hand came back up. She was holding a bag of some kind—like a potato chip bag. At the same time, a dog appeared. It was a perfectly manicured white Pekinese, a lap dog with a bright red collar. It stood on its hind legs, its front paws on the seat back, its head turned toward her.

"You've got to be kidding me," I groaned.

She transferred the bag to the hand she had on the steering wheel, then reached delicately into the bag with her other hand and extracted something. She held it just above the dog's nose, who lunged for it and took it out of her hand.

"She's feeding it doggy treats." I let off the gas again and looked at the speedometer. Our speed had dropped to fifty-five miles per hour.

"Danni, don't."

"Don't what?" I snapped.

"Don't honk at her."

As she fed the dog another treat, I fell back another car length or two. Who knew what this ditz was going to do next? I was fuming. "Come on, woman!" I muttered through clenched teeth. "Wake up and drive."

At that moment, the woman jerked upright. The bag of doggy treats went flying. She groped blindly for the steering wheel, then gripped it so hard I could see her knuckles turn white.

"What's she doing?" I cried.

And then she hit the brakes.

"Watch out, Danni!" Rick yelled.

Both brake lights lit up, and there was a horrible screech. The car's nose dropped sharply. Blue smoke billowed from beneath the car as she laid down two black strips of rubber on the pavement.

As I stood on my brakes with all the strength I had, I saw the back end of her car start to skid to the right. No! If she hit the gravel shoulder moving sideways, she'd roll for sure. My tires were screaming but I was still closing on her much too fast. And there was a semi coming straight at us in the opposite lane. There was no going around her. All of this flashed through my brain in a millisecond.

Out of the corner of my eye, I saw Rick's hands shoot out and brace himself against the dashboard. Everything was happening so fast, but I was seeing every detail like it was slow motion. The sports car straightened itself with a jerk—probably with the help from the Beamer's braking system. Then I saw her eyes in her mirror. She was looking right at me, and her eyes were wide with shock. She could see me coming at her.

In that instant, her brake lights went off and the Beamer shot forward like a stone from a slingshot. Three seconds later, with me far enough back not to hit her, her right blinker came on, and she pulled off the road onto the shoulder in a cloud of dust and spraying gravel.

I shot past her, even though I was decelerating so rapidly I could feel my seat belt cutting into my stomach.

"Stop the car, Danni!" Rick yelled.

"I am!" I yelled back. I turned on my blinker and pulled onto the shoulder as well. Before I had fully stopped, Rick was out and sprinting back toward the BMW. I slumped forward, willing myself to let go of the wheel. I couldn't. My heart was hammering in my chest, my mouth was dry, my whole body was shaking. Behind me, I heard Cody moan, and then he sat up, one hand rubbing his head. He had been asleep on the seat, and I realized I had probably sent him crashing to the floor when I braked so hard.

I looked in the rearview mirror. Rick had disappeared into the cloud of dust, but a breeze was clearing it away fast. I saw him reach the sports car and bend over to talk to the woman. She was still gripping the wheel, forehead resting against it.

There was an angry honk as a car whipped past us. Then another one followed. I barely heard them. I watched as Rick talked to her. He reached out and touched her arm. She looked up finally, and I could see her face was white.

Cody leaned over the seat, looking dazed. "What happened?"

"It's all right," I said, opening my door. "Stay here. We'll be right back."

I had to walk slowly because my legs felt wobbly. To my surprise, the woman was pointing at her windshield. Rick leaned over, probably so he could see better; I saw him visibly flinch. Somewhere in the back of my mind, I was aware of the stench of burnt rubber in the air and that the dog was barking wildly.

As I approached the car, Rick leaned over again to peer at the windshield. Then he opened the door for the woman.

"I'm all right, I'm all right," she said, her voice trembling. She undid her seat belt and got out. The dog was still in a frenzy. She turned to it. "Candy! Be quiet."

To my amazement, the dog instantly shut up. As the woman stood, I saw several things all at once. She wasn't just beautiful, she was stunning. She wasn't in her thirties or forties. She was more like twenty-five. It would be years before any plastic surgeon would be getting money from her. Her eyes were a light blue, and her skin was flawless. She wore short shorts and a halter top. Her fingernails were perfectly manicured.

Rick took the woman by the elbow and led her around to the back of the car, getting her away from the road. Another car whipped past us, and the wind buffeted us a moment later.

I slowed my step, then stopped a few feet away from them.

She gave me a shaky smile before turning back to Rick. "Really, I'm all right now. Thank you for stopping."

To be honest, I felt pretty crummy. "What happened?" I asked.

"I . . . I'm not sure. It was so strange. It really frightened me."

"What frightened you?" I asked.

Rick came over and took my elbow. "Come here. I want to show you something." We waited for three more cars to pass before he could lead me to the driver's side door. "Look at the inside of the windshield. On the driver's side."

Leaning in, grateful the dog was gobbling up the scattered treats and ignoring me, I peered at the glass. I wasn't sure what I was look-ing for. When I saw it, my jaw went slack. There, in letters about two inches high, nearly transparent but clearly visible, were the words:

COME ON, WOMAN. WAKE UP AND DRIVE!

I felt chills shoot up and down my spine, and the hair on the back of my neck stood up. Then, even as I watched, the letters slowly faded away and disappeared.

CHAPTER 36

Rick offered to follow Miss BMW to Price, but she waved that off. She had recovered quickly and said she needed to call her husband. The imp in me wanted to hang around and hear her side of the conversation, but then I saw Rick watching me, his eyes hooded and troubled, so I just waved good-bye. As we walked back to the truck, I didn't dare look at Rick. He said nothing, and his face was unreadable. As we reached the truck, I meekly said, "Do you want to drive?"

He turned in surprise. "Do I need to?"

"No, I'm all right."

"That's not what I meant."

"I know." I walked around to the driver's side and got in. A few moments later, we were headed north again. I set the cruise control for sixty-eight miles-per-hour and, with a growing sense of dread, settled in to wait for Rick to ask his questions.

Cody didn't wait. "What happened?" he said. "What did I miss?"

I looked at Rick. He shook his head. So I gave Cody a one-minute summary, leaving out the part about the changing bumper stickers and mysterious writing on the windshield, of course. Rick didn't volunteer to fill in the details.

When I finished, he shrugged. "No more dumping me on the floor, Danni. All right?" He sat back and stared out the window.

About five minutes later, when we passed a sign and saw that we were still forty-five miles from Price, Rick turned in his seat so he was facing me.

"All right. I'm waiting. Tell me what happened back there."

My first impulse was to play coy. But we were way past that. Knowing what we were possibly facing, it wasn't fair to keep secrets from him anymore. "Why don't you ask me questions, and then I'll fill in from there."

He gave a curt nod. "Okay. What about the bumper sticker? Did you do that?"

"No. Not in the way you mean it."

"Which means what?"

"I didn't look at the bumper sticker and say, 'Turn into something different.' And when I told her to wake up and drive, I didn't shout it at her. I was just frustrated and said it to myself. You heard me."

"But it showed up on her windshield."

Cody shot forward, his head poking between us. "Say what?"

"Not now, Code, I'll tell you later." I turned to Rick. "That's right. But I didn't ask it to, or tell it too. Or even wish that it would. What? You think I'm some kind of a witch or wizard or something?"

"Of course not, but something very strange is going on." He frowned. "Tell me about the money in your purse."

"It's not my purse. It's the pouch Grandpère gave me."

"That's your answer? Come on, Danni. I know what it is and where you got it from. Stop stalling. I want to know what's going on here."

"It *is* the pouch," Cody said. "It's a magic pouch."

"Cody! You want to get out and walk?"

"Well, it is," he muttered, but he sat back and shut up.

"You're kidding, right?" Rick said, turning around to face Cody directly.

"Code. Not another word, unless I say." Then I swung on Rick. "If I tell you, you have to promise not to interrupt until I'm through."

"Agreed. Just don't stop before you're done. I want to know everything."

"Okay, okay." I leaned forward, hunching over the steering wheel, feeling a headache coming on. "Grandpère gave me the pouch three years ago. You were there. He never said anything about it being strange or enchanted in any way."

"You think it's enchanted?"

I shot him a dirty look.

"Sorry. Go on."

"You know it's called *Le Gardien* in French—the Guardian in English."

"Yeah, but I just thought it was kind of a family name. Are you saying that's what it does? It guards you?"

"That's what Mom thinks. That's why I fought her about taking it with me everywhere. I resented the idea of having some weird, invisible escort watching my every move. It was like having a nanny, and I didn't like it. Then when everyone started giving me a hard time about it—calling it 'The Nanny Pouch'—I really didn't like it. I came to hate it, actually. So it's just hung there in my room for years, gathering dust. It never did anything strange."

Except when it told Cody to build a fort in the hay two weeks ago—a fort that kept us out of El Cobra's clutches.

I debated whether I should tell Rick about that but decided I had enough to explain right now. Maybe later.

"Go on."

"Then suddenly, these last three days, strange things have started to happen. Like the speed limit sign."

"That was the pouch?" he yelped.

"I think so. Uh . . . I'm not sure." I sounded like an idiot. "Probably."

"But—"

I held up my finger. "Remember, in the Grand Gallery, when Grandpère said I had a gift? He said I could feel things, like danger, or evil."

"I remember."

"I'm not sure how the two things are related. Or even if they *are* related. But sometimes they do seem to work together."

And so I told him everything I could remember. The speed limit sign. The eerie feeling I had up at the mine when I thought we were being watched. The premonition that Mom and Cody were in danger. Several times I could tell he wanted to ask questions, but he held his tongue, listening carefully. However, when I described what happened up to me and Cody in the attic, it was too much for him to contain.

"Wait!" he cried. "You're telling me you became invisible?"

"Yes," Cody exclaimed.

"No," I said at the same time. "We weren't invisible—not in the strict sense of the word. Mom and Dad could see us, and so could Grandpère. But the bad guys couldn't see us. Maybe a better way to say it is that their eyes were blinded momentarily."

"But that's impossible."

"Yeah, that's what Cody said too. But if you think that's hard to swallow, hang on."

To his credit, he did remember his vow. Though I could see him visibly become more and more incredulous, he held back any further questions. As I talked quietly, Cody confirmed what I was saying, even adding details I had forgotten. And even as I listened to myself, I couldn't believe it: The attic lights suddenly not working. The garage lights exploding. My sudden, sporadic understanding of Spanish. The loss of our invisibility even though we were still in danger. A toy gun with no barrel that fired real bullets and continued firing even after the magazine should have been empty. A voice in my head telling me what to do. A truck alarm that wouldn't shut off until we were away safely.

When I stopped, Rick was staring straight ahead. He murmured something, but I couldn't tell what it was. "Say that again?"

"Two thousand dollars in cash appearing out of nowhere. A bumper sticker that rewrites itself. Ghostwriting on the inside of a woman's windshield."

"Yeah, that too," I said glumly. By this time, I wasn't sure I believed any more of it either. It was simply too fantastic.

"There was actually writing on that woman's windshield?" Cody broke in, awed. "Awesome! Dad would love that. He's always talking to other drivers, making comments about their driving and stuff."

I glanced at Rick. He put his face in his hands and started massaging his temples with his thumbs. I smiled sadly. It seemed I wasn't the only one with a headache.

No one spoke for about five more miles. Finally, I looked at Rick. "So, that's the whole story."

Straightening, Rick laid back against the headrest. Then, to my surprise, he reached out, took the pouch, and handed it to me. "Can you make it do something right now?"

I took it, shaking my head. "What?"

There was a fleeting grin. "Another couple thousand would be nice."

I sighed. "You don't believe me, do you?" I knew it. Not that I blamed him.

"Actually," he said after a couple of moments, "what's giving me a headache is that I can't *not* believe you. And yet how could anyone believe a story like that?"

"El Cobra did," Cody said quietly.

Rick's head whipped up. "Say that again."

"El Cobra. He knows there's something strange about the pouch. He almost took it away from Danni."

Rick looked to me. I nodded. "While we were hiding in the barn, he told his men to be sure they got the pouch when they caught us."

Rick's sigh was a long-drawn-out expulsion of air. Then he put his head down again. "Sorry," he finally said. "I need some time to process this."

CHAPTER 37

None of us spoke again until we entered the town of Wellington, just six miles south of Price. Like hundreds of other communities founded by the Mormon Pioneers back in the 1800s, Wellington, Utah, is mostly a farming community with fewer than a thousand people.

When I saw the reduced speed limit sign, I let off the gas. It was then, from the back, a meek little voice finally spoke. "I gotta go."

I glanced at Cody. "Okay." Then to Rick. "I wouldn't mind a stop either."

He nodded, but said nothing.

I pulled into the next service station and took one of the parking places up front by the convenience store entrance. "Want a drink or a snack or something?" I asked Cody.

"Yeah, in a minute."

I laughed. As he headed for the restroom door, I noticed he was doing a little dance as he walked. "Hurry," I called after him.

———

Reluctant to get underway again, the three of us stood in the shade of the convenience store, munching on our snacks. Rick's cell phone rang. "That'll be Dad," he said. But as he looked at the number, he reared back. Giving me a puzzled look, he put the phone to his ear.

"Hello?"

I could hear the tinny voice of a man, but couldn't make out any of the words.

"Yes, I'm Ricardo Ramirez."

More tinny voice.

Rick's eyes shot to me, and suddenly they were tinged with fear. "Yes, she's right here." Slowly, he extended the phone to me.

"Who is it?" I whispered.

He hesitated, then in a low voice said, "It's El Cobra."

I recoiled as if I'd been struck.

"He says he wants to let you talk to your parents," Rick said.

I knew I had to do it, but I was paralyzed for a moment. Then a thought came to me. I looked at Cody. "Get me the pouch." As he raced to the truck and yanked open the door, I took the phone. But I waited until Cody had placed the pouch in my hand before I punched the speaker phone icon so Rick and Cody could hear. "Hello?"

"*Hola, chiquita.* How is my little friend?"

"Let me talk to my parents."

"All in good time, *señorita.* You've been a busy girl since we last talked. Where are you now?"

"Do you want an exact address, or just the general neighborhood?"

There was a bark of laughter. "Ah, *señorita,* you are a cool one, I'll grant you that."

"I want to talk to my parents."

"But of course," he said expansively, "of course. Actually, I've been trying to call you all day so you could talk to them. Why did you turn off your phone? That was foolish of you." He had to know that we had not just turned off the phone, but taken out the battery too, otherwise he would be tracking us right now.

"I dropped it when we were getting away. I've done something to the battery. It's not working."

Rick's eyebrows went up, then he nodded and gave me a thumbs up.

"So you took it out of the phone, of course," he said, the sarcasm heavy in his voice.

"Had to," I shot right back. "It was leaking gasoline, or whatever it is that batteries have in them."

Again he laughed. "Very good, *chiquita,* very good. Here's your father."

I clasped the phone more tightly as Dad's voice came on the line. "Danni?"

"Dad! Are you all right?"

"Yes. We're fine. All of us are fine."

"Where are you?"

I heard a sound, then El Cobra's voice. He must have his phone on speaker as well. "Would you like the exact address or just the general neighborhood?" Another laugh. He seemed to be enjoying himself immensely. But immediately Dad spoke again.

"Are you and Cody all right?"

"Yes. We're good. What about Mom and Grandpère?"

"We're all okay."

"Promise?"

"Yes. Here's Mom."

A moment later, Mom was on the line. Her voice was strained, but filled with relief. "Carruthers, are you really all right?"

"Yes, Mom. We're with Rick. He's helping us. We're doing fine. Really." Cody was waving at me. "Here's Code," I said, and handed him the phone. As he started to talk, I stepped closer to Rick. "He knows we took out the battery. And why."

"Of course he does. What we have to do is make absolutely certain he hasn't put anything on my phone too."

"How do we do that?"

"If we can find a phone store in Price, we'll have them check both phones." Seeing my look, he quickly added, "I'm almost positive he hasn't tampered with my phone, but let's be sure."

"You're right," I said, surprised at my certainty. "If your phone was bugged, they'd have us by now."

"Bye, Mom," Cody said. He handed me the phone.

"Mom, are you okay? Have they hurt you?"

"No, Danni, we're all right. They're treating us well."

Danni? She must be in a bit of shock to have used my nickname like that.

"Grandpère wants to talk to you. Bye, my love. Be safe."

"I will, Mom," I whispered, my eyes suddenly burning.

"Danny Boy, is that you?"

"Hi, Grandpère." My voice caught. "Are you all right? I saw them hit you."

"I'm fine. El Cobra hurt his hand though. You don't hit solid rock without doing some damage." I heard a bark of laughter in the background.

"Oh, Grandpère," I cried, laughing through my tears. "You're wonderful."

"Danni, listen—" he started. I heard Doc's voice cut in over the phone, a low hiss. "Don't try to be cute, Old Man."

"I'm a long ways past cute," Grandpère replied, then he was talking to me again. "Listen, Danni. I meant to tell you this before, but in the excitement of finding the rhodium and all that followed, I completely forgot."

"Forgot what?"

"I put a little something for your birthday in the bottom of your overnight bag before we left. It's a manila envelope with some papers in it."

"An envelope?" I had opened that bag while we were camping and again this morning, but I hadn't seen an envelope.

"Yes, it's not much. Just some papers I thought you'd enjoy."

"Okay." It seemed strange that under the present circumstances he was worried about an envelope.

"There's one more thing, Danni."

"What?"

"*Il est un menteur,* Danni. Don't forget that. Be very—"

"No French." I couldn't tell if it was El Cobra or Doc who shouted it, but the words were followed instantly by the sound of a hard slap across skin. Grandpère grunted in pain. The phone cracked loudly as it dropped onto something hard. In the background, I heard Mom shout something.

I closed my eyes, gripping the phone so hard it felt like my knuckles would break. "Grandpère?" I cried. "Grandpère!"

A moment later El Cobra was on the phone again. He was breathing hard. "What did he say?"

"I don't know. I don't speak French."

"What did you say, old man?" he shouted.

I was straining to hear, trying to picture what was happening. I heard heavy footsteps moving across the room. There was another sharp slapping sound, and I heard Grandpère grunt again. And again.

"What did you say?" screamed Doc.

For a moment, I could hear only Mom's sobbing and Grandpère's heavy breathing. Then, in a low voice, Grandpère answered, "I told her that you are a liar."

Several seconds passed. I heard voices talking in Spanish. Then

El Cobra's voice came on again. He was breathing hard too. "Your grandfather is a foolish and stubborn old man. He is very lucky that we need him for what is going to happen next week. But understand one thing, *señorita*. If you do not do exactly as I say, you will never see your family again. In this, I do not lie."

"And if I do?"

"On Tuesday, you will be reunited with them, and we shall simply disappear."

Grandpère's voice was suddenly in my mind again: *"Il est un menteur."*

"So listen, and listen good. To make this work, we need your father and grandfather back in Hanksville immediately so no one gets suspicious. We need them to meet the Canadians in Moab on Saturday afternoon and take them up to the mine. We also need them to be in Salt Lake City on Tuesday for the closing."

I saw what was coming. "I understand. You want to trade me and Cody for them."

"Exactamente." His voice was like the whisper of a knife blade across silk. "And I am out of patience." He paused. "Are you familiar with the Temple of the Moon and the Temple of the Sun?"

"In Capitol Reef National Park?"

"Sí. The same."

"Yes, I know where they are. We've been there many times."

"That's what your father said. Here's what you're going to do. You, your friend Rick, and your little brother are going to—"

"Rick stays out of this," I cut in. "He's just giving us a ride."

Rick shook his head at me.

"Oh, I think he's doing much more than that, but that's fine. As long as he keeps his mouth shut, he's free of this. If he doesn't, tell him we know where his Aunt Shauna lives in Moab."

Rick's face registered shock and then horror.

"You and your brother will go to the Temple of the Sun and the Temple of the Moon. Enter at the Cainsville turnoff, not the river crossing road. *¿Comprendes?*"

"Yes, I understand. I'm not four, you know."

He ignored me. "Come alone. Just the two of you. We will see to it that no one else will be around. Go past the Temple of the Sun to the Temple of the Moon. Stop in the turnaround circle and get out of the car. If we're satisfied you're playing it straight, we will appear a short time later. We will have your father and grandfather with us and will park next to the Temple of the Sun."

"But not my mother?"

"Oh no, she's enjoying herself here and doesn't want to leave. She's working on her tan. Polishing her nails." He laughed at his own joke. "She is anxious to see you again. And by the way, Luke," he added, turning away from the phone for a moment, "just so you and Grandpa don't get any ideas, you'll be accompanied by a couple of my men who will be your 'employees' while you are with the Canadians. Wouldn't want you tempted to do anything foolish."

Dad murmured something I couldn't hear. My mind was racing. The Temple of the Moon and the Sun were in Cathedral Valley in the north end of Capitol Reef National Park. It was a spectacular area of high, red sandstone cliffs that were sculpted into fantastic spires and battlements. But the formation is isolated and, despite being in a National Park, visited by relatively few people. That part of the valley held pretty much only the two monoliths he had named, sand dunes, and scattered low brush. Once we turned off the highway at Cainsville, El Cobra would know if anyone was following us. As with everything El Cobra seemed to do, it was brilliant. He could easily keep control of the situation.

He came back on the phone. "When you see your father and grandfather coming with their escorts, then you and Cody will start walking toward us. You'll get in our car, they'll get in your SUV, and everything's *muy bien* once again. *¿Comprendes?*"

"When?"

"How soon can you get there?"

"Saturday morning. Nine o'clock."

He swore. "You think we are playing a game, *chiquita? Tomorrow* morning, nine o'clock."

"Sorry." I was hugging the Guardian like I was suffocating and it was my oxygen mask. And it was working. Rick, who was hearing both sides of the conversation, was watching me with growing alarm, but my mind was racing with that same marvelous clarity I had felt earlier.

"Do you understand me, Danni?" El Cobra shouted. "Tomorrow morning."

"Oh, I understand you all right, I just don't trust you. I have no guarantee that you won't hurt them or us anyway."

"Ah, but you have twenty million guarantees, *señorita*. Don't forget that."

"Only until those guarantees are deposited in your bank account on Tuesday. Then I have nothing. *Nada.* You've got to give me more than that."

There was a long pause, then, "I told you before. Hurting your family doesn't benefit us at all. *If* you cooperate, we'll disappear, and you'll never see us or hear from us again."

He is a liar. I drew in a deep breath. "Sorry, *señor*," I said, "it's going to take more than that. Not that I doubt you are a man of honor and integrity."

I heard him grunt, then mutter something to someone else. I thought I heard the woman's voice answer. He finally asked, "What are you suggesting?"

Rick and I exchanged glances, me imploring him for help, him shrugging helplessly. "We're still trying to work something out," I finally said. "As soon as we do, I'll call you back, and we'll set up an exchange. But it will be on *our* terms, not yours."

"No, *señorita* Danni, that smells very much like a trap."

I paused, wanting him to think I was wrestling with this. "All right. We'll come to Cathedral Valley as you say, but we say when and where."

"And you will put the battery back in your phone so I know you are not playing games."

"I will. That is, when I get a new battery. Remember, it's leaking gasoline."

There was a snort of derision. "Tell them to put in a gallon. Or maybe you could find a very small set of jumper cables and charge it up again." Then his voice went very soft. "One more question, *chiquita,* and I want you to think very carefully about this before you answer."

"Go on."

"Have you, or anyone with you, made contact with any law enforcement officers of any kind?"

"We have not," I said without hesitation. "Not in any way. I am fully aware of the consequences of doing so. I'm not stupid, you know."

"Your parents tell me you are an honest girl. Do you swear this on the grave of your grandmother?"

"I do." I held my breath, praying he wouldn't push the issue.

"All right," he said, and I sighed in relief. "I believe you. We shall call you again. *Hasta luego.*"

As I handed the phone back to Rick, I said, "Be sure you write down his number. The FBI will want it."

"It's on my phone," he said, "but it won't be traceable. I bet he's using one of those throw-away cell phones or something like that." As he returned the phone to its case, he gave me a funny look.

"What?" I said, suddenly embarrassed.

"Was that you or the pouch talking?"

"I . . . It wasn't me. I was scared to death."

"You were Wonder Woman," Cody said.

Laughing, I threw my arms around him and hugged him tightly. "Mom and Dad and Grandpère are all right, Code. They're all right." I looked up at Rick. "Did you hear what he said about Mom working on her tan?"

"Yes. Do you really think she is?"

"No, but where's the best place to get a tan? At the beach. They're at Lake Powell, Rick, I'm sure of it."

He considered that for a moment, then nodded. "I think you're right."

"Good. Then we'd better get going. Let's go find us a phone store."

He didn't move. "Danni, why do you think your grandfather told you that El Cobra is a liar? He had to know that was going to cause trouble."

"Because he wants me to know that we can't trust him."

"Yes, but . . ." He was squirming a little.

"What? Do you know something I don't?"

"While you were sleeping this morning, I got on the Internet and did some research on secret bank accounts."

A sudden dread swept over me. "And what did you learn?"

"They are carefully protected, but the banks have an agreement with US law enforcement. If they can prove a crime has been committed and the criminals are using the banks to hide that crime, then the banks must turn over the records and access to those accounts."

I was tired, but I understood what he was saying. "So all this talk about them disappearing once their money is safe is just to keep us going along with them."

He shrugged. What other conclusion was there? Fighting hard not to let discouragement completely wash me away, I reached in the pocket of my jeans, took out the keys, and tossed them to him. "I'm really, really tired, Rick. You drive."

He caught them. For a long moment, he searched my face, looking into my eyes. Then he reached out and laid a hand gently on my arm. "It's going to be all right, Danni," he said quietly. "You're every bit as smart as El Cobra." He laughed softly. "And if you can make writing appear on windshields and change speed limits signs, then everything will be okay."

"Promise?" I said, my voice barely audible.

This time he laughed aloud. "You're sure asking for a lot of promises today."

CHAPTER 38

Caitlin, our salesperson—or technical support associate, or token cutie, or whatever they were called in this particular phone store—gave me a long look, sizing me up. She also kept glancing at Rick, who, for now at least, was letting me take the lead. Caitlin was an attractive brunette, probably nineteen or twenty. I wondered if she knew her stuff or was just a pretty face. One thing was for sure. She was impressed with Rick. I was getting used to that.

"Now," she said, "I have to warn you, in order to find out if there is malware on your phone, we're going to have to—"

"Malware?" I cut in.

"Yes, that's what we call it instead of spyware. *Malware* is an abbreviation of 'malicious software.' Anyway, what I was about to say is, once I hook your phone up, whoever it is that's monitoring you will know where you are."

Rick had already warned me about that. We had decided that our stay in Price would be short enough that El Cobra's people couldn't get to us before we were on the road again.

"Yes, I know. We'll take the battery out again as soon as it's confirmed. We're on our way to Denver to meet our parents, so I think we'll be all right." I saw Rick and Cody register a flicker of surprise, but then nod.

"Okay, then let's find out for you." She gave another sidelong glance at Rick, then offered me an awkward smile. "You sure your parents didn't put it on your phone? That's the most common explanation. They want to monitor where their kids are and what they're saying to their friends." She emphasized the word "kids" just enough to raise my hackles. "That," she went on quickly, "or employers who want to monitor their employees." She sized me up and down. "Are you employed?"

"Yeah, I own a mine with my father," I said as if that were the most common thing in the world. "And my parents didn't put anything on my phone."

She nodded. I think the mine ownership bit went right past her. As for my parents, it was obvious she had heard that line before. "Follow me," she said, businesslike.

She led us back to a counter with several desktop computers lined up.

I handed her the battery and the phone. "The battery is about dead," I said. "Would it make any difference if you put in a new one?" I was still worried about El Cobra swooping in and grabbing us.

"No, the tracking is done through the wireless signal that is sent to the phone. Once the battery is out, there's nothing to track. But it doesn't matter which battery it is."

"Hold on," Rick broke in. "So there doesn't have to be malware on your phone to track it?"

"Oh no. All cell phones register their location with their home networks several times a minute. Those service providers can track the phone to within a few meters if they choose to do so. That's how law enforcement agencies are able to track someone who's lost, or a child who's been abducted."

Okay, she wasn't just cute, she knew her stuff. I looked at Rick to see what he thought, and was surprised to see sudden fear in his eyes.

"What's wrong?" I asked.

He barely heard me. "Do law enforcement agencies have to get permission to track someone's phone?"

She frowned. "That's a big issue right now. They're supposed to get a warrant, but the law is fuzzy, especially in cases of an emergency. Cell phone companies, including the ones we represent, charge a pretty hefty fee for tracking services. They're making a lot of money from police departments all across the US."

My mind was suddenly spinning. So could the FBI track El Cobra's location through his phone? How simple would that be? We'd just wait for him to call, then . . .

But Rick's mind was going down another track. "Can anyone buy that service from the phone providers? Like a private citizen?"

"Supposedly not," she said, less sure of herself. "But I guess, theoretically, if a person had enough money and the right contacts, they could bribe an employee to provide that for them."

I was suddenly weak in the knees. Rick wasn't thinking of the FBI tracking El Cobra; he was thinking about El Cobra tracking *his* phone. The same phone that El Cobra had called him on in Wellington less than half an hour ago.

"And is there anyway to protect against that?" he asked in a low voice.

"Not that I know of. But I don't think you need to worry about that." She gave him a strange look. "Unless you're running from the law."

Oh, great! Now she was suspicious. I almost grabbed Rick's hand and bolted. But good old Rick gave her a rueful smile and moved in closer. "Actually, we've got a guy stalking my sister here. At first, it was just an annoyance, but now he's really starting to worry us."

She looked at me, her dark eyes suddenly full of compassion. "How awful. Have you called the police?"

"Our parents have," I said, thinking fast. "We're going to see them as soon as we get home."

Rick still wasn't satisfied. "I'm pretty sure there's no malware on my phone, but if this guy can track the phone anyway, that's a real concern. I guess I could remove the battery from my phone too, but we have to stay in touch with our parents."

"I understand. I'm sorry, but I really think the chances of someone getting access to that information are pretty remote."

Not if you're El Cobra and you have twenty million dollars at stake, I thought.

Caitlin shrugged. "If you're really nervous about it, you could always buy a temporary phone. It's still traceable, but it has no recorded ties to you."

"And do you carry those here?" Rick asked.

"Yes."

Rick looked at me. I nodded vigorously. "Let's do it."

"Do you want one or two?"

I didn't wait. "Two." I remembered something else. "And we'll need a car charger."

"All right," Caitlin said.

Rick took out his phone and started to remove his battery.

Caitlin spoke to me. "Do you still want me to remove the malware from your phone? They may be able to track your phone, but if we take the software off, they can't listen in on your conversations or intercept your text messages." She shuddered. "That would give me the creeps."

"Me too. Take it off," I said.

To my surprise, she touched my hand briefly. "I'm so sorry." She removed the case and started to replace the battery. As she did so, I suddenly held up my hand. My mind started correcting itself just like it had after I'd knocked Gordo out in the barn. "No, wait. Don't take it off."

Her eyebrows shot up.

I turned to Rick. "Once we're with the police, maybe they can use it to lure the guy into a trap or something."

He saw instantly where I was going. "Good thinking, sis. We'll just leave the battery out until we're ready." He turned to Caitlin. "Thank you, Caitlin. You have been most helpful."

"Yes. We really appreciate it." And I meant it. She had been great. I reached in the pouch, felt around, then brought out two hundred-dollar bills and handed them to Rick. "You get the phones," I said. "I'll wait outside. We'd better hit the road as soon as possible."

Though I was feeling much more kindly toward Caitlin, it still gave me great satisfaction to see her eyes widen at the sight of that much cash. Maybe now she would think I really did own a mine.

As I started for the door, I had another thought. "Hey, Caitlin?"

"Yes?"

"Could I ask a special favor of you?"

"Of course. What is it?"

"You'll have the numbers of our throwaway phones, right? Could you give us a call if someone happens to come here asking about us?"

"Sure," she promised. "I'll call you immediately."

"Thank you. Just ask for Carruthers."

"I'm sorry?"

"So am I," but I smiled as I said it. "Carruthers. C-a-r-r-u-t-h-e-r-s." She scribbled quickly. "Got it. I'll call you."

CHAPTER 39

When I rejoined Cody, who was waiting outside, I opened the back of the 4Runner and started rummaging through our gear.

"Whatcha lookin' for?" he asked.

"My overnight bag. I'm want to see if I can find that envelope Grandpère talked about." I found the bag and started going through its contents.

Rick came out of the store carrying a sack with the store's logo on it. "You want me to drive again?" he asked.

"Ha!" I cried, straightening and waving the envelope at them. "He *did* put it in here. But I could have sworn it wasn't there before."

"I drive, you drive? Your call."

"You drive. I want to see what Grandpère is up to."

As we got underway, I opened the envelope. It held a pack of papers about a quarter of an inch thick. I looked at the first page, then frowned. "It's a note from Grandpère. Written on my birthday." I read it aloud.

Sunday, June 12
My Dearest Danni,

*Happy sixteenth birthday—another milestone in your jour-
ney of life. For the past few days, I have felt a desire to share some
things with you, things you are not familiar with yet, but which
are part of yours and Cody's heritage. If you are reading this and
I am not with you, it is likely because you are in some kind of
difficulty. I know not what form this difficulty will take, but for
more than a week now, I have had a growing sense that some
great challenge is coming to our family.*

I stopped and looked at Rick. "That's amazing. How could he
know that?"

There was no good answer for that, so I continued.

I have included the following items with this letter:
*Some brief excerpts from my life history. It was written by
my father as though it had happened to someone other than his
own son. He said it was easier that way.*

*Some extended excerpts from the journal of Monique La-
Roche—my mother and your great-grandmother.*

*Some handwritten notes of my own to answer any possible
questions you may have about what you read.*

*The story of my mother's experience in Paris as told to me
when I was sixteen years old. After we emigrated to America, she
asked that I write it for her because she said that if she wrote it
herself, the tears would blot out the words. I wrote it exactly as
she dictated it to me.*

*And finally, I have written some brief concluding comments
for reasons that will be clear after you read them.*

*I recommend you read what I have given you in the order
listed above as this will make the most sense.*

Danni, it is time you know the full story of Monique La-Roche. Since you bear her name, I pray that her story will give you strength in whatever challenge you may be facing at this moment, or in the years which still lie ahead of you.

De tout mon coeur—*with all my love,*
Grandpère

PART SEVEN

Resistance

CHAPTER 40

Le Petit Château, France
Friday, August 11, 1944

Jean-Henri LaRoche and Louis Girard were playing war. It was a beautiful summer day with a light breeze. The sky was perfectly clear. Even the smudge that usually hung over Strasbourg, about six kilometers north of them, was not there today.

Their "battleground" was the dirt lane that led past Le Petit Château, Jean-Henri's home. Blocks of wood were their tanks. Round stones from the creek behind the château were the trucks. Short lengths of willow sticks stuck in the soft ground were the supporting infantry. Their "air force" consisted of one plane each, a gift to Jean-Henri from his grandmother.

Louis Girard was Jean-Henri's best friend. His father was the village butcher, and his family lived over the butcher shop in the heart of the village. He was a couple years older than Jean-Henri, but in the village school, all the grades met together so age differences didn't warrant much attention. Because Louis's home was small, he usually came out to the château—good weather or bad—once his chores were done.

As Jean-Henri's plane swooped in, suddenly Louis held up his hand. "Shh!" He cocked his head to one side, looking to the northeast.

"What is it?" Jean-Henri cocked his head too.

"Bombers," Louis said after a moment.

Jean-Henri went up on tiptoes, straining to hear better. "*Oui.* Many of them."

Both boys searched the sky to the north. The sound was definitely getting louder, but there was no sign of any planes. "Stuttgart, do you think?" Jean-Henri asked.

"No. Listen. They're closer than before. I think it's Strasbourg."

Jean-Henri stared at his friend. "You really think so?"

"Boys?"

The voice of Monique LaRoche brought them both around. She was standing on the front veranda of the château, wiping her hands on her apron, looking anxiously up into the sky. "I would like you to come closer to the house to play."

"But, Mama, we can see better from out here."

Suddenly Pierre LaRoche appeared at the barn door. He had a pitchfork in his hand. "Jean-Henri," he called. "You heard your mother."

"*Oui,* Papa."

The two boys left their armies in place and moved to the grassy area directly in front of the house. Both mother and father joined them. They all turned to the north to watch. What had been a faint hum at first was now a dull roar, heavy enough that the sound took on a life of its own. And then the bombers appeared—first just three or four, then row after row after row. They were no more than two kilometers north of the château, coming in fast. Planes had never flown so close to their little village before.

Suddenly, bright flashes of light and splotches of jet-black smoke speckled the sky in front of the bombers. A couple of seconds later, the sound of the explosions reached their ears. The aircraft batteries surrounding Strasbourg had opened fire. Each blast came as a sharp crack of sound, like repeating claps of thunder. *BOOM! BOOM! BA-BOOM! BOOM!* The explosions were coming so rapidly they were almost blending into one continuous sound. The sky was pockmarked with black smoke, but to Jean-Henri's astonishment, the bombers kept going, flying directly into the firestorm until they were partially obscured by the smoke.

"Look," his father exclaimed. "Here comes the Luftwaffe."

From high above the bombers, black specks appeared. Streaking downward at incredible speeds, they pounced on the fat, old bombers. Tail gunners, turret gunners, and waist gunners opened fire on their attackers even as the attacking fighters opened fire on them. Brilliant tracers laced across the sky in every direction. Then more fighters appeared, coming in from the other direction—American this time, escorts for the bombers. In seconds, dogfights raged in and around the lumbering bombers.

For the parents, who understood the reality of what they were watching, the next few minutes filled them with a growing sense of horror. For the young boys, who had been playing at war just minutes before, it was a spectacular sight. There was a large flash of fire, and one of the bomber's wings sheared off, pulling the aircraft into a steep dive, trailing smoke as it went down. A German fighter exploded, and seconds later the roar of the blast reached their ears.

The family flinched as another bomber disintegrated in a ball of fire. Another fighter went spiraling downward, leaving a curl of smoke across the sky. They couldn't tell if the plane was American or German. Monique turned to her husband. "We need to go inside the house."

"No, Mama," Jean-Henri cried. "Not yet."

Pierre put an arm around his wife's shoulder. "They're not close, my dear. We're at no risk."

"There go the bombs," Louis yelled. Tiny clusters of black dots were falling from the bellies of the lead bombers. *CRUMP! CRUMP! CRUMP!* The high explosives made a much deeper sound than the antiaircraft guns. Moments later, the ground shook beneath their feet.

For the next five or six minutes, as the faraway rumble became one continuous roar, pebbles danced on the ground, and little puffs of dust could be seen in the lane as the earth trembled and shuddered and shook.

Monique LaRoche crossed herself and bowed her head. "May God have mercy on them," she murmured.

When it was finally over and the bombers had gone, the silence seemed surreal, almost like a dream. No one spoke. Even Louis and Jean-Henri were silent as they realized that for Strasbourg, death and destruction had rained from the sky.

Pierre had started back toward the barn when two simultaneous sounds jerked him around—the roar of aircraft engines and the rat-a-tat of machine gun fire. Eyes wide, he scanned the sky. "There," he shouted.

In the sky to the east, at an altitude of two or three thousand feet and coming fast were two black blobs against the blue. They bobbed and darted in and out, jerked upward, then dove away again. For a moment, Jean-Henri thought it was two Stuka bombers, coming to pay him a return visit, but he could see orange and yellow tongues of fire from the front of the second plane. The lead plane jinked hard to the left, and the tracers shot right past him.

Jean-Henri, who could recognize the silhouette of any plane—

Allied or Axis—saw that the lead plane was a P-51 with white stars on its fuselage and the underside of its wings.

"It's American," he cried.

"Get down," Pierre shouted, diving for his wife, pulling her down, and covering her with his body. The boys reacted instantly. Louis fell on his stomach and buried his face in the grass. Jean-Henri did the same, but rolled over on his back to watch.

The two planes flashed past them, just a few hundred yards south of where they lay. Jean-Henri groaned as he recognized the silhouette of the second plane. It was the Messerschmitt 109, a mainstay of the Luftwaffe. Without being consciously aware of what he was doing, Jean-Henri was up on his knees, fists punching the air. "Go, Yank! Go!" he shouted.

"Jean-Henri. Get down!"

He barely heard his father. As if in slow motion, he saw the M-109 fall in line behind the American plane. Tracers erupted again. And this time the pilot walked them right into the tail of the Mustang. The plane shuddered as the bullets struck. The Mustang wheeled sharply over, trailing a stream of dark liquid.

Jean-Henri gave a low cry as his father slammed into his body, tackling him and throwing him down.

"Stay down, son!" he shouted.

He fought like a wild man to get his head free. When he did, it was just in time to see the engine of the Mustang burst into flames. A second later, what looked like a dark, round ball separated from the plane. It tumbled downward as the fighter arced steeply, then dove straight into the ground behind a hill not half a mile a way. Jean-Henri held his breath. Then a white parachute blossomed in the sky and floated gently down to earth. He gave a cry of triumph.

They got to their feet, scanning the sky, but the Messerschmitt was gone.

Jean-Henri's father sprang into immediate action. "Mother," he called. "Get some bandages from the house. Hurry! The Germans in the village will have seen this too. We can't let the pilot fall into their hands."

A look of horror crossed Monique's face, but to Jean-Henri's great surprise, his mother didn't protest. She turned and sprinted for the house.

"Watch where he lands," Pierre barked, then he turned and hobbled awkwardly for the barn.

Louis and Jean-Henri were stunned by what they had just seen. Using a small outcropping on one of the higher hills as a marker, Jean-Henri mentally noted where the pilot was going down. His mother and father came back at about the same time. Monique carried some folded cloth, a tube of ointment, a small leather pouch of wine, and two *torches électrique.* She also had a cloth purse with a wooden button and rope handle over her shoulder. Pierre returned with his shotgun, which, since the occupation began, he kept hidden in the attic of the barn. The boys ran over to join them.

When Pierre held out his hands for the items, Monique shook her head. "No, Pierre."

Pierre's eyes narrowed. She rushed on quickly.

"They will instantly suspect any adult male in the forest today, especially one with a gun, and you will be arrested." She forced herself not to look at his leg, or point out that if soldiers did come, there was no way he could outrun them. "But two boys playing in the woods? It is not the same."

With great reluctance, Pierre finally nodded. Monique removed the pouch from her shoulder. "May I send *Le Gardien* with them?" she asked.

"Of course," he said. "You don't have to ask."

"It is your pouch, not mine."

"Send it with them, by all means."

Monique handed the supplies to Louis but hung the rope strap of the pouch off Jean-Henri's shoulder.

"What am I to do with this?" Jean-Henri asked, puzzled.

She gathered him in her arms, hugging him more fiercely than he could ever remember. "Just keep it with you," she said softly. Finally pulling free, she kissed him on both cheeks. *"Que Dieu te garde, mon fils,"* she whispered. "Go with God, my son."

CHAPTER 41

As I lowered the papers, Cody spoke from the back. "Awesome."

My eyes were on Rick. "Did you catch that? Monique called the pouch *Le Gardien.*"

"I did," he said. "Read the date again."

I flipped back to the first page. "It says 1944. So almost seventy years ago. That's amazing."

"Read some more," Cody said. "I want to know if they saved the pilot."

I smiled at his excitement, which matched my own. "Okay. These are in Grandpère's handwriting. They must be his notes."

A full account of how I, and my friend Louis Girard located the downed American pilot, First Lieutenant Arnold Fitzgerald of Ogalalla, Nebraska, can be found in my life history. I have not included it here, for reasons that shall become obvious shortly. In the near future, though, if you so desire, perhaps we can read it together.

Before I begin, however, I must say a word or two about my

father's pouch which my mother handed to me that day before
sending us into the woods. I think you know what pouch it was.
Though I did not recognize it then, I realize now that it played
an important part in the events of that night, and also in what
followed. For example, as I look back on it now, it is quite
remarkable to me to realize how clearly my mind functioned that
night. I knew exactly what to do and where to go. Sometimes I
was warned to stop, and moments later we saw Germans passing
nearby.

I stopped and looked up. "Yes!" I cried. "I know exactly what he
means. That's what I was trying to tell you, Rick. It's like someone
turned on a light in a darkened room and suddenly you can see everything clearly."

Rick nodded, but he had a funny look on his face.

"What?"

"Is that what you felt when you changed that woman's bumper
sticker?"

My face fell. "Uh . . . no. No, it's not. That part I don't understand."

He reached across and touched my hand. "Sorry. Keep reading."

Three times that night, the pouch became our protector
from German patrols in the forest—once before we found the
pilot, and twice as we helped him back to the château. Once, the
soldiers were so close I could have reached out and touched their
boots.

Most remarkable to me was how we found Lt. Fitzgerald.
Louis and I searched until dusk to no avail. I grew discouraged,
knowing that when dark came, our search would have to end.
As we sat down to rest, without consciously thinking about it, I
clutched Le Gardien tightly to my body. I guess I was looking for

a little solace. It was at that precise moment that we heard a soft moan nearby. We leaped to our feet and went in the direction of the sound, calling out softly, "Américain. Américain."

We heard nothing more so we stopped and looked around. And that is when Louis saw blood on the forest floor. As we stared at it, another drop splattered from above. We looked up. There was the pilot, unconscious and dangling from his parachute in a large sycamore tree. He was bleeding from a severe gash to his head. I shall only say that we managed to get him down and take him to where the partisans of the Resistance movement were waiting with my father.

When we reached home late that night, my mother asked for the pouch back. I did not see the pouch again until I received it from my father on my thirteenth birthday.

My purpose in mentioning this is because by now, in whatever difficulties you are facing, I suspect you have learned that this simple pouch is indeed a remarkable gift. You know its name. I hope you are beginning to sense its worth. Use it well. Use it wisely.

One caution. Be careful for what you wish, for the pouch responds to the desires of your heart, even if those desires are not to your benefit.

And with that brief admonition, I return to the story as told to me by your great-grandmother.

CHAPTER 42

Le Petit Château, France
Saturday, August 12, 1944

Yesterday, Pierre and I, and our son, Jean-Henri, and his friend, Louis Girard, witnessed an air battle over Strasbourg. This was a horrible thing to watch, even though it was distant enough that we did not see the suffering or the dying firsthand. As it ended, an American fighter plane was shot down near our home. Fortunately, the pilot was able to bail out.

As we watched the pilot floating down from the sky, my beloved husband shouted at me and told me to run and get bandages. We had to find the pilot before the Germans did. His words stunned me. How could he ask that of me? The punishment for helping the enemy in any way is instant execution.

We were already in great danger. Since the Allied invasion of continental Europe, the French Resistance in our area has been very active. Though he never spoke of it, I knew Pierre had joined the Resistance. He doesn't know that I never sleep on the nights he is gone, not until he is back safely in bed with me. I say this only to show that we were already living each day under a great cloud of fear. Twice in the past three months, German soldiers have come to our house and questioned my husband at great length, searching the house for anything that might give him away. But the fact that he is crippled seems to convince them he could not be part of the Resistance.

All of this flashed through my mind in an instant as he called out to me. But at that same moment, as I watched the pilot floating down helplessly in the sky, I knew what I had to do. This was my time. This was my war too. Mothers in America were sending their sons across the sea to France to risk their lives to help free my people from tyranny. How could I not help one of their sons?

When I returned with some things to help the pilot in case he had been injured, something strange happened. My son and his friend were standing next to my husband, who had fetched his shotgun and was preparing to leave. Contrary to all emotion and reason, I knew, as surely as I knew anything, that it was my son who must go in search of the pilot and not my husband. One part of my heart cried out in anguish at the thought of sending my boy on such a dangerous mission, but I knew that this war was my son's war too.

That night was yet another long night without sleep. But, thanks be to God, the boys found the pilot and brought him back to our home. They arrived here just before dawn. The pilot had landed in a tree and had not only been badly cut but had also broken his leg. We discussed sending him immediately south into Switzerland, but he could not travel on foot, and the roads were much too dangerous because the Germans knew an American pilot was down.

When the boys arrived at our home with the pilot, Pierre took me aside. Was I willing to hide this man here on our farm until the Resistance could find a way to smuggle him west to the Allied lines? My blood ran cold, but I answered yes without hesitation.

As my husband left to get help from others in the Resistance, I looked away, wondering if I had just made a terrible mistake. It was then that I saw Jean-Henri looking at me. His eyes were filled with so much pride and so much gratitude that everything was suddenly all right. We hugged each other and cried together as the men carried the American into the barn, found him a hiding place, and then set to work erasing any trace of him.

That day was awful beyond belief—trying to act as if everything was normal; fearing the soldiers would come at any minute; hoping against hope that we had not missed any bloodstains or left any other evidence that a wounded man had been treated in our kitchen.

Just before noon, the soldiers came. They had found the parachute in the tree and the blood on the ground. They knew the pilot was alive and were searching every farmhouse, every outbuilding, every shop and home in the village and the surrounding area. They were savage in their anger and threatened to kill ten people for every person who aided the downed flyer.

But they did not find him. Unbeknownst to me, Pierre had built a false half wall in the hayloft. After putting the bandaged lieutenant in there, the men moved enough hay in front of it to cover it completely. The soldiers searched, threatened, ranted, and raved, but in the end, they went away with nothing.

Last night, our little family knelt together and gave thanks to God for his overwatching care. We also pled for Him to protect us and the pilot until we could get him to safety.

CHAPTER 43

Moselle, France
Sunday, August 13, 1944

Today is my twenty-ninth birthday. And today has been the worst day of my life.

This morning at 3:37 a.m., the Gestapo came to our little château.

Gestapo. The State Secret Police. The very word sends stark fear into the hearts of people all across Europe.

A full day had passed since we brought the American pilot to our home, and we had relaxed somewhat, thinking we were safe. We were not. Looking back now, obviously someone betrayed us. Who would do such a thing in this community of ours? One of the villagers? A collaborator? A family member hoping for some leniency for one of their own? It doesn't matter. It was done.

When the police battered on the door, Pierre and I leaped out of bed. We barely had a moment before they burst into our room with guns drawn. They threw Pierre against the wall, and the officer in charge shoved me into a chair. Moments later there was a crash from down the hall, followed by a scream from Jean-Henri. I leaped to my feet, and Pierre hurled himself at his captor. Colonel Horst Kessler, the officer in charge, was from Strasbourg. We had seen him in the village on more than one occasion. He had always been pleasant and courteous to me. But as I tried to stand, he struck me across the face with the back of his hand, cutting my cheek open with his ring. The soldier guarding Pierre clubbed him on his bad leg, and he went down, screaming in pain.

When another soldier marched Jean-Henri into the room, I started to get up again.

"Madame," Kessler said coldly. "If you move again, I shall have you taken out and shot. Do you understand me?"

I sank back down, fighting hard not to break into tears.

"Get him up." The colonel motioned with his pistol at Pierre. Two soldiers stepped forward and dragged him to his feet. The colonel stepped over to Jean-Henri. He smiled, then bent down and looked into our son's eyes. "*Petit gar-çon*—little boy," he said in a conversational tone, "where has your father hidden the American airman?"

Jean-Henri met the officer's gaze with open defiance. "I do not know."

I had never been so proud, or so frightened, as I was at that moment.

The officer's hand moved in a blur, and instantly he had the barrel of his German luger pressed against our son's forehead. "What was that you said?" he asked pleasantly, leaning in closer.

"I do not know."

"He doesn't," Pierre cried out. "Do you take me for a

fool? Do you think I would involve my wife and children in this? They know nothing." His head dropped. "Nothing."

"So," Kessler said, holstering his pistol, "does this mean you are ready to cooperate?"

"Fully." Pierre looked at me, weeping. "I am so sorry, *ma chérie*. I am so sorry."

———

It is night now as I write in my diary. There have been many tears shed this day, and much anguish experienced because of the desperate nature of our situation. Yet, in the midst of our sorrow, there have been blessings as well and for that we are grateful.

Blessing number one. Though my beloved husband is now in the hands of monstrous and evil men, my son and I are not. I fully expected that Colonel Kessler would arrest me for questioning and perhaps take Jean-Henri into custody and send him off to a camp where he would become part of the Hitler Youth movement. When the colonel did not return right away, I feared he might change his mind, so we set out immediately for Moselle, where my parents live. We told no one, and we slipped away through the woods without passing through the village. If they come for us, they shall find no one there.

Second blessing. A woman in our village serves as a housekeeper and cook at the German garrison. When she arrived there this morning, the whole garrison was in an uproar. The local cell of the Resistance had been totally broken up and arrested. (More evidence that we were betrayed from within.) From what she heard, Colonel Kessler planned to conduct the interrogations himself and then summarily execute all the prisoners. But when he wired to Paris to inform the Gestapo of these developments, they ordered him to escort all the prisoners to the capital. As things grow increasingly worse for them, the German High Command is anxious to break the back of the Resistance if at all possible. So Pierre is still alive, thanks be to God. And thanks be to God for a woman who risked her life to call my parents and let them know what she had learned. If she had not done so, Pierre would have been shipped off without me knowing, and I might never have heard from him again.

Moselle is a small town a few kilometers east of Metz. We found all there to be well. Moselle has been largely bypassed by the war. My parents were overjoyed to have their only child and grandchild with them again. And he is overjoyed to be with them. If something happens to me, I take comfort in knowing he shall be well cared for.

When the call from our friend came, I immediately determined that I must go to Paris to try to intervene in Pierre's behalf. Both Father and Mother are trying very hard to dissuade me from such a dangerous mission, but I am resolute. I cannot stand idle if there is any hope—even the tiniest hope—that I can do something to save Pierre from execution. Tomorrow, I shall try to obtain rail tickets, or some other form of transportation, to Paris. It is 350 kilometers to the west. With the war, I am not sure if it is even possible to make such a journey. But I must try. I am fully aware of the danger, but my heart is set upon it, and my mind will not be changed.

I weep even as I write those words, but I must not—I cannot—sit back and do nothing.

CHAPTER 44

My entry tonight must be brief. It has taken much longer than I thought (more than a week) to make my way here. With the Allies drawing closer to the capital every day, there are roadblocks and checkpoints everywhere. The closer I got to Paris, the more chaotic things became. Vast numbers of refugees clogged the roads. The German High Command has preempted all rail traffic, and it is dangerous to even try to purchase a ticket. I had brought what little money we had saved, but few people were interested in money. All they cared about was escape. So I rode in cars, trucks, carts, and wagons; mostly I walked.

Paris is a nightmare. The Germans are frantic. The French Resistance, emboldened by the approaching Allies, has risen up, and there is fierce fighting in some districts. Rumors fly that the Free French and an American division will reach the city any day now.

I am one of only three guests in a small hotel; one of

the hotel wings is gone. The owner looked at me as if I were mad when I asked for a room. I pray that the Germans have not taken Pierre away with them. Or that they have not taken action against him because of the urgency of the situation. Tomorrow, I will go to Gestapo headquarters to find my husband. I have little confidence that I will succeed, or, if I do, that I can save him. I find it difficult tonight to maintain even a sliver of hope. But I will never give up. Not until—

No! I will not give up. I will not.

"O Dieu, ne m'abandonne pas maintenant." O God, do not abandon me now.

CHAPTER 45

I sat back, laying the papers on my lap. "That's the last from her journal. The next part looks like it's her history that Grandpère wrote for her."

"Go on," Cody exclaimed. "I want to know what happened."

I didn't answer him. I was thinking of the black-and-white photograph of his mother and father on their twenty-fifth wedding anniversary that Grandpère kept on his nightstand. Even though she had been in her fifties by that point, she was still beautiful, with long dark hair and dark brown eyes. But even in the grainy photo, there was a scar on Monique's right cheek—a jagged white streak against her olive flesh. It always made me shiver a little to look at it. I had asked Grandpère about it more than once, but he would always put me off with, "Maybe some other time, but not now, dear." Well, that other time had come.

I told Rick and Cody about the picture. Cody said he remembered the picture, but hadn't noticed the scar. Rick's response was more thoughtful. "If she left immediately to escape the colonel, she wouldn't have had time to get the cut treated." Then, very softly, he added, "That's a noble name you carry. I would like to have known her."

"Me too," I murmured. I picked up the papers again. "This next entry is dated August twenty-fourth." I flipped back through the pages. "So that's . . . eleven days later. Eleven days after she was at her parent's home."

"Read it to us," Cody said.

I had a sudden idea. "Rick, are you getting cell phone reception up here?"

We were nearing Soldier Summit, the high spot and the dividing point between Price Canyon and Spanish Fork Canyon.

"Dunno," Rick said. "Hold on." He pulled out his phone and swiped it. He peered at it closely. "Yeah, I've got two bars. What do you need?"

"So you can get Internet access?"

"I assume so." Then his expression soured. "Oh, but not on these throwaway phones. Uh . . . do you want me to put my battery back in? It would only take a few minutes."

"No!" I barked. The last thing I wanted right now was to have El Cobra knowing where we were. "Never mind. It's not that important. It can wait."

"There's a service station at the top of the summit, just a mile or two from here. We could stop there, see if they would let us use their computer for a few minutes."

"You think they would?"

Cody half stood and reached over the seat to where the pouch sat between me and Rick. He lifted the flap and fished inside for a moment. When he withdrew his hand, he waved a hundred dollar bill at me. "They might."

In the end, the woman was willing to let us use the computer for free. She took us back into a tiny office and logged us on to her computer. "Just stop by and say hi again sometime," she said with a smile. "Maybe fill up with gas here instead of down in Price."

"Deal," Rick said. Once she'd left, he turned to me. "So what am I looking for?"

"I want to know what day the Americans liberated Paris."

CHAPTER 46

Paris, France

Thursday, August 24, 1944

"Monsieur?"

"*Oui*, madame?"

"How much do I owe for the room?"

"Nothing, madame. I cannot in good conscience charge you for a room with no heat, no lights, and no running water."

"But, monsieur—"

One hand came up, cutting her off. "Madame LaRoche. You are a brave woman, and my heart aches for your tragedy, but I beg of you. Wait for the Allies to come. They grow closer every day. They will help you find your husband."

"Only after many days," she said. "By then, it may be too late. But I thank you for your concern. Please, can you tell me how to find Gestapo headquarters?"

"This is madness, madame. Even I can hardly find my way through all the rubble. And there is still fighting in the streets. You cannot go."

She nodded. She appreciated his concern for her safety, but

realized he wasn't going to help her. "*Merci,* monsieur. You have been very kind." She turned and walked out the door.

"Madame!" His call was insistent, but she didn't look back. All she had left was a few francs, a hard roll, some cheese, and half an apple, which she carried in the old pouch.

As she walked out into the street, she marveled again that she had felt compelled to bring the old pouch. It was not hers, but Pierre's. It had been in his family for generations, and she knew the great reverence her husband had for it. She remembered that day when Jean-Henri had been protected from the Stuka dive-bomber. And just a few days ago, it had helped Jean-Henri and Louis in the forest. Perhaps . . .

But she didn't finish the sentence. All she could do was hold the pouch a little closer to her body.

———◆———

It was worse than the hotel owner had said, even worse than Monique had imagined. She had been to Paris only twice in her life—once as a little girl, once as a teenager—so she didn't know the city at all. She sought for a map without success. Not that it would have helped anyway in the war-torn city. She had assumed she could just ask for directions, but that proved far more difficult than she had thought. The streets were mostly deserted. Except for the distant rumble of artillery, a pall of silence lay over the city. Occasionally, she would catch a glimpse of a face at the window, but it would quickly turn away. The few people she did meet either refused to stop, or shook their heads and said they didn't know, or ran when they heard the word *Gestapo.*

By midafternoon, she was totally and completely lost. Exhausted and rapidly losing heart, she huddled in the doorway of a bombed-out building. She ate her remaining food, saving the apple for last. She ate it, seeds, core, and all.

Sick with worry, nearing physical collapse, and fearful that she might run into German soldiers, the last of the resolute courage which had driven her was rapidly ebbing away. Leaning back against the wall, she drew her legs up and laid her arms across her knees, using the pouch for a cushion. Her head dropped; she buried her face against the rough cloth as the tears began to flow.

"I can't," she cried. "I can't do it." A shudder shook her body as the floodgates of her emotions burst. "I'm sorry, Pierre. I'm so sorry. I'm so sorry."

She wasn't sure how long she wept, but when her body finally spent itself, she was too weary to care anymore. A great numbness settled upon her. She laid her head back against the brick wall behind her, surrendering to the nothingness.

It was somewhere at that point that the voice came into her mind. It was softer than the whisper of a breeze across the grass, more soothing than a damp cloth on a fevered brow, sweeter than the choirs of Notre Dame.

Why do you weep, Monique? Have you forgotten that there is purpose to your life, even in the midst of your suffering? Do you think that because you have been stretched beyond your capacity to endure, that you have lost the right to choose who you are and what you will be?

Her head lifted as the tears began afresh, only now they washed away the despair, washed away the weariness, washed away the hopelessness.

"No," she whispered. "I have not forgotten."

When the voice spoke in her mind again, it filled her with such joy that she felt as if her heart would burst. *Then go forth. And remember, you are not alone.*

When she stepped out into the rubble-strewn street again, she was at peace, but she still had no idea where to go or what to do. Placing the pouch over her shoulder, she stood for a moment, one hand resting lightly upon it, waiting, listening. This time it was not a voice, but only a feeling. She looked both ways, but chose to turn left.

She had not gone a block before a noise ahead of her startled her. She ducked into the shadows of a ruined building. Not ten feet ahead of her, a young man stepped out from the doorway of an apartment building. He had a French beret pulled low over his eyes and a World War I rifle in both hands. Glancing furtively in both directions, he turned and started away. She stepped out. At the noise of her footsteps, he spun around, rifle coming up as he dropped into a crouch.

She raised her arms slowly, holding his eyes with her own, letting him see that she was not a threat to him. She was sure he belonged to the French Resistance. The stubble on his face was thick and dark, his clothes were stained with mud and torn in a few places. She guessed he was maybe eighteen or nineteen.

He recovered quickly. Seeing she was alone and unarmed, he lowered his rifle. "Mademoiselle," he said urgently, "you should not be here. It is too dangerous. Go back inside."

She smiled. To have him mistake her for a young, unmarried woman instead of a weary, terrified wife and mother lit up her soul like a ray of light. "It is *madame*," she said, "not mademoiselle. Please, can you help me?"

She had done better than she had thought. She had already reached the eighth *arrondisement,* or district, of Paris and was only ten minutes from rue de Saussaies.

The young man stopped as they rounded a corner. "There," he said, pointing. "Number eleven is the white stone building with the green doors." He touched her arm. "But you will find no one there. The Germans loaded their prisoners onto trucks and left about two hours ago."

All she could do was stare at him. Only two hours ago? Had she come so close only to have failed? "Do you have any idea where they were taking them?"

He could not meet her gaze. He turned away, pretending to examine the building ahead of them. But Monique had seen what he could not bear to tell her, and she could not bear to ask.

"I am sorry, madame. I cannot help you," he finally said.

Her head came up. "I understand. *Merci beaucoup.*"

His face was stricken. "I am sorry that I cannot go farther, but others are waiting for me. There are things yet I must do. I must go."

"I shall never forget what you have done for me," she whispered.

"And I shall never forget my angel in the rubble, madame. Your image in my heart will remind me of that for which we fight this day."

To her surprise, he took her by the shoulders and kissed her quickly on both cheeks. "And may God grant you success in the search for your husband. *Adieu,* madame."

As he strode away, she realized that he had said *adieu* rather than *au revoir. Au revoir* meant good-bye, but *adieu* literally meant "to God." It was not used as a farewell often in everyday life, because it carried with it an implication that by commending the other person to God, one recognized they might never meet again.

Straightening her shoulders, filled with both fear and dread, she started down the street.

CHAPTER 47

No. 11, rue de Saussaies, 8th Arrondisement, Paris, France

Thursday, August 24, 1944

Monique approached the entrance to the Gestapo headquarters slowly. The doors were wide open. One hung crazily from one hinge. Stepping carefully, trying not to make a sound, she moved inside. What greeted her was a scene of chaos, destruction, and flight. Papers and rubbish were scattered everywhere. Chairs were overturned or smashed in pieces. Filing cabinets stood askew, drawers half-opened. In one corner there was a desk with a typewriter and phone on it. The phone was overturned. A sheet of paper was in the typewriter, abandoned by an unknown clerk.

She felt a growing chill as she moved through the large room. This was not just any office. This was where the everyday aspects of the work of horror began. It was over these phones that unthinkable orders were given, and on these desks that certificates of death and torture were signed and certified, and in these cabinets that a record of unthinkably ghastly deeds was meticulously filed in alphabetical order.

She wanted to scream—scream to the world so that all might see what man had done to their fellow man.

She forced herself to push the horror away. Her quest was all that mattered. She stopped, looking around, listening intently.

"Bonjour," she called after a moment. "Is anyone here?" Her heart was hammering so loudly that she wasn't sure she would hear an answer if one came. But there was nothing.

Bending down, she picked up a piece of paper half-filled with lines of German—a language she could neither read nor speak fluently. She discarded it, and tried another with the same results. This one had an official-looking stamp at the bottom with the Nazi swastika in a circle. She flung it away from her like it was acid on her flesh.

Feeling her despair rising, she moved toward a hallway. The likelihood of finding some clue to Pierre's whereabouts was remote. But perhaps the boy was wrong. Perhaps, in their rush, the Germans had not been able to take all of the prisoners with them. The chilling silence in the room belied that hope, but she had to know. She began looking for stairs; perhaps there were prison cells in the basement.

She entered a long corridor with doors on both sides. Most were open. Here too, the evidence of flight was everywhere. As she passed one of the rooms, she stopped. Inside, two plain wooden chairs faced each other. A single light fixture hung down from the ceiling. She saw the barred windows and a thick metal ring attached to the far wall. Shock jolted her as she realized she was passing the interrogation rooms. She saw dark stains on the walls. She turned and fled in horror.

When she finally found a set of stairs that led down, her steps faltered. *"Allo? Bonjour?"* Is anyone down there?" She was shivering violently. Only silence answered her call.

She took a deep breath, then plunged down the stairs. And there she found the cells. She increased her pace, wanting to see them all to be sure. They were empty. Every door was thrown open.

She spun around, anxious to be free of this place. Had Pierre and

Lieutenant Fitzgerald been put in one of these cells? Had she come this close only to find them gone? Then something caught her eye. She stepped into the cell on her right. In the plaster above the built-in cot she read three words: *I am afraid.* She turned slowly, her eyes searching. There was another inscription near the hole in the floor used as a toilet: *Never confess.*

She went quickly to the next cell. She found more words, only this time longer, and written in pencil. She shuddered when she saw a woman's name: *Yvette Mari-Jo Wilbort.* What followed was a verse from the famous French poet, Alfred de Vigny.

> *Wailing, pleading, crying—these are the coward's call.*
> *Assume your heavy and onerous burden,*
> *The one that fate has cast your way.*
> *And then, like me, suffer and die in silence.*

Bile rose in her throat, and she felt like she was going to suffocate. But she had to know. Almost running, she went from cell to cell. Two cells from the stairway she found what she was looking for. This time the words were scratched deeply into the plaster with something dull, perhaps a spoon handle: *June 20, 1944. Pierre LaRoche. Farewell, my beloved Monique.*

————

She was still sitting on the stairs three minutes later, weeping quietly, when the floor over her head creaked. She jerked up, heart exploding into a thunderous pounding. Heavy footsteps crossed the floor, coming down the corridor toward the stairs. She leaped to her feet, shrinking back against the wall. In her haste, her own feet scraped heavily across the cement. The other footsteps stopped, then broke into a run.

"Halt! Who goes there?" It was said in French, but with a heavy German accent.

Her heart plummeted. She looked up, frozen in place. A dark figure filled the doorway at the head of the stairs. She could see the German luger in his hand.

"Stop where you are, *Fräulein*."

Her legs were suddenly weak, not just with fear, but because she had recognized the voice instantly. Standing above her was Colonel Horst Kessler, most recently the commandant of the Gestapo unit stationed in Strasbourg.

"Stop here, *Frau LaRoche*."

Monique stopped, her hands still resting on her head. Without a word, Kessler had dragged her up the stairs and back into the main office. Now he let go of her arm, but he kept the gun pointed at her.

"Please, do not move." Kessler stepped away, moving toward a filing cabinet behind an overturned desk. He took a key from his pocket and unlocked the case. Bending down, he opened the bottom drawer and withdrew a black briefcase. "Very foolish of me to go off and leave this," he explained as he came back to her. "Now, please, out the back door and into my car."

"Is my husband still alive?" she asked as she started walking forward again.

When he didn't answer, she half turned her head. "Have you no humanity at all? Would it jeopardize the Third Reich to tell me if you shot my husband?"

"Eyes front," he barked. He jabbed the pistol against the small of her back. As they approached the door, he pulled her to a stop. *"Moment mal."* He stepped around her, opened the door a crack, and looked outside. Satisfied, he motioned to her. "Into the car. Quickly."

They drove for several minutes before he spoke again. Kessler's driver often had to slow almost to a crawl to get through or go around the rubble in the streets. Once he even had to back up and find another way. Kessler sat in the front seat beside him, but turned so he could keep his pistol trained on Monique.

"You knew about the American flyer hidden in the barn, didn't you?"

She looked away.

"To aid an enemy combatant is high treason. The penalty is death by firing squad."

"And the torture? What about that? That is forbidden by the Geneva Convention."

He shrugged. "War is war, madame. Be grateful that things right now are such that you will not be joining your husband in the mass grave we have dug. But you shall spend the rest of the war in a work camp, paying for your crimes against the state."

"Which won't be long," she said, head up, eyes defiant.

His eyes were glacial, and his smile was little more than a thin hard line. "You and your little son," he said easily. "So brave. So innocent." His voice was cold. "'A tale, told by an idiot, full of sound and fury, signifying nothing.'"

She felt her stomach lurch.

He laughed aloud at her expression. "Does it surprise you that a monster such as myself quotes Shakespeare?"

She turned away, not wanting him to see her reaction. He hadn't said "the mass grave we dug," but "the mass grave we *have* dug." That suggested its purpose was not yet fulfilled. Not daring to hope and yet unable not to, she closed her eyes, determined to say nothing more.

"Colonel?" The tightness in the driver's voice brought Monique up with a jerk. They had left the part of the city that had been bombed and were moving faster. They had just turned a corner into a broad boulevard when the driver lifted his foot off the gas pedal and the car rolled to a stop.

The tableau before Monique would be forever fixed in her mind. Four heavy German transport trucks were parked along the curb. Soldiers in German uniforms were lined up in front of them, hands high in the air. Ten feet in front of them, American soldiers had their weapons trained on them. Behind them, stretching back along the boulevard as far as she could see was a column of heavy armor, tank after tank after tank. Jeeps and armored personnel carriers were parked alongside them. The lead tank, the only one she could see clearly, had a big white star painted just below its cannon.

"Back! Back!" Kessler screamed at his driver.

There was a grinding of gears, and the car careened backward, throwing her to one side. "Halt!" She couldn't tell who had screamed it. Men were running hard toward them.

"Go! Go! Go!" Kessler screamed, dropping into a crouch on the floorboards.

But it was everlastingly too late. A burst of machine gun fire exploded from the lead tank. Bullets blasted into the pavement to the left of the car, ricocheting away with angry snarls. Not waiting for orders from his commander, the driver slammed on the brakes and threw his hands in the air. *"Ich ergebe mich! Ich ergebe mich!* I surrender! I surrender!"

———

One of the American soldiers opened the car door and said something to her. Monique couldn't understand him, but it didn't matter. With tears streaming down her face, she clambered out of the car, then threw herself into his arms, laughing, crying, and shouting for joy. Suddenly, all around them, the buildings began to disgorge their inhabitants. Men, women, and children flooded the streets, yelling and shouting and waving their arms. "Yankee! Yankee! *Les Américains! Les Américains!*"

In moments, the GIs were swarmed. Grandmas fell at their knees and kissed the soldiers' hands. Old men wept unashamedly. Little children were lifted up to sit on the tanks and Jeeps. Young women kissed their liberators joyously. Stunned, but equally joyous, the GIs kissed them back.

———

It was almost an hour before Monique saw a small group of US soldiers coming toward her. She was sitting in Kessler's staff car. Kessler and his driver, of course, were nowhere to be seen. As the Americans drew closer, she saw that the man in the lead had three stars on each shoulder. A young man in a French uniform walked behind him.

She stood, shutting the door of the staff car behind her, her hands trembling.

"Mrs. LaRoche?" the man said, saluting her. The French officer translated quickly. "I'm Lieutenant General George S. Patton, commander of the US Third Army. We have all the prisoners unloaded from the trucks. We're giving them food. Would you like to come with me?"

When she heard the translation, she could only nod. As she fell in behind them, her vision was so blurred with tears that she had to reach out and lay her hand on the arm of the young Frenchman.

The prisoners were in the shade of the trees that lined the boulevard. As she saw them, milling around folding tables, still fifty or sixty feet away, her step slowed.

"It's all right, madame. We will go slowly. Take your time."

But at that instant she heard a strangled cry. "Monique?"

A figure was moving toward her in a hobbling run. His hands were swathed in bandages, and his nose had been broken.

"Pierre?" Monique cried out.

"*Ma chérie!* Is that you? Can it possibly be you?"

With a strangled cry of joy, Monique flung herself across the grass, skirts billowing, hair streaming behind her. As she threw herself into his arms, all around them everything came to a halt. French, German, American—everyone turned to witness this momentary deliverance from war, this miracle of love and faith and courage. And all around them, both jaded Parisians and hardened combat veterans were suddenly finding it equally difficult to see.

CHAPTER 48

Soldier Summit, Utah
Wednesday, June 15, 2011

"Amazing!" Rick said, his husky voice tinged with awe.

I could only nod. My throat was too choked to get anything out. We were still parked beside the service station on the top of Soldier Summit.

I laid Grandpère's envelope aside and took the paper Rick had printed from the woman's computer. Clearing my throat, I read it as best I could. "'After four years of German occupation, largely due to the success of American Forces under the command of General George S. Patton, US Third Army, on August twenty-fourth, 1944, the first of the Free French, British, Canadian, and American forces rolled into Paris. By midnight, virtually every church bell in Paris was ringing. After four years of occupation, Paris was free.'"

"And she was there," Rick said.

"Incredible," I whispered. "I never personally knew my great-grandmother," I said, picturing her as I had seen her in Grandpère's photograph. "She died when I was a baby. But Great-Grandpère Pierre lived until I was about six. He came out from Boston several times and stayed with Grandpère and Grandmère. I don't remember much from those visits, but I do remember his fingers. They were stubby, twisted things with no fingernails. The knuckles were all swollen and deformed. Mom thought the Germans had broken every bone in his hands trying to get him to talk. She also told me that he never took off his shirt in public because of the scars on his back."

The car was quiet for a moment. Then I picked up the last few pages from Grandpère.

A few postscripts.

When Colonel Horst Kessler, commanding officer of the Gestapo in Strasbourg, France, was told to transfer his prisoners to Gestapo headquarters in Paris, the name of First Lieutenant Arnold Fitzgerald of the United States Army Air Corps was not on the list.

Once the war ended, my father and mother began an inquiry. When they were finally allowed to see the records of the Strasbourg Gestapo office, Lieutenant Fitzgerald's name was not found anywhere. Nor was there any record of an American pilot being captured at that time.

However, the same woman who told my mother about my father's transfer to Paris later testified that she overheard some of the soldiers saying that Colonel Kessler had tortured Lieutenant Fitzgerald for information concerning the design and performance of his aircraft. He died under interrogation. The soldiers had been ordered to bury the pilot in the Strasbourg cemetery in an unmarked grave.

The news was a devastating blow to me and my parents and my friend, Louis. Though we had only known Fitzgerald for two days, we had established a lasting bond with him. My mother especially grieved over his death.

Due mostly to the tireless efforts of my father and mother, the body of Lieutenant Fitzgerald was eventually exhumed by French authorities. Once they had confirmed his identity and the cause of death, his body was returned to his family in Nebraska.

Colonel Horst Kessler was brought before a military tribunal in 1948 and charged with war crimes, including the murder and torture of an American pilot—a combatant who is protected under the articles of the Geneva Convention—and the torture and execution of French civilians.

My father, mother, and I flew back to Germany to testify against Kessler. This was very difficult for my mother because she had to face him once again in the courtroom. After nine days of testimony, including that from the housekeeper, Kessler was pronounced guilty on all charges and sentenced to life in prison. He died in 1951, reminding us once again that there is evil in the world, but eventually, under God's watchful eye, justice and truth will prevail.

May these things which I have shared with you stay with you in the hours and days to come, providing you strength, hope, and inspiration.

With deepest affection,
Grandpère

PART EIGHT

Partnership

CHAPTER 49

After I finished reading Grandpère's writings, we all fell quiet. My mind and heart were both full of memories and histories, and when I finally roused myself back to the present, almost an hour had passed. We were still in Spanish Fork Canyon. I turned to Rick. "Now that you've had a chance to think about all we read, tell me what you're thinking."

He gave me a quick look. "So what about the FBI?"

I wasn't expecting that, but I had made up my mind already. "Call them right now."

"Can't right now. No cell phone coverage yet."

"Then as soon as we're out of the canyon. Set up a meeting for first thing in the morning."

"Good for you, Danni. I think your grandfather would be proud."

"It's not just him I'm thinking about."

"Monique?"

"Yes. If she can take on the Gestapo, I'm ready to hand El Cobra a few surprises."

"Like what?" Cody asked.

"I don't know," I admitted. "I need to think about that. And right now, my brain feels like dried mud."

"I've also got to call Dad and give him our new numbers," Rick said. "Why don't you try to get a little more sleep? We're still about an hour and a half from Salt Lake. I'll wake you up when we get closer."

I squinted at him, giving him a warning look. "I'll try, but you're not forgetting about stopping somewhere to get some clothes, are you?"

"You think I have a death wish?"

"Good," I murmured. I was surprised how good it felt to relax and how quickly I fell asleep.

I came awake with a start, groping wildly for a grip on something. My brain finally registered that I was in the front seat of Rick's 4Runner. I noted that the sun was still up, but getting lower in the sky. And when I heard a cell phone ring a second time, I came fully awake and sat up.

"Mornin', sunshine," Rick said with a grin.

"Feel better?" Cody asked.

"No. Worse."

Rick pressed the answer button on his throwaway phone. "Hi, Dad." Pause. "Yeah. We're passing through Utah Valley now. We'll be in Salt Lake in about an hour, depending on traffic. Glad you got my message. I was—" He stopped, nodding. "Yeah, there are some dead spots along that stretch. Did you get my earlier message about what El Cobra said about Aunt Shauna and the girls? Good, good." Long pause. I could hear his dad speaking Spanish. "Great!" Rick said when he finished. "Hold on, let me tell Danni."

He moved the phone away. "Dad has Aunt Shauna and my sisters with him. He's bringing them to my Uncle Fernando's house in West Valley City. They'll be safe there. That's a huge relief."

"I'm so glad." El Cobra's threat was probably an empty one, but I didn't want to be wrong.

Rick got back on the phone. "How far behind us are you?" Brief pause. "Oh, okay, that'll work. We're gonna make a short stop to get Danni and Cody some clothes, then we'll find a motel. I'll call you with the number and address as soon as we get it." More from his dad. "No, no. Danni's got some cash"—he shot me a quick look— "from a family fund." Then his eyes widened. "*What?* Why not?"

He put his hand over the phone and said, "Dad says we can't pay for the motel with cash."

"Of course we can. Everybody takes cash."

He waved me to silence. "Okay. Understood. Listen, Danni's made up her mind. I called the FBI and have an appointment with the agent in charge tomorrow at nine. What's that? Sorry, Dad, you're breaking up." He pressed the phone more tightly to his ear. "Oh, that. No. We didn't tell him what it's about, only that it's important."

This time even I could hear the static. "I'm losing you, Dad. Call us when you get out of the canyon."

He tapped one of the keys, then put the phone back in his pocket. "He just passed Soldier Summit, so by the time he takes the girls to Uncle Fernando's he'll be probably three hours behind us."

"Why can't we pay cash?"

"He said that most motels require picture ID and a credit card as a way of discouraging drug dealers and others from falsifying their identities. He said to call him when we find one, and he'll call in with his credit card and tell them we're coming."

"He's not paying for this, Rick."

"Are you kidding? When the pouch is generating cash faster than you can spend it?" He laughed. "You can pay him back. He knows your dad is good for it."

"And speaking of cash," I said, "who authorized you to say that our shopping stop was going to be 'short'?"

He had that momentary "deer in the headlights" look, but quickly recovered. "Ma'am, I invoke my right to remain silent as guaranteed by the Fifth Amendment lest I incriminate myself and end up in deep trouble."

I couldn't help but laugh out loud. "I'll say this for you, Ramirez, you're quick on your feet." Then instantly my humor was gone. "Did you tell your father how much I appreciate what he's doing for us?"

"I did. He brushed it off like it was nothing. But he knows."

"And you too," I added. "We'd be lost without you. I can't believe what I said earlier."

"Good. Maybe if you're stricken with guilt, you'll take mercy on us males and not spend forever when we get in the store."

"Ha!" I cried. "Dream on."

———

By 5:45, we had entered the south part of the Salt Lake Valley and ran headlong into a major traffic jam. I had been rereading Grandpère's materials and hadn't been watching. "What's up?"

"Can't tell. Maybe road construction, maybe an accident."

I made a face.

"But all is not lost," Rick added quickly, pointing to a large sign up ahead. "There's a Kohl's at the next exit."

"Well done, Ricardo," I said. "You have redeemed yourself."

Rick shrugged. "While you're shopping, I'll call Dad and check in with him."

"Coward." I didn't add that I really didn't want him with me, hanging back, looking at his watch every ten seconds, wondering how long it was going to take. This wasn't a major shopping trip. I just needed something that wasn't already old, dirty, or smelly. I had way too much on my mind for anything else. My plan was to go in fast, find what I wanted for me and Cody, and be back out in under half an hour. "But thanks," I added, and went back to reading.

"Man, what a mess," he said a few minutes later.

"It looks like we're going down to one lane," Cody said, leaning over the seat.

"And right before the exit," Rick agreed.

I put the papers away and surveyed the situation. "The thing that makes me crazy," I said as I watched the cars on our left slip by us, "is that even though they can see what is coming, there are always those who stay in the inside lanes as long as possible so they don't have to wait like the rest of us."

"That's my dad's favorite gripe too," he said.

I peered ahead. We were about a hundred yards from where the lanes merged, and another hundred yards from the exit. "Since you're getting off here, can you get on the shoulder and squeeze by?"

He shot me a dirty look. "And slip by all these others who are waiting their turn, you mean?"

I felt my face flush. "You're getting off at the exit. It's not like you're trying to cut ahead of them."

No answer to that, but no movement either. I decided that in light of what had happened with the speed limit sign and our experience with the sports car, I was treading on thin ice, so I clamped my mouth shut and settled in to wait. Which was not my strength. I had always thought that the old saying about patience being a virtue was highly overrated.

But I couldn't let Rick get by with that last snippy comment. "If you were really smart, you wouldn't pick a fight me with right now, Mr. Ramirez. I'd wait until you've fed me and got me some new clothes."

He laughed. "Got it."

We moved forward slowly, one car length at a time. Cars were passing us on the left, squeezing in up ahead and forcing our lane to a bare crawl. We went from four lanes to three, then from three to two. One more merge to go. I was happy to see that most people had already merged in with us.

Then movement caught my eye. Behind us in the inside lane, a guy driving a red pickup was moving up on us. It had at least two feet of ground clearance, huge tires, and spotlights on the rack above the cab. As he passed, I saw there was a woman with him and wondered if she needed a hoist to get into something that high. But the guy was the perfect fit for the truck: shaved head, three-day-old whiskers, white tank top, biceps like a quarter of beef.

He passed another four or five cars, then braked and turned on his right signal.

"See what I mean?" I exclaimed. "That bugs me so much."

The guy edged in, trying to stick the nose of his truck between two cars.

I rolled down the window. "Close it up! Close it up," I yelled. "Don't let him in."

"Danni! Roll up the window."

I ignored him. To my great joy, the other drivers, seeing what the guy was up to, closed ranks until front and rear bumpers were almost touching.

I looked at Rick. "Don't you let him in."

"For crying out loud, Danni. Maybe his wife is having a baby or something."

"Yeah, right. You don't even know if that lady *is* his wife."

We were three cars away from the red intruder. His right front fender was just inches from the other cars. There was a long, angry honk that I was pretty sure was from him. *Honk all you want. Wait your turn like the rest of us.*

He was going to have to do something, because just ahead of him was a sign blinking the words SINGLE LANE AHEAD along with a flashing arrow pointing right.

Foot by foot, we moved closer to the merge point. I was elated. One more car length and we would be past him.

"If you yell at him as we go by," Rick said, "I'm getting out and walking."

I glanced at Rick, not sure if he was kidding. I didn't think he was.

And in that split second of lost focus, a five-foot gap opened up between us and the next car. Instantly, the Ram lurched forward, inserting his nose between us and the next guy. Rick had to tap his brakes to avoid hitting him. Then, adding insult to injury, the woman rolled down her window and gave us a cheery wave of thanks.

Fuming, I reached across Rick and laid on the horn.

Rick knocked my hand away. "What is the matter with you?"

My anger flashed at him. "It's not right that he can get away with that," I muttered. "It's not fair."

Rick shook his head.

I knew my reaction was partly due to my lack of sleep and a truckload of stress, but I didn't need another lecture from him. Then I had an idea. I picked up the pouch, clutching it to my chest.

Seeing the movement, Rick shot me a look. "What are you doing?"

"I'm not doing anything," I fired back. But even as I said it, I pulled the pouch closer, closed my eyes, and made a wish. The flashing sign momentarily blacked out. I held my breath. When it came on again, I punched the air. "All right!" I crowed.

The sign was now blinking a new message. And while I felt a little twinge of guilt, I could easily ignore it. The sign now read

HEY BLOCKHEAD IN THE RED PICKUP.
TAKE YOUR TURN LIKE EVERYBODY ELSE.

I stole a glance at Rick, whose lips were pulled into a thin, hard line.

"Now that's what I'm talking about." Then, to my satisfaction, all up and down the line, cars tapped their horns to express their total agreement.

———◆———

We finally exited the freeway and left Johnny Redneck moving north. Which, to be honest, was a big relief. As we had crept forward, I suddenly wondered what would happen if the guy somehow decided it was us who had made the sign change. I could picture him grabbing a crowbar, jumping out of his pickup, and pounding poor Rick into a two-inch high mound of pulp while I looked on helplessly. But the guy had no way of knowing who had changed the sign, and a minute or two later, we turned off and headed for Kohl's, and I relaxed.

Cody and I were in and out of the store before Rick had finished talking with his father. I wasn't after something spectacular. Anything was better than what I had on. Though Rick seemed surprised—and pleased—to see us so quickly, he said nothing as we got in and started north again.

The rest of the way into Salt Lake was like riding in a hearse. I didn't dare look at Rick, and as near as I could tell, he never took his eyes off the road. Sensing the tension, Cody sat in the back and said nothing.

As we pulled into the motel's parking lot, I finally spoke. "Just say it."

"I've nothing to say."

"Yes, you do. You've been saying it all the way here in your head. So you may as well say it out loud."

He just shook his head, but as we reached the front door and he held it open for me, he finally spoke. "First the woman in the sports car. Now a guy that looks like a refrigerator in a T-shirt. That's not right up there with saving downed pilots or rescuing your husband from the Gestapo, is it?"

I said nothing, but I felt my face go hot.

"And that's all you've got to say?"

My shoulders lifted and fell. "It was a stupid thing to do. Do you want me to turn in my driver's license?"

To my surprise, his face softened. "It's been a rough two days for you, Danni."

"That's no excuse for being a jerk."

"I know. But it is an explanation."

Not only that, but it was an offer of a truce, and I took it gladly.

CHAPTER 50

"Well, don't you clean up nice?"

"Thank you," I said, blushing a little. I wasn't used to seeing such open admiration in his eyes.

"Nice . . . umm . . . capris."

I laughed. "These aren't capris. These are just shorts. But thanks anyway."

"Oh."

Walking over to the edge of the pool, I called to Cody. "Okay, little bro. It's your turn in the tub."

He came over. "After swimming? You gotta be kidding."

"On your way. Get the smell of the chlorine off."

He kicked off from the side, floating on his back.

"I mean it, Code. It's almost nine thirty, and there's no sleeping in tomorrow."

"Sheesh!" he said in disgust. "I'm just getting my towel. Gimme a break."

"I left the door open a crack. I'll be up in a few minutes."

He waved, climbed out of the pool, grabbed his towel, and went inside.

I sat down beside Rick. "Did your dad make it back yet?"

"Not yet. He wants to make sure the girls are asleep first. It's been a long day for them."

"And for you? Aren't you tired?"

He shook his head. "I wasn't up all night. I'm okay. Oh, by the way, Caitlin called."

"Caitlin?"

"You know, from the phone store in Price?"

"Oh." That seemed like days ago. "And?"

"A man showed up just before closing time. Short, plump guy."

"Gordo," I said, my pulse suddenly racing.

"I think so. She said he had black hair and dark eyes that sent shivers up her back. She said she was glad she wasn't in the store alone. He claimed to be an employee of your father, who had sent him to make sure you got home safely."

So they had been able to track Rick's phone. "Did she happen to see what kind of vehicle he was driving?"

"Guess."

"A black Hummer."

"You got it." He shook his head. "We can't underestimate these guys, Danni. They're not missing much." He snapped his fingers. "Oh, and one other thing. Caitlin said he asked if you were carrying an old-looking purse."

"Really?" So El Cobra did suspect there was something unusual about the pouch. Maybe we could work that to our advantage somehow. I was tired of running from Doc and Gordo and El Cobra and of being sick with worry about my parents and whether or not we were being tracked every second. "So what does your dad make of all this?"

"He's relieved you're meeting with the FBI tomorrow. Though he thinks we shouldn't have waited."

"Do you agree?"

"Not anymore. Who knows what tomorrow's going to bring? You and Cody need to get a good rest."

"Thank you. I was starting to wonder if it was me just being stupid or not." I pulled a face. "Again!" I turned to face him. "I don't know what got into me today, Rick. First the lady in the sports car, then the guy in the pickup truck. What's the matter with me?"

"I'd rather focus on another question."

"Okay. Just know I'm getting tireder by the second."

"Tireder? That's pretty serious."

"Okay, more tired. So what's the question?"

He reached down beside his deck chair and picked up a thin pad of paper; it had the motel's logo at the top, and it was covered with writing.

"What?" I teased. "You've been making notes?"

"A list, actually." He wasn't smiling as he peered more closely at the paper. "A list of all the important things in this equation. I wanted to see if we could make sense of them. Feel free to make comments or corrections, or stop me if I'm making you mad."

"Okay. Go ahead."

"Number one. Three years ago, your grandfather gave you a very old pouch that has been in your family for umpteen generations—*Le Gardien,* or the Guardian. At the same time, he also gave you four charges, or the Four Remembers, as he called them, and said they would be influential in your life if you let them."

"Check."

"Two. Up until the day before yesterday, the pouch was just a quaint family heirloom hanging on your wall. Then suddenly, all sorts of strange things began to happen." He shot me a sharp look.

"Some of which seem to have been instigated by—well, let's just say they didn't spring from the noblest of motives on your part. These include changing speed limit signs, a—"

"I got it, Rick," I cut in quickly. "Check."

"Third. This remarkable change happened on the same day that a gang of violent and dangerous men decide to invade your home and hold your family for ransom. A very big ransom."

"Check."

"I'm not done with number three."

"Sorry. Uncheck."

"The Guardian further 'comes to life,' for want of a better term, and starts doing all kinds of impossible things." He smiled faintly. "I was going to say magical things, but that doesn't feel quite right. Now, the plot thickens. After a quite miraculous escape—"

"Quite."

"You learn from Grandpère that he has put an envelope in your overnight bag without you knowing it."

"Or seeing it until he told me about it."

"Yeah, that too." He took a quick breath. "In the envelope, you find a letter of explanation from your grandfather, an excerpt from his life history, a journal entry from—" He stopped. "What?"

"Do you always think like this? I mean, I'm not complaining. I think it's wonderful. As I sat in the tub tonight, I was trying to sort it all out in my head, and it's still one big jumble to me."

"Then stop making fun of me," he shot back. "This is serious."

"I wasn't making fun. I mean it. This is what I need. Keep going."

"Okay." He found his place on his list. "And entries from your great-grandmother's journal and life story," he concluded. "Does that about cover it?"

Reaching across, I touched his hand. "Excellent work, Sherlock. I am very impressed."

To my surprise, he took my hand, interlocked his fingers with mine, and then continued. It was a good thing he was reading from the paper, because I was gawking at his hand on mine. This was the first time he had ever held my hand.

"With your permission, I would like to ask you some questions about your grandfather. I hope they will clarify the issues further."

I smiled. "Permission granted."

"Okay. First, I—"

"I can keep track of them without you numbering them," I said, squeezing his hand. I smiled to let him know I was only teasing. He squeezed it back, and I decided he could ask me as many questions as he wanted. And number them any way he wanted to.

"First, how did your grandfather know that what he included in that envelope would be of great significance to you?"

"That's easy. What he shared is incredible. Even if nothing bad was happening, it would still be of great significance to me."

"Right, right. Let me say it a different way. He writes you this letter, saying that he feels like something bad is going to happen. He doesn't know what, just that he has this bad feeling."

"Do you find that hard to believe?"

"Not at all. Especially since it's your grandfather. But it does seem strange that he hasn't told you any of this before. You're right—it's an incredible story, so why wait until you're sixteen? No, why wait until you're sixteen *and* in a crisis similar to your great-grandparents'?"

"This is nothing like what they faced."

"Isn't it? I agree that it's not as sweeping, not as horrible, not as devastating, but your parents are in real danger, Danni. And so are you and Cody. Don't you find it remarkable that he gives you these stories right at this moment?"

"No. That's just how Grandpère is. As Dad likes to say, Grandpère doesn't do random. He's a deep thinker, and he always waits for just the right time to teach me something, even if it takes years. He's a . . ." I shook my head. I wasn't sure what word would accurately complete my thought.

"A mystic?"

I snorted in derision. "Come on."

"Then what? A sorcerer? A magician? A wizard?"

"If Grandpère were here, he'd be laughing at you."

"This from the girl who changes speed limit signs, rewrites bumper stickers, becomes temporarily invisible, makes things appear magically out of nowhere, and nearly creates her own road-rage incident by rewiring a traffic warning sign? Am I missing anything?"

I said nothing.

"Obviously, he knew that what was in those stories would be helpful to you right now. I mean, come on, Danni, surely you see this was the perfect message for you at this time."

"To remind me that I'm not alone in all of this?"

"Yes."

"That I too have a purpose to fulfill that has to do directly with saving those I love?"

"That too."

I looked away. "And that the choices I make can influence how this whole thing turns out?"

"Right again. That's what I mean, Danni. It's the Four Remembers to a T. What he sent you is perfectly tailored for this situation, but he admitted that he didn't know what the situation would be when he gave it to you. Wouldn't you agree that's more than just a grandfather's intuition? More than just a fortunate coincidence? There's something really significant going on here."

"Yes," I said, withdrawing my hand from his; it was making it hard for me to concentrate. "But here's something that's bugging me.

I've been thinking about this too." I smiled sweetly at him. "I didn't make a list, but . . ."

"Go on," he growled.

"Grandpère told me that the pouch responds to the desires of your heart, even if those desires are not good for us. But the thing I want the most is to have my family free. And that is a good desire. So if the pouch is such a wonderful thing, why didn't it warn us beforehand that gunmen were waiting at our house? Then we could have called Mom and Cody and warned them. Or, for that matter, if it can produce a gun out of nowhere, why not make it so we all could escape? Why only me and Cody?"

"Maybe because . . ." His voice trailed off. Finally, he shook his head and motioned for me to continue.

I was working up a head of steam, feeling frustrated and upset all over again. "*Le Gardien* won't free my family, but it will let me do stupid things with bumper stickers and windshields and traffic signs. How do you explain that?"

He waved the paper at me. "Dunno, but that's one of my questions too. Here's one possibility. Why do we let go of a toddler's hand so he can walk on his own, even if we know he's going to fall and bump his nose or scrape his chin?"

"I . . . Wait, say that again."

He did.

"So you're saying that the pouch is letting me learn from my mistakes?"

"No, I'd switch that around. What if the pouch is letting you make mistakes so that you can learn from them?"

"Like a nanny," I said after a moment.

"Exactly. Maybe that's why your grandpa told you that it sometimes grants you things that may not be wise."

"That doesn't make sense," I said. "It isn't working. If the pouch can create money out of nothing, why doesn't it just yell at me? Why doesn't it say, 'Hey, stupid! Stop being such an idiot'?"

"Because you're not stupid."

"Come on, Rick. You know what I'm talking about. What desires have been driving my use of the pouch? Get Rick to drive faster. Get Miss Perfect to speed up. Tell the blockhead that he's a blockhead. How stupid is that? Can you imagine what Grandpère would say about that if he were here?"

"I think so."

"No, you don't," I snapped. "You're just trying to be nice."

"I think he'd ask you one question."

"What question?"

"*Are* you learning from your mistakes?"

I looked at him. I was so tired, but I had to at least try to answer his question.

Was I learning from my mistakes? I didn't think so. I didn't feel like I was doing anything right. I was just being Danni McAllister at her worst—impulsive and immature, with too much Irish temper.

Rick took both of my hands and held them between his own. He looked directly into my eyes. "Tell me this. What do the stories of your great-grandmother and Aron Ralston have in common?"

The answer was simple and obvious. "Never give up," I said in wonder.

"So you *are* learning something," he said with a smile.

CHAPTER 51

When I got back to the room, Cody was already in bed. He was so far gone that even when I turned on the lights it didn't wake him. So much for a bath. Oh, well. I could live with a little chlorine smell for one night. I was ready to call it a day, too.

Yet when I got in bed a few minutes later and turned out the lights, my mind wasn't ready to shut off. There was something back there that I couldn't quite catch hold of, and I couldn't push it away. It was something that had occurred to me while I was talking with Rick, but now I couldn't remember what it was.

Friggatriskaidekaphobia.

I sat straight up in bed. Where in the world had that come from? We hadn't said anything about Friday the thirteenth. Why would I think about Mom's fear of it now? I started to lay back down again, when I remembered what Grandpère had said that day at the Grand Gallery. My ever-so-great-grandmother, Angelique Chevalier, had lost her parents on her thirteenth birthday, which was on a Friday the thirteenth. And then I realized exactly why that word had popped into my head.

I threw back the covers, turned on the lamp beside my bed, and got up. Moving quietly, I went to my overnight bag and retrieved Grandpère's envelope.

And there it was. The American pilot was shot down on Friday, August 11. Two days later was Monique LaRoche's twenty-ninth birthday—the thirteenth of the month. All three of us had birthdays on the thirteenth of the month. And that was also the day the Gestapo had come and taken away my great-grandfather and Lieutenant Fitzgerald.

Suddenly I wished I knew our family history better. How many others in my family had been born on the thirteenth? Was this some kind of family curse? Or a blessing, as Grandpère seemed to think? And did Mom know all this? Was what I thought was merely superstition really part of that same gift that ran through our family? A sensitivity to danger? Premonitions about evil?

My mind was swirling. I wished Mom was here so I could ask her. Maybe there was much more to this situation than I thought. Maybe that was why she always brushed my questions aside. I went to the dresser where I had left the pouch. I picked it up, then, feeling silly, I checked to make sure I had locked and bolted the door. As I climbed back in bed and turned off the light, I held the pouch close to me, finding great comfort in its rough surface.

Come on, Danni. That inner voice of mine started up again; it was pointing its finger at me. *When El Cobra came it wasn't a Friday and it wasn't the thirteenth. You had a good birthday, and everything was fine. You've had a lot of birthdays where nothing unusual happened.*

Feeling more and more frustrated, I turned on the light again. I dug in my overnight bag until I found my journal. Then I went to the desk and began to write.

It was an hour later when I finished. My eyes were suddenly heavy and my mind exhausted. I turned off the desk light and crawled into bed again. As my eyes closed and I started to drift off, my great-grandmother's prayer, offered in a bombed-out hotel in Paris, came back into my mind: *"O Dieu, ne m'abandonne pas maintenant."*

O God, do not abandon me now.

CHAPTER 52

Bountiful, Utah
Thursday, June 16, 2011

I woke with a start when I heard someone knocking on our door. Sunlight was coming in around the corners of the blinds. I came up on one elbow. "Who is it?"

"It's me," Rick said. "You up?"

"Yes." I raised my head enough so that I wouldn't be lying.

"Breakfast's in fifteen minutes," he called.

I sat up completely, rubbing my eyes with the backs of my hands. I noticed the other bed was empty. "Is Cody with you?"

"He's swimming."

"Okay. I'll hurry."

"Good." I heard footsteps moving away so I called again, this time louder. "Rick?"

The footsteps came back. "Yeah?"

I got out of bed and moved to the door, leaning up against it. "Thanks for that list last night. I was going over it in my head, and it really helped me get to sleep."

He laughed and moved away. I stifled a yawn and headed for the bathroom. Maybe I would wear the turquoise capris today.

353

Though we had looked for a motel in downtown Salt Lake, everything around there was pretty pricey. The two thousand dollars the pouch had produced was down to about sixteen hundred after we'd purchased clothes, gas, food, and phones. I had learned enough about the way the pouch worked to know it would be a mistake to assume I could make it produce more money anytime I wanted it. So when Rick found a cheaper motel in Bountiful, we opted for that one.

My sleeping in had made us later than we had hoped, so it was already 8:30 before we pulled out of the motel, with Rick's dad right behind us. I wasn't ready for big city traffic yet, so Rick drove, heading for the I-15 southbound on-ramp. Both Rick and I groaned when we saw the line-up of cars waiting to get on the freeway. The ramp had three lanes, but they were all backed up to the bottom. Up ahead, we could see the monitoring lights for each lane turning red and green in a regular sequence.

"Man," I exclaimed, "I thought the traffic would be lighter."

"You're just used to Hanksville traffic. Or non-traffic," Rick said with his usual "nothing to be done about it" attitude. "We'll make it." That was said with less assurance.

"Thanks. Now I'm supposed to be patient too?"

"Use the pouch," Cody said from the backseat.

Both of us snapped around.

"Well, why not?" he said defensively. "We don't want to be late for the FBI."

Rick and I exchanged glances. The pouch was on the seat between us. He finally shrugged. "It's up to you."

"Do you think it's wrong?"

"Not under the circumstances."

I picked it up. The results were almost instantaneous. About ten or twelve cars ahead of us, the light for our lane turned green for a moment, then back to red. But instead of the next lane turning green in sequence, ours came on again. Then it did it again. We moved up, gaining two car lengths on the lady next to us.

"All right!" Cody crowed. "Way to go, Danni!"

Then my elation disappeared. "Oh no!" I cried. "It can't be."

"What?" Rick said.

"Look. In the lane next to us. About seven cars ahead of us. Surely, that couldn't be—"

But it was. A large red pickup truck with spotlights on the rack over the cab was waiting its turn in the center lane.

"No way!" Rick exclaimed.

But I knew it was. I couldn't see the driver yet, but I knew. And I knew something else, too. This was *Le Gardien*'s way of teaching me a lesson. I put one hand to the side of my face and slid down in my seat.

"It'll be all right," Rick soothed. "Just don't say anything."

Was he kidding? I was terrified. The image of that guy and the crowbar was back in my head.

"Come on," Rick urged, speaking to no one. The 4Runner moved up another space. We were just five spaces behind the red truck. Horns were starting to honk as drivers went from baffled to angry. Then, to our surprise, when our light went red, the outside lane's light went green. And it stayed that way for three cars. Then once again, ours turned green. For one car. Then back to the outside lane. The center lane, the one where Big Red was, didn't change. Horns grew louder and angrier.

"Uh-oh."

I looked at Cody, not liking the sound of that. "What?"

"Look."

The driver of the pickup truck had stuck his head out the window and was looking at us. And we were close enough that I could tell he was not a happy camper.

"I think he recognized us," I said in a tiny voice.

"Just ignore him," Rick said. "Keep the window up. If the traffic keeps up, we'll be past him in about three more light changes."

Not only did I make sure my window was rolled up, but I locked the doors, too.

The green lights were still alternating between our lane and the outside lane, and with the next change, we drew alongside the pickup. The guy was still leaning out the window, glaring at me. He motioned for me to roll down the window. I didn't move a muscle.

"Hey, kid," he yelled. "This is your blockheaded friend speaking. Roll down your window. I wanna talk to you."

We moved up a space. We were two cars away from being the lead car in our lane. Ten more seconds.

"Pull over. I know you can hear me. I wanna talk."

Then, to my utter horror, the center monitoring light flashed green. The lead car shot forward. The red truck moved alongside us again. It was like a nightmare being played out in slow motion. We moved forward. He moved forward. Finally the semaphores were working properly. Of all the times. And there was nothing I could do to stop them.

I flung the pouch at Rick. "You take it. I'm just making things worse."

He started to protest, then picked it up and placed it on his lap. Both cars were in the lead position, like we were at the starting line of the Indie 500.

"Pull over!" the guy shouted. He was close enough that I could see how mad he was. I had a sudden vision of tomorrow's headline:

UTAH TEENAGER KILLED IN
ROAD RAGE INCIDENT ON WAY TO FBI.

I turned to Rick. "Do something!"

He clung to the pouch with one hand, but looked totally helpless. And then there was a loud clanking sound, a couple of loud bangs as the pickup's engine backfired, and then, with what sounded like steel grinding on steel, the engine died. Smoke poured out from under the hood. Our light changed to green, and Rick jammed the gas pedal to the floor. As we shot forward, I could hear the guy yelling and saw him pounding on the steering wheel.

Once we were on the freeway, I realized Rick's dad had been right behind us through it all. Feeling my heart slow down, I turned to Rick. "What are you going to tell your dad?"

He grinned. "I'm going to tell him it was all your fault and that I had nothing to do with it."

CHAPTER 53

On the way to the FBI's office building, the mood in the truck was pretty somber. We were back to reality. In a few minutes, Cody and I would tell our story to the Federal Bureau of Investigation. That would start a whole different clock ticking. And that clock had an ominous sound to it. I kept hearing El Cobra's voice in my head: *If you go to the police, you will never see your parents again.*

I had planned to spend some time this morning outlining the events of the last three days, but then I'd overslept. But with both Cody and Rick willing to help me, I decided it would be all right. The bigger question was how to explain our escape from El Cobra and his gang.

"You all right?" Rick said, watching me closely.

"Yeah. I—Well, no. Uh . . . I don't know what I am, to be honest."

"You're doing the right thing, Danni."

"Am I? Are you absolutely positive about that?"

"Yes."

"Then why do I have this sick feeling in the pit of my stomach?"

"Because there's so much at stake. It's only natural. But this *is* the way to help your family. You have to do it."

I grunted something and fell silent, checking the rearview mirror to make sure Mr. Ramirez was still behind us. He was, but for some reason that didn't help my nerves much.

"Will we have to move to another state?" Cody asked with such sadness that I looked around in surprise.

"Why would we have to do that?"

"Because we're witnesses now. Remember that movie about the husband and wife who witnessed a murder in New York? The police put them in the Witness Protection Program and sent them to Wyoming so they would be safe."

"We're here," Rick interrupted. "It's the big white building up ahead. The FBI is on the twelfth floor." He slowed and flipped on his turn signal.

"That's different, Cody. The FBI will help *us* find Mom and Dad."

"I know that," he said, irked. "But we're still witnesses, aren't we?"

Not sure how to answer that, I shrugged as we pulled into the parking lot. A couple of minutes later, the four of us were standing outside the main entrance to the office building.

"Are you really going to take the pouch in there with you?" Rick asked.

I barely heard him. Once again I was clutching it like a drowning man—or rather, a drowning girl. My warning bells were clanging like crazy. Something wasn't right. I looked at Cody. He was beside me, waiting patiently, fully trusting that I would do the right thing.

The gift that Grandpère said I had was a strange thing. It was never exactly the same. Sometimes I felt a clear, immediate danger. Other times it was a feeling of being in the presence of evil.

Occasionally it had been nothing more than a general sense of un-easiness.

This was different. This was clearly a warning. My first thought was that the FBI had been infiltrated by El Cobra's gang after all. But I shook that off. That didn't feel right. Was there danger nearby? Had El Cobra's men somehow followed us? I rejected those as quickly as I had the first idea. I had to believe that if El Cobra's men were nearby, I would have felt it sooner and more strongly.

"Are you ready?" Rick asked.

I shook my head. "Just a minute." I stepped away, not wanting to be distracted. My gaze returned to Cody. This was what he had wanted from the beginning. In fact, he had thought of the FBI before I did, but now he looked nervous and frightened. And no wonder. He was still a kid, and this was a lot to ask of a kid. Add to that the fear of being ripped from his home and put into a Witness Protection Program, and it was no wonder he was nervous.

"Danni?" Rick asked. "You're not changing your mind, are you?"

Surprisingly, his father stepped in before I could answer. "What's wrong, Danni?" he asked kindly.

"I'm not sure. Something doesn't feel right."

He considered that for a moment. I expected him to tell me it was just the jitters, or something like that. So his next question took me by surprise. "This is more than just being afraid something might go wrong, isn't it?"

I started to shake my head, then changed it to a vigorous nod. "Yes. I know this is the best thing to do, but suddenly it's not right. And I don't know why."

Cody was watching me, but he didn't seem to want to come over and join the conversation. He looked lost and forlorn. I wondered if he was thinking about Mom. *It's not just himself he's scared about. He's just a kid.* That last thought came quite strongly.

And then I knew. When Aron Ralston said he'd had an epiphany about how to perform the amputation of his arm, I had wondered what he meant. It hadn't been something he'd seen in a vision, like when he saw his future little boy. It was something he saw, or understood, in his mind. Now I knew what he meant.

Like a sudden flood of light in a darkened room, I understood my anxieties. All along, I had been picturing me and Cody and Rick loading up into black, government SUVs and roaring off into the desert to find Mom and Dad and Grandpère. I pictured me and Cody in this working partnership with the FBI, going along with the agents, helping them when they got stumped, making sure El Cobra and his gang were brought to justice.

What a fantasy. And Cody had seen it first.

"What is it, Danni?" Rick said, peering deeply into my eyes. "What's the matter?"

His father held up his hand to ward him off, but I wanted to answer him. I *needed* to answer him. "We're just kids," I said.

Both father and son reared back a little.

"I'm sixteen, and Code's only thirteen."

"So what?" Rick asked.

"So our parents are being held for ransom. We have no legal guardians right now."

"I'm not following," Charlie said.

"What do you think the FBI is going to do with us once they have finished questioning us? Send us home? Take us with them? No, they'll take us into protective custody. And because we're just kids, they probably put us with foster parents somewhere out of state until all of this is over."

Realization dawned in Rick's eyes. He turned to his father. "Dad, we can take them home with us, can't we?"

"Yeah, right," I shot back, "when El Cobra's men are already watching your place?" I turned to his father. "Do you think I'm wrong?"

His dark eyes were filled with sadness. He finally shook his head and answered Rick's question. "I have no legal status here, son. Danni's right. It will very likely be protective custody for them."

"I can't do that," I cried. "I can't. I won't."

Cody came over to stand beside me. I took his hand. "Did you hear all that?"

He nodded, then squeezed my hand hard. "I don't want to be in protective custody."

"But you can't do this alone," Rick exclaimed. "It's too dangerous."

I said nothing. He was right. But so was I.

After a moment, Charlie straightened. "I would like to propose something to you, Danni. I think we can make it work, but you have to be the one to decide."

I searched his face for a long moment, and as I did, understanding came into my mind with that same crystal clear clarity as before. I could trust his wisdom and maturity. I knew that was what Dad would want me to do. "All right," I said. "I'm listening."

———— • ————

Five minutes later, Charlie Ramirez went inside the building, heading for the twelfth floor. At the same time, Rick, Cody, and I went back to Rick's 4Runner and returned to the motel.

We had one hour to pack up before Rick's father called.

———— • ————

At precisely ten thirty, Rick's phone rang. He snatched it up, then handed it to me. I took a quick breath, looked to Cody for encouragement, then put it to my ear. "Hello?"

"Danni?" Mr. Ramirez's voice was calm.

"Yes?"

"There's someone here I want you to talk to."

"I'm not going to change my mind, Mr. Ramirez."

"I know. And he knows. Can he speak with you?"

"Of course." I was already dreading what I knew was going to be a lecture on the dangers of going it alone and being foolish, and—

"Miss McAllister?" It was a pleasant voice of an older man.

"Yes?"

"This is Agent Clay Zabriskie. I'm the AIC, or agent in charge, of the Salt Lake Regional Office. I understand you have a story to tell me."

"Yes."

"May I call you Danni?"

"Yes."

"Danni, Mr. Ramirez has explained to me your concerns about being taken into protective custody."

I said nothing, bracing myself.

"And you are right. That is the protocol in a situation like this. And personally I believe that is the wisest thing to do, but—"

"I'm not going to be kept out of it," I cut in.

"I understand. I also understand that we have a very unusual set of circumstances here. Mr. Ramirez assures me that nothing I can say is going to change your mind."

Meaning you're a very stubborn young woman. "Yes, he's right about that."

"Of course, we cannot force you to do something against your will. However, to give you the help and support you need in this very dangerous situation via telephone connection alone, as Mr. Ramirez has suggested, isn't going to work. It's too problematical. In the first place, I need to spend time with you and your brother. I need to

GERALD N. LUND

interview you in person and help you recall every detail. That's not going to work over the phone."

"Go on."

"In the second place, what if things start to unravel and we're a hundred or two hundred miles away from you? Or what if you're in a dead zone for phone service and you can't contact us at all?" He hesitated. "I could give you a dozen other 'what if' scenarios that are just as scary."

I had no answer for him. All I knew was that Cody and I couldn't be taken out of this. But I liked his voice. He sounded kind and wise and competent.

"I have a counterproposal which I think will honor your wishes and also answer these other concerns at the same time."

"What is that?"

"That I come with you."

"But—"

He rushed on. "Just me. I won't be bringing a whole bunch of agents with me. Not yet. I'm not sure that would be wise at this point anyway. But I'll have a satellite phone and laptop with me. I can keep in touch with my agents no matter where we are. I can keep them apprised of the situation, and I can also tap into the vast resources of the FBI as needed. For example, I'd like to slip someone into your house to see if we can pick up any fingerprints. Find out who these guys are."

"There won't be any prints. They all wore surgical gloves."

"See, that's the kind of thing I need to know." Long pause. "What do you say? Will you let me come with you?"

This was a no-brainer. My relief-meter was going through the roof. "Yes."

"Wonderful. It's going to take me an hour or two to get organized, then Mr. Ramirez and I will come to the motel. Stay together

364

in one room. Put out the Do Not Disturb sign. I'll post some men in the area to make sure there's no one around."

"But what if—"

"I can assure you no one will see my men," he said. "This is what we do. Okay?"

"Yes. All right. Thank you, Mr. Zabriskie."

"It's Clay. We'll see you in a couple of hours. I'm looking forward to meeting the three of you."

CHAPTER 54

Clay Zabriskie was about ten years older than my dad, and he looked more like a kindly grandpa than a senior FBI agent. His features were pleasant—not particularly handsome, just one of those faces you liked immediately. His hair was dark brown and cut short but graying around temples. There were smile wrinkles around his mouth and eyes, which were a blue-gray color.

Other than that, he was FBI through and through—lean and muscular. His face and arms were deeply tanned. I expected him to be in a suit, but he had dressed so he could go with us—hiking boots, Levis, a sport shirt, and a baseball cap with the Pittsburgh Pirates logo. Most of all, he had a look of supreme confidence—and competence—about him.

I took all of this in as he shook hands with Cody and Rick. I liked what I saw. This was someone I could work with.

Finally, he extended his hand to me. "Danni, Clay Zabriskie. It's a pleasure to meet you. I'm sorry about your parents and your grandfather. Sounds like you've been through a lot. "

"Thank you. It's been a rough few days."

"Well, I'm here to help." He took out a laptop from his briefcase. "Mind if I take over the desk? I'd like to record our interview and type up some notes, okay?"

"Fine."

As he set up, we got settled ourselves—me and Cody on the extra chairs, close to the desk, with Rick and his dad behind us on the bed.

"We have some good news," he said as he booted up his laptop. "In a preliminary search, we found seven other kidnapping cases over the last three years with a similar MO to your case. One in Brazil, two in Paris, one in Spain, two in England, and one in Arizona. All of them were carefully planned and flawlessly executed."

"Really? And that's good?"

"In one sense, yes. It looks like it's the same guys, probably an international cartel or gang. None used the name El Cobra that we know of, but there were a lot of other similarities. A mixture of nationalities, including some Europeans and others from Latin America. No Americans have been identified. Their trademark is extortion through holding family members hostage. Except, in the other cases the families were wealthy. You're the first to have them go after what amounts to a business fortune." He shrugged. "It doesn't solve anything for us, but it does give us a leg up."

"And did they let the hostages go in the other cases?" Charlie Ramirez asked.

"In all cases but one—the one in Arizona. That one fell apart when they spotted a member of the surveillance team and opened fire on him. One of our agents was wounded; one of their men was killed." I could see he was uncomfortable telling us this. "A family member was also wounded. He was hospitalized, but recovered. But yes, they were all freed."

Seeing the dismay on my face, he went on quickly. "I was tempted to hold that back from you, Danni, because I thought you might ask. But if you and I are going to make this work, we need to be totally honest with each other." His eyes dropped for a moment. "I was the head of the surveillance team who got shot."

"Oh."

"No one is more motivated than I am to make sure that never happens again. But if you would like me to bring in someone else, I'll understand."

I glanced at Rick, who gave a quick shake of his head, then to his father, who was more emphatic about it.

"No," I said. "Thank you for being honest."

"Good. I can also tell you that this gang has extorted about twelve million dollars from people."

"Whoa!" Rick cried.

"Yeah. This is a lucrative business. The ransoms have ranged between one to five million dollars. It was clear they had done their homework and knew what each family could afford to pay. Your case almost doubles their total. But I see that as a positive. These guys are not radical extremists. Their motives are not political or stem from some fanatical cause. This is purely a business to them. Which means that if they start killing hostages, it will greatly increase the likelihood that life will get more difficult for them. People will refuse to cooperate. It also means that countries that might otherwise turn a blind eye to people like them would have a different reaction if it involves murder, especially of families."

"That is good," I said, "but if I'm hearing you right, if they were to find out we have gone to the police, then . . ." I couldn't say it.

He was grave. "Yes, it could mean all bets are off. We have to assume that possibility, but we'll go to great lengths to keep our involvement secret."

He could see I wasn't happy with that, but then there wasn't much about the situation I was happy with. "Okay. Thanks again for being honest."

He gave a curt nod, then turned on the recorder. He spoke briefly, giving the date and time and our names. Finished, he set it on the desk, then turned to the laptop. "Okay, I'm ready. Why don't you and Cody start from the beginning. Just talk it out first. Then we'll go back, and I'll start asking questions."

I picked up the pouch. This was the first thing on my mental list. "Before we do that, I have sort of an odd request."

A little puzzled, he glanced back and forth between my face and the pouch. "Go on."

"Would it be possible to have your people make a duplicate of this pouch?"

It said a lot about him that he didn't ask why. He held out his hand, and I gave him the pouch. He put it under the light of the desk lamp, turning it over and over, examining the embroidery closely. He opened it, peered inside, then came back to the flap. He leaned in. "Are these letters here?" he asked.

"Yes. They spell out *Le Gardien,* which is French for the Guardian."

"Hmm." He set it beside the laptop, took out his cell phone, and began snapping pictures of the pouch from every angle. When he was done, he turned back to me. "The fabric and the wooden button are unusual. The biggest problem will be duplicating the embroidery." He shrugged. "I think we can come close. Has anyone in the gang actually held this pouch?"

"Yes, a couple of them. But only briefly, and they were more interested in what was inside it than what was on the outside."

"And you feel that getting a duplicate is important?"

"I'm not sure. El Cobra is definitely interested in it. It could turn out to be important."

He nodded. He made a quick call, explaining what he wanted and telling them he was sending pictures. "Okay," he said. "Tell me what it is about this pouch that is so important."

My shoulders lifted and fell. "It is important, but before I tell you why, you need to know something else. There are some things in our story that you'll find strange. In fact, you'll wonder if we aren't all a little crazy. So I think it's important we get something settled up front. And it has to do with this pouch."

"Okay," he said slowly. "Go ahead."

"You may want to turn off the recorder for this."

He reared back. "Do you want me to?"

"No, but I think you'll erase this part later." I took a deep breath. "If you'll look in the pouch, you'll find something of particular interest to you."

"I did look in it. The pouch is empty."

"Please." My hands were resting on my knees, and I had crossed my fingers. I didn't have the slightest idea what I was doing, or why. I was just going with my gut.

He started to say something, then shook his head and turned back to the desk. He picked up the pouch, and immediately I saw his eyes widen. Even I could see the small lump inside of it. He shook it, then felt it. Gingerly, he set the pouch on his lap and lifted the flap.

"What is this?" he cried. He gaped at the black wallet in his hand for a moment, then opened it, revealing the FBI badge attached inside of it. "This is my wallet." He reached inside his jacket. "How did you—"

"Why don't you look again?" I said.

He didn't move. His eyes narrowed into slits. "What kind of game are you playing?"

"Please. Just look again."

He reached in the pouch again. This time he withdrew a key ring with several keys on it. His jaw dropped even further. "But—" He felt his pants pocket.

"Again," I said.

In quick succession, he pulled out Rick's wallet, Charlie's wallet, Rick's car keys, Charlie's car keys, a small shampoo bottle with the motel's logo on it, the Bible from the dresser drawer, and a shower cap, also furnished by the motel.

By that time, he was looking quite dazed, as was Charlie.

Satisfied that we had his attention, I said, "Okay, Clay, now we're ready to tell our story."

Cody and I talked for nearly fifteen minutes, with occasional additions from Rick and his father, while Clay recorded us all on his digital recorder. Several times, he shook his head, muttering something to himself, but he held back until we finished. When we did, I stood up and started pacing, knowing what was coming.

"This is impossible."

"I know," I said cheerfully.

"What are you doing, Danni? *How* are you doing this? Is this a setup? I want to know how you really got away from them. No more of this invisibility, or toy guns shooting at people, or money materializing out of nowhere." He picked up the pouch. "This is some kind of magician's pouch, Danni, and it's not funny."

I sighed and walked to the bathroom, stopping in the open doorway so he could still see me. "Where's your wallet now, Clay?"

He slapped his jacket again. A look of anger crossed his face. He snatched up the pouch, reaching inside. Then he turned it upside down and shook it. Nothing came out.

"Where is it?" he barked at me.

"On the television."

He leaped up and grabbed it.

"Convinced?"

"No. Tell me how you're doing this."

What was it going to take to convince this guy? The answer came immediately. "Do you always keep your gun loaded? You have it with you, right?"

"Of course. Why?"

"Take out the clip."

Wary, he got to his feet, then reached beneath his jacket for the shoulder holster under his arm. He pulled out a pistol and ejected the clip. We could all see the bullets in it. "It's loaded. I checked it this morning."

"No, it's not."

He looked down, then fell back a step. The clip was empty.

"Oh," I said, feigning surprise. "I was wrong. Look."

His eyes jerked back to the magazine. The clip was full again. After what seemed like a long time, he put the clip back in, slid the pistol back in the holster, then sat down slowly at the desk.

Cody grinned at him. "Magicians can't change things they've never touched. The pouch really is magic," he said.

"I prefer the word *enchanted*," I said. Clay had to accept this, or we weren't going to get anywhere.

"That's not possible," he murmured again, but from the look on his face, it was clear he wasn't sure about that anymore.

"We don't understand how it works, or why," I explained, "but it does work. That's the only reason Cody and I are here. That's why you have to know about the pouch. It's a factor in how we go after these people. It can help us. I mean, really help us. And you need to take that into account as we talk about how to free my parents and grandfather."

CHAPTER 55

After another hour of interrogation, I knew that Clay had finally accepted the reality of the pouch. He was still having trouble believing it, but he had accepted it. And more important, I could tell he was starting to include the pouch in his plans.

Charlie had left, anxious to check on his girls. We promised to call and keep him up to date. Unless Clay decided otherwise, he would not be involved, but would stay and watch his girls. Around-the-clock protection was being furnished for the whole family.

"How sure are you they are at Lake Powell?" Clay asked me abruptly, after typing for several minutes.

"Ninety percent. No. Ninety-five percent."

He cocked his head.

Rick jumped to my defense. "One of the ways the pouch works is by helping her feel and sense things."

He nodded, took out his cell phone, and punched a speed-dial number. He began speaking rapidly. My heart soared as he started talking about Google Earth and requiring live satellite data for scanning the entire length of Lake Powell. When he finished, he listened for a couple of moments, then hung up. He turned to me.

"There'll be a lot of houseboats out, but we're assuming this guy will choose an isolated spot and stay to himself, so that should help a little."

"Thank you," I said. "Thank you for believing me."

"Actually," he said with a twinkle in his eye, "I don't believe you. Not in my head. But . . ." He blew out his breath in wonder. "You are a remarkable young woman, Danni."

"A little stubborn at times," Rick said, "but yes, quite remarkable."

Clay leaned forward, his face earnest. "I was going to wait before I proposed something to you, Danni. But this changes everything."

"What?"

"We can't do this alone—just the four of us. Let me pull in the full resources of the agency. Start putting teams on the ground. Have a chopper standing by. Do a full-court press on identifying who these people are and how they came to target your family."

I was already shaking my head.

"I know what you're afraid of, Danni, and rightly so. But with the pouch and your abilities, we'll let you and Cody stay with us. We can't wait until we find these guys to call for help. My men have to be in place ahead of time. I know—"

But I guess he decided he had said enough. He looked at me, imploring me to seriously consider his offer. I turned to Rick.

"You already know how I feel. Same for Dad."

"Me too," Cody chimed in. "We need to trust him, Danni. We need their help."

"You have my word," Clay went on, "that if you're getting feelings of danger, or warnings from the pouch, or ideas that you think we need to try, we'll listen." He paused. "In the agency, we have a phrase that we use with each other: 'I've got your back.' Let us do that for you. Let us cover your back."

"All right," I said. "I agree. Let's do it."

A sense of relief filled the room, which Cody broke almost immediately. "Good," he said. "I'm hungry. Can we get something to eat?"

We all laughed. Cody was always hungry, but it confirmed to me that what we were doing was right. He wasn't so worried about Mom and Dad and Grandpère that he wasn't thinking of his stomach.

Clay turned to Rick as he pulled out his phone again. "There's a pizza place not far from here that delivers." His fingers moved across the screen. "Order enough for everyone. Breadsticks and drinks too. My treat. I need to make some phone calls. By the time the food gets here, we'll be done and can hit the road." He gave Rick the number.

As Rick made the call, Clay motioned me to join him. "All right, Danni, it's time to talk strategy."

I jumped up and retrieved my journal from my overnight bag. "I agree. Last night, when I couldn't sleep, I had some ideas." I opened the journal. "See what you think." As he took it, I grabbed my cell phone and waved it at him. "Remember, we don't have to find out where they are. All we have to do is put in the battery and they will know where I am."

I could tell he didn't like that idea, so I went on quickly. "I know that in some ways we're just naive kids who think they can solve everything by themselves, and I know you're trying to protect us."

He started to protest, but I rushed on. "But remember, we know this country. I don't know how many times my family has camped in and hiked through Cathedral Valley. This is our ground. And if we control where we meet—and when and how—then, with your help, we control the game."

He was impressed, but still not convinced. "I won't put you and Cody in harm's way."

"My whole family is in harm's way already."

"I know, but . . ." He shook his head. "No, you're right. Tell me what you're thinking."

———

As we finished the last of the pizza an hour later, Clay sat back, dusting off his hands. "Okay? You two ready?"

I took a deep breath, looking first to Cody, then to Rick. Both of them nodded. "Ready," I said.

Rick inserted the battery into my phone, plugged in the charger, then handed it to me. I saw Clay glance at his watch, so I did the same. It took less than ninety seconds before the phone rang. I put it on speaker then touched the answer button. "Hello."

"*Hola, chiquita. Cómo estás,* little one?"

"I want to talk to my parents."

"But of course," El Cobra said expansively. "Keep it short. We have much to talk about."

A moment later Mom's voice come on. "Carruthers?"

"I'm here, Mom."

"Is everything all right?"

"Yes. We're fine. Everything's fine." *Except for you being held hostage, and us being on the run, and men with guns after us, and . . .*

"Thank the Lord," she said.

"Are *you* all right, Mom?"

"Yes. We're being treated well." There was a short, mirthless laugh. "Except that I'm cold. You know me, Carruthers. Middle of the summer and my feet are like blocks of ice. I suppose it's because of the stress."

I heard someone mutter, and then she gave a low cry as the phone was yanked from her hand.

Another voice came on the line. My dad.

"Hello, Danni. Are you sure you're all okay?"

"Yes, we are. Really. Rick's dad has been helping us, but we're ready to come back now. Put Mom back on. Cody really wants to talk to her."

I handed the phone to Cody, then saw Clay scribbling a note: *Keep him talking. Trying for a trace.*

They must not have been concerned about Cody trying something funny because he was allowed to talk for thirty seconds or more. Then he handed the phone back to me.

El Cobra came on the line. "Okay, *chiquita*. We're running out of time here. On Saturday, your father and grandfather must be in Moab to meet the Canadians. We've got no more time for your little games."

"I want to talk to my grandfather. I need to know he's okay."

"The old man is fine," someone growled in the background. But a moment later, Grandpère came on the phone.

"I am okay, Danni. But they're not going to let me talk very long." Wry chuckle. "Maybe I'll try texting you sometime."

Even I laughed at that. "You texting? That will be the day, Grandpère."

"Just listen to your mother, Danni."

El Cobra was back on in an instant. "Where are you now, *chiquita*?"

"Now who's playing games? You know where we are because you're tracking my phone. But as soon as I hang up, the battery comes out again, and we're moving to another location. So call off your dogs, Cobra. They're not going to find us. Not until we're ready."

"And when is that, *chiquita?* No more stalling."

"We're ready. We'll make the exchange for Grandpère and Dad on Saturday in Cathedral Valley, following the directions you gave to us before."

For a moment I thought he would protest us waiting until Saturday, but all he said was "When?"

"When I say." Even as I snapped that out, another part of my brain was yelling a warning. *This guy is a hardened criminal. He holds a gun to your family's head. And you're talking to him like he's a bug on a rock. Don't make him angry.* But it wasn't just me talking. Once again I was feeling the influence of the pouch. So I went on in that same imperious tone.

"One other thing. We'll be trading Cody for Dad and Grandpère. *Only* Cody. I'm not going to be part of the bargain."

"What?" A string of Spanish followed, almost certainly profanity. "Don't you dictate terms to me," he yelled. "You want to see your mother alive again?"

I hit the screen and terminated the call.

Clay about choked. "What are you doing?"

I held up a finger, the phone poised by my ear. It rang almost immediately.

"Hola, señor."

"Don't you hang up on me!" he screamed into the phone.

"I didn't. You don't hang up a cell phone. You simply hit the end-call button."

"You little witch," he started. "I'll—"

I hit the end-call button again. This time Clay smiled, though it was somewhat strained.

The phone rang again a few seconds later. I spoke before El Cobra could start yelling again. "Are you ready to talk, or do you want to keep screaming at me?" I was amazed at how calm I was and that I was talking to him like this. No question but that the pouch had kicked in.

He didn't answer.

"Good. Here's the deal. If I send Cody, you'll have him and my mother. Since you're sending two of your men with my father and grandfather, that means that they're still your hostages too. So if I surrender, you'll hold all the chips, and I'd have nothing left to bargain with. So count me out."

He started ranting again. I overrode him. "I'm sure you're thinking you're dealing with a stupid kid, but you should know I'll be bringing my dad's rifle with me, and I know how to use it."

"Oh," he sneered. "There's something to lose sleep over."

"And there's one more thing. You know that old purse I carry with me?"

This time there was only silence. Then, "Yes. What of it?"

"I think you know by now that it's much more than just a purse. Among other things, it allows me to sense when danger is near. How do you think we knew you were coming to Rick's house and escaped in time? And we know about fatso going to the phone store in Price. So if you send somebody out looking for us now, it's over. I'll call the FBI and tell them everything."

"I think you've already talked to the FBI, little one." His voice was like the hiss of a snake. "That's why you went to Salt Lake."

Clay wrote furiously, then held up the note: *He's fishing. He doesn't know.*

I laughed into the phone. "We came to Salt Lake because you threatened Rick's aunt and his little sisters. We had to get them to a safe place. And by the way, they got the message. Rick's out of it now. He's staying here. So is his dad."

"It wasn't a threat," he shot back. "And what I am about to say is not a threat either, *señorita*. It's you with your brother, or nothing. *¡Nada!* And you'll never see your family again."

"Okay," I said, "then it's *nada*." And I cut him off a third time.

This time almost two minutes went by, and I was starting to sweat. Had I pushed him too far? Clay didn't seem too concerned.

"Be patient. You've got him hooked. And you've wounded his pride. You're one step ahead of him at every turn." The respect in his eyes made me feel that maybe I wasn't being an absolute fool.

When the phone finally rang again, I waited for three rings. "Are you ready to talk about Cathedral Valley now?" I said.

"What guarantees do I have that you're coming—that this isn't a setup?"

"Saturday morning, no later than eight o'clock, I'll put the battery back in my phone, and you can track us from then on. You have my word we will come alone. And by the way, Rick will do the same thing with his phone at that time, so you'll be able to see that he's still up in Salt Lake." Actually, Rick had given his phone to his dad, and Charlie would turn it on when we told him too. A minor detail.

"What about the exchange?"

"It goes down exactly like you said before, only I don't go with you. I'll find another way home."

"Will you have your little pouch with you?"

"Yes. I always have it with me."

"*Muy bien.* So nine o'clock?"

"No, eleven o'clock."

There was a howl of anger. "That's not enough time for your dad to get to Moab. It's nine o'clock or nothing."

"Go whenever you want. Cody and I will be there at eleven." I hung up on him a fourth time and removed the battery before he could call back.

CHAPTER 56

For what seemed like a full minute we all sat there, a little dazed by what had happened. Finally, Clay shook his head. "You know, Danni, for a girl who looks like she sings in a church choir, you're like tangling with a pit bull."

Cody sang out. "Dad says it's more like trying to stop a bulldozer under full power."

I sniffed haughtily. "Thanks. I find both of those comments seriously less than flattering."

Clay's smile broadened. "I didn't say you looked like a pit bull. Just the opposite, in fact. That's what catches people off their guard." Then he sobered. "Seriously, Danni, you played that brilliantly. Absolutely brilliantly."

I extended my hands so he could see how badly they were trembling. "It was kind of like I was on autopilot and just went with it."

"Why Cathedral Valley?" he asked. "I'm not a native Utahan, and I've never been there. Why would he choose that location? And why the Temples of the Sun and Moon specifically?"

"Simple. First, it's not that far from Hanksville. About thirty miles is all. Probably more important, it's isolated. Though Capitol Reef is a National Park, you can go there even in the summer tourist season, spend a day in the valley, and never see another person."

"That would be important for him."

Rick broke in. "And it's an easy place to make sure you're not walking into a trap. It's open and flat around the two temples. No one's going to be sneaking up on you."

"What are these temples?"

"They're two freestanding rock formations that jut up out of the desert floor. They're massive, hundreds of feet high. Big enough that you can hide someone behind them where they can't be seen."

"Big enough to hide my team?"

"No." I said it more sharply than I had intended. "You're going to have to stay back."

"Draw me a map," he said, pulling out a notepad from his briefcase. "Show me what you're thinking."

<hr>

Over the next fifteen minutes, we laid it all out—how Cody and I would come in, where Rick would be, where Clay's team would wait. The fact that he would have a chopper at his disposal was a big relief. When we finished, Clay reached in his jacket pocket and pulled out a car key and remote. "We think your Toyota is too recognizable now, Rick. Here's a trade. We'll see that yours gets back to you when the time's right." He tossed him the key.

"What is it?" Rick asked as he caught it.

"We wanted you to blend in, so we got you a 1997 Chevrolet Silverado. It's pretty beat up and has about a hundred and fifty thousand miles on it."

The disappointment on Rick's face was so evident that Clay

laughed out loud. "Actually, it's almost brand-new with less than a thousand miles on it. It's a rental, so try not to beat it up too badly."

"I can live with that!" Rick said, trying to suppress a grin.

"Will it hold the four-wheeler?" I asked. The four-wheeler was critical to our plan.

"It will. Ramps are in the back. We've already transferred all your stuff into it. More important, there's a satellite phone in the backseat. You can call me anytime on that, no matter where you are. Also, there are two hand radios in the glove box. They are encrypted and have a range of about twenty miles, so we can stay in contact with each other. If something goes wrong, we'll be three minutes away by chopper."

"But *only* if something goes wrong," I warned.

"Yes, ma'am." He flipped me a salute.

I gave him one of my brightest smiles. "I am totally going to have to take back all those mean things I've been thinking about you, Mr. Zabriskie," I teased. Then the smile faded. "Seriously, Clay, thank you for being here with us. It's a huge load off our shoulders."

"Yes," Cody said from the bed. Rick was nodding vigorously.

"Danni, I've got to be straight with you. The only reason I am consenting to this whole idea is because I am certain that El Cobra will not hurt either you or Cody. He's got twenty million reasons not to."

"I know," I said quietly. "There are many things you could say about him, but he's not stupid. If Cody and I get so much as a scratch, my mom and dad will fight him every step of the way."

"I agree. So I'm going along with this plan because I think it's the best option we've got to stop him. Maybe even the only option. But I'm still worried about sending you out there alone. You know there's no way El Cobra is going to walk away and leave you behind. He's got something up his sleeve."

I reached down for the pouch. "And we've got something on my shoulder. We'll have a surprise or two for him as well."

He nodded slowly and thoughtfully. "If it weren't for that, you wouldn't be going."

At that moment, my cell phone chimed, alerting me to a text message notification. I was pulling my phone out to check it when I saw Rick's face.

"What?" I asked.

"Your phone is dead, Danni. You took out the battery, remember?"

My jaw dropped. "But how—" I looked more closely. I had at least a dozen text messages, mostly from my friends. Not too surprising since I'd had my phone off for a couple of days. But the latest message had no name on it. Puzzled, I opened it. There was no name or number showing in the sender box. And the text itself was blank.

"Who's it from?" Clay asked.

I held it up for him to see. "Nobody," I guess. Then I looked more closely. "Wait. There's something at the bottom." I scrolled down quickly and saw a series of numbers. The first was 21-11-1934. That was followed by a seventy-eight enclosed in a hexagon and a seventy-nine enclosed in a circle. The others moved in closer to see.

"That's strange," Rick said. "The numbers 1934 sound like a year, but it can't be a date. There's no twenty-first month." He snapped his fingers. "Could it be GPS coordinates?"

"No," Cody said. "Wrong format. And there's only one number. You need two for GPS."

I was still staring at the first number. I leaned forward to peer at it more closely. And then I suddenly knew what it was. "It's Grandpère's birthday. But written in the European way, with the day first and the month second. He was born on November 21, 1934. This is a message from Grandpère. I know it is."

"So what's the next part, then?" Clay asked. "Why are those other numbers enclosed inside those shapes? I didn't even know you could do that on a cell phone."

"And I didn't know Grandpère knew how to text. Or that a cell phone without a battery could still work, either," I said. "I know it's from him. That's why he talked about texting me. He's trying to tell us something."

"I taught Grandpère how to text," Cody said smugly. "And those numbers are channel markers for Lake Powell."

"What?" I cried. Would this kid never cease to amaze me with his gift for numbers?

"The odd numbers are in circles, and the even ones are in hexagons. That's how you mark how many miles you are from the dam. The hexagons are for when you're going upstream, and the circles are for when you're headed downstream."

"Grandpère's telling us where they are!" I nearly shouted. "I'll bet the entrance to the canyon is between channel markers seventy-eight and seventy-nine."

Clay whirled to his laptop and typed rapidly. "I think we have a detailed map of Lake Powell in our database."

I barely heard. I was pacing back and forth, trying to remember exactly what Grandpère had said, and how he'd said it. His joke about texting was clear now. But why the charge to listen to Mom? I had thought it odd at the time because Mom had barely said hello to me. Except she'd said how cold she was. And how her feet were like blocks of ice.

I whirled around. "I can tell you which canyon it is."

"Just a second. I've got the map." He was moving the image on his screen with his fingertips.

"It's Iceberg Canyon."

He looked skeptical. "How could you—" He turned back to his laptop. He zoomed in, then swiped it more slowly with his fingertips. The map was blue print on a white background, with red numbers showing GPS coordinates, key sites, and channel markers. He zoomed in some more. He leaned forward, unintentionally blocking my view. I heard a soft intake of breath. When he turned, his eyes were filled with astonishment. "The opening to Iceberg Canyon is at channel markers seventy-eight and seventy-nine."

I did a little bow, acknowledging my just dues.

He hit a speed-dial number on his phone. "Gus. Clay here. I need a current satellite scan of the full length of Iceberg Canyon at Lake Powell. Yeah, that's right." Pause. "No, it's not a national emergency, but there are several lives at stake." Another pause. "Right. Let me know as soon as possible. And also, when we have a man on the ground at Bullfrog Marina, have him discreetly start nosing around, see what he can find out. Thanks."

As he put his phone down, he was shaking his head. "How did you know?"

"Because of what Mom said. A couple of years ago, we stayed in Iceberg Canyon. It was the middle of July and seriously hot, but Mom kept saying how cold she was." I turned to Cody. "Remember? She told us that now she knew why they called it Iceberg Canyon." Back to Clay. "And it fits what they'd be looking for. It's got a narrow entrance, easily guarded. There are only a few places to beach a houseboat, so it's never crowded. The high vertical cliffs come right down to the water. I'm sure that's it."

Clay sat back, appraising me and Cody with even greater respect. "Okay, my confidence level keeps going up." He flashed a grin. "I have *got* to meet this grandfather of yours. In the meantime, we'll get to work and check things out."

I was soaring. We knew where my family was. And the FBI was taking us seriously.

"We're going to make this work, Danni. There's only one problem I haven't solved yet," Clay said with a rueful smile.

"What's that?" Rick asked.

"I'm not sure how I'm going to write all this up in my official report."

PART NINE

Entrapment

CHAPTER 57

Wellington, Utah
Friday, June 17, 2011

I didn't think I'd get back to my journal quite so soon, but in some ways, I'm like a little kid with her favorite blanket. The journal gives me something to cling to, something that helps me feel some semblance of normalcy, which is something I very much need right now.

So, here's what's going on now. (In brief. It's going to take a long time to write everything that's happened.) We—Rick, Cody and me—are in a small motel in Wellington, just south of Price. We got in last night and crashed. We have two rooms. Rick and Cody are in one, and I'm in the other by myself. Pure heaven! It's the first time I've been alone in four days. This morning we're just hanging out, getting things ready for tomorrow.

And BTW, checking in and paying for the rooms wasn't a problem. Clay called ahead and set everything up. And the FBI's paying for it! Good thing. The Guardian isn't being much of a guardian at the moment. It absolutely refuses to make any more money for me.

At the moment, Rick and Cody are out gassing up the truck and replenishing our supply of water and food. I've

389

been doing some laundry. I volunteered. It gives me time to write. When they get back, we'll check out and head south.

Tonight, there'll be no motel and no bed. We'll all be sleeping outside. Here's the plan. Rick is going to drop me and Cody and the four-wheeler off in Cainsville with our sleeping bags, etc. Though we know people in Cainsville—it's only twelve miles west of Hanksville—and I'm sure we could find someone to put us up for the night, we can't let anyone know we're there. So we'll find a place where the willows and undergrowth are heavy enough to conceal us from the highway and do our best to cope with the ten gazillion mosquitos who anxiously await our arrival.

Rick will then go on to Cathedral Valley, but he'll use a back way that will take him up on the mesa rather than down in the valley itself. Then he'll hike the four or five miles under cover of darkness to the temples. He'll stay there until we arrive.

Later today, Clay is bringing in his team over the west road into Cathedral Valley. That's a long and brutal way into the valley and few people use it, so they should be able to come in pretty much unobserved. They'll be in place before dark tonight, but staying back where there is no chance they will be seen.

Tomorrow morning, I'll turn on my cell phone as promised, but Cody and I will hang there by the river in Cainsville until about ten. On full alert, you can be sure. We'll then get on the four-wheeler, taking some water and Dad's rifle, and head north for the valley. At eleven, the game begins.

Since we can't pick up the four-wheeler from where we left it down by Rick's house until tonight, we have all of today to kill. Rather than sit around in the motel and go bonkers, we're heading for Leprechaun Canyon, which is about twenty-eight miles south of Hanksville. That's the second part of the plan, and I'll say more about that in a minute.

Unfortunately, we have to pass through Hanksville to get there, but me and Code will hide in the backseat of the truck, and Rick will have his hat pulled way low so no one can recognize him. Since he's not driving his 4Runner, we're pretty sure we'll be all right.

Good news. Clay just called. Satellite photos show a single houseboat moored in Iceberg Canyon. No sign of my family, but that's not a surprise. There are a couple of men visible. Clay's going to send a team in by chopper this morning and drop them off up at the head of the canyon. They'll hike in along the cliff tops and set up a surveillance station. One other thing. Clay's man at Bullfrog Marina posed as a tourist from California and said he'd heard Iceberg Canyon was a good place to take a houseboat, and asked the staff about it. They agreed, but said they had received some reports that two park rangers were turning people back at the mouth of the canyon. The rangers said that some severe water pollution had been found and that the canyon would be closed for a few more days while they tested things.

Thank you, Grandpère. This is great news. Clay is already starting preliminary plans for going in to get them. But again, none of that happens until we finish the opening round tomorrow.

Side comment: Clay is the best thing that could have happened. He's honoring his promise to make sure Mom and Dad and Grandpère stay safe. He's great, and it's such a relief that he—in his words—"has our back."

While our clothes have been washing, I got out all the stuff Grandpère sent me and read everything again. It was a great way to put things into perspective. It inspires me to do all that I can to honor the name of Monique. Knowing the role the pouch played in that whole experience is also a comfort. I need all the inspiration I can get right now, and I'm—

———

A knock on the door brought my head up. "Who is it?"

"It's me," Cody called out. "And Rick."

I got up and opened the door. "Is it time to go already? The laundry's not quite done."

"No," Rick said. "Cody and I still have to pack. Let's plan to leave in half an hour."

"That works for me." I told them about Clay's call, which lifted their spirits as well as mine. As they started for the door, I had another thought. "Rick?"

He turned back. "Yes?"

"Would you think it was silly if we . . . umm . . . if we like had a prayer before we go? We keep saying we're not alone, so maybe it wouldn't hurt if we acknowledged that fact openly and asked Him for a little help over these next few days."

He shut the door again. "Good idea. I should have thought of that."

I sighed. "You're not nearly as scared as I am."

"Oh?" He held out his hand, palm down. "Look at me shake." His hand was rock steady.

Before I could comment on that, he reached out and caught my hand. Then he took Cody's hand as well. "Do you want to stand or kneel?"

"Kneel," Cody and I said together.

———

Have to close. We're leaving. May not have time to write again until this is all over.

CHAPTER 58

Cathedral Valley, Utah
Saturday, June 18, 2011

Cathedral Valley occupies the north end of Capitol Reef National Park. The valley includes a fantastic array of brilliant red cliffs sculpted by the wind and the rain into hundreds of enormous spires and towers. There are also freestanding monoliths, as tall as fifty-story skyscrapers, scattered throughout the valley.

Two of those monoliths on the very eastern border of the park are known as the Temple of the Sun and the Temple of the Moon. Made of the same soft sandstone as the cliffs, they resemble Gothic cathedrals with their needlelike spires, imposing battlements, and vertical drops of hundreds of feet.

One of the easiest ways to access the valley is via the Cainsville Wash Road, which takes off from Highway 24 at the little hamlet of Cainsville and follows the wash for about ten miles or so. The road crosses the wash in several places. In those places, the road becomes quite rough and makes for slow going. But that was all right. Cody and I left Cainsville early so we would be sure to meet the scheduled time.

About five or six miles in, I pulled the four-wheeler off the road where it crossed one of the higher ridges. As we stopped, red dust swirled around us, but was quickly dissipated by the light breeze. The temperature was relatively mild for this time of year, probably only eighty or so, but by this afternoon, when the breeze died, it could easily be pushing a hundred degrees.

I shut off the engine and both of us climbed off the four-wheeler. Turning slowly, I rotated three hundred and sixty degrees, scanning the landscape for any sign of dust plumes, vehicles, or human life. There was nothing. I took the handheld radio off my belt and clicked the transmit button. "Rick, this is Danni. Do you copy?"

Radio static sounded for a moment, then Rick's voice came on. "I'm here. Good morning."

"Are you in place?"

"Have been for about eight hours."

"Clay, do you copy?"

"Ten-four," came the immediate reply. "We're in the cliffs about two and a half miles west of the temples. In place and out of sight."

Cody came up beside me. In a hushed voice, he asked, "Is it smart to be using our real names?"

"Cody, this is Clay. The radios are secure. They not only use a restricted frequency, but the signal is also encrypted. Even if someone were to tune us in, all they would hear is static."

I came back in. "Last night, Cody and I camped where we could see the Cainsville Wash Road turnoff. About seven thirty this morning, we saw two vehicles turn off the highway and head north. A dark green, four-door Jeep Rubicon and a white GMC Yukon SUV. We were too far away to read the license plates. Also too far away too see how many people were in each vehicle, but they were definitely traveling together. There has been no other vehicles since then."

"The Jeep arrived here about eight fifteen," Rick said. "Alone.

There were four men in the Jeep, and they immediately started scouting the area, including the parking area around the Temple of the Moon. But about half an hour later—I assume when they got the all-clear signal—the Yukon joined them. The man I assume is El Cobra was in the Yukon along with two more men plus Danni's dad and granddad."

"Are they all right?" Cody blurted.

"I'm looking at them through the binoculars right now. They're in cuffs, but they look fine."

"Good," Clay said. "Then everything is as we hoped."

"Uh . . . Clay?"

"Yes, Rick?"

"None of the men are wearing ski masks. Should that concern us?"

Long silence. *Remember, Clay. You said you'd be honest.*

Finally the radio clicked again. "It says that the situation has changed in their minds, which I don't like. But not only would the masks be stifling in this heat, if anyone happened to see them it would mean trouble for them. I'm not overly concerned."

I tried to put a smile in my voice. "You're just saying that to make me feel better, aren't you?"

No answer.

"Well, don't stop. Make me feel better."

"Danni, I want you to go ahead and activate the listening device on the ATV. Be sure the red light comes on. You're still too far away for us to pick up the signal, but I don't want you having to turn it on while they're watching you. Oh, and be sure you turn off the engine when you get there or it'll drown out everything else."

I reached under the four-wheeler's gas tank and flipped a switch on a small black box. "Okay, it's on. Will you be able to hear everything once I get there?"

"Only what takes place within a thirty- to forty-foot range of you. Try to keep El Cobra within that radius, if you can."

"Okay."

I guess he read the tone of my voice, because he came right back, his own voice calm and soothing. "Danni, you don't have to do this. If you're feeling that something's wrong, then . . . You have the pouch, right?"

I sighed. "I do. And so far, I'm fine."

"Which reminds me," Clay went on. "I got a call early this morning. They'll have a duplicate pouch ready for you by this afternoon. It'll be in your truck by the time you and Rick get back."

"Great. Thanks."

"Anything else?"

There was no answer from either of us.

Clay came on one last time. "It's going to work, Danni. I feel it."

"And if it doesn't, do I get a refund?"

I heard a soft chuckle, then the radios went dead.

CHAPTER 59

We left the wash several miles later and crossed the South Desert, which was mostly flat, sagebrush-covered landscape. I braked and pulled to a stop. In the distance, about a mile away, we had our first view of the two monoliths. I also saw the Jeep and the Yukon, though they were small specks from this distance. I half turned my head. "Okay, Code. Here we go." I twisted the throttle and we shot forward. I was ready to get this over with.

The road into the temple area forked to the left from the main gravel road. We took it, moving slowly so as to give El Cobra and his men plenty of time to see us coming. A short distance later, we passed the marker for the park boundary. I could see the two vehicles more clearly and several men standing around them. I slowed down a little more.

"Possible problem," I said to Cody, looking down in the direction of my hidden transmitter. "I don't see Dad and Grandpère."

There was no answer from the radio, even though Clay and Rick were both monitoring us. Nor would there be. We were under strict radio silence. All we needed for this to become a major disaster was for El Cobra to know I was talking to someone.

As we approached, one of the men stepped out into the middle of the road, a pistol in his hand. I didn't recognize him, of course, but from his build, I guessed it was El Cobra. I increased my speed and kept going at a pretty steady clip straight at him. At about thirty feet, I saw a flash of panic in his eyes. I squeezed hard on the brake levers, sending the four-wheeler into a long slide, creating a spray of sand, dust, and gravel. I was pleased to see that I had stopped no more than fifteen feet in front of him.

As the dust drifted away, I had my first clear look at the man I had come to fear and hate. Instead of green scrubs, he was dressed in black slacks, a red shirt that showed how muscular his upper body was, and fancy designer shoes. The top three buttons of his shirt were undone, revealing two heavy gold chains around his neck. He also had what looked like a Rolex watch on his wrist.

His skin was olive brown, but not dark—about the same color as Rick's. His eyes—just as I had seen them through the ski mask—glittered like black marbles. His hair covered the collar of his shirt and glistened like oiled ebony in the sunlight. When he smiled, which he did as he put the pistol back in his shoulder holster, I saw that his teeth were flawless. I estimated his age as thirty. He was strikingly handsome, in an Italian Mafia kind of way. I guessed he was no more than half-Hispanic, maybe only a quarter.

"Hola, chiquita." His voice was so warm and welcoming you would have thought Cody and I were honored guests at a family reunion. As soon as I heard that voice, there was no more question. This was El Cobra. And that brought my thoughts back to the situation at hand.

I looked around. The man nearest the Jeep was almost certainly Gordo—short, fat, balding—though he was younger than I had pictured him. But none of the others were tall enough to be Doc. That didn't bode well. What rock was he hiding under?

I got off the four-wheeler, motioning for Cody to stay where he was. I reached down and got the pouch, slinging it over my shoulder. Then I withdrew the rifle and levered a shell into the chamber. The men behind him stiffened, but he waved them away with a nonchalant flick of his hand. I might as well have pulled out my electric toothbrush and aimed it at him for all the concern he showed.

"Stand easy, *compadres,*" he called over his shoulder. "She's not going to shoot anyone."

"Not *anyone.* Just you, if somebody does something stupid. Where are my father and grandfather?"

Without turning around, he snapped his fingers. One of the men opened the door to the Jeep, and Grandpère and Dad climbed out. Both had their hands cuffed behind their backs.

"Dad, are you all right?"

"Yes. We're okay."

Immediately, they were pushed back into the Jeep.

"Satisfied?" El Cobra sneered. When I nodded, he waved a hand in the direction of the Jeep. "With your permission, then, they'll be on their way or they won't make their Moab connection in time. They'll be accompanied by their two new 'employees,' of course."

I nodded and lowered the rifle a little.

Two of the men got into the front seats, started the engine, and the Jeep roared away in a cloud of sand and dust.

El Cobra was oozing confidence. "Okay, Cody, your turn. Walk over to the other vehicle."

I raised the muzzle of the rifle. "Don't move, Code. We're going down to the Temple of the Moon. The exchange will take place there as previously agreed."

"Sorry, *chiquita.* Change of plans. I think we'll just take *both* of you with us right now. I don't like the idea of you running free for the next few days." His voice turned icy. "You were a fool to come alone. *¿Comprendes?*"

I heard footsteps behind me and jerked around. A tall, muscular man with a face pitted and scarred from acne was coming up behind us. He had a large pistol in his left hand pointed directly at Cody. He brushed dirt and sand off his clothes with his free hand. Without the ski mask, he was even more chilling than with it. It was Doc, no question about it.

I tried to repress the shudder that went through me. I held up the pouch and waved it at El Cobra. "Do you never learn?" I said. "If he comes another step, you'll be the first one to go down. *¿Comprendes?*"

He tossed back his head and laughed. "Did you hear that, Raul? Our *chiquita* here claims to have claws."

I tipped my head back and called out loudly. "Did you hear that, Rick? El Cobra thinks I am alone."

The crack of the rifle shattered the silence. The bullet ricocheted off the gravel road with a sharp whine. It hit no more than a foot away from El Cobra's designer shoes. Cries rang out as the men sprinted for cover. I turned my head in time to see Doc drop into a crouch, looking around wildly.

I spun around to face El Cobra. His right hand was hovering near the holstered pistol, but his face registered his shock.

"I wouldn't do that," I said easily. "He won't kill you, but waiting for an ambulance to get here from Green River might."

His hands lowered slowly, but otherwise he didn't move.

"Tell Raul to drop his weapon," I commanded.

He sneered. "You tell him."

I turned, holding the pouch up high, as if I were shielding myself from Raul's presence. There was another sharp cry, only this time it was one of agony. Raul immediately dropped the pistol and clutched his hand to his chest, moaning and whimpering in pain. At his feet, a wisp of smoke curled up from the pistol. There was the distinct smell of burning flesh in the air.

"Pick it up," El Cobra screamed. But Doc was backing away from the weapon, his eyes stark with fear.

"Tell him to join the others," I commanded. "Then we'll talk."

Doc didn't wait for permission. He scuttled away from Cody and me, still holding his hand against his body. I waited until he joined the group, then looked at El Cobra. I held up the pouch in front of me. My voice was cold when I spoke. "Now, would you like to go back to the original plan?"

I held up the pouch again, extending it toward him. He shrank back with a gasp. I opened the flap, turned the pouch upside down, and shook it hard. "As you can see, *señor*"—I spoke the title with utter contempt—"the pouch is empty, just as it was the other night in our house." I reached inside. I wasn't sure what I would find, but was gratified when my fingers touched a small packet. I withdrew it and flipped it in his direction, where it landed softly in the dust.

He jerked away, staring at the item. Then he gingerly bent down and picked it up. His eyes went even wider than Doc's. He held another packet of hundred dollar bills.

I kept my voice light and conversational as he ripped off the wrapper and counted quickly. "I believe you'll find that to be two thousand dollars, but feel free to count it."

When he was finished, he caressed the bills with his thumb. Then he held it up so his men could see what it was and waved it back and forth in triumph. There were a few smiles, but mostly they looked spooked. But not him. What I saw in his eyes was naked greed.

Suddenly there was something else in the pouch. "Hold on," I said, reaching in again.

He jerked up, clawing for his pistol with his free hand. "Don't! Keep your hands where I can see them."

I didn't, of course. I brought my hand out, and held up the next surprise. And surprise it was. When I saw it, I laughed out loud.

For a moment, there was dead silence, then the titters and chuckles began, turning quickly to open laughter. El Cobra was staring at my hand, looking bewildered. I turned the item around. I held a bobble-head doll, about six inches tall. The body wore clothes that exactly matched what El Cobra was wearing. The oversized head, which bobbed and danced in the sunlight, was capped with thick black hair combed straight back, just as his was. And the face? I could scarcely believe my eyes. It was El Cobra in miniature. Correct in every detail.

I pulled it closer. On the base I saw two words in block letters: *Cobra Pequeño*. For a moment, it didn't register. When it did, I laughed with delight. The title meant "little cobra." It couldn't have been more perfect. After all of the times he had called me *chiquita*—little girl—this was sweet justice indeed.

The men were still laughing, though nervously, as they watched El Cobra for what his reaction would be. He swung around and instantly the laughter died in their throats. When he turned back to me, his eyes were murderous. "Is this your idea of a joke?"

"A joke? No, I think it's a pretty good likeness, actually." I tossed it to him. He made no move to catch it, and it fell to the road. With a cry, he stomped on it, crushing it with the heel of his boot.

The time for playing around was over. "Now do you understand, *Cobra Pequeño?*" I shook the pouch at him. "In Spanish, I think you would call this *la bolsa encantada,* the enchanted purse." *Wow! Where had that come from?* It even sounded like I'd pronounced it perfectly. "It *is* enchanted. You saw it before when it produced a pistol. Now you see it again. This pouch has great power. And that is why you will not take me back with you today. I will honor my word, even though you have dishonored yours. Do that again, and you will live to regret it."

His tongue flicked out, and he licked his lips quickly. "Go on."

I nodded. "This is how it will play out. Day one—today—Cody and I will drive to the Temple of the Moon and park in the turn-around area, as you previously instructed. You—and only you—will come halfway down the road between here and there, and then I will send Cody to you. If you make any more attempts to take me with you, you will see for yourself the full power of the enchanted pouch."

Wow! Even I was impressed with how ominous that sounded.

"You will then leave with Cody. As a guarantee to you that I have not—unlike you—gone back on my word, you will leave two of your men here at the Temple of the Sun. All the rest can go with you. I will stay at the turnaround until your two men hear from you that you are safely out. That way you will know I have not set a trap for you. Once they give me the signal, I will leave on my four-wheeler."

He started to protest but I kept talking. "If they should attempt to hold me against my will, then . . ." I shrugged.

His eyes were hooded and dark. "They will have no vehicle."

"Ah, yes. That. Well, I see several options. One, they can walk out. It's only about eighteen miles to the highway. If they're lucky, maybe someone will happen along. Two, you can send someone back for them. Three, you can call for a limousine service. I really don't much care either way."

He finally nodded. "Then what?"

"Day two. Sunday. Grandpère and Dad, along with your two thugs, will show our Canadian clients the rhodium mine. If they finish in good time and all is in order, they may go up to Salt Lake that afternoon or evening. If not, they will drive up on Monday."

The lines around his mouth were pinching tighter and tighter. "You think you've got this all figured out, don't you?"

"Yeah, I think so. Day three. Monday. While Dad and the others make sure everything is in order for the closing on Tuesday, you and I will work out the details of the *next* exchange."

"What exchange?"

"Me for my mother and Cody." I smiled innocently. "I'm sorry. Didn't you see that coming?"

"You are *muy loco*. Why would I exchange two hostages for one—especially one who has been nothing but trouble?"

I held up the pouch and wiggled it a little. "Because with me, you get this."

I heard several gasps, including one from Cody. One thing was certain, I had everyone's undivided attention.

"Day four. Tuesday. Once the sale of the mine is closed, we'll make one final exchange. Me, my grandfather, and my father in exchange for twenty million dollars and *la bolsa encantada*."

That finally broke through his veneer. The hunger in his eyes was palpable, but he was still suspicious. "You would give that up? I do not believe it."

To my surprise, Cody suddenly burst out from behind me. "She would to save our family."

El Cobra's eyes narrowed, and I could see his mind was weighing what that would mean. "Tell me, *chiquita*. What game are you playing?"

I gave him a pitying look. "You have my family. This is not a game. Think about what I'm offering. I'll be waiting for your answer." I climbed back on the four-wheeler, started it up, shoved the gearshift forward, and gave the machine full throttle. He jumped to one side as Cody and I roared past him.

CHAPTER 60

The Temple of the Moon was another hundred or hundred and fifty yards down the road. As I swung the four-wheeler into place and turned off the engine, I looked around. Then I called softly, "You there?"

Off to my left, I heard Rick's voice, low and soft. "I'm here. Fifty yards to your left, behind the sand dune. I've got your back."

"Great." Cody and I climbed down.

"You were awesome, Danni!" Cody said.

I didn't feel awesome. I was shaking pretty badly. "It was the pouch, Code. Not me."

"How much did you hear, Rick?"

"Most of it. I agree with Code. Awesome. You really had him off balance."

I looked back toward the Temple of the Sun where El Cobra and his men were gathered in a tight circle. "Will he buy it?" I asked.

"Only time will tell. All we can do is wait."

———

It didn't take long. Three or four minutes later, Cody poked me. "Here he comes."

I looked up. Sure enough, El Cobra was walking down the middle of the dusty road toward us. I turned to Cody. "Okay, big guy. You up for this?"

He nodded, but he looked pretty scared.

"This is for Mom, Code. She'll be so relieved to have you with her. When it's safe, tell her everything that's happened."

"Okay."

I pulled him close and clung to him. "I love you, Code."

"I love you too, Danni."

Fighting not to choke on my tears, I turned him around, laid a hand on his shoulder, and gave him a gentle shove. "Take care."

"I will," he said as he started away. I took the rifle out of its case, then knelt down behind the ATV and rested it on the seat, training the sights on El Cobra's chest.

El Cobra came more than his half of the way. He came almost to the turnaround, stopping in the center of the dirt road about thirty feet from me. He had a sardonic grin on his face, as if he found the idea of me pointing a rifle at his chest amusing. He had fully recovered his swagger and his coming so close to me was nothing but "in your face" bravado. Mostly for the benefit of his men, I guessed.

Cody went to him. El Cobra tried to lay a hand on his shoulder but Cody jerked away.

El Cobra stepped in front of him, then turned back to me. "One more question, *chiquita*."

"No more questions. And just for the record, I don't like being called *chiquita*."

It was like spitting into the wind. He totally ignored me. "Could it be that the reason you offer me the pouch so willingly is because you know it will work only for you?"

I had expected this question and had rehearsed the answer in my mind. "I am not the first to own the pouch, nor will I be the last. It has been in our family for nearly two hundred years. The pouch responds to whoever carries it. The reason I am willing to give it up is to get you out of our lives and to have my family together and safe again."

I could see in his eyes that his mind was examining the issue from every angle.

"But there is one thing."

His eyebrows lifted.

"Before I turn it over to you, I will require that you take a solemn oath."

He didn't like that. "What kind of an oath?"

"That so long as you live, you will never come back into our lives again or seek in any way to use the pouch to bring harm upon me or my family. As long as you honor that oath, it will be yours to do with as you will. But know this—before I turn it over to you, I will place a curse on the pouch that should you ever go back on your word, your life will become one of endless torment."

I would have given anything to be able to see inside his mind at that point. His face was unreadable, but at last, he nodded. "Okay, *chiquita*. You leave me little choice. We'll do it your way." He motioned for Cody to move. "Back to the car." As they started away, he turned back. "We'll see you again soon, *chiquita*." And then with a smile that sent a chill up my back, he added, "You are like the chipmunk, little one. You stand on your hind legs and chatter at anything that moves. But underneath you are afraid. You are frightened. The tiniest thing makes you scamper for cover." He grinned, and his face was filled with hatred and pure malice.

Then, quick as the snake for which he was named, both hands

shot up, his fingers curling into talons. He leaped forward one step, clawing the air. "Boo!" he cried.

I jumped. It was so unexpected that I couldn't help it.

Laughing at his joke, he strode quickly to catch up with Cody, then waved back to me over his shoulder.

I gritted my teeth. If he wanted to play macho, I was game. I was tired of his condescension, his superiority, and his arrogance. I bent down, took careful aim, and squeezed the trigger. BLAM!

The bullet hit about eighteen inches to one side of him. He jumped and swung around, his eyes wild. "You are *loco*!" he yelled.

I stood up and cupped my hands to my mouth. "Boo!"

CHAPTER 61

Once the Yukon left, leaving two men sitting in the shade of the temple with their rifles, Rick came in. I heard a soft rustling in the sand, and I knew he was right behind me. I didn't turn around, but about a minute later, he came crawling on his belly, his dad's rifle cradled in his arms.

"Hi," I said with great feeling. Though I had known he was out there, it was wonderful to have him right here beside me.

In a soft, spooky voice, he said, "Listen to me, *El Cobra Pequeño,* if you ever threaten my family again, I shall place a curse on the magic pouch and your life will become one of endless torment." Then he laughed softly. "Holy cow, Danni. You ought to be in the movies."

Clay's voice crackled softly over the radio. "Amen. You even gave me the chills."

"Oh, stop it," I said, holding back a laugh. "My hands are still shaking like crazy."

Rick reached up and took one of them. "Liar. You're steady as a rock." He started to release his grip, but I hung on.

"It takes a few minutes to detect it," I said.

"Like how many?"

"About thirty."

He laughed, but he didn't let go. And it felt good.

After a minute or two, he carefully peeked around the ATV's front tire. "Do you know if they have binoculars?"

"I don't think so. All they're doing is sitting there smoking cigarettes. They're not very happy."

Clay came on again. "We're moving in."

"Don't get too close," I said quickly. "El Cobra probably left them with a satellite phone."

There was a soft chuckle. "Ah, Danni. Does the fox really think she needs to teach the weasel how to steal eggs?"

I laughed. "Sorry. Force of habit."

"Actually, I think it's wonderful. You're doing great. And we'll stay well out of sight until you call us in. In the meantime, tell us exactly what happened. We only caught part of what he was saying."

"Yeah," Rick said. "What did you give him after the money? He was really mad."

I told them.

"Say that again," Clay blurted.

"I gave him a bobble-head doll that was a perfect miniature of himself. It even had a name on the base: *Cobra Pequeño*. Little Cobra."

Rick let out a low whistle. "The pouch did that?"

"It did."

There was a long silence. "Are you still there?" I asked.

"Yeah, sorry," Clay said. "Just thinking there is yet another thing I'm not sure how to include in my report. But well done, Danni. Excellent work. You've not only thrown him off stride, you've got him angry. And greedy. Obviously, he's thinking about the pouch now and not just the twenty million. That can only work to our advantage."

"I hope so," I said.

"Hold on a sec. I've got a call coming in."

It was more than a second. It was three or four minutes before the radio popped softly again.

"Okay. That was from my guys in Hanksville. The Jeep came through about ten minutes ago. They stopped briefly at Danni's house and got some things. Your father and grandfather were with them. Then they took off again. How far is the Yukon behind them, Danni?"

"Maybe ten minutes or so."

"Okay, we'll watch for them."

———— ◆ ————

It was almost exactly ten minutes later when Clay came back on the radio. By this time I had angled the four-wheeler around enough to provide a little shade. I was sitting in the shade, but on the side of the ATV where the two men could still see me and I could watch them. Rick was sitting on the opposite side, hidden from view of the two men.

"Danni?" Clay called.

"Here."

"Just got word that the Yukon is in Hanksville. They're stopped at the gas station at the junction. No sign of Cody."

"They wouldn't let him out," I said. "Everyone in town knows him. But they'll regret not letting him stop. He's got a bladder the size of a bean."

Clay chuckled, then went on. "They left two men behind."

That caught me up short. Then I nodded. "Let me guess—Gordo and Doc."

"Say again."

"My names for them." I briefly explained how I had nicknamed them at the house. "Gordo is at least a foot shorter than Doc, and obviously likes to eat. Doc is tall and dark, very muscular, very buff. Ugly face, rough complexion. Gives me the creeps. Probably has a bandage on his right hand."

"How did you know that? He didn't have it on when he went in the station, but he did when he came back out."

I explained how the pistol had turned hot and burned his hand.

There was a soft exclamation of surprise. "Man, you are something else."

"Not me. *Le Gardien.*"

There was a momentary pause. "The Yukon filled up with gas before heading south. But these two—Doc and Gordo—had another vehicle waiting for them at one of the motels."

"A black Hummer?" I asked.

"No. Probably too recognizable. It's a silver Ford Explorer, Colorado plates. They were headed in your direction, then holed up in the willows along the river where they can see the highway. We assume they're waiting for you."

"Perfect!" I exclaimed. Rick and I exchanged looks. He nodded. "Then I'd say let's give the UHP a call."

"Already did. And by the way, she said to say hello."

"*She?*" Rick asked.

"Yeah, Officer Blake. Said she'd already met you two. Said I needed to hear that story some time."

I laughed softly. Maybe this was going to work after all.

"She'll be waiting at the Shell station. Drive by slowly so she sees you. And so she can see if anyone is following you. You're stopping for lunch, right?"

"Right. I'm famished, and Rick looks as though he's about to faint."

"I'm betting our two guys check out your vehicle while you're eating. So don't leave it unlocked. Too obvious. And, Danni, I would—"

"Clay. Are you forgetting that Hanksville is my town? Would you really try to teach the fox how to get into the henhouse?"

His laughter was a bark of delight. "Right. Sorry."

"Okay," I said, straightening. "We're moving."

"Ten-four. The chopper is standing by for your signal. Good luck."

I started the engine, put the ATV in gear, and started to roll. Up ahead, I could see both men come out to stand in the road. Both assault rifles were pointed at me. I drove slowly. The last thing I wanted to do was spook them. When I was about thirty or forty feet away from them, the nearest man held up one hand. I immediately brought the four-wheeler to a stop.

"Your boss should be out by now," I called. "Have you heard from him?"

They exchanged glances. Clearly, they were skittish. They were staring at me like I was wired with a bomb around my waist. Finally, the nearest one nodded. "You are free to go, *señorita*."

"I need to talk to El Cobra." I reached into my pocket and took out my cell phone. "I can't get reception out here, but I need to talk to him. So you call him and tell him that.'"

They conferred briefly, then the nearest guy punched some numbers into his satellite phone. He put the phone to his ear. As he did so, I touched the pouch with my fingertips. In a moment, his expression became perplexed. He entered the number again, but with the same result. He looked at his companion. They exchanged words in Spanish. Then he said, "No signal."

"I was hoping you'd say that." I raised one arm high and waved.

BLAM! Again the crack of a rifle shattered the stillness. A spray of sand shot up from between them. They jumped and whirled around, dropping into a crouch.

I yanked my rifle out and fired a round into the air. "Drop your weapons! Put your hands in the air."

Rick and I watched as Clay's men loaded the two men into the chopper, hands cuffed behind them. They were guarded by two agents in addition to Clay. I was holding their satellite phone. I hit the power button and heard a dial tone. "It's working again. You two ready?"

Both Rick and Clay nodded. I hit the redial button and the phone started beeping immediately. It only rang once before someone picked it up.

"Hola." It was Eileen's voice.

"This is Danni. Put El Cobra on."

She muttered something in Spanish, but a few moments later, El Cobra was on. "What are doing?" he demanded.

"Just so you know, your two guys are so spooked by the pouch, they want nothing more to do with you and your deal."

"What have you done with them?" he screamed, his voice cracking with rage.

"Never laid a hand on them. Last I saw, they were headed west, putting as much distance between you and them as possible. They're hoping they can find someone who will give them a ride out to the west entrance. I have their phone. I'll keep it with me so if we need to talk we can."

As he began cursing and raving, I terminated the connection. I handed the phone to Clay. "Can we go now?"

Clay was beaming. "Well done, guys. Want a lift to your truck?"

I shook my head. "We'll take the four-wheeler. We may need it for phase two."

"Right. And by the way, as promised, the item you requested is in the truck."

I gave him a thumbs up. "See you in Ireland."

CHAPTER 62

By the time we took the four-wheeler around to Rick's truck on top of the mesa, got it loaded in the back of the pickup, and drove out to the highway, it was coming up on two o'clock. We turned east. Hanksville was about twelve miles away.

"We could have a problem," Rick said. "They'll be looking for my truck, not this one. Be a shame if they missed us."

I took out my cell phone and waved it in front of him. "They won't miss us. They already know we're coming."

***

Rick let the truck slow as we passed the reduced speed limit sign on the west outskirts of Hanksville. A minute later we both saw it at the same time. A silver Explorer was parked in the shade of a tamarisk tree about twenty yards off the road.

Rick watched the rearview mirror as we continued into town. About thirty seconds later, he nodded. "They just pulled onto the highway, coming our way."

A few moments later, we slowly rolled past the Shell station. Parked on the east side of the building was a white Utah Highway Patrol car. I nudged Rick. "There she is." A woman in uniform was standing beside the car. As we passed, she raised a hand and waved. I waved back. "All right," I said. "Let's get some lunch."

We pulled into the station at the junction, the famous one with the convenience store carved out of a cliff face. "Give me a minute," I said. As Rick waited, I checked to make sure my blouse was pulled out and hung loose around my waist.

"You can't tell," Rick said. "Not unless you really look close."

"Okay. Let's go."

After filling up the truck, Rick went in to pay, and we both took a bathroom break. When we came back out, I looked into the front seat of the truck. The pouch was still on the seat where I had left it. Not a big surprise. There were too many people around and the truck was right in the middle of the parking lot. Without being too obvious, I glanced around. No Explorer in sight.

"I'm ravenous," I called to Rick. "How about some lunch?"

"I'm with you on that one." We moved the car away from the pumps over to the restaurant, which was next door. There were several cars out front, so Rick pulled around to the side and parked beside an old truck rusting in the sun; it partially obscured our truck from the highway.

I hid the pouch under the seat, then reminded Rick to lock the doors as we got out and headed inside.

We were warmly greeted by some of the locals—both staff and customers. We were back in home country. The good thing was nobody seemed to have noticed we'd been gone all week.

When we came out forty-five minutes later, I stopped on the veranda of the restaurant and stretched, using it as an opportunity to look around. Still no sign of the Explorer or anything suspicious.

As soon as Rick unlocked the doors, I checked under the seat. The pouch was gone. They had taken the bait. I felt a thrill of elation, but for anyone possibly watching, I gave a loud cry. "Rick, the pouch is gone."

"Are you sure? I thought you put it under the seat."

"I did. But it's gone. Didn't you lock the truck?"

"I did. You saw me do it."

"Then how can the pouch be gone?"

"I don't know, Danni. But we can't just stand here wailing about it. We've got to keep moving."

"What'll I do?" I cried. "That pouch is our only hope against these guys."

Shaking his head, he told me to get in the car. I did so reluctantly, but once we drove away, turning south onto Highway 95, I gave him a shaky grin. "Okay, so far, so good." I checked the bulk around my waist. The rope handle was digging in a little, so I readjusted it, then looked at Rick. "Round two."

About five minutes later, Rick looked up, staring in his rearview mirror. "Danni?"

"Yeah?"

"I think that's the Explorer behind us. Maybe three quarters of a mile back."

I looked out the back window. The vehicle behind us was far enough away that it was pretty small, but I could tell it was a light-colored SUV. "I think you're right. Okay. Hold it right at sixty-five. It's Saturday afternoon. With all the Lake Powell traffic, they're not going to run us off the road. Especially if there's a highway patrol car between us and them."

This was one of the trickiest parts of the whole plan. We needed things to happen at the right time and in the right place. That was critical. If El Cobra's men decided to run us off the road or something like that, it would change everything. To ensure that wouldn't happen, Clay's plan was that Officer Blake would leave Hanksville while we had lunch. She would stop alongside the road a few miles south of town, looking like she had set up a speed trap. Once we passed her, she'd pull out, putting herself between us and the Explorer. We hoped that would ensure that our two pursuers didn't try something before we wanted them too.

It sounded great, but there were so many ways things could go wrong that my stomach was doing flip-flops, handstands, and somersaults. I knew it would be a major mistake to underestimate El Cobra's determination or his ingenuity. Everything depended on Officer Blake.

"Okay, there she is," Rick said as we crested a low rise and could see the highway ahead for some distance. Up ahead, about half a mile, a white Utah Highway Patrol car was pulled off on our side of the road. Officer Blake was right where she was supposed to be.

"Tap your brakes. We all do that when we see a cop ahead of us."

He did so, then took a quick breath. "I hope this works."

As we flashed by her at sixty-five miles an hour, I saw that she was sitting behind the wheel. "Not too quickly," I murmured, watching her in the side view mirror. "We need you right between us." Then, to my astonishment, the lights atop her cruiser came on, and she roared onto the highway behind us.

"What?" I cried. "No. Wait."

But it was too late. She was in full pursuit, gaining on us quickly, red-and-blue lights flashing ominously.

Rick started to brake, heading for a place where the shoulder was wide enough to accommodate us. "What's going on?" he said, watching his mirror.

I didn't answer. The Explorer was still a ways back, but it was slowing too.

"What is she thinking?" I said through clenched teeth. "Didn't Clay tell her how critical this part of the plan was?"

"Well, we're about to find out," he said as Officer Blake opened her door and got out. Leaving the lights flashing, she started toward us. Rick rolled down the window.

"Sorry," she said as she came up and leaned in. "Change of plans. Zabriskie called on the satellite phone. Your brother is in a speed-boat with El Cobra headed downriver toward Iceberg Canyon. But four men left Bullfrog about ten minutes ago in the white Yukon. Clay thinks they're on their way to help the two guys behind you. This increases the risk tremendously, and he recommends we abort. He told me to pull you over, let our guys pass, then get you back to Hanksville."

"No!" I cried. "We can't abort. We won't get another chance like this."

She glanced back, and I turned to look. The Explorer was five or six hundred yards back and still coming, but not much faster than a crawl. I could only imagine what was going on in their vehicle right now.

Blake turned back to me. "Zabriskie knows you're disappointed, but he says that six men changes the whole equation."

I had to look away. Disappointed didn't come close to describing how I felt. I had pulled off a major coup this morning and reduced El Cobra's forces by two men, and now Clay was getting cold feet? This was what I had been afraid of in the first place. That was the bottom line, wasn't it? The kids couldn't handle it.

Officer Blake saw the dismay on my face. "I'm sorry. The risks are just too high."

"Wait a minute," Rick said. "We're what, twenty miles from the turnoff to Bullfrog? But Bullfrog is forty miles past that. We'll be way past the junction by the time they get there and can meet up with those guys behind us."

I reached for my the satellite phone. "I'm calling El Cobra. I'll tell him we know about the men and have him back off."

"That won't work, Danni," Rick shot right back. "Supposedly, you don't have the pouch anymore. There's no way you could know about the other men unless you're working with the police. And that could be disastrous." He glanced in the rearview mirror. "Besides, here they come."

As I started to turn, his hand shot out and grabbed my arm. "No! Don't look at them. Let them pass."

Officer Blake turned her head as well, and she suddenly stiffened. "Uh-oh."

I couldn't help myself. I had to see what she had seen. When I did, I went rigid too. The Explorer's turn signal was flashing, and they were pulling off the highway about twenty yards behind the patrol car.

Blake reached down and unbuckled her holster. "Stay here. I'll handle this."

As she started toward them, the Explorer came to a full stop. Blake held up a hand. The driver's door opened and Doc got out.

"Sir," she called. "Please move on. This is a routine traffic stop. We don't need any help. Get back in your vehicle and move on."

Doc started forward, smiling. "Officer, that's my niece and nephew in the truck," he said, smooth as oil. "I wanted to make sure they're all right."

Blake glanced back. I shook my head emphatically. "It's them," I cried in a low voice. But when Blake turned back, already pulling her weapon from its holster, it was too late.

Doc held a pistol in his bandaged hand. Behind him, Gordo was out of the car with an assault rifle trained on her.

"Oh," Doc said easily, "I think this is anything but a routine traffic stop. Hands off your weapon. Now!"

She hesitated for a moment, then complied. Gordo moved in quickly, coming around behind her to cover the three of us.

Doc motioned with his pistol. "Ma'am, we don't want any trouble. Unbuckle your gun belt with your left hand and let it drop to the ground. Then step away from the truck."

She did as she was told. As Gordo collected the gun belt, Doc moved to my side of the truck and yanked the door open. He waved the gun at Rick. "Out! Both of you." We got out of the truck. Doc's eyes were murderous as he glared at Rick. "You're the one who shot at me, boy. I'd love an excuse to even the score."

"Car coming," Gordo sang out. "Everybody look natural." He lowered his rifle and turned his back to the road.

The car whipped past us, and instantly we felt the blast of wind from its passing.

"All right," Doc said. "We can't stand out here. Listen up. I would really rather not shoot anyone today, so here's what we're going to do. Officer, get back in your vehicle. Don't be foolish enough to touch your radio. Danni, you get in the back of the patrol car. Lew, you'll ride with her. Ramirez, you'll drive your truck until we find a place to ditch it. Patrol car will go first. You second. I'll bring up the rear."

He turned to Blake. "Do you have nylon strap handcuffs?"

Her eyes flicked to me, then away. "Yes. There are four sets in a bag in the trunk."

"Get two pair, Lew. Cuff the girl, hands in front. Hold off on the kid until he's no longer driving." As Lew started moving, he called after him. "And once Danni is secure, look in the truck. She had a rifle. Ramirez may have one too. Make sure the truck is clean."

As Lew jumped into action, Doc motioned to Blake with his pistol. She got back into her car. He reached across her, grabbed the microphone from its hook, and ripped it hard, snapping the coiled wire. He then leaned farther in and took her satellite phone. He looked at it suspiciously. "Satellite phones are now issued to the UHP?"

I jerked up, resisting the urge to look at her, to warn her not to say anything about Clay. But I had underestimated her. Without a moment's hesitation, she said, "Some places out here are so remote they can't even reach us by radio."

That seemed to satisfy him, and I resumed breathing. Lew was back in a minute and cuffed me. "I'm going to leave these loose enough that they don't bite into your flesh," he said, "but mess with me, and I'll pull 'em so tight your fingers will turn blue. Understand?"

"Yes."

He grabbed my elbow and steered me into the back of the patrol car, slamming the door behind me. Moments later, he emerged from our truck holding up both of our rifles for Doc to see. "The little bees have stingers," he chortled.

Doc looked at Rick. "We're going to ditch your truck and the ATV, but not here. In the meantime, you'll stay exactly four car lengths behind the patrol car. I think you understand what will happen to Danni if you decide to be a hero."

"I do."

"Then let's go. Officer, hold your speed at exactly sixty-five miles an hour. We'll be stopping at the turnoff to Ticaboo and Bullfrog and waiting for some company there."

So El Cobra had already told them help was on the way. That was a major complication. Leprechaun Canyon was two miles beyond that junction. We absolutely could not stop at that junction.

Doc was still talking to Blake. "Sorry you had to get involved in this, but behave yourself and all you'll have is a long walk in the desert. Otherwise . . ."

"I understand."

He looked more closely at Rick's belt, and then yanked the radio from it. He waved it at Lew. "See if the girl's got one too. If so, get it."

"Right," Gordo called. He got in the backseat, leaned over and took my radio, then sat back and put on his seat belt. He turned to me, laughing. "Buckle up, sweetheart. Don't you know riding in a car without seat belts is dangerous?"

I held up my hands, reminding him they were cuffed. Bad mistake.

Grinning wickedly, he undid his seat belt and leaned across me, his face inches from my own. His eyes never left mine as he fastened my seat belt. Still very close to me, he pursed his lips as if he were about to kiss me.

A shudder ran completely up and down my body.

He roared with laughter and moved away from me, fastening his own seat belt. "Ah, *señorita*," he crowed. "It is a great day, no?"

Thirty seconds later, our little convoy was underway.

CHAPTER 63

Lew, or Gordo, was in a good mood. He sat directly behind Officer Blake, humming some nameless tune to himself, and glancing at me and grinning.

"What's so funny?" I finally snapped.

"You."

"You must be easily amused."

"Little Wonder Girl, waving her wand around, shooting lightning bolts from her fingertips. You even had El Cobra on the run there for a while. Now look at you. Take that pouch away, and you're just a skinny little kid, no different than anyone else."

"I'm skinnier than you, that's for sure."

He patted the roundness of his belly. "But not nearly as jolly, no?" His stomach jiggled as he laughed loudly.

"Where are you taking us?"

He laughed again. *"No comprendes."*

"Where's my mother?"

"No comprendes, señorita." He leaned forward and poked Officer Blake's arm. "She's a funny one, no?"

I looked out the window, despair filling my throat with bitterness. If only Clay had let things be and not told Blake to warn us that the plan was aborted. Okay, so it was nice that he was concerned about our safety, but that wasn't the only issue here. What had just happened probably created a much greater danger.

Stop it! I told myself. *Save the "poor me" routine for later. If you insist on worrying, worry about Rick and Officer Blake. You know El Cobra's not going to have Doc bring them out to the houseboat. You will be fine, at least until Tuesday, but they're nothing but excess baggage.*

Another shudder started, but I shook it off. I was angry with myself, and it felt good. *Get back on task, Danni. Time's running out. If your great-grandmother were here right now, you know what she would say: "Never give up."*

I could see the top of Officer Blake's forehead in the rearview mirror. What was she thinking? Did she know how much danger she was in? Was she waiting for me to do something? And what about Rick? Was he back there vowing to himself that he would never again be sucked into something involving Danni McAllister?

Maybe he was making another list right now: "Stupid Things Danni Has Done." Number one: Her stupid obsession with pushing the speed limit. Number two: Assuming that once invisible, always invisible. Number three: Coming to our house and dragging my family into all this. Number four: Writing on a woman's windshield to try to get her to go faster. Number five: Picking a fight with the guy in the red truck.

I sighed heavily. *Number six: Thinking you could make everything go exactly as you planned today and—*

Oh, stop it, McAllister. Give me a break.

Then another thought came, and my eyes flew wide open. What

about that sports car? Similar scenario, right? You have a woman in a car, and you want to say something to her, but you can't talk to her directly. So . . .

I glanced at Gordo. His eyes were focused straight ahead. He was alert but bored. I sat up straighter in my seat, drawing his attention. His head swung around, eyes wary.

"Ow!" I moaned. "These cuffs are killing me. Can't you loosen them up a little?"

"I am sorry, *señorita*," he said, his voice dripping with phony concern, "nylon handcuffs don't have keys. They have to be cut off. Do you really want me to get my knife out?"

I looked away. He relaxed and went back to humming. After a moment, I looked at the rearview mirror again. It had worked. By sitting up straight, I was tall enough that I could see Officer Blake's eyes. She was looking at me. She seemed relieved to finally be doing so.

I glanced at Gordo. Could he see her too? No. He could see the mirror, but not her in it. Wrong angle.

I dropped my hands into my lap, then, when I was sure he was paying no attention to me, I felt along my waist, touching the extra thickness of the pouch—the real pouch—beneath. I thought of Grandpère searching in the forest for a downed pilot. I thought of Great-Grandmother Monique inside the Gestapo headquarters in Paris. I felt my confidence surge. What was a fat guy with bad breath compared to that?

I pinched a corner of the fabric between my thumb and forefinger and focused intently on the mirror. I nearly shouted aloud when I saw the first white letters appear. *Yes!* For some reason, this time the words were written in upper and lowercase letters, not all caps.

Officer Blake. This is Danni. If you can read this, blink once.

Instead of blinking, she physically jerked, her eyes startled and frightened.

I released my grip on the pouch. The writing faded away.

Gordo shot forward, his pistol jerking up. "Something the matter, baby?"

She tensed, then shook her head quickly. "No. I . . . I'm not sure what it was. Maybe a pinched nerve or something."

"Well," he growled, "just remember, if you get jumpy then I get grumpy." He hooted aloud, delighted with his play on words. I wondered if he and Doc had enjoyed a bottle of tequila in their Explorer. He was certainly having a good time.

I squeezed the pouch again.

Can't explain. Can you read this? Blink once for yes, twice for no.

Which was stupid, really. If she couldn't read it, how would she know to blink twice? But though she was looking very bewildered, her eyes blinked once.

Good. Did the FBI tell you about the Irish Canyons?

One blink.

Just east of the junction of Utah Highways 276 and 95, Highway 95 enters a long, red-rock canyon known as the North Wash. Eventually it drains into Lake Powell, not far from Hite Marina. Running off from that canyon is a series of other canyons, all feeding into the wash. Three of the more spectacular slot canyons are known as the Irish Canyons because they all have Irish names—Shillelagh, Blarney, and Leprechaun Canyons. That was where Rick and I had decided the second stage of our plan would take place.

As I watched the mirror, I was totally blown away when my message faded out and another appeared, this time in all caps.

YES. HE SAID WE'RE GOING TO LEPRECHAUN CANYON. RIGHT?

She could communicate back to me? That was seriously amazing.

Yes. It's critical we get there.

One blink, then *HOW, IF WE'RE FORCED TO STOP AT JUNCTION?*

Still working on that.

GIVE ME SOME WARNING?

Yes. How far to the junction?

Nothing for a few moments, then *FIVE TO SIX MINUTES.*

Great. Leprechaun is close.

I KNOW IT WELL.

Will distract Gordo. Don't stop at the junction! Turn off at Leprechaun parking area.

One blink. Long pause, then *ARE YOU SURE?*

I blinked back at her twice. *Not in any way. Just be ready.*

After another long pause, she blinked once.

I jumped as Lew's elbow dug into my left arm. "You praying?"

Not sure what he meant, I gave him a blank look.

There was a wicked grin. "I can see your lips moving. May as well admit it."

That jolted me. Had I been so engrossed in my conversation with Officer Blake that I was actually forming the words silently? Evidently so.

"I'm praying for your soul," I finally said. "I'm asking God to have mercy on you and not leave you in hell for more than ten thousand years."

There was a short bark of laughter, but not before I caught the look of fear that flickered in his eyes.

———

As we passed mile marker 25, I cleared my throat. "Officer Blake, I'm thirsty. Do you have any water?" I had seen a bottle of water in the cup holder by her seat.

"I do." She turned to look at Gordo. "May I?"

He thought about it for a moment, then switched the pistol to his left hand. He reached over the seat and grabbed the bottle. Clamping it between his legs, he twisted off the cap. He looked at me for a moment, amusement dancing in his eyes. Then he lifted the bottle and took a long swig. "Ah," he said, as he finished. Then he peered more closely at the top of the bottle. "Oh, dear. It looks like I spilled a little."

His grin was a horrible grimace. He brought the bottle to his mouth and, with exaggerated care, ran his tongue all the way around the edge. "There you go, *señorita*. Still thirsty?"

I was close to gagging, but I held his gaze. This might be the opportunity I needed. I swallowed hard, then nodded.

No!

I drew back, surprised by the sharpness of the voice in my head.

"What's the matter, *chiquita?* Weak stomach?"

Refuse him. Goad him. Make him angry.

"Better a weak stomach than a weak brain, Gordo."

His eyes narrowed dangerously. "Watch your tongue, little one."

"Or what? You'll breathe on me and make me throw up?"

He jammed the pistol between his legs, switched the bottle to his left hand, and grabbed me by the neck. He yanked me toward him and forced the bottle up against my teeth, pressing so hard that I felt the plastic cut my lip. "Drink it!" he yelled.

Blake turned to see what was happening.

"Unless you want a bullet in the head," he screamed, "keep your eyes forward."

I was fighting him like a wildcat—kicking at his shins, jerking my head back and forth, trying to punch him with my cuffed hands. But his grip on my neck tightened. Pain shot down my back and arms. I screamed.

He laughed. I surrendered, going totally limp in one instant. It startled him, then he gave a cry of triumph. He took my face in both of his hands and this time when he leaned in, it wasn't the bottle he was going to press to my lips.

Now!

My hands shot forward and I grabbed the pistol from between his legs.

Startled, he fell back, trying to block my hands. Too late. Clutching the gun tightly in both hands, I pointed the pistol directly at his nose. "Move back! Move back!"

He didn't just move back. He literally fell back, pressing himself against the opposite door.

"Are we to the junction yet?" I yelled at Blake.

"Just ahead."

"Don't stop!"

We blew through it at sixty-five miles an hour. Instantly, the radio popped. "Lew! Stop! We're stopping here."

Using both of my thumbs, I cocked the hammer. "Take out the radio and hand it to Officer Blake," I hissed. "Now!"

He did so, his eyes glazed with shock.

"Tell him this pig just tried to kiss me. That's why we missed the turnoff."

She took the radio and clicked it. "This is Officer Blake."

"What's going on?"

"Your man just tried to kiss Miss McAllister. She has his pistol pointed at his head."

"*What?* Lew, are you there?"

I said to Lew, "Tell your friend what you tried to do. Or I'll shoot you right now."

Officer Blake held down the transmitter button, and Gordo barked out a couple of sentences in Spanish, none of which I understood.

"Danni?" Doc said. "I apologize for my associate. You're right. He is a pig. But put down the gun. Otherwise I press one button on the phone and your mother and little brother will die."

"I know that. I'll surrender the pistol, but you tell this animal to stay away from me."

There was another burst of Spanish, this time from Doc. A very subdued Gordo kept nodding and saying, *"Sí. Sí. Sí."*

"All right. Give Lew back the gun."

"No way," I shouted. Turning, I rolled down the window and threw away the pistol.

There was a screech of tires. Behind us, Rick had swerved sharply to miss the pistol coming at him. I turned and saw it still bouncing as the Explorer swerved as well.

"There's your pistol," I shouted into the radio.

"Stop the car," Doc yelled. "I'm coming up."

"Not until you promise to get this creep out of here."

"Officer Blake, stop the car. Now!"

"I can't do that, sir," she said, "not until we have your assurance that Danni will not be harmed."

I waved at Blake to get her attention. When she looked back, I mouthed, *How much farther?*

Half a mile, she mouthed back.

"You have my word," Doc shouted over the radio. "Now stop the car or I will."

When Blake pressed the button to answer, Lew screamed, "Raul, they're up to something."

I kicked at him, catching him in the knees. His hands formed into claws, but as he lunged at me, he stopped then dropped his hands again. I don't know what Doc had said to him, but it must have been pretty serious. He sat back, breathing hard, watching me with baleful eyes. Then he turned to Blake. "If you do not stop the car now, it will go very badly for you."

Intervene! cried the voice in my head.

Intervene? What did that mean?

Remember the red truck.

I pinched *Le Gardien* hard. As I did so, the patrol car's engine coughed, and the whole car shuddered. It coughed again, making that same horrible grinding sound the red truck had made on the on-ramp.

Seeing that Blake was absorbed in dealing with this new crisis, Lew snatched the radio from her hand. He pressed the transmit button. "Raul! Something's wrong with the engine. We're stopping."

If Doc answered, I didn't hear it. I peered out the front window, looking for the turnoff into the parking area for Leprechaun Canyon. Nothing. I suddenly remembered it was around the next curve. I let go of the pouch. The engine roared into life and leaped forward. Tires squealed as we leaned into the curve. The parking lot was about a hundred yards ahead. I gripped the pouch, and the engine lurched again. Instantly we were slowing.

Lew was going wild. "Pull over, pull over," he shouted.

I hope you're ready, Rick. It was a silent shout. Who knew what was going through his mind? He didn't have a radio and therefore had heard none of this. I looked back. Thick blue smoke was pouring out of our exhaust, half obscuring Rick's truck. That would help. *Remember the red truck, Rick.*

"Look," Blake shouted. "There's a turnoff. On the left. Let's get off the highway."

Fortunately, there was no traffic coming in either direction. Blake turned on her blinker and, a moment later, one by one, we turned onto a narrow dirt road. She continued on it for about seventy-five yards before coming to a small parking area. As soon as we reached it, the engine made one last awful sound and died.

I already had my hands on the door handle. I yanked it hard, threw my shoulder against the door, and tumbled out. I was up and running before the car stopped rolling.

CHAPTER 64

As I raced away, I saw three things simultaneously: Gordo shouting and hammering on the door handle, trying to get it to open; Rick tumbling out of the truck then racing away in a hard sprint; and Doc, looking startled. He was yelling and waving his pistol. I saw him throw himself against his door, but his door wouldn't open either.

All we needed was a short head start, and we'd be into heavy brush that would make it hard to see us. And that's what the pouch was giving us.

At the east end of the parking area, which was only large enough to hold five or six cars, the road abruptly narrowed into a walking path. I could hear Rick coming right behind me. Staying low, we ran at full speed. I watched the ground carefully because if I tripped and fell, I knew I would go down hard; my hands were still held together by the nylon strap.

The parking area was actually part of the dry wash that was at the mouth of Leprechaun Canyon. But because it was a wash, even in the full heat of summer, the occasional rainstorm brought enough moisture to keep the wash a green oasis in the desert. There were a few scrubby trees with thornlike needles, a lot of tall sagebrush, scattered willowy bushes five and six feet high, and lots of reeds. The foliage would be our protection until we reached the canyon itself. Our pursuers would find it relatively easy to follow us if we stayed on the path, but they had no way of knowing if we would or not, so they would, of necessity, be slower than we were. That was an important advantage.

The path moved up the side hills a little to avoid the more clogged parts of the wash. At one point, we stopped to catch our breath. I turned around, scanning the trail behind us. Just as I spotted Doc's head coming through the underbrush, a rifle cracked. There was a sharp slap as the bullet hit the rock face ten or fifteen feet above my head.

I yelped and dropped into a crouch. Had that been a warning shot, or had Doc just not had a clear shot? One thing was sure: Doc and I did not get along.

"Let's go," I cried. "They're about two minutes behind us."

"How far to the canyon?"

The Irish Canyons were a favorite camping place for my family, but Rick had never been here. "Maybe half a mile or so. But they'll have to go slower than we do."

As the path quickly narrowed, we dropped into single file, trotting briskly. "Danni," Rick called.

"What?"

"Do you think they'll hurt Officer Blake?"

"No. She didn't do anything. They probably just cuffed her to the steering wheel."

"Good. Try not to be a target anymore. I think this Doc guy is through playing around."

"Got it," I said. I was coming to the same conclusion.

———

Ten minutes later, I stepped off the path and scampered up the steep rock face on our right. The canyon walls were closing in fast and getting much steeper. This time, I kept low, staying in a crouch until I reached a place where I could peek over and see down into the wash below us. I looked at Rick, putting a finger to my lips. When I scanned the wash below, it took me only about ten seconds to see Doc's head again. I couldn't see Gordo, but I guessed he was right behind Doc.

I came back down, jumping the last five or six feet into the soft red sand. "We're gaining a little on them. They're maybe three minutes behind us. That's good. We'll be into the canyon in another minute or so, and to the junction where the canyon splits in maybe five to seven more. If we can make it that far, we're home free."

"You sure that *free* is the right word in this context?"

I didn't laugh. "Rick?"

"Yes?"

"Be careful. They're not going to hurt me. They won't risk that. But you are of no use to them, I am sorry to say. So if they catch us, don't fight them. I think they'll just tie you up and leave you somewhere."

"Are you suggesting I can't keep up with you?" he asked dryly.

"No. I'm suggesting that, to them, you're excess baggage."

He smiled wanly, and we continued on.

One of the things that makes Southern Utah so breathtakingly beautiful is the nature of its geology. Millions of years ago, it was covered by a great inland sea. When it receded, it left thousands of square miles of soft sandstone, much of it a deep reddish-brown from the iron. Carved by the forces of nature, the land became an endless variety of plateaus, mesas, canyons, upthrusts, and deep gorges.

Slot canyons are formed when rainwater and snowmelt follow the natural pull of gravity, relentless as time itself, and cut their way into the soft sandstone. In some places, deep fissures form in the rock. If the fissure is deep enough, it becomes a canyon of its own, eroding ever deeper, until it creates a canyon that can be hundreds of feet deep, yet no more than a few feet wide in some places.

The slot canyons of the Southwest United States are infinite in their variety and stunning in their beauty. The Irish Canyons are just three of hundreds of such marvels, and Leprechaun Canyon is considered by most to be the best of the three.

When Rick and I entered Leprechaun Canyon, the walls had closed in to where they were only twenty or thirty feet apart. The deep vermillion cliffs rose two or three hundred feet straight up above our heads, making us feel like we were ants in a cathedral. The canyon floor, which was actually the sandy bed of the water channel, was serpentine, turning and twisting every few yards, allowing us to see only a short distance ahead or behind. The lower portions of the walls were striated, showing the action of the water on the stone.

We moved along at a trot, side by side, not speaking, listening intently for any sound of pursuit. Fortunately, the narrow walls of a slot canyon served as amplifiers, sending sound echoing up and down the narrow passages. If our two pursuers were closing in, we would know it soon enough.

As we rounded yet another twist in the canyon, we could see where the canyon pinched down to a very narrow slot.

"That's a pretty tight stretch up ahead, but it's not a long one," I explained in a low voice. "Both of us can get through it, though it'll be a squeeze for you. Doc too. Gordo, though? I'm not sure. Depends how flabby his tummy is."

"So what will Doc do if Gordo can't come through?"

"Not sure. There's a fairly easy way up and around the spot, but they won't know that. Doc will come after us alone if he has to, but I'm sure he'd rather not. Not with two of us to contend with."

"Knowing Doc," Rick said, "he'll kick Lew hard enough to get him through, even if it means leaving a couple of pounds behind on the rock."

"Agreed. After we get through there, I know a spot where we can wait to see if they both make it."

"Isn't that cutting things a little close?"

"It's close, but not too close. You okay with that?"

"If you think it's important, then it's important."

"I think it's important. We need to know what we're up against."

"Then let's go."

I let Rick go first in case I needed to give him a shove, but while he had to really suck in his stomach in one place, he made it through without much difficulty. I followed without any trouble.

As we broke into a trot again, Rick said, "I hope that's the tightest place we have to go through."

"Don't tell me you're claustrophobic."

"No. Just a little fatter than you."

Smiling at his joke was a relief, because I knew what was coming and was feeling a touch claustrophobic myself. I thought it was ironic that I hated being in an underground mine because they cause me to experience some mild to medium claustrophobia. But slot canyons don't freak me out, even though they are often much tighter and more confining than a mine shaft. I'd asked Dad about it once, and he thought it was because the slot canyons are open to the sky. And he was right. The thought of all those thousands of tons of rock over my head made me crazy. But I'd been through Leprechaun Canyon before and there was only one place where it was almost totally dark. The sky was up there somewhere, but it was so far up and hidden by the twist of the canyon walls, it didn't feel like it. I knew I'd have to force myself to really focus on there being sky above me to stop me from freaking out.

"Here," I said, pointing to where a low ridge of rock jutted out into the canyon. "We can wait here."

As we settled in, Rick touched my arm. "*Are* there tighter places than that?" he whispered.

I flashed him a quick smile.

He shook his head, serious. "We've got two guys with guns after us, Danni. And you're still handcuffed. How tight is it?"

I sobered. He was right. Keeping my voice low, I said, "Be sure you take your wallet out of your back pocket before you start."

"Come on, Danni. I'm serious. Have you been through here before?"

"Just once. Mom didn't come with us. She found a place to paint and waited for us outside. Dad and Grandpère couldn't make it. They had to go around on the top. My uncle Glade, Dad's younger brother, took me and Cody through. Glade's built like a greyhound, but he still lost two buttons off his shirt. Cody's a worm, so it was a piece of cake for him. But I can show you where I left some flesh when we came through. And I tore the button off my shorts and had to hold them up by hand until we got back to the car."

"Way too much information," Rick said in dismay. "Why didn't you tell me all this before? If you could barely make it, then how in the world—"

I punched him softly on the shoulder. "The narrowest place in the canyon is a little more than twelve inches wide, but—"

"Twelve inches!" he yelped.

"Shh!" Then I smiled. "Did I happen to mention that we're not going that far into the canyon?"

He glared at me. "Speaking of worms," he said, "you're pretty much a worm yourself."

"It's still going to be a tight fit, Rick. I wasn't kidding about the wallet. Put it in your front pocket so it's out of the way. The canyon will be about fifteen inches in one place."

Before I could say more, we heard sounds from below us. We both dropped on our bellies, peering over the rock at the spot where the slot opened up and became a full canyon again. There was definitely a murmur of voices, and I estimated Doc and Gordo were still four or five minutes away.

I spotted a rock with a jagged edge. I scooted over to it and started sawing the nylon cuffs on the edge. It seemed to be working. If only I had another week to keep at it. "I should have kept the pistol," I grumbled. "We could use it about now."

Suddenly we heard a cry. Gordo. "I can't get through there."

"Shut up, fool!" Doc's voice hissed in Spanish. "You can make it. Don't hold the rifle in front of you. Hold it out at arm's length."

With a start, I realized my gift of interpretation was back. I cocked my head to one side, listening intently.

A few seconds later, Gordo wailed again. "I'm stuck, Raul. Don't leave me."

"How can I leave you, stupid? I'm behind you, remember? Keep your shoulders turned sideways. If the Ramirez kid made it, you can make it."

I glanced at Rick and smiled. Doc's logic was somewhat faulty, considering the size difference between Rick and Gordo. I raised up higher. If Gordo was stuck, I wasn't worried about anyone popping out and surprising us, and I wanted to see what they were doing. As I moved, I saw the top of a head with wisps of dark black hair covering a large bald spot. It was Gordo. And out in front of him, I saw something else—the barrel of his assault rifle.

My hand shot out and grabbed Rick's arm. "I've got an idea."

"What are you doing?" he said into my ear.

There was another burst of Spanish. I grinned. "Doc says he's going to shoot Gordo if he doesn't keep moving. I think he's pushing him." Before Rick could react, I leaped up and scuttled away in a low crouch.

"No, Danni!" Rick's cry was involuntary, but Gordo's head jerked up and he saw me instantly.

"There she is, Raul. It's the girl." Then panic. "She's coming."

"Go, you idiot!" Doc screamed. "Push!"

I gasped as I felt someone grab me around the waist and toss me aside. "I'll get it," Rick said and shot past me.

There wasn't time to be mad. Another foot and Gordo would be through the tight spot and able to raise his rifle.

Gordo was stuck in an unusual part of the canyon. The slot itself was only about seven feet deep on one side because the south cliff face opened up there, leaving a rock slab that formed a shelf parallel to the slot for several feet.

Rick scooped up a handful of sand, then darted onto the shelf. As he reached Gordo, he flung the sand into his face.

The fat man let out a howl and started cursing.

Ignoring him, Rick leaned down, grabbed the rifle barrel, and yanked it free.

"Raul! He got the rifle."

"Go!" Rick yelled at me, waving wildly as he sprinted back toward me.

As I stood up, I heard a loud thump, a whoosh of air, and a cry of pain. Gordo popped out of the slot like a cork from a champagne bottle and went sprawling on his face.

"Get him! Get him!" Doc was yelling. I could see his dark shape pushing through the slot as rapidly as he could. I could also see that he was holding a pistol in his bandaged hand.

"Go! Go! Go!" Rick shouted. But I had already decided that I had seen more than enough and took off running.

CHAPTER 65

"We've got to slow them down," I cried as we ran up the canyon. A short distance above the first slot, the canyon abruptly opened up into an area called the Subway. It roughly resembled a subway tunnel and was big enough to hold a pair of parallel tracks. We were coming up on it fast. In one place, the Subway was at least a hundred feet long, a straight shot that had no significant cover.

Rick swung around and dropped behind a desk-sized boulder. "Keep going," he called. "I'll catch up."

I nearly stopped too, but knew this was no time for an ego contest. Rick pulled back the lever on the rifle and put a shell in the chamber. As I reached the other end of the Subway, I heard the rifle crack once, then twice. The sound was deafening as it echoed up and down the length of the Subway. Another crack. Then the lighter sound of pistol fire followed.

Rick came into view, running hard. "That'll make them think twice before coming on a dead run. How much time do we need?"

"Just enough to get far enough into the slots so they can't see us."

Or shoot at us. "There's a junction about five minutes ahead of us. At the junction, the left fork becomes a narrow slot. No more than fifteen inches wide. That's where we're going. The right fork is virtually impassable without climbing gear."

After the straight stretch of the Subway, the canyon curved to the right. As soon as we were out of sight, I slowed to a stop, then bent down, drawing in huge gulps of air.

"See—if—they're—coming," I managed to get out the words between gasps.

But Rick was already sidling along the wall. He peeked his head around. "Not there. We're gaining on them." He raised the rifle and fired again. The shot was thunderous in the narrow gorge, reverberating off the walls. "Just to let them know we're still here."

Then he stepped to me. "We've got to get those cuffs off you before we go into that slot canyon. Try the pouch."

"I have tried the pouch," I snapped. "I've been telling it to get me out of these cuffs for the last mile. Nothing! Don't ask me why. Maybe it's reminding me that I can't boss it around." Suddenly, I had another idea. I stuck my hands out in front of my body. "Shoot them off."

"What?"

"Come on, Rick. Those guys are coming, and they're coming fast. I'll hold my hands up in the air as far apart as I can. You put the barrel right up against the nylon and shoot them off."

"No. I don't like that idea. Sure a bullet would cut through nylon, but it's too dangerous. It could jerk the cuffs so hard it breaks your wrists."

I hadn't considered that. In the movies, the hero would just shoot them off.

He looked around wildly. Suddenly he grabbed my elbow. "Look, that rock has a sharp edge. Start sawing."

I leaped forward. Too eager! My foot slipped in the loose sand and gravel, and I pitched forward.

Quick as a cat, Rick's hand shot out and grabbed for me. He reached for my hands but missed, his fingers catching the nylon strap between the two cuffs. There was a soft snap, and the cuffs came away in his hand.

For a moment, we gaped at the cuffs, then at each other. The strap itself hadn't broken, but both cuffs had snapped cleanly in two. Nylon thick enough to resist several hundred pounds of pressure had simply broken.

Rick gave me a strange look. "I think you owe Nanny an apology," he said.

I touched the pouch beneath my waistband. I said nothing. I didn't have to. I had learned another lesson from this strange companion of mine, and I knew that was what it was all about with *Le Gardien*. I glanced down the canyon. "We'd better go. We've got to get into that slot before they catch up to us."

We started moving again, but this time in a steady trot. "You go in first," I ordered. "Remember to move your wallet. Put your back against the right wall. Turn your head to the right. Once inside, you can't turn back."

"No!" he said. "You go first. You know the way."

I knew what he was thinking. He was the one with the rifle, and it would be better if he was between me and Doc.

"We'll have to leave the rifle. This canyon is too narrow. Besides, the last thing we want in a slot canyon is a gunfight. The good news is only Doc can follow us. Three feet in and Gordo would be stuck like one big pea in a very small pod."

"Good."

"Once we're through that first slot, they'll be a twelve-foot vertical rise. The rock fall is too steep to climb, but the slot is still narrow enough we can shinny up it by placing our feet on one side and our backs on the other."

"Been there, done that," he said. Even though he had never been to Leprechaun Canyon before, Rick was no stranger to climbing in canyons.

"Right. It's pretty dark in there. It will take a few minutes for our eyes to adjust."

"Got it."

"Once we're on top of the rockfall, we stop. That's where we wait for Doc. Okay?"

He nodded, panting hard.

We slowed down as we approached another narrows. It was pretty tight for a short stretch, but by turning sideways, we got through it without much trouble. I led, keeping the pace brisk. When we came to where the canyon widened to about four feet, I raised my hand and pointed ahead of us. "There's the junction."

As we reached it, Rick removed the clip from the rifle, propped the rifle against one wall, then, using the toe of his boot, he buried the clip in the sand. He took a quick breath, forced a ragged smile, gave me a thumbs-up, and slipped into the left fork.

The junction's left fork was maybe three feet wide, but it quickly doglegged to the left and closed in to less than half that width. While this wasn't the worst place in the canyon, it was still pretty daunting. The slot was not strictly vertical, but tipped about ten degrees to the right of center. That meant we had to lean backward as we shuffled our way into the opening.

I took a quick breath, then slid in after him. "Here we go," I said.

"Next time we go on a date, I get to choose the place," he replied.

"If you're still willing to ask me on a date after this, I'll go anywhere you say. Deal?"

"Deal."

From that point on it was total concentration. In less than a minute, we were in what felt like total darkness. I had my head facing forward, so I could make out Rick's dark shape from time to time. But with the twists and turns, that wasn't very often. As I slid through a particularly tight spot, where the clearance was narrowest at waist level, I felt the lower button on my blouse catch on the rock and pop off. Only then did I remember that the pouch was still wrapped around my waist.

Idiot! You tell Rick to take out his wallet and then you leave that around your waist? Brilliant, Danni. Absolutely brilliant. But there was nothing I could do about it now.

I pushed ahead, planting my left foot and thrusting myself sideways to the right. I could feel the fabric scraping across the rough rock, hanging up, then springing loose again. "Rick?" I said softly.

"Yeah?"

"Bad news."

"Are you stuck?"

"No. You're going to have to take me shopping again. I should have picked out jeans with a metal button and not a plastic one."

He chuckled. "Never a dull moment with you, Danni."

Somewhere behind us, we heard the soft murmur of voices. I stopped and so did Rick.

"They're at the junction," I whispered. "They'll have to check out the right fork, but barely a minute into it and it ends in a nearly vertical drop. They'll know we didn't go that way. Doc will leave Gordo there to stand guard."

"You really think Doc can make it through here?"

"He'll donate some blood to the Irish cause, but he'll make it."

We said no more as we started forward again.

———

The rock fall was an easier climb than I remembered. There was enough room for Rick to give me a leg up, and I quickly shinnied up the rest of the way. Rick came up easily by himself. The narrow canyon continued on from where we were, but the top of the rock fall provided a small platform where we could stretch out. I felt like we were in a small cave. It was still pretty dark, but our eyes were adjusting, and I could make out Rick's shape in the darkness.

"All right," I said. "We wait here." My heart was pounding, my mouth was dry, and I felt nauseous. Rick took my hand, and I put my other one over his. "Sorry for dragging you into this," I said, keeping my voice low.

He said nothing, but I could feel his disapproval in the darkness. "I mean it."

"I know you do."

And then I saw his shape looming closer. Before I could react, he leaned in and kissed me softly on the forehead. As he started to pull away, I tipped my head back. "I think you missed," I murmured.

This time he took my face in both of his hands, leaned in again, and did it exactly right.

CHAPTER 66

It took nearly five minutes before Doc reached the bottom of the rock fall. We could hear him coming. We could hear him breathing. We could hear his clothes scraping on the rock. Our eyes were adjusting to the dim light, but when I finally saw his shape fill up the narrow crevasse, I couldn't tell if he had the pistol with him or not. Best guess was yes.

Both Rick and I were breathing in slow, shallow breaths, hands covering our mouths, so as not to be heard, but even still, Doc stopped right as the slot opened up to give him access to the rock fall. I nudged Rick's arm.

"Hold it right there," Rick said. "I have a boulder ready to drop on your head."

There was a short laugh. "And I have a pistol pointed at your girlfriend's head."

I couldn't tell if he did or not, but the sudden chill I felt told me that he very likely did.

"You put your pistol down," I said, "and we'll put down the rock. Then we can talk."

Doc let the hammer down with a soft click. Rick let the rock fall to the ground.

"So talk."

"It's over," I said. "We give up."

If he was surprised, I couldn't hear it in his voice. "And why is that?"

"I thought we could get out of here and escape. The last time my family was in this canyon, we came down from the top. There are four major drops where we had to rappel down. We used deadman anchors and webbing to get down, but we left them in place for others to use, or for when we might came back again. But someone has taken them out. At least on the first vertical. We can't go any farther."

"And you propose what?"

I took Rick's hand. "I'll surrender to you if you let Rick and the highway patrol officer go. It's over. I'm exhausted. I can't do it anymore."

Silence.

"No other conditions. Just take me to my mother and brother. I want it over with."

Longer silence. Then, "All right. Ramirez? You stay up there until I call for you to come out. Danni, you come down now. Step past me and head toward the entrance. I'll have the pistol pointed at you the entire time. You will stay no more than three feet ahead of me. Is that clear?"

"Yes."

I stood up and, with Rick's help, descended until I was standing next to Doc. I could smell his sweat and the dust on his clothes. I tensed, remembering what El Cobra had once said about Doc: *"He's not the only one who would love to get his hands on you, so behave yourself.*" But he stepped back, letting me move past him as he waved the pistol in my face. "No more than three feet."

I turned sideways and slipped into the slot, head turned away from him.

At about the halfway point, Raul suddenly yelled, "Lew!" In the closeness of the slot, his voice boomed like a shotgun, and I jumped a little, scraping the skin on one knee.

"Yeah!"

"I've got them. We're coming out."

"Okay. I'm here."

Then Doc yelled in Rick's direction. "All right, kid. You can come out now. But slow."

"I hear you," Rick called. "Coming down now."

As we moved toward the entrance, the light began to grow brighter. In a couple of places, I could have turned my head and looked back if I chose to, but I didn't want to look at Doc for one second longer than I had to.

I scraped up against the rock wall pretty hard and I felt the fabric of my pants rip and the button fall off.

I panicked for just a moment. I didn't want to be standing there with my pants falling down and Doc and Gordo looking on. So the moment the slot widened enough for me to reach down, I did so. Just as I feared. The button was gone, and it felt like the remaining material was pretty much shredded.

Since we were nearly to the junction, I worked the pouch out from beneath the waistband. Holding it in one hand and clutching at my pants with the other, I stepped into the area where the two side canyons joined. I glanced back. Doc was only a few feet behind me with the pistol pointing at me.

I squinted at the sudden burst of sunlight, but as I did so, I looked around in feigned surprise. The passageway was empty. No Gordo.

"Lew?" Doc called out.

I looked down and saw that one corner of my shirt was gone along with the two bottom buttons. The waistband of the capris right around the zipper looked like a dog had been chewing on it. But the zipper was still holding and, for the moment, I was okay. Not that I was about to let go and test it.

"Lew!" Doc's voice was sharper. Louder. No answer. He started muttering under his breath. I heard the words, *el baño,* which meant "the bathroom." Doc glanced at me, then did a double take, staring at my left hand. "What are you doing?"

"Stopping my pants from falling off," I snapped.

"No. In your hand." He waved his pistol, the bandage on his hand flashing like a semaphore in the sunlight.

"Oh, this?" I held up the pouch.

He gaped at it as though it was something from one of his night-mares, then fell back a step, his other hand coming up as if to shield himself from it.

"How did you get that?" He pointed the pistol at my head.

"Surprise!" I said. "What you and Lew stole wasn't the real thing."

"Give it to me!"

"No."

He cocked the pistol.

"Are sure you really want it?" I said, trying hard to keep my voice steady. "You've already got one bad hand." I put the strap over my shoulder then quickly added. "I'll give it to El Cobra. No one else."

"If you so much as reach for it, I'll kill you. Do you hear me?"

"I do." And I knew that he meant it.

Just then there was a sound behind us. He whipped around, pis-tol jerking up. "Lew?"

The sound had come from the right fork. We both peered into it, but we couldn't see very far inside.

"Lew! Is that you?" Doc called.

"Coming." A moment later, Lew appeared. He reached out a hand to lean against the wall as he started to descend.

I stepped back to make room for him, a sudden rush of panic hitting me. Lew was where he was supposed to be, but he wasn't supposed to be alone. Not if Clay had carried out the plan.

"I told you to stay here!" Doc shouted, his face twisted and ugly. It was clear he was not having a good day.

Then I relaxed, trying not to smile. His day was about to get worse.

As Lew squeezed through the narrow place, a head appeared just behind him, along with a rifle barrel aimed at Doc's chest.

"Drop your weapon!" one of Clay's agents barked. "Now!"

Too stunned to react, Doc just gaped.

I spun around as the sound of running footsteps reached us. Clay Zabriskie and two more of his agents, along with Officer Shayla Blake, were coming up the main channel, pistols drawn.

"FBI! Drop your weapon!" Clay barked.

I turned around in time to see Doc looking at me in complete shock. I smiled my prettiest smile at him. "I think they mean you."

PART TEN

Confrontation

CHAPTER 67

Rick and I stood side by side, watching as they loaded Doc and Gordo into the FBI van. Clay had brought four agents with him. Always the thorough one, he had left the fourth agent with the vehicles to make sure no one came along to complicate matters. Now, three were taking the two captives in the van; the other one would drive the Explorer back.

Officer Blake came over. "Well, I'm off." She gave me a funny look. "Assuming my car will start."

"It will," I assured her.

"I've got about a hundred and twenty-five supervisors at Green River waiting for my report. We rarely get this much excitement down here."

Laughing softly, I asked her, "And what are you going to tell them about the handwriting on your rearview mirror?"

"You tell me," she said. "What *am* I going to tell them? What *was* that? How did you do it? And the car?"

"It's a long, long story."

Her eyes narrowed. "Has this got anything to do with our last time together and that speed limit sign?"

"It's a long, long story." Rick repeated my words with a smile. "When this is all over, Danni and I would like to buy you lunch, Officer Blake. We'll tell you the whole thing." His smile broadened. "But I'm warning you, you're not going to believe it."

We turned as Clay came over. He had our two handheld radios. "I think you two will want these back."

As we each took one, I asked, "What about the four men that are coming up from Bullfrog?"

"We decided it would be better not to take them. They could see us coming and alert El Cobra. This way they'll know something's happened to our two friends, but won't know what. We've got to keep out of this—as far as El Cobra's concerned—for as long as possible."

I nodded in relief. I was glad to know that Clay was still taking every precaution to keep my family safe.

Rick raised his radio. "I know these have special long-range capability, Clay, but once we get into Iceberg Canyon, it'll be too narrow for them to carry very far."

"Right you are, Rick," Clay said. "That's why the surveillance team on the cliffs will have a relay transmitter."

"You think of everything, don't you?" I said, amazed.

His face slackened. "I didn't think Raul and Lew would take you guys hostage. That could have been a disaster." He shook his head. "Officer Blake told me what you did."

"Not me. The Guardian."

"Thank the good Lord you had it with you."

"I already have," I said fervently.

He turned to Rick. "The bigger problem will be getting those radios past El Cobra and his people. You know they'll search you thoroughly. If we can't communicate with you, it's really going to handicap us."

It was my turn for a solution. "If the pouch can make Cody and me invisible, I think two small radios shouldn't be too much of a problem."

"Say what?" Blake said, jerking around.

Clay intervened smoothly. "I'll join you guys for that lunch and try to help explain that, too. Danni, I put the rifle back in your truck. We don't care if they find that."

He held out his hand to Blake. "Officer, thank you for all you've done today. I'll write a commendation to your supervisor. We deeply appreciate your help."

"Yes," both Rick and I chimed in.

"Thank *you*." She flashed a grin. "It's been fun. It'll be hard to go back to the normal routine." She touched the brim of her hat with one finger, slid her finger into a "pistol," and pretended to shoot it at me. "I'm going to hold you two to that lunch," she said. Then she chuckled. "Either that, or I'll have to write up that ticket for Rick being fifteen miles an hour over the speed limit."

———————

As we watched the two vehicles leave, Doc's satellite phone rang. Clay picked it up and looked at the number. "It's him. He's been calling steadily. Are you ready to talk to him?"

I shook my head.

"Why not?" Rick asked. "You're going to have to do it sooner or later."

I stuck my nose in the air and sniffed loftily. "Because I'm going to change clothes first." And with that I stalked to the truck, climbed up in the back, and started rummaging in my bags. I found the other pair of capris I had bought at Kohl's and jumped down again. As I passed by the two of them, I raised a finger in warning. "Not a word."

Smirking, they pretended not to hear.

———

When I returned a few minutes later. I looked around for a trash barrel to throw away my ruined pants.

"You're not going to throw those away, are you?" Rick asked.

"I'm not?"

"No, you're going to take them home and put them in a drawer." He withdrew the two pieces of nylon cuffs from his pocket. "And you're going to put these with them. Someday you'll be Grandmother or Great-Grandmother Danni, and you'll show these to your grandchildren as you tell them your story."

I was touched by that. "You're right," I said. Why hadn't I thought of that?

We walked together to the truck. Rick rolled the cuffs inside the jeans and put them beneath the seat of the truck. Then he rolled the radios into a tight ball in one of his shirts before putting them in the bottom of my overnight bag. Just then, the satellite phone rang. We looked at each other as Clay pressed the speaker phone switch, tapped a button, and handed it to me.

"Yes?"

There was a soft gasp, then silence. *"¿Chiquita?"*

"Sorry, I'm out of cell phone range here. I was going to call you."

The voice exploded with rage. "Where are Raul and Lew?" I heard scuffling noises, then a cry from Cody. "You listen to me, *chiquita*. I've got a gun to your little brother's head, and if you don't start explaining, I'm going to pull the trigger."

I fired right back. "I warned you not to try anything. I told you that the pouch would warn me if we were in danger."

458

"But—"

"Oh, that. The pouch your men stole, you mean? Did you really think I would be so foolish as to leave my pouch in the truck for anyone to steal? What they stole was something we picked up at the Salvation Army store for a buck. I'm holding the real pouch even as we speak."

"Let me talk to Raul or Lew."

"Sorry. They're on their way to the nearest Utah Highway Patrol station."

"What?" he screamed. "I warned you about bringing in the police—"

I could feel the power of the pouch behind me, driving the conversation. I cut in, shouting. *"I* didn't bring the police in on this. Your stupid guys did. Whose brilliant idea was it to have them kidnap a highway patrol officer?"

I could hear him breathing heavily on the other end.

"I want to talk to my mother. And to Cody."

"No way. Not now. Maybe not ever. I'm missing four of my men. You think I will overlook that?"

"You listen to me, El Cobra, or whatever your real name is. That highway patrol officer pulled me and Rick over because she thought we were speeding. Then your guys came up and took us all prisoner. How stupid was that? Rick and I managed to get away and grab Lew's pistol. When we had your two guys tied up, the officer wanted to know why they were after us. We told her we didn't know. So she knows nothing about you or what you've done to my family."

"I don't believe you."

"I don't think she did either. So don't be surprised if, when she gets back to Green River and reports all this to her supervisor, they issue a warrant for Rick and me and come looking for us." I took a quick breath. "So if you want us to stand around while you yell at us, have it your way."

There was no answer.

"Let me talk to my mother and my brother and make sure they're still okay, then we'll talk about how to undo the mess you've made of things before the police show up."

"If they do, then your mother dies."

"If she does, you'll lose twenty million dollars. So come on. What'll it be?"

More silence. I heard voices in the background whispering urgently. Then he came back on. "You tell me what you propose, then I'll decide if you speak to your mother or not."

I looked at Clay. He nodded vigorously. "Okay," I said. "It's nearly six o'clock. Are you still tracking my phone? I've left the battery in it the whole time."

"Yes."

"Even though we're out of cell phone range?"

When he answered, it was with open contempt. "You and your boyfriend think you're so clever. You don't need cell phone coverage to track the GPS on your phone. I know exactly where you are. You have stopped on the side of the road next to Highway 95."

Okay, so he wasn't bluffing. "We're at Leprechaun Canyon. If we leave now, we can be to Bullfrog in little more than an hour. We'll come straight to the large parking lot near the boat ramp. We'll meet you by the restrooms."

"And why would you choose to come to Bullfrog Marina?"

"Do you really want to play dumb?" I snapped. "I know you're somewhere on Lake Powell. I've even got a pretty good idea of which general area you're in. If I'm right—or better, if the pouch is right—you're on a houseboat within fifteen or twenty miles of Bullfrog. So that gives you plenty of time to get to the marina by speedboat before we do."

I heard Eileen's exclamation of surprise. Good. It wouldn't hurt for her to be a little spooked by the pouch as well.

"But I also know about the four guys you sent off to meet us at the junction. Call them off. If they try to stop us . . ." I left the rest hanging.

"*Sí,*" El Cobra finally said. "They'll follow you at a distance. We'll meet at the restrooms at the parking lot. What time?"

I glanced at the time displayed on the phone. "We can be there by seven fifteen."

"Not 'we.' You."

"Rick's coming with me. He's my transportation."

"Last night you told me he wasn't going to be involved."

"Yeah, and this morning you told me you would leave me alone."

"He doesn't come. He can drop you off at the parking lot and leave."

"You don't listen very well, do you? Do you want me there or not?"

"All right. We'll play it your way. Seven fifteen. Don't be late."

"Wait! What about my mom?"

But he had already hung up.

CHAPTER 68

We leaned on the hood of the truck, talking quietly.

"This is going to rush us a little," Clay said, "but I think we can be ready." He looked at me. "I haven't told you the latest from Iceberg Canyon."

"What?"

"The surveillance team on the cliffs has seen your mother several times now. She's fine. They also saw the speedboat deliver El Cobra and Cody. From what they could see from above, your mom was pretty elated to see Cody."

That was good. We now had absolute confirmation that we had the right houseboat.

"We've transported half a dozen men to the upper end of Iceberg Canyon by helicopter. They're making their way down now."

"That won't do them any good," I said. "Once they reach the water, there's no beach to walk along, except for a couple of places."

"That's what our observers report too. They're carrying three small inflatable rubber rafts. Two men will have scuba gear. They'll move in tonight and stay far enough back that there's no chance they'll be seen or heard."

"And they stay out of sight until I say so, right? Just like today."

Clay's eyes dropped and he studied his hands. "Uh . . . we need to talk about that, Danni."

"No, Clay," I interrupted. "We play it the same way. You promised."

"This is different, Danni. Once you're on that boat—even if Rick is with you—it's not going to be the same as being out in the open, or trapping someone inside a narrow slot canyon."

My lips pressed into a grim line. "No."

"Just listen, Danni," Rick urged.

When I didn't answer, Clay went on. "Our spotters have identified five people on board with your family—El Cobra, the woman, and three other men. We also know about the two men who are with your dad and grandfather. That makes seven."

"But those two guys aren't on the boat. They're with Dad and Grandpère."

He let out his breath in a long, weary sigh and reached in his pocket. "I received a text message this afternoon. We think it's from your grandfather." He looked at me carefully. "Have you talked to him or let him know you're working with us? Did you give him my number?"

I laughed. "None of the above. Are you sure it's from him?"

"The message had no name or phone number listed with it, but the contents are pretty clear."

"What does it say?" Rick asked.

He unfolded the note and began to read. "'Will finish with Canadians by Sunday am. Some evidence EC'"—he looked up—"'I assume that means El Cobra—'will return us to the boat immediately after. Will stay until Monday pm when all come to Salt Lake for Tuesday's signing.'"

I marveled that not only had Grandpère learned how to text but he was also sending out messages when, as far as we knew, his phone had been taken from him. Not only that, he was sending messages to numbers he didn't know and to people he'd never met. That kind of made a candle that kept bursting into flames look pretty trivial.

"When all this is over," I said to Clay, "I want you to meet Grandpère."

"I look forward to that." Folding up the note, Clay leaned forward. "Anyway, the message makes sense. It's much safer for El Cobra to have your father and grandfather right there under his thumb. But it changes everything. It complicates things in one way—we have two more men to deal with—but it also gives us a great opportunity. Thanks to you, they now have four fewer men overall."

"No, five."

"Five?" Both he and Rick looked confused.

"Yeah, Doc is worth two men. Having him out is a big plus."

"Right. So if we can free your family on Sunday, then the whole extortion plot is over. And we'll have the gang in hand so they can't cause you any more trouble."

"No."

"No?"

"What are you planning, Clay? A SWAT team rappelling down the cliffs? Guys roaring in on their rubber rafts? Scuba divers springing onto the deck?" My voice caught and I had to clear it quickly. "My family going down in a hail of gunfire?"

"I think we deserve more credit than that, Danni."

"I give you all the credit in the world, but it's too dangerous. The houseboat gives them a clear field of fire. They'll see you long before you can get to them."

"You're not thinking clearly, Danni," he said gently. "El Cobra lost four men today. He's raging. You're not going to catch him off guard again. Your family is already in grave danger."

I ignored him. "I told you we had to do this differently, Clay. This can't be some glorious, Hollywood-type hostage rescue. There's too much at stake." I leaned forward. "Look, once I'm on board I'll figure something out. The pouch will help me. Maybe I can take out two or three of their people before Grandpère and Dad arrive."

"Danni," Rick said, touching my arm. "Can we talk?"

I whirled around. "So you can make me change my mind? Are you going to stand with Clay on this, Rick? Or are you going to support me?"

"That's not fair."

"Neither is life, Rick."

He took me by the arm. "Let's talk." He turned to Clay. "Can we have a few minutes?"

"Of course." He walked away, taking his phone out of his pocket and starting to dial.

Rick found a place with some sparse shade, and we sat down in the soft sand. "Don't, Rick," I said. "I already know how you feel, so just don't."

"Oh? And does that come from the pouch too?"

"What?"

"Knowing how I feel?"

"No, I . . ." I shook my head. I was suddenly exhausted beyond belief. And scared and frightened and terrified.

"Tell me, then. What am I feeling right now?"

I blinked a couple of times, taken aback by him going on the attack. And then I got mad. "All right, I will. You think that just because I let you kiss me, you think you can tell me what to do, tell me what's right and what's wrong."

"*Let* me kiss you?"

"All right, I wanted you to kiss me. But that doesn't mean you can take advantage of me because of it."

His look was so incredulous and so hurt that I kicked myself for bringing up the kiss. But I wasn't about to apologize.

"You didn't tell me what I was thinking," he finally said in a low voice. "You told me what you are thinking."

"All right, then," I said, unable to keep the sarcastic bite out of my voice. "Tell me what *you're* thinking."

I could see him debating about whether to say it. I could see his own temper was starting to rise. But he finally nodded. "I was thinking that what happened today was brilliant. You're right. The odds against us have changed significantly, thanks to you. But I was also thinking about the last few days. I was thinking how you nearly caused a major accident with that woman in the sports car because she wasn't driving the speed limit."

I opened my mouth to protest, but he went on quickly.

"And how you nearly triggered a road rage incident because some jerk tried to get in line ahead of us. What if that happens again on the houseboat, Danni? What if you make another mistake?"

"Mistake? Maybe those things were wrong, Rick," I cried, deeply hurt, "but if I hadn't done that with the sports car, I would never have thought about communicating with Officer Blake in the same way. It was my so-called 'mistake' that helped us escape today."

That took him aback. "What do you mean? Communicating in what way?"

I remembered he hadn't been in the police car with me, so I quickly explained what had happened.

"You didn't tell me that."

"You didn't ask," I said bitterly. "I also made the engine stop,

Rick. Where do you think I got that idea from? From what happened on the on-ramp the other morning."

"Oh," he said in a small voice.

"Yeah, Rick. So maybe I'm not quite as stupid as you think."

He looked down, unable to meet my eyes.

"Apology accepted," I said angrily.

His chin came up, and there was sadness in his eyes. "Let me ask you one question, Danni, and then I'll shut up. Was it you who stopped the engine? Or the pouch?"

"It was . . . uh . . . what's the difference? It was my idea."

"And it was a great idea. But you didn't say that. You said, '*I* made the engine stop.'"

"So you're going to hang me because of a slip of the tongue?" I cried hotly.

"Slip of the tongue? Can you not even hear yourself, Danni? '*I* did this,' and '*I* did that. *I'll* figure something out. The pouch will help *me*. Maybe *I* can take out two or three more men. All you professionally trained agents should just stand back and let *me* handle it.'"

I shot to my feet. "That's not fair."

"Neither is life, Danni." He shook his head. "Clay won't say that to you, but someone has to."

I started to walk away, so mad I could hardly speak.

He called after me. "I think it's wonderful that you learned from your mistakes, Danni, I really do. But that doesn't change the fact that they *were* mistakes."

Spinning around, I bowed low. "Thank you for enlightening me, Mr. Ramirez."

"I know you don't want to hear this, but sometimes what you do with the pouch is wrong, Danni. The Guardian is remarkable. It's a gift that was entrusted to you, and it was wrong to use it as you did."

He got to his feet, forcing himself to speak more calmly. "And thinking that you and the pouch are invincible is wrong, too. Don't you see that? And you can't be wrong this time, Danni. We're all depending on you. Clay, me, your mother, Cody—"

"I get it, Rick." I was teetering between throwing myself into his arms or picking up a rock and throwing it at him. Finally, I shook my head. "Maybe El Cobra is right. Maybe it's best if it's not *we* who goes tonight."

He flinched as if I had slapped him. "Maybe so," he finally said. "Maybe so." He turned and cupped his hands. "Clay! We're ready to go." When the agent waved, Rick started walking swiftly away.

"Rick, I . . ." I broke into a run, closing the distance between us in great strides. I grabbed him by the arm and spun him around. "I'm sorry, Rick. I'm really sorry."

He gave me a fleeting, momentary smile, but it didn't make the sadness go away.

"That was stupid of me. I didn't mean it. Don't walk away." I took his hands. "I don't mean to sound cocky and arrogant, but I am being protected. I am being guided. I am being told what to do, and—"

I stopped as my own words rang in my ears: *I am. I am. I am.* I felt sick at heart. What was happening to me? But something else in me was crying out that I had to help him understand. "Grandpère once told me to trust my feelings, Rick. Sometimes they're the only things that make sense. And I have a bad feeling about the FBI taking over this operation and coming in like they're storming the castle. I know it doesn't make sense, but maybe this isn't the time for logic and reason, Rick. I have to trust my feelings."

"I understand."

My shoulders fell. He didn't understand. Nothing I had said swayed him.

"We'd better go if we're going to get you to Bullfrog by seven fifteen."

"You don't agree, do you?" I said, the dejection so real I could taste it.

"I never said that."

"Yes, you did."

His eyes probed mine. "Do you really want to know what I'm feeling right now?" he asked.

"Yes."

"All right. I know you have to trust your feelings. They've been right *most* of the time." I lifted one of my eyebrows, but he ignored me. "But right now *I* have a bad feeling too, Danni. And mine doesn't come from the pouch. And mine isn't about the FBI."

I didn't want to, but I couldn't not ask. "What is it, then?"

"I have this feeling that when you and I step onto that boat, you're going to be so hell-bent on delivering your family that you'll make another mistake. And this time, maybe everything won't work out exactly as you have planned."

CHAPTER 69

It was Saturday night and even though it was past seven in the evening, Bullfrog was jumping—no pun intended. There was a long line of boats at the ramp waiting to enter the water. The gas station had cars clear out into the street, and the store was packed with people. The bay was dotted with houseboats, motorboats, and jet skis—dollops of white on the deep blue expanse. We drove slowly to the upper parking lots near the boat ramp.

The parking lot by the restrooms was full, but we found a place near the far end of the lot just east of it. As we eased into the lot, Rick shut off the engine. Neither of us moved. We hadn't said much in the hour since we'd left Leprechaun Canyon.

Now Rick asked. "What do you want to take with us?"

I shrugged. "My overnight bag. You?"

"Maybe just the gym bag."

Several seconds ticked by in silence. "Rick?"

"You don't have to say it, Danni. We were both pretty stressed out there at Leprechaun. Let's just focus on what happens now."

There was so much I wanted to say, so much that needed to be said, but he was right. Now wasn't the time. I reached for the door handle just as my phone chimed. Another new text message. I drew in a quick breath. No name, no number.

"Your grandfather?"

I nodded. He must have gotten access to a phone somehow. I scooted over in the seat and held out the phone so we could read the message together.

DANNI & RICK. THE CRITICAL HOUR HAS ARRIVED. BUT YOU ARE NOT ALONE. OUR THOUGHTS AND PRAYERS ARE WITH YOU EVERY MOMENT.

"I hope so," I whispered.

THERE ARE SOME THINGS YOU MUST REMEMBER.

"You are unique," I intoned. "There is purpose to your life. You are free to choose." I knew it would be the Four Remembers. He had given them to me for times like this, so I fully expected him to remind me of them again.

I was wrong.

1. IF GRANDMÈRE MONIQUE WERE HERE, SHE WOULD PUT HER ARMS AROUND YOU AND TELL YOU HOW PROUD SHE IS OF YOU.

Tears filled my eyes and I had to swipe at them with the back of my hand so I could continue reading. Into my mind came the image of Monique LaRoche walking into the deserted Gestapo headquarters, crying out to God not to abandon her. And strangely, that mental image immediately brought a sense of peace to my heart.

2. I SENSE MUCH CONTENTION BETWEEN THE TWO OF YOU. YOU MUST PUT IT FROM YOU NOW! CONTENTION ROBS YOU

OF THE POWER OF DISCERNMENT. YOU MUST BE UNITED IF
YOU ARE TO SUCCEED.

We looked at each other. Rick nodded soberly. He slid a little closer. I laid my head against his shoulder.

3. THE POUCH IS A TOOL TO BE TRUSTED, NOT A WAND TO
MAKE THE WORLD CONFORM TO YOUR WILL.

Ouch! I looked up at Rick, but he was concentrating on the screen.

4. "A WOMAN USES HER INTELLIGENCE TO FIND REASONS TO
SUPPORT HER INTUITION."—GILBERT K. CHESTERTON.

"Who's that?" Rick asked.

"I have no idea." I read the quote again, softly and more slowly. "'A woman uses her intelligence to find reasons to support her intuition.'" My shoulders lifted and fell. "That's me. My mind can think up a thousand reasons why I should do what my heart has already decided to do."

"Wait," Rick said. "I don't think that's a chastisement. I think he's reminding you that you have a great gift of intuition, Danni. I think he's saying, 'Trust it. But be wise too. Use your mind along with your heart.'"

I looked at Rick in wonder. I wanted to throw my arms around him for sharing that insight, for expressing his trust in me. "Thank you," I said.

5. THE DIFFERENCE BETWEEN INTELLIGENCE AND STUPIDITY
IS . . .

The answer came in the next message. We both leaned in, watching the screen closely.

THERE IS A LIMIT TO INTELLIGENCE.—Grandpère

"Oh, Grandpère," I cried out, laughing. "I love you so much. Thank you. I hear you." I looked at Rick. "I can't believe it. It's like he was sitting there listening to us argue. Listening to me say how *I* was going to do everything."

I was trying to put on a brave face, but down deep, it hurt. Was that what Grandpère thought? That I had been incredibly stupid? That I still *was* being incredibly stupid?

"Call Clay," I said. "Tell him I'll do whatever he thinks is best."

Rick turned in surprise. "What?"

"You heard me."

Turning to face me, Rick took me by both shoulders. "You did it again. Why do you think your grandfather is talking only to you, Danni? Put those two sayings together, and I think you'll understand what he's trying to tell us. It's good to have feelings, to trust in them, but we have to be intelligent about it. Not do something stupid, which is something we all do."

"Like saying I should do this alone?" I murmured.

He shook his head. "Like saying all you cared about was yourself."

We laughed together and it felt so good. As the sound died away, we were looking deep into each other's eyes. I started to lean in toward him. He responded. Then, suddenly he pulled back and turned to look out the window.

To say I was disappointed would be an understatement. But the moment he moved away from me, I remembered something I had shared with Rick about a month ago. I'd been in the cafeteria with a bunch of my friends, including Lisa Cole. She and Jaren Abbott had been dating for almost a year, and everybody knew they made out a lot. Some of the other girls were a little envious and were asking her questions about it. You know, things like, was he a good kisser and did she always keep her eyes closed? Lisa was basking in the attention, but then she got kind of wistful and said, "Jaren and I used to talk a lot when we first started dating. Now all we do is make out."

As I watched Rick out of the corner of my eye, I wondered if he was remembering that too. Had he thought I was putting him on notice when I told him that? I hadn't meant it that way. I'd shared it with him because we were friends.

So what was going through his mind now? I knew what was going through mine. One part of me wanted him to kiss me so badly that I could hardly stand it. After our battle royal a few hours before, this seemed like a perfect way to make up.

I realized our friendship had changed significantly over the past few days. This crisis had brought us closer together, and the shared stress of dealing with El Cobra had actually deepened the bonds of our trust. I wasn't sure we could have had that argument a week ago. But now, we felt confident enough in our friendship that we could say what we were feeling. We could be totally honest with each other, even if it hurt like fury. It wasn't the sweetness of a kiss that had brought that about. It was heat of the fire.

So, if we started kissing now, would things change between us? I didn't want that. I loved being with Rick because I could be completely and totally me with him. He knew me for what I was and *still* liked me. And that was a wonder.

Then another thought hit me pretty hard. Just a moment ago, all he and I were thinking about was kissing for the second time. Yet we were minutes away from surrendering ourselves to a vicious criminal. In a few hours, we could be facing a confrontation that might turn deadly. My family was being held hostage, and it was possible I might never see some of them again. And all I could think about was if Rick was going to kiss me?

I guess that was the answer to my question. In sudden gratitude, I reached out and rubbed his arm for a moment. "Thanks, Rick."

"For what?"

"For being you." Then, embarrassed, I looked at my watch. "It's seven ten. Should we go?"

He nodded and we both reached for the door handles. But at that moment my phone chimed. We looked down. The screen was filled with two more paragraphs.

AS DAVID DID MANY CENTURIES AGO, YOU GO NOW TO MEET YOUR OWN GOLIATH. THE BIBLE SAYS THAT DAVID CALLED TO GOLIATH AND SAID: "THOU COMEST TO ME WITH A SWORD, AND WITH A SPEAR, AND WITH A SHIELD: BUT I COME TO THEE IN THE NAME OF THE LORD GOD OF HOSTS. THE BATTLE IS THE LORD'S, AND HE WILL GIVE YOU INTO OUR HANDS."

MUCH LOVE,

GRANDPÈRE

My hand withdrew from the door handle. I slipped the pouch over my shoulder, then took Rick's hand. I bowed my head and closed my eyes. He did the same. *"O Dieu, ne nous abandonne pas maintenant."* O God, do not abandon us now.

"Amen," Rick murmured.

When we both looked up again, I said, "I'm ready. Let's go."

CHAPTER 70

El Cobra and Eileen were waiting for us off to one side of the restrooms. She was beautiful—petite, with deep auburn hair that glowed in the evening light, and eyes so green they were almost startling. She was dressed in black slacks and a tailored turquoise blouse. Half a dozen gold bracelets dangled on one wrist, and more gold was around her throat.

When they saw us coming, El Cobra jerked his head for us to follow, and we fell in behind them, moving through the cars until we came to the very last row of the parking lot. They stopped at a white Lexus with Arizona plates.

He motioned us to move around to the far side of the vehicle, putting us farther out of sight.

"Eileen," he said. "Search her. Make sure she's not wearing a wire." He looked at Rick. "Hands on the car. Spread your legs." Very quickly and very professionally we were both searched. Eileen tried to remove the pouch from my shoulder, but I grabbed it and held on. She looked to El Cobra, but he shook his head and she let go.

"You two. In the backseat. Stay apart."

Eileen produced a pistol, holding it down low so it couldn't be seen by anyone but us. She waved it at us, and we got into the car as El Cobra took our bags from the truck. He went through Rick's bag thoroughly, then turned to mine.

I clutched the pouch and held my breath. *Blind his eyes to the radios. Please, not the radios.*

He pawed through the contents of my bag then zipped it up. Satisfied, he threw both bags in the back. "All right, let's go."

Rick and I looked at each other, and I breathed a sigh of relief.

We drove around and parked at the marina parking lot. They made us get our bags and walk ahead of them toward the slips. It was obvious that El Cobra liked nice things. The Lexus. The Rolex. Gold necklaces and bracelets. A sleek, expensive speedboat that looked like it could do fifty or sixty miles an hour on the open water.

Eileen took the front seat opposite the steering wheel, still keeping the pistol low and pointed directly at us. She reached over to the driver's console and pushed a button. The engine sprang to life, settling immediately into a low rumble that resonated with the promise of power.

"You next, *chiquita*," El Cobra said. He took my bag and tossed it in the back. He offered his hand, but I ignored it, hopping lightly down into the boat. El Cobra turned to Rick. "Sorry, kid. This is where we part company."

"No!" I cried. "You promised."

He whirled, eyes flashing with anger. "I promised you nothing. He stays here." He swung back to Rick. "And if you make any attempt to contact the authorities, your girlfriend will die. *¿Comprendes?*"

Rick said nothing. I leaped to my feet. "If he doesn't go, we don't go." I thought of the driver in the pickup. I remembered the highway patrol car. I closed my eyes. Instantly, the boat's motor died.

Surprised, Eileen pressed the starter button again. The engine ground loudly, as if someone had dropped something into its gears.

"Stop!" El Cobra yelled. He hopped down into the boat and pushed her aside. "Watch them," he barked. He tried starting it again, pulling on the choke. The grinding sounded worse. He glared at me.

My chin came up and my jaw set. "If Rick doesn't go, we don't go."

Muttering under his breath, he looked up. "Get in."

As soon as Rick was beside me, El Cobra tried the engine again; it roared into life, smooth as silk. Eileen stared at me with what I thought looked like open fear. I gave her my best "don't mess with me" smile and sat down.

El Cobra cast off the lines, and we pulled away from the slip.

Five minutes later, we were out in the bay. El Cobra shoved the throttles forward, throwing us back in our seats, and in moments we were skimming across the water like a launched torpedo.

As we raced across the bay and entered the gorge of the Colorado River, Rick and I said nothing. Eileen stood beside El Cobra, and they spoke Spanish back and forth. Rick, who spoke fluent Spanish, watched them but said nothing.

After another few minutes, Eileen came back and sat in the seat across from us. She studied us for what seemed like a full minute—mostly focusing on me—before she spoke. "I think you have put an enchantment on my husband," she said abruptly.

Husband? That was a surprise.

"I'm not an enchantress," I said.

"A witch, then?"

"Depends in what sense you mean the word."

The humor went right past her.

"May I see this pouch of yours, if I promise to give it back?" The last was said with a sneer. She didn't like me. That was all right. I was having trouble warming up to her too. I found it hard to believe that these two were husband and wife. They were so different. I guessed she was Irish. What I had thought was a British accent had a different lilt to it, which fit with the auburn hair and green eyes. How in the world had these two ever become a match?

With a shrug, I removed the pouch from my shoulder and handed it to her.

She unbuttoned the flap, opened the pouch, and gave it a thorough examination. She even ran her fingers along the inside seams to make sure it was empty.

"There is nothing here," she said, closing it up and handing it back. I didn't take it; I just watched her steadily. Then her eyes widened, and she jerked back, feeling the fabric with her thumbs. There was now a flat lump beneath the fabric.

She turned. "Armando. There's something inside now."

Ah, so El Cobra had a name. That was good. Armando didn't seem quite so ominous as El Cobra.

"Open it," he commanded.

She was clearly fearful, but she tentatively drew back the flap and reached inside. It was another bank packet, but instead of a stack of money, the stack of paper was multicolored, like abstract art. I looked more closely, then gave an "oh" of delight. It was strips of newspaper cut from the Sunday comics.

Eileen was staring. Armando was staring. I was trying to keep from laughing out loud. This was almost as good as the bobble-headed *Cobra Pequeño*. I saw Rick trying to hold back a smile too.

She erupted, cursing in English at me. "You would make a fool of *me?*" she cried and flung the packet at my face.

My hand shot up and snatched it out of the air. Beside me, Rick was warning me with his eyes: *"Don't mess with this one."*

But I wasn't messing around. Both of these two needed to know that I wielded a force to be reckoned with. I wanted them to be afraid of the pouch. No, I *needed* them to be afraid of the pouch. I held the packet in front of me, then passed the flat of my hand over it, like magicians do.

"Oooh," I said in a spooky voice, "behold the enchantress at work."

It was Rick's gasp that brought me out of it. He was gaping at the packet. I looked down to see why, then jerked back. The comics were gone. Green bills had replaced them. I stared in disbelief, then looked up.

Eileen's eyes were like saucers. She leaped forward and snatched the packet out of my hand. Ripping off the packet wrapper like a madwoman, she spread out the bills in her hand. It wasn't hundred dollar bills this time. It was thousand dollar bills!

"How much?" Armando shouted in glee, glancing back at her.

She waved the bills in front of his nose. "Twenty thousand dollars!" she cried. "Twenty thousand!" She whirled back to me. "Make some more!"

I folded my arms. "We'll see," I said. I looked up at Armando. "We'll see tomorrow."

———

As we turned into Iceberg Canyon, I immediately saw where the canyon began to narrow. Two men were in a small powerboat and dressed in ranger uniforms. One was smoking a cigarette; the other rested a hand on his pistol. I poked Rick, then pointed. "There are two we didn't count," I whispered.

He stared at them as we went by, then nodded. "How many more surprises are there?"

I had no answer.

The houseboat was three or four miles up the canyon, clear of the main channel. It was anchored on a small, narrow strip of sand that quickly gave way to sheer rock walls on either side. I could see two domed tents on the sand and a blackened fire pit.

My eyes lifted. The cliffs were so high I had to tip my head back to see the sky. I tried to picture men rappelling down from that height and found the thought dizzying.

The canyon was as spectacular as I remembered. And the air was noticeably cooler. I guessed it was because the canyon was so narrow that it didn't get as much sunlight during the day and so the water was colder than other parts of the lake. Mom had been right.

As we came into sight of the houseboat, I saw figures standing on deck. Two of them immediately began to wave wildly. I found myself swallowing hard to try to deal with the lump which had lodged in my throat, and brushing away the tears which had filled my eyes. This would be the first time I had seen my mother since Tuesday night— which now seemed like years ago—and I was suddenly overwhelmed with a desire to hold her very, very close for a very, very long time.

CHAPTER 71

Iceberg Canyon, Glen Canyon National Recreation Area
Sunday, June 19, 2011

I couldn't see my watch, but I guessed it was well past midnight.

After a light supper, Armando gave orders for rearranging the sleeping quarters. This was a large, luxurious houseboat with five bedrooms and three baths. He put me in with my mom, and Rick and Cody bunked together. He and Eileen would stay in the master suite, of course. Since he made all of the men sleep outside, either on top of the houseboat where they took turns standing guard, or in the tent on the beach, that left two bedrooms empty. I wondered if he was holding those for Dad and Grandpère. I felt a warm spot in my heart when I realized that Doc and Gordo would be sleeping on a bunk in a jail cell tonight.

Though I was exhausted—it had been a long and full day—sleep was far from me. I slid close to Mom so I could whisper into her ear without being overheard. I told her everything that had happened since Cody and I had fled into the night. She listened carefully, murmuring her approval from time or time, or making sounds of concern. But the only questions she asked me were about the FBI and what they planned to do. I stalled a little on that, saying we hadn't decided yet.

When I was through, I moved back onto my side of the bed and turned on my side, facing her. The houseboat was quiet except for the murmur of voices from the two guards up top. Moonlight filtered through the small window and the thin drapes, allowing me to see Mom's face clearly. She was on her back, staring up at the ceiling.

Sensing I was watching her, she smiled at me. "So was that the first time you've ever been kissed?"

"Oh, Mom!" I laughed. "I love you." Of all the hundreds of questions that were surely racing through her mind, *that* was the one that had floated to the top. "Yes, except for when I was in kindergarten and Bobby Walker had his friends hold me down so he could kiss me."

"Oh yes. I remember. His mother called to complain about you giving him a black eye."

I chuckled. "He still kind of steers clear of me."

She reached out her hand. "I wish you weren't here, Carruthers."

"Why?" I cried, totally surprised.

"You know why. At least before, you were free."

"Well, I *am* here, Mom. And we're going to see this through." Then I remembered something. "By the way, the FBI thinks El Cobra will bring Dad and Grandpère here this afternoon, rather than letting them go to Salt Lake by themselves."

"I know."

"You do?"

"Yes. They know that, because I speak fluent French, I can understand a lot of their Spanish, so they're careful what they say in front of me. But this afternoon, I was on the roof. I told them that I wanted to do some suntanning. Anyway, the two men on the beach were talking about Dad and Grandpère. They didn't realize that the water magnified their voices."

Suntanning as a cover for eavesdropping? Who but Mom would think of that? She was amazing. The coolest ever. Then I saw the look on her face. "What is it, Mom? What's wrong?"

"I don't know what's going to happen on Tuesday. Remember what Grandpère said about El Cobra being a liar."

"I do."

She squeezed my hand tightly, and her lip began to tremble. "I don't think they plan to free us, Carruthers. Especially not now when so many things have gone wrong. You weren't here, but El Cobra knows those two men just didn't walk away in Cathedral Valley. And now he's lost two more."

I squeezed her hand back. "We're not waiting until Tuesday. It's going to be okay, Mom, I promise."

"That's what the dentist always tells you just before he does the root canal."

I laughed. At least she still had her sense of humor.

"Mom, since we're trapped here, and you won't be able to make up some crazy excuse and duck out on me, I have a few questions for you."

"I beg your pardon," she retorted. "When have I ever done that?"

"Only every time I ask you questions about our history."

"Well, you're certainly right about being trapped here. So fire away."

"Okay. You once read me the story of my great-great—I don't know how many greats—grandmother Angelique Chevalier, and what happened to her on her thirteenth birthday." I hesitated, then went for it. "The other night at the motel, while Rick and Cody were swimming, I got on the motel's computer and Googled a perpetual calendar."

"I think I know where you're going with this."

"Her birthday was October 13, 1871. That was a Friday. She lost both her mother and her father on a Friday the thirteenth. And that's not all. Grandpère gave me a bunch of papers, stuff from his mother."

"Yes, I know. I'm the one who suggested he include his mother's history."

"You were?" Would the surprises never stop coming? I went on. "Anyway, the day the pilot was shot down over the château was Friday, August eleventh. And two days later—the day the Gestapo came and arrested Grandpère's father—was the thirteenth of August." I stopped, hoping she would respond. She didn't, so I made my point. "And that was her birthday. Do either of those two events have anything to do with your feelings about Friday the thirteenth?"

She didn't answer for almost a minute. I could see there was a faraway look in her eyes. When she came back to me, she said, "I would like to hold off answering that question for now. What else do you want to know?"

"Dad says that he wanted to call me Angelique after you, at least for my middle name. You said no. He also said that because it meant so much to Grandpère you agreed to name me Monique, but not as my first name."

"That's true."

"Was that because you thought if Monique was my first name, it might be bad luck?"

"No. I wanted Carruthers to be your first name so that my grandmother, Louise Carruthers, would know she was loved too." She giggled. "I had to go with Carruthers because I never liked Louise very much as a name."

I rolled my eyes. That was pure Mom.

"Besides, Carruthers is an honorable name."

"It is, Mom, but that's not the question. I'm just trying to understand why you feel so strongly about these things."

"Would you like me to call you Danni? I will, you know."

I stopped and considered her question thoughtfully. To my surprise, I found myself shaking my head. "No. I like how Carruthers is special just between us."

She shot me a look of pure skepticism.

"I do, Mom. Really. It was really nice the other day when you called me Danni, but no. Don't change." I flashed her an impish grin. "I can live with it. And I'm big enough now that I can whip anyone who makes fun of it."

Her eyes glistened in the semidarkness. "Thank you. That's part of your heritage too."

"I know. Though you've ducked my question about why you don't want to call me Monique."

"Any other questions?"

"Yes." This was the big one, actually. "Is our family . . . uh . . . I mean, are we really . . ." I shook my head and finally just blurted it out. "Am I an enchantress? A witch of some kind?"

"Oh, my dear girl," she exclaimed. "No, not in any way. And neither was Angelique nor Monique."

"What about Grandpère? Remember the candle on my thirteenth birthday?"

"That was just a trick candle he bought at some magician's shop in Salt Lake. He just loves having people think he's mysterious."

"Oh, really? And what about this? Even though they took his cell phone away, he's been texting us messages."

She reared back a little. "Grandpère? Texting?"

"Mom. Answer my question."

"He does have a phone. When the pistol went off in the house and pandemonium broke out, I saw him roll across the floor and take

his phone back. I guess he's managed to keep it hidden ever since."
Then she became serious. "Carruthers, listen to me. If you had asked
me about the pouch, that would be a different matter. Is it enchanted?
Yes, in some ways. Is it magic? Grandpère doesn't like that word, and
I'm not sure I do either. But it certainly does magical things some-
times. This much is sure—it has a power that we don't understand.
But it is a power for good, not evil."

"Why do you think it's called *Le Gardien?*"

She smiled. "Oh, so you're not calling it Nanny anymore?"

"No. I regret that I ever did, and I will tell Grandpère that the
first chance I get."

"That will please him very much."

"So?"

"So, I think you already know the answer to your question. The
pouch becomes a wise and powerful guardian for whoever is the
keeper of the pouch."

"It's function is to protect me? And our family, too, of course?"

"Oh, it is much more than that. It will teach you things if you let
it. Guide you. Sometimes even rebuke you, if necessary."

"I know what you mean."

"I don't understand it entirely, Carruthers. Obviously, it's because
of *Le Gardien* that you have been able to do what you have done. I
don't know how to describe it. Somehow it becomes interactive with
us, extending its power to us. It watches over us, protects us, warns of
us danger—"

"Put thoughts into our minds, or helps us think clearly."

"Exactly. And it is this relationship, this invisible bond between
the pouch and its owner, which empowers and enables us. This is
why we can do things greater than ourselves. It is a gift given to very
few, but it is the pouch which makes the gift a reality."

"Why does Grandpère still have some of those powers when he's no longer the keeper?"

"Because if you are wise, you learn and grow and mature, and you don't need it the same way anymore."

She turned on her side so we were looking directly into each other's eyes. "I guess one of the reasons I don't like the word *magic* is because it brings up images of wizards and witches. But that's pure fantasy. The pouch isn't like that. There are no magic wands or love potions or invisibility cloaks. We can't cast spells on someone, or curse them. As far as I know, it doesn't help us see around corners or foresee the future."

"But, Mom, sometimes I know when something bad is going to happen."

"That's not the same as seeing the future. The pouch works more through giving us feelings—premonitions, feelings of danger, or a strong confirmation that we need to do something. But it also engages our minds, inspiring us at just the right moment to do what needs to be done. And occasionally, it does something quite remarkable."

"Like putting a pistol in a pouch?"

"Or making thousand-dollar bills. Did you know that the US government hasn't made a bill larger than the one hundred dollar bill since 1969?"

"Really?" I grinned. "It also made a bobble-head doll of El Cobra."

"It did what?"

I realized I'd left that part out in my narrative, so I told her quickly about *Cobra Pequeño*.

She put her hand over her mouth to stop from laughing out loud. "No wonder he hates you so much."

"Well," I said, "you've got to admit. That's hardly normal."

She sighed. "I know. That's the part I don't understand. But, as I've thought about it, I decided that those things only happen when something is required that we can't do ourselves."

As she spoke, I realized something with a start. "Why do you keep saying 'us' and 'we'? Were you a keeper of the pouch once?"

She gave a deep, pain-filled sigh. "Yes."

"But I thought—"

"You thought I had been skipped over because I'm too superstitious."

"Well . . ." She had nailed it. That was exactly what I thought.

"So, that brings us back to your first question. Why do I feel like I do about Friday the thirteenth?" She sighed, and it was filled with sorrow. Then she laid on her back again, staring up at the ceiling. "I think I'm ready to answer that now."

CHAPTER 72

As Mom spoke, her voice was so low that I had to move closer to hear her. As I did so, she took my hand, clutching it tightly.

"On the day I turned thirteen," she began, "which was not a Friday, and certainly not the thirteenth, Grandpère took me into the back country of Rocky Mountain National Park. There he taught me about the Four Remembers, then gave me the pouch, just as he did with you."

I was astonished. Grandpère had said that not everyone had the gift and sometimes the pouch skipped a generation, so I had just assumed he meant Mom.

"He actually began to show me how it worked. Later, he admitted that had been a mistake, that it was best to let people learn from the pouch itself. I was dazzled by the whole concept, actually. In fact, I decided I was a sorceress, a good witch, sent to right the wrongs of the world." She turned her head, and I could sense her sadness. "I'm afraid I became quite prideful about it. Pretty headstrong."

I winced, not sure I wanted to hear any more.

"One day, when I was about your age, I was with a group of boys and girls at a party. We were just hanging out, having a good time. There was one boy there that I had my eye on. But so did my best friend. We had this quiet competition going on between us. Without really meaning to, I decided to put her in her place by taking her down a peg or two. So I told the group I could read people's thoughts. That was an exaggeration, of course, but I could often discern what people were thinking. So we started a game. They'd think of something, and I would tell them what they were thinking."

"And the pouch let you do that?"

"Was it the pouch or me? I'm not sure. But I will say this. I didn't know it then, but the pouch sometimes grants us things even though they may not be good for us or wise."

"I know," I said in a whisper.

She gave me a quizzical look, but went on. "When it was my friend's turn, she didn't want to play. I mean, she *really* did not want to play. She wouldn't say why. So we pressed all the harder. Then . . ." She stopped and closed her eyes. "Then suddenly I knew what she was thinking."

"What was it?"

"She was thinking about him. About the boy. She had such a terrible crush on him. She had his picture on the wall with hearts around it. She wrote a love poem to him in her journal. She would drive by his house late at night and sit across the street fantasizing about him asking her to the prom, or them running off to Las Vegas to get married."

A sense of horror was creeping in me. "And you told the others that?"

Her eyes closed. "I did. I told them all of it."

"What happened?"

"Well, she fled, of course, absolutely humiliated. The rest of us thought it was hysterical. The boy left the party a few minutes later and never spoke to me again." One tear appeared at the corner of her eye and trickled down her cheek. "That night, my friend went home and took a whole bottle of her mother's sleeping pills."

I gasped. "No!"

"Thank heavens her parents discovered what had happened and rushed her to the hospital. They pumped her stomach, and she was fine." She was speaking so softly, I had to strain to hear her. "It took me almost two years to regain her friendship, but eventually, we became best friends again. We still write regularly. I was maid of honor at her wedding."

"Kendra?" I burst out. "That was Kendra?" Kendra Wilson was one of my favorite adult people in the whole world. She and my mom were closer than sisters.

"Yes," she said, staring at her hands. "The next morning, I gave the pouch back to Grandpère. Nothing he could ever say or do changed my mind. I knew I wasn't worthy of it." She met my eyes. "There's one more thing, Danni."

I waited.

"The morning I gave back the pouch back to Grandpère was Saturday, October 14, 1995." She stopped, waiting for my reaction, but I was drawing a blank. And then I knew.

"The party was on Friday night?"

"Yes."

"Friday the thirteenth." It wasn't a question.

She laid her hand on my cheek. "I know it's silly. Even neurotic. Up until then, it was nothing more than this nagging uneasiness. We had people in our family line who were born on Friday the thirteenth, and we had those to whom bad things happened on the thirteenth day of the month. But after that night, I was convinced that there was a curse on me, on Fridays, and on the thirteenth day of the month."

She sighed. "Did you know that in high school, I never went out on a date on a Friday? Or when it was the thirteenth? I made up some excuse or another, but I didn't dare do it because I thought I would be punished." She gave another weary sigh. "I'm better now, but—" She shrugged. "But I still can't help feeling nervous about it. What do you call it again?"

"Friggatriskaidekaphobia."

"The name is almost scarier than the disease."

I smiled. "Thanks for telling me, Mom. I won't bug you about it anymore."

"I find that hard to believe," she teased, "but I'll hold you to it."

"Mom, you said that you'd let me read Grandma Angelique's journal someday, when I was older. After this is over, could I do that? Read all of it?"

"After this is over, you will definitely be older."

"And I'm going to ask Grandpère if I can read Grandma Monique's life story too."

"Would you mind if we read them together?"

I snuggled against her. "I wouldn't mind that at all," I said happily.

CHAPTER 73

The next morning, I was brushing out my hair in front of the tiny mirror over the equally tiny bathroom sink that was in one corner of our bedroom.

Mom came over to stand by the door. "Your hair is getting so long, Carruthers. It's beautiful."

"Thank you." I looked at her in the mirror. "Can I ask you something else, Mom?"

"My goodness, so many questions. What has gotten into you?"

"I think you've been there most of the times when El Cobra has called me on the phone, right?"

"Yes, as far as I know."

"Am I being stupid or just plain nuts?"

"I'm not sure what you mean."

"Let me put it this way. I'm a sixteen-year-old kid who's bumbling her way through this whole thing. Armando is a professional criminal."

She started to say something, but I held up my hand. "No, let me finish. But when I talk to him, something comes over me, and it's like he's the sixteen-year-old kid and I'm the adult. I'm glib, flippant, insulting. I disagree with him, tell him what he will and won't do, hang up on him."

A tiny smile appeared around her eyes. "You just described almost every sixteen-year-old kid in America."

I couldn't help it. I laughed out loud, then clapped a hand over my mouth.

She sobered. "When you kept hanging up on him the other day, he was absolutely livid. I thought he was going to burst a blood vessel."

"That's just it. What am I thinking? It's like I have this crazy woman in my head who starts speaking for me. The words just pop out of my mouth, and sometimes I'm as surprised as he is. I'm not normally like that."

Our eyes locked in the mirror, then a slow smile stole across her face.

"Well, I'm not," I cried. "Am I?"

"I guess I'd have to say that you're easy to get along with—as long as I don't ask you to wear a dress, put a ribbon in your hair, or wear high heels. And nylons? Forget it—that would be like starting World War Three."

"Mom," I wailed, "no one my age wears nylons. They're for old ladies."

"Yeah, old ladies like twenty-five and thirty."

"All right, I get it, Mom. But this is different. I can't stop goading this guy, needling him, digging at him, trying to get a rise out of him. What if I push him too far and he snaps?"

She sobered immediately. "You're right, Carruthers. I shouldn't treat it lightly." She pursed her lips, deep in thought. "Let me ask you a question. Is it possible that some of what is happening is happening under the influence of the pouch?"

"Yes, I think so. At least sometimes." I came out of the bathroom and joined her in the bedroom. "Why?"

"I don't know, the thought just occurred to me. If it is, that would make a difference in my mind. El Cobra is a very dangerous man, Carruthers, but he is also a very vain one. And while you often infuriate him, I think he has some respect for you, too. You've met Eileen. Do you think she's a doormat?"

"You're kidding, right?"

"That's just it. She's a spitfire—hot-tempered, tongue like a branding iron, full of passion and courage. I've seen her tear into him like a terrier taking on a Great Dane. And he takes it." She looked at me directly. A frown creased her forehead. "When you talked to him yesterday about you and Rick giving yourself up, it occurred to me that sometimes he treats you with more deference than he does his own men."

In a way that made me feel better, but in another way, it was troubling. "You talk like the pouch has . . . what? Intelligence?"

She cocked her head. "Was it you who thought up the bobble-head doll? I don't think so. Yet that was so absolutely perfect for him and his inflated ego. And when you and Cody ran and hid in the attic, did you decide that invisibility was the perfect solution? No. You just wanted not to be found. What is intelligence if not the ability to make choices that determine outcomes?"

"Hmm." I flopped backward on the bed, my mind spinning with possibilities. She sat down beside me. "Just be careful, Carruthers. Don't push him too far. He is quickly coming to the end of his patience, and I fear that if he really loses his temper, it could be very ugly." She sighed. "On the other hand, stand your ground. It gives you an advantage with him. Do whatever you have to do to get us out of here."

"I will, Mom. I will." I sat up, then got up. "Which reminds me—I need to go swimming today."

"Swimming?"

"Yeah. The sooner the better." I leaned in and dropped my voice. "I've got to contact Clay and talk about what happens today and when. So back me up, will you?"

"El Cobra's not going to let you do that."

"We'll see." I retrieved the pouch from beneath my pillow. "We'll see."

Her eyebrows creased, and her eyes were suddenly troubled. She came to me and touched my shoulder briefly. "Just remember. They didn't name him El Cobra for nothing."

CHAPTER 74

Rick and I volunteered to do the dishes after breakfast, but Armando was in an expansive mood and made his men do it. He and Eileen left us with two guards and went out to confer with the other men. Mom, Cody, Rick, and I sat around for almost two hours with our heads together, the two guards watching us in obvious boredom.

The phone rang shortly before noon, and El Cobra came running. From what we gathered from our side of the conversation, Dad and Grandpère were down off the mountain. Everything had gone smoothly at the mine. The Canadians were pleased and had left for Salt Lake. El Cobra's men were on their way to Bullfrog and would deliver the hostages to the houseboat in about an hour and a half.

That put El Cobra in a good mood. Things were finally working according to *his* plan. And having all of the chickens in the coop would put him fully back in control again.

I decided it was time to act. "Armando?"

Eileen, who was near the door, whirled. "His name is not Armando. Not to you. It is El Cobra."

"And my name is not *chiquita*. Not to him. It is Danni."

He laughed. "What is it you want, *chiquita*?"

"I'm going for a swim this morning."

"No swimming. The water is too cold."

"That's the point," I shot right back. "This boat is an oven. I need some space."

"No one is going swimming," he snapped.

I pointed out the window. "I'm only going to that rock slide. I'll be in sight the whole time. And if it makes you feel better, I'll wear a life jacket." Which I planned to do anyway. It was critical for what I had planned.

Rick stood up. "I'm going with you."

Cody also got to his feet. "Me too."

Mom chimed in. "Let's make it a family swim."

"Silence!" he roared. "Do you take me for an idiot? No one goes swimming today. No one."

I started for the bedroom. "All right, no family swim," I said. "But *I* am going for a swim."

"Then one of my men is going with you."

I stopped at the door and turned around. I pulled the pouch in front of my chest as if it were a shield. "Are you really going to fight me on this?" I asked wearily.

The boat's generator, which provided constant background noise, sputtered. The overhead lights flickered. I looked up at them. "Are you?"

He glared at me, his chest heaving. "No more than half an hour," he conceded.

"No, Armando!" Eileen cried. "Don't let her go. She's up to something."

He shook his finger at her. He never said a word, but her eyes dropped and she turned away.

"Half an hour," I agreed. "If it makes you feel safer, put a man with a rifle on the roof to watch me. He can shoot me if it looks like I'm having too much fun." I went over to a chest and grabbed a life jacket, then went back in the bedroom, shut the door, and locked it.

———

When I returned a few minutes later in my new swimming suit, every eye in the room turned to look. The suit was pale lavender with a dark purple floral pattern. The moment I had seen it, I knew it would set off my dark hair and tan skin. And I knew Rick would like it. Of course, the bright orange life jacket didn't add much class, but since that held my radio wrapped in a plastic bread sack in place under my arm, I had to live with it. I also had the pouch over my shoulder, under the jacket. Come to think of it, maybe the overall effect wasn't quite as stunning as I thought.

However, I immediately saw that El Cobra's men didn't agree with that assessment. The two of them stared at me openly, unashamedly. El Cobra was at the kitchen table with Eileen, looking at some papers. When he looked up, his eyes widened, and he actually gawked at me. It was embarrassing. I wasn't used to being looked at like that.

Eileen watched her husband for about five seconds, then slugged him hard on the arm. *"Eres un cerdo,"* she spat. "You are a pig! She is a little girl." Then she leaped up and stomped out of the room.

Pretending that I hadn't noticed, I headed for the door, the pouch over my shoulder. Rick followed me out. As soon as we were outside, he said under his breath, "Do you have the radio?"

I nodded and patted the pouch. "I pinched a bread sack from the garbage this morning."

"Hey! *Niñito,*" El Cobra's voice barked from behind us. "Get away from her."

Rick turned, keeping me shielded from view. My heart was suddenly hammering, and my hands trembled. But I managed to appear calm as Rick stepped away and headed back for the door.

"I'm not a little boy," Rick said as he passed El Cobra, who raised one hand as if he was going to cuff him across the back of his head. Rick never even glanced at him.

Before Armando could come any closer, I ran lightly down the gangplank and onto the beach. It was close to noon, and the sand was hot. I hopped back and forth down to the water, then sighed with relief when I stepped into the lake.

"Hey, *chiquita*," Armando called. "Surely you do not want to get your pouch wet. Bring it to me, and I'll keep it safe for you." He cackled loudly.

I neither answered nor turned to look at him. Wading out quickly, gasping as the cold hit me, I dove forward and broke into a strong breaststroke.

He shouted something else, but I was making too much noise to hear.

———

The rock slide was rougher than it looked from a distance. Clambering about like a crab, fully aware that El Cobra was watching me through binoculars—the thought made my flesh crawl—I finally found a slab big enough to let me stretch out. Turning my back to him, I removed the life jacket and the pouch and laid them beside me. I took a minute to shake the water from my hair, then stretched out on my stomach.

I waited a full three minutes before I turned my head enough to see the houseboat. El Cobra was still there, but he was not looking through the binoculars anymore. He and Eileen were having a battle royal, judging from the sound of their voices drifting across the water.

I suspected I knew what it was about and briefly wondered if I could use it somehow to my advantage.

The instant that thought came, I thrust it away. I would not—could not—play up to this guy, no matter what leverage it gave me. The thought of having him touch me, or even be close to me, made me shudder.

I turned away from the boat. Then, moving slowly and deliberately, I went to work. I took out the bread sack and unwrapped the radio. I checked the volume control to make sure it was on low, then hit the transmit button.

"Clay Pigeon, this Danny Boy. Do you copy?" Clay pigeons were Frisbee-like plastic saucers that machines hurled up in the air that people used for target practice. Clay had probably shot more than his share of them.

There was a soft crackle, then almost immediately Clay's voice came on. "Ah, Danni," he said with real pleasure in his voice. "Clay Pigeon. Nice touch. How are you doing?"

"Everything here is as expected. Oh, except there are two guys in ranger uniforms in the boat guarding the entrance to the canyon."

"Not anymore," he said, sounding pleased with himself. "We took them totally by surprise about half an hour ago. We now have two of our men in identical uniforms in their boat."

"What if El Cobra checks in with them by radio?"

There was a soft sound of exasperation. "Come on, Danni. Give us a little credit. A gun to the head buys a lot of cooperation, even from bad guys."

"Sorry. How many men do you have?"

"Five on the cliffs, including one sniper and four mountaineers. Six more coming in the rubber boats, two of those with scuba gear. Then there's me and two other agents with your father and grandfather. So counting our two substitute rangers, that's eighteen in all. Are those good enough odds for you?"

I felt an enormous weight lift from my shoulders. "That's wonderful. Thank you, Clay. Will you have Dad and Grandpère by then?"

He laughed softly. "Hold on."

Another voice came on the line.

"Hello, Danni."

"Dad!" Tears sprang to my eyes. "Is that you?"

"It is. And Grandpère's right here beside me."

"You're free? But how?"

"Clay's team was waiting for us at the parking lot. Our two guards never even saw them coming. Both of them are in the boat with us, maintaining radio contact with the houseboat."

Clay came back on. "I'm glad you called in, Danni. We're moving the timeline up, but weren't sure how to let you know."

"Wonderful. How soon?"

"Hold on."

A moment later another familiar voice came on. "Monique?"

Monique? It was Grandpère's voice, but why had he called me Monique? I brushed it aside. "Oh, Grandpère, it's so good to hear your voice again."

"And yours too, Danni. How's your mother?"

"Fine. Cody too. They've been treated well."

"Wonderful. We're anxious to see you all."

"Me too, Grandpère. More than you can know."

"Monique?"

"Yes?" I answered hesitantly.

"Remember Tuesday night, as we were coming home from the mine? You and me and Mack were talking about what we might do with the money from the sale. Do you remember that?"

"Uh . . . yeah." What was Grandpère talking about?

"Then, just as we were almost home, you had this wonderful feeling come over you. Remember?"

Wonderful feeling? It was an awful, terrible feeling.

"Well, I just wanted you to know I have that same feeling right now. We're so anxious to see you again, and so happy, even if everything isn't working out as planned."

I stared at the phone in horror. Goose bumps popped out on my arms and chills ran up my back. Something was wrong. He was trying to warn me. At that instant, the feelings of that night came sweeping back—a feeling of danger, of evil, of something being terrible wrong. I clicked the radio again.

"I understand, Grandpère. I'm having those same feelings too. I'm so excited to see you again. I love you."

"I love you too, Danni," he said softly. "Be wise. We'll be there in about an hour."

I immediately sat up and grabbed the pouch. As I started to replace the radio in the plastic sack, the feeling came that doing so would be a mistake. They were going to search me when I got back. I knew it! I dropped the radio and the bag in a gap between the fallen rocks. Wincing as the cold, wet fabric of the pouch touched my warm skin, I hurriedly put it over my shoulder, then strapped on the life jacket.

I stared across the water at the houseboat. Everything seemed normal. Armando and Eileen were no longer in sight. One guard was pacing on top of the houseboat. Another guard was standing in front of the tent. Both were smoking cigarettes and looked very alert. There was no one else in sight.

That should have been reassuring, but alternating waves of dread and fear were washing over me, wrenching my gut and making my whole body tremble. Scrambling across the rocks, I reached the water and waded out into the water. Then I dove and started swimming as fast as I could toward the houseboat.

As I pulled myself through the water, Grandpère's words echoed over and over in my mind. *Be wise.* I didn't have any trouble translating what he really meant. *The difference between intelligence and stupidity is that there is a limit to intelligence.* Rick's voice chimed in. *Just because we learn from our mistakes, doesn't mean they weren't mistakes. I have this feeling that when you and I step onto that boat, you're going to be so hell-bent on delivering your family that you'll make another mistake. And this time, maybe everything won't work out exactly as you have planned.*

I pushed myself harder and harder; I had never felt so alone, so inadequate, so forlorn, so . . . so stupid. And I realized I was crying bitterly as I cut through the water.

As I approached the beach, I heard Grandpère's voice again. But this was more than just remembering what he had said. I actually heard his voice in my mind.

You are Angelique Chevalier. You are Monique and Pierre LaRoche. You are the young King David. You are Aron Ralston.

As my feet touched bottom and I stood up and pushed forward toward the shore, his words concluded in slow cadence, each word emphasized with great solemnity.

You are Carruthers Monique McAllister. You are the keeper of the pouch. And you are not alone.

CHAPTER 75

The first thing I noticed was that the guard contingent had doubled. The one on the roof was now two. The one by the tent had moved closer to the cliffs, and a fourth guard was standing at the front door. All four had their weapons up and ready. All four were on full alert.

With a sense of gnawing uneasiness, I went up the gangplank and onto the boat. As I approached the door, the guard stepped back, his eyes never leaving me. The front door led directly into the main living area of the houseboat. It was airy and spacious. All of the drapes were drawn back, so the room was flooded with sunlight. I stopped short as I entered the room.

The first thing that caught my eye was Mom and Cody sitting at the dining table, against the window. Mom's cheeks were stained wet, and her eyes were red and swollen. Cody sat beside her, rigid as a steel pole. At the end of the bench, Rick sat with his face turned away from me. I was surprised when he didn't look up.

Eileen was seated at the table too. El Cobra stood behind her, one hand on her shoulder, the other one holding a pistol. Both of their faces were hard as flint. The sharp sound of me drawing in air was the only sound in the room.

"Come in, *chiquita*," El Cobra said, his voice tight and strained.

"What's going on here?" I said, but it came out sounding pretty feeble.

And then I saw it. On the table directly in front of Eileen was Rick's handheld radio. It was designed to easily fit in the palm, but at that moment, it looked as big as a wheelbarrow. Armando came around the table. He picked up the radio, tossing it lightly up and down in his hand. "Did you really think I would be so blind as to not see the radios you had hidden?"

I didn't answer. I was too stunned. The pouch had betrayed me again. The radios had not been invisible. El Cobra had simply left them for this very purpose, to trap us. Had he found them in time to listen to everything I'd said out on the rock? Of course he had. That was why he hadn't fought any harder to stop me from going swimming.

Stupid! Stupid! Stupid! But why didn't Le Gardien *warn me?*

Eileen stirred. "Tell her to put some clothes on."

We all jumped as he swung around, raging at her. "Don't tell me what to do, woman!" he screamed. "Who cares what she's wearing?"

She shrank back, as stunned as we were. I glanced at Rick and openly gasped. Rick dabbed at his nose with a crumpled napkin that was spotted with blood. Across his left cheekbone was a bright red, nasty-looking welt about three inches long. I whirled back to El Cobra. "What did you do to him?" I cried.

"Search her," El Cobra barked at Eileen. "And be thorough about it."

She came over to me. As she approached, I took off the life jacket and let it drop to the floor. She ripped off the pouch, wrenching my shoulder, and tossed it to her husband. Then she patted me down very thoroughly. When she turned and shook her head, he stalked forward.

"Where is it?"

No more flippancy. No more pushing his buttons. I could tell his fury was on the verge of exploding. "I left it on the rocks."

"Why?"

"Because I was afraid you might search me."

In a blur, his free hand shot out and grabbed me by the hair. He yanked back so hard my back arched. I bit my lip to stop from crying out.

"No!" Mom yelled. "Don't hurt her."

He bent over me, his face no more than an inch from mine. "What happened to my men in Cathedral Valley? And don't give me some story about them being frightened of the pouch."

I could smell cigarettes and liquor on his breath. "Once you were gone, the pouch made their phone go dead. Rick was hiding behind a sand dune with a rifle. They surrendered without a struggle, and the FBI took them away."

"So the whole thing was a trap?"

"Yes."

"And Raul and Lew?"

"We led them into the canyon long enough to let the FBI move in behind us. It was really quite simple, actually."

He let me go, but as I straightened, his hand flashed again. The back of his hand caught me full across the right cheek. I screamed, and staggered back, reeling from the blow. The thought flashed across my mind that if he wore a ring, I would have a scar like Monique.

Rick leaped to his feet and charged, fists swinging. Calm as a summer morning, El Cobra raised his pistol and fired. Rick went down like a scythe had cut his legs out from under him, clutching at his left thigh. I screamed. Mom screamed. Cody screamed.

El Cobra was back on me, like a pouncing wolf. Again he grabbed me by the hair, yanking my head back hard. "Stop fighting me, or the next one goes into his heart," he hissed.

"Okay. Okay," I cried. "Don't shoot him."

Mom rushed out from behind the table and dropped to her knees beside Rick, who was writhing on the floor, holding his leg and moaning in pain.

"Stay away from him," El Cobra shouted at her, raising the pistol again.

I kicked out at him with all my strength. He stepped aside and laughed as I missed him, then yanked even harder on my hair until I was bent backward. "I'm not playing, Mrs. McAllister. Get back. Now!"

Cody was sobbing, begging her to come back. She did lean back, but she stayed on her knees beside Rick. She looked up at her captor, eyes calm, face expressionless, staring at him, daring him to fire.

He was breathing heavily and, from my position, I could see his finger twitching on the trigger. But gradually, sanity returned. He lowered the pistol and looked over his shoulder at his wife. "Get her the medical kit. See if you can stop the kid's blubbering."

He turned back to me. Hauling me back up until only my neck was bent backward, he glared at me, eyes seething. He leaned in until our faces were nearly touching. His grin was feral, evil, more horrible than anything I could imagine. I went totally cold. And then he kissed me. It was not a kiss of passion. It was a kiss of domination—hard, brutal, crushing my lips against his teeth. When he finished, he let me go and gave me a hard shove. I nearly stumbled as I fell away from him.

"Now, *chiquita*," he said, handing me the radio, breathing hard. "Now, we're going to make a call to your friends in the FBI."

PART ELEVEN

CHAPTER 76

"Clay Pigeon, this is Bright Star Two. Over."

"Yeah, Danni. We're here. What's up?"

El Cobra yanked the radio from my hand and shoved me away. "I'll tell you what's up, *señor* FBI man," he screamed into the radio.

I ran to Rick and dropped down beside him, clutching tightly to one of his hands. I was crying, sick at heart. The wound was in his upper left thigh, off to the right of center. Mom had her hand clamped over the wound but blood still oozed out from between her fingers. Rick looked up at me as I took his hand and managed a wan smile.

As El Cobra continued screaming orders into the radio, Eileen returned with a white tin box with a red cross painted on it and a pair of scissors. She knelt down beside us and began cutting up Rick's pant leg. I lifted my head and started paying attention to what was going on over the radio.

El Cobra had finally stopped screaming and released the transmit button.

Clay came on immediately. "Is everyone all right?"

"Everyone except the boyfriend," he hissed. "I shot him."

I heard Dad cry out in the background. "Danni!"

"That's right, Luke," Armando screeched. "Call for your little girl, because she is in grave danger. As are you."

"Am I talking to the man they call El Cobra?" Clay asked. He was trying to sound calm, but it was clear he was deeply shaken.

"I am not the man they *call* El Cobra. *I am El Cobra!* And you are about to see the cobra strike." Drops of spittle sprayed from his mouth as he shrieked into the radio. "Do you understand me? I will kill them all, one by one, and let you and the father and the grandfather listen to their screams as they die. *¿Comprendes?*"

For several seconds, there was no response. Then Clay quietly asked, "What do you want us to do?"

"We heard your conversation with Danni, *señor*. Every word of it. I know your plans. I know how many men you have. So here is exactly what you will do. I hope you and your agents are taking notes because I am only going to say this once."

"I'm listening."

"You will pull back immediately," he spat. "If I hear one shot fired, see one head poke up, hear the whisper of one boat engine, or see one aircraft within five miles of this position, I will open fire on the family. Tell them, *señor*. Tell them to back off."

"You heard the man," Clay said. "Pull back to your original positions and wait for pickup. Marty?"

"I'm here, boss," said a deep voice.

"Call Salt Lake. Have them contact the airport at Bullfrog. We need the airspace over this part of the lake totally cleared."

"Ten-four." Brief pause. "Good luck." Then he clicked off.

El Cobra was back on immediately, but he was calmer. "That's better. Second. You and the men with you will, this very moment, surrender your weapons to the four men of mine that you hold captive. You will also give them back their satellite phones and have them call me immediately to confirm this is so."

Almost immediately, a cell phone rang. El Cobra snatched it up. "¿*Sí?*" He listened for a couple of moments, then started firing off questions in Spanish. He kept nodding, so I assumed he was hearing what he wanted to hear.

By this time, Eileen had cut away the rest of Rick's pant leg. When she pulled the fabric back, I gagged and nearly fainted. There was blood all up and down his leg, and the hole where the bullet had entered showed raw flesh inside of it.

"I've always had that effect on girls," he croaked.

I laid my cheek against his. "I'm so sorry, Rick. It's my fault. It's all my fault. I'm so sorry."

"There you go again, taking all the credit for yourself."

He raised his head a little, grimacing with pain, until his mouth was near my ear. "Did you hear it?"

I reared back. "Hear what?"

"Your grandfather's voice."

"You heard it too?" I asked, astonished.

He began quoting softly. "Angelique. Monique. Pierre. King David. Aron Ralston."

I could scarcely believe it. He *had* heard. I started to straighten, but he pulled me back. "And Yogi Berra."

My eyes widened. Yogi Berra? The famous baseball player? For a moment, I wondered if Rick was in shock. I looked down at him to see if he was joking, but he nodded vigorously at me. And then I understood. Dad quoted Yogi Berra all the time. Things like "The future ain't what it used to be," and "When you come to a fork in the road, take it." But the one he quoted more than any other, especially when things looked bleak, was this classic: "It ain't over 'til it's over."

I sat back on my heels. I wanted to lay my hand on Rick's cheek, bend down and kiss him, lay down beside him and hold him. But instead I slowly nodded. "Thank you," I said. "I understand." I got to my feet.

"Don't talk, " Eileen said to him. She looked at Mom. "There is no exit wound. The bullet is lodged somewhere inside his leg." She looked down at Rick, and I thought I actually saw sympathy in her eyes. "We have to bandage your wound. It's going to hurt very badly." She straightened. "Armando, we have to get him to a doctor."

He hooted in disgust. "Oh yeah, that one's high on my priority list." He immediately went back to speaking Spanish into the telephone. Finally he said, *"muy bien,"* then switched to English and spoke into the radio.

"Okay, *señor.* My men are in charge. Do not try anything foolish."

"We are not fools," Clay said.

"Bueno. That is *muy importante* if you want anyone to come out of this alive." He released the transmit button and walked to the table where he sat the phone and the radio down beside the pouch. Then he looked to the nearest guard. "Get everyone in here. *¡Pronto!"*

As the man rushed out and started hollering, El Cobra turned to us. Mom and Eileen were wrapping Rick's leg. He grunted softly each time they moved him. Beads of sweat stood out on his forehead, and there were tears in his eyes.

Mellower now that he was back in control, El Cobra came over and watched for a moment. Then he reached down and grabbed Mom by the elbow. "Up. Eileen will finish."

She jerked her arm away angrily. "You're a monster."

"No," he said thoughtfully, "actually, I'm a snake." Then he pulled hard, dragging her to her feet. She cried out in pain. "I told you to get up," he snarled.

I leaped forward. "Leave her alone!"

"Be patient, *chiquita*. I'm coming back for you."

As he started to herd Mom back to her seat, I went after him, hands up like claws. Quick as a cat, he spun around, and I had the barrel of his pistol pointing at my nose, no more than six inches away.

"Don't!" he yelled.

But I was swept up in an emotion I had never experienced before—pure, undiluted rage. I spun around, and, before he could stop me, I was to the table. I snatched up the pouch, clutching it tightly against my chest with both hands. I dropped into a crouch as he came after me lunging for the pouch. He stumbled over my feet, and we both went down. We sprang back up to face each other, panting heavily. His smile was a horrible grimace.

"Give me the pouch," he said, his chest heaving.

"Come and get it," I hissed.

He spun around and took two steps to where Rick was on the floor. With a swipe of his hand, he knocked Eileen away. Then he leveled the pistol at Rick's head. The sound of him cocking the hammer was like an explosion going off in the room. "Give me the pouch or he dies."

He's going to kill him anyway. I remembered what I had said to Rick earlier: *You're a liability. You're excess baggage.*

Grabbing the pouch in both hands, I held it out in front of me. One word burst from my mouth, and I shouted it with all the force in my lungs. "Stop!"

An invisible force slammed into him. The pistol fired as it was knocked away, the bullet hitting the wall. He went flying—literally flying—backward. He hit one of the chairs and flipped backward onto the floor.

Eileen screamed and ran to him in three steps. She dropped down beside him, helping him get up. He was dazed, momentarily disoriented.

He wasn't the only one. My hands were tingling like I had stuck them in a wall socket. The pouch felt hot to the touch, and I dropped it where I stood. I backed up a step, then another.

Eileen helped El Cobra to his feet. He looked at me as if he wasn't sure who I was. Then, with an animal roar, he came at me again. This time I said nothing, but scooped up the pouch and flung it at him, flat like a Frisbee. The rope strap was flying out behind it, and it caught him squarely in the chest. There was a great whoosh. He dropped to his knees, eyes bulging, frantically gasping for air. Eileen started for him again, but when she saw me coming at him, she threw her hands in front of her face and screamed.

I snatched up the pouch, then crouched down so that I was looking directly into his eyes. He was still gasping desperately for air. His face was turning purple. I leaned in. "I will go with you. I will give you the pouch. I will teach you how to use it." I slapped him across the face. That broke things loose and he gulped in air like a drowning man. "But if you try to kill anyone, or hurt them in any way, or if you touch me again, you will die. Do you understand me, El Cobra? You! Will! Die!"

CHAPTER 77

From where Mom, Cody, and I were sitting at the dining table, we could look out the window onto the lake. When we heard the sound of motors, we turned and watched three motorboats approaching. Rick was stretched out on the bench, his head in my lap. He started to get up, but I pushed him down again. "It's all right, Rick. It's Dad and Grandpère. They're here."

He fell back, his breath coming in quick, shallow bursts.

"Is the pain terrible?" I asked softly.

He shook his head. "Actually, it's going numb."

"You lie!" I said.

He didn't deny it.

El Cobra got up and went out on deck, pistol in hand. I could hear the guards above us moving around on the roof and assumed their rifles were pointed at the incoming boats. Dad was driving the first boat. Grandpère and Clay were beside him. They each had a man with a rifle trained on them. In the second boat there were four men, all dressed as park rangers. Two were seated, cuffed hands clasped on top of their heads. Clay's agents, I assumed. One of the original "rangers" drove the boat; the second kept guard with his rifle.

The final boat had only one man at the helm. They all cut their motors and glided into the beach, one alongside the other. We saw them get out of the boats one by one. El Cobra's men came down off the roof and swarmed around them. The four agents were marched over to one of the tents and forced to sit down back-to-back before being handcuffed together. Dad, Grandpère, and Clay were shoved roughly toward the gangplank. I could see they'd been cuffed too, with nylon cuffs like the ones I had been secured with. Moments later, we were all together in the houseboat's main room.

Dad gave a cry and started for Mom, but El Cobra leaped in front of him and stiff-armed him, hard. Dad crashed against the wall and nearly went down.

"Stay over there," El Cobra barked. "You'll have your reunion soon enough."

The guards lined up Dad, Grandpère, and Clay along the front bulkhead, then stepped back a few paces. Their rifles never wavered.

Barking orders like a drill sergeant, Armando sent Eileen back to the bedroom to pack, and ordered the men who were not standing guard inside, to pack up and prepare to leave.

Then, with a grim smile, El Cobra turned to us. "At last, we are all together."

He took out his satellite phone and dialed a number quickly. Then he held up a finger at us. *"Un momento."* We heard the faint, tinny sound of someone's voice answer, and he began speaking. My mind translated his words effortlessly. He was calling for a helicopter to meet him in one hour at the airport at Hall's Crossing. That was not good.

Hall's Crossing was across the lake from Bullfrog Marina, but was much smaller, with only a small marina, some campgrounds, the ferry ramp, a service station, and tiny convenience store.

El Cobra paused, listening to a question, then started speaking again. As my mind translated, my insides twisted into a tight knot. He had evidently been asked how many people he was bringing with him. His answer? Three. Himself. Eileen. And a sixteen-year-old girl.

Ten minutes later, satisfied with how the loading of the boats was going, El Cobra came back inside, Eileen at his side. He was all business.

"This is how it's going to work."

Every eye was turned to him. "First of all, *señor* FBI man. You will make another call to Salt Lake, and you will tell them that the four men they hold in jail at the moment are to be released no later than tomorrow morning."

"I'm not sure they will—" As Armando's head came up, eyes like cold steel, Clay changed his mind. "I will do my best."

"Oh, you will do much better than that," came the cold answer. Then he turned to Dad and Grandpère. "Though there have been many efforts to thwart our plan, we now return to it—only we're going to move things up a bit. Luke, you will call your Canadian contacts and tell them that due to a family emergency, the closing must be tomorrow afternoon."

Dad frowned. "I'm not sure all the documents can be ready that soon. Besides, it's Sunday and—"

His eyes went hard. "You're depositing twenty million dollars. I think the bank will accommodate you. You will be there when the bank opens, and you will make this happen, is that clear?"

"Yes."

"Good. You and Grandpa here will go with your two escorts in one boat. They will take you back to Bullfrog where you will pick up your vehicle and leave immediately for Salt Lake City. That will get you there tonight so you can be at the bank when it opens tomorrow morning. And by the way, you will leave your phone on at all times so we can track your every movement. If it were to be turned off . . ." He shrugged, a simple gesture, but filled with terrible menace.

"What about my family?"

"Since it is your family which has complicated everything, we shall simplify things."

That sent a shiver of fear through me.

"What do you mean, simplify?" Mom asked.

"You and Cody will stay on the houseboat. I'll be taking Danni with me."

"No!"

He went right on. "The rest of my men will be taking the other boats and dispersing themselves as quickly as possible so they can be in Salt Lake by tomorrow afternoon. That will leave you two here safely in the hands of the FBI."

He turned to Clay. "Of course, you will have no means of communicating with your agents. With the wiring removed from the houseboat's motors, there is also no way to get out of here before tomorrow. Should you somehow surprise me and be rescued sooner than that, I am sure you will not try to further interfere with our activities. Otherwise, this young girl you seem to admire so much will die. And it will not be pretty."

Clay's mouth pinched into a tight line. Mom dropped her head in her hands. Cody shot to his feet, fists clenched. "You leave my sister alone!" he cried.

"Sit down, little bantam rooster. Your courage is commendable, and if everyone here does as they are told, you shall be reunited with your sister by tomorrow evening."

He's lying. The thought came as clearly as if someone had spoken it. He wasn't going to let me go. At least not until they were safely out of the country. Which meant they would probably take me with them. I raised my hand.

He looked at me, instantly suspicious.

"What about Rick? He has to see a doctor and get that bullet removed."

"Sorry, mercy is not on the agenda today."

I changed tactics. "May I at least change back into my clothes before we leave?" I asked, forcing my voice to stay steady.

He reached down to where my life jacket still lay on the floor. He scooped it up and tossed it to me. "This will be sufficient. I think lavender is a good color on you." Eileen's head jerked around, and she glared at him. He laughed. "A very good color on you."

Grandpère took one step forward. Instantly rifles and pistols snapped up. "I will not let you be alone with my granddaughter."

El Cobra was incredulous. "Oh? You will not?"

"If you insist on having it your way, no motor will work, no radio will operate, no telephone will have a signal. And you will not meet the aircraft that is coming for you."

Once again, with that swiftness that had earned him his name, El Cobra leaped forward, his hand a blur. An instant later, he pressed the tip of a knife hard against Grandpère's throat. The room went totally still. "I don't like threats, Grandpa."

Grandpère did not so much as blink. "I think you are not a killer," Grandpère said through clenched teeth. "But should you choose to thrust in the blade, know this. The moment that happens, police departments all across the state of Utah will be alerted to the situation and will converge on you like an army even as you try to escape. Don't ask me how that will happen. I don't know. I just know it will happen. And your grand plan will end here in Iceberg Canyon on this day, and your life will come to an end in an electric chair."

As I watched this man with the gray hair, gentle face, and kindly eyes in amazement, I also saw in my mind's eye a little boy standing in a meadow, looking up into the sky. As the screams of a Stuka dive bomber filled the morning air and the German pilot bore down on him, the little boy raised a hand and waved. And a short distance away, his mother exclaimed in soft amazement, *"Enchantement."*

Eileen broke in. "You don't need her, Armando. Not once we have the money. Let it be."

Grandpère spoke again. "I am not needed at the signing. Mack can handle that by himself. And in case you doubt my word, have one of your men try to start one of the boats. Any one. It doesn't matter. Or pick up your phone and try to call someone." He spoke as casually as if he were giving instructions on how to do yard work.

El Cobra lowered the pistol and stepped back. He jerked his head at one of his men who darted outside. A moment later, we heard the starter of the nearest speedboat grinding. It went on and on, but nothing happened. At the same time, Armando snatched up his phone, punched some buttons, then put it to his ear. After a moment, he lowered it again slowly.

Grandpère spoke again. "I only want to ensure my granddaughter's safety. You have my word that I shall not interfere in any other way."

"Including no more magic?"

"I don't believe in magic," Grandpère replied.

As he stepped back against the wall and El Cobra lowered the pistol, my legs nearly buckled. I had to steady myself on the table. I looked at Grandpère through a blur of tears. *"Merci,"* I whispered.

He nodded, then smiled. *You are not alone,* he mouthed back at me.

CHAPTER 78

When we came through the narrow opening that led out of Iceberg Canyon into the main channel, Armando turned the boat sharply to the right—upstream. As soon as we reached forty miles an hour, he motioned to Eileen to take the wheel.

Grandpère was in the backseat, next to the cover which housed the twin motors. He had tried to sit down by me, but El Cobra wouldn't let him. He also had refused to let Grandpère wear a life jacket.

"You so much as blink in a way I don't like and I'll throw you overboard," he snarled. "We'll see how well your magic works underwater."

Grandpère had said nothing in response, nor had he since. But when I turned to look at him, he smiled at me. He seemed perfectly calm.

Armando picked up the pouch from the driver's seat, then stepped back and took the seat across from me. I still had my life jacket on, but I also had a towel over my legs. I had said I was cold, which was true. But it wasn't from the air temperature.

He leaned forward so his face was only a foot or so from mine. He held up the pouch and shook it a little. "Okay, *chiquita*. It's time."

I was ready. I had been thinking about it since we had left the houseboat. "There are a couple of things you have to understand about the pouch."

"I'm listening."

"You've got to get it out of your head that this is like some magic wand you just point and shoot, or that it works on some kind of rigid formula. The pouch works on what we really desire."

He cocked his head, giving me a dubious look.

"Somehow, it senses what we want or need, then responds in a way that helps us get that."

"You wanted to give me a silly doll that looked like me?" he asked, openly skeptical.

"No, I wanted to make you look ridiculous in front of your men."

He grunted and his eyes narrowed, but he said nothing.

"And it wasn't my idea to have it produce money, either. What I wanted was to let you know that having the pouch made me something much more than some silly teenager."

"Well, it did that," he admitted.

"The pouch determines how things are done. And that's just it. Often, you cannot predict what it will do. It really surprises me sometimes."

"I saw as much on your face."

"One caution. If what we want is foolish, or even wrong, the pouch may not grant it. But sometimes it does, and then it will not be for your good. You'll reap the reward of your own stupidity, if I may say it that way." I was strongly tempted to add some quip about stupidity being a natural gift of his, but I didn't.

"Yes, yes," he said, brushing that aside. "So do I have to be actually touching it to make it work?"

My nose wrinkled as I considered his question. I quickly thought back over the times when it had worked for me. I couldn't remember a time when I wasn't holding it, or when it wasn't against my body. "I don't know," I finally said. "I think so, but I'm not positive."

"It does not have to be in your hand," Grandpère spoke up. "But it is helpful, especially when you first begin to use it."

"All right." He was eager, almost little boyish. "I know what I want. Make it happen."

"No," I said. I wasn't sure if I could make this work or not. I was in over my head. "*You* have to make it happen. You've got the pouch. Hold it tightly in your hands."

I noticed that Eileen kept turning to watch what was going on. We were going at least forty-five miles an hour; I hoped she remembered to look forward from time to time.

He held it up, squeezing the seams of the pouch with his fingers. "It's hot," he said.

"That's a good sign. It often generates heat when it's working."

"I want it to make gold."

That took me by surprise. I half-expected he'd ask for more packets of thousand-dollar bills.

"Why not rhodium?" Grandpère asked.

"Rhodium?"

"It's worth about twice what gold is."

His eyes were dark with sudden anger. "And so much harder to sell on the open market without calling attention to yourself. Good try, old man. But gold will do."

I was watching Grandpère's eyes, and I saw that El Cobra's answer actually pleased him. I wasn't sure why.

El Cobra held out the pouch in front of him. "Make gold!" he commanded.

I snorted in disgust. "I told you. You're not some wizard. You don't have to shout at it. Just focus on what you want."

He considered that for a moment, then half closed his eyes. His lips began to move. For several seconds nothing happened. All four of us had our eyes fixed on the pouch. Then suddenly it was ripped from El Cobra's hand, crashing to the bottom of the boat with a heavy thud. Instantly he was down on his knees, clawing at the flap of the pouch. A moment later, he withdrew a full-sized gold bar, and, with some difficulty, got back to his feet. The gold was a stunning sight. It glowed like he was holding a piece of the sun in his hands.

He set it on the seat behind Eileen. Then, holding on to the wheel with one hand, he swept her up in the other. His expression was one of pure ecstasy. Laughing, she tipped her head back and cried, "Kiss me, you magnificent fool." Then she turned to us. "How much is it worth?" she cried.

"Current price is roughly fifteen hundred dollars an ounce," Grandpère said.

"And how much does this weigh?" Armando demanded.

"Twenty-seven point five pounds. Or about four hundred forty ounces," Grandpère said. "That bar is worth about six hundred and sixty thousand dollars."

El Cobra was stunned. For a moment I thought he was actually going to cross himself in order to thank God for his good fortune. But he had another idea. In three steps, he was back to the pouch. He picked it up, gripped the edges, and spoke to it like it was a living thing. "Again!"

This time he was ready for the weight. It took maybe ten seconds, then his arms sagged sharply. He ripped back the flap and extracted an identical bar. "One million two," he shouted at Eileen. He started to set the pouch down when it was ripped from his hands again. This time it hit the cushioned seat and bounced to the floor with a heavy crash. He stared at a third gold bar in wonder. "Two million!" There was a soft grinding sound. Another bar was pushing the other one out of the pouch. He stopped dead, staring at it in disbelief.

I looked at Grandpère. He had that same enigmatic smile on his lips, as though to say, "Be patient, my dear, and you will understand."

Armando was quickly on his hands and knees, lifting the bars and putting them on the seat across from me. As he took each one out, the end of another one would appear. In a matter of minutes, his face was bathed in sweat, and there were dark stains under his armpits and around his collar. And one after another, as if they were coming off an assembly line, the bars kept appearing.

"Move back," Armando shouted at me. The boat had three sets of seats. I was in the right middle; Grandpère was directly behind me. I stood up and moved back with him. Armando grabbed the pistol from the seat across from me and waved it at me. "Help me move these bars. Both of you."

"Are you sure you want us touching the pouch?" Grandpère asked softly.

That startled El Cobra. After a moment, he shook his head and waved us back.

Eileen turned around. "Stop it for a minute, Armando."

He grabbed the pouch, dumped another bar out, then gripped it around the edges. "Stop!" he exclaimed. And it did.

As Armando began distributing the bars evenly on the seats, I counted quickly. Eleven bars. More than five million dollars. When he was done sorting the bars, he surveyed his work. Satisfied, he touched the pouch again. "More!" he barked. Moments later, another bar clunked on the boat's bottom.

I looked around. We were in a much wider part of the main channel. Just ahead, on our right, Slick Rock Canyon led off to the south. It was a much smaller canyon, just east of Iceberg. But near its mouth there was a sandbar just off shore. It was about thirty feet long and maybe five or six feet out of the water. It was marked with a shallow water obstacle marker.

"Eileen," Armando said, pointing. "Over there."

As she swung the boat to the right and headed for the sandbar, Armando picked up the pistol again and waved it at Grandpère. "You're getting out, old man. We need the room."

"I'll be there in a minute," Eileen said.

"Out!" Armando shouted. "Now!"

I leaped up. "No! You can't do that. He doesn't have a life jacket."

"It's all right, Danni," Grandpère said. And not waiting for another prod, he jumped over the side and started swimming toward the bar in long, even strokes.

"Grandpère! Come back!"

Once Eileen saw that he was going to make it to the sandbar, she veered away and gunned the boat forward again.

"You, *chiquita!* Sit down. And don't move."

Immediately, he went back to work stacking the bars. I kept watching Grandpère anxiously, but then I saw him stand up and wade out of the lake onto the sandbar. He waved to let me know he was all right.

"I told you not to harm anyone," I said to El Cobra.

He ignored me, but he kept the pistol close at hand. Now that he had the pouch, his confidence—his *arrogance*—was back in full strength. I watched as the pouch produced another ten bars of gold. They were rapidly approaching what they hoped to get in ransom money. I did a quick calculation. The pouch was producing a new bar about every thirty seconds. *A million dollars a minute!*

Then suddenly I understood. This was the answer. Now it all made perfect sense.

"El Cobra," I said, leaning forward.

He lugged another bar in place before he looked up. "What?"

"Forget about the mine sale. Before this day is over, you'll have five times the ransom. Ten times!"

His teeth showed white in a wicked grin. *"Sí, señorita."*

"So let us go. You don't need another twenty million dollars."

He hooted in derision. "Everyone needs another twenty million dollars."

"No, Armando," Eileen said. "She's right. There's too much risk. Let her go and let's go home."

"No!" He bent down for another bar.

I lifted my hand and pointed at the pouch. "Stop!" I said.

He spun around, grabbing the pouch and clutching it to his chest. It was a flat, empty, crumpled piece of fabric. He gave an animal howl in pain. "No! More. More! Don't stop!"

When nothing happened, he grabbed his pistol and came at me, raising it to the level of my eyes.

"That's your answer to everything, isn't it?" I said in contempt.

"Make it start again, or I'll shoot."

I looked at the bars stacked on the seats ahead of me, thinking that if he shot me, he would lose the twenty million anyway. I decided it wasn't wise to point that out to him.

He took a step closer. "I mean it, *chiquita.*"

How ironic. Almost forty million dollars, and it wasn't enough. Then another thought came like a flash of light. *Twenty-one bars at twenty-seven pounds per bar*— We now had about five thousand pounds of gold in the boat.

It was like a brilliant light had just been shown in my mind. "All right," I said. "Have it your way." I looked at the pouch. "More," I said quietly.

As Armando's hands sagged downward with the sudden weight of the next bar, I stood up and rolled over the side.

———

As I neared the sandbar, Grandpère waded out to me and reached out his hand. I dropped onto the sand beside him, my chest heaving. Then I looked around. "Are they gone?"

There was a soft chuckle. "No, I wouldn't say that." He pointed.

I turned, then drew in a sharp breath. The boat was coming straight for us, but they were still about two hundred yards out in the channel. Eileen was at the wheel, but Armando was beside her, shouting and waving his pistol wildly. I got to my feet, tensing.

His words floated to us over the sound of the motor. "*Chiquita.* Stop it. Stop the pouch. We're going to swamp."

Eileen suddenly left the wheel and bent down. A moment later, there was a flash of gold and a big splash. I wanted to laugh as I saw Armando do the same. "Please, *chiquita.*" His voice floated to us across the water. He bent down and another bar plopped into the lake and sank to the bottom.

I watched closely as the boat pushed its way slowly toward us. The water was only three or four inches from the top edge of the boat. Then a noise caught my attention.

"Look!" Grandpère called out.

Coming from the opposite direction and rounding a bend in the canyon about half a mile away was a large ski boat. It was coming fast, its front end clear up out of the water. I could see several people inside.

El Cobra turned around to look. The ski boat must have been

coming at close to fifty miles an hour because it was closing in on us. A moment later, the roar of the motors abruptly cut off.

The nose of the boat dropped back into the water, sending out a wash of water ahead of it. The driver of the ski boat must have seen Grandpère and me on the sandbar and El Cobra's boat riding low in the water because it immediately swerved toward us.

Someone stood up and started waving. A woman's voice carried to us across the water. "Need some help?"

El Cobra spun around. "No!" he screamed. "We're okay. Go away."

The ski boat kept coming, but slowly. "You look like you've got problems," a man called.

They were about fifty yards away. Armando was still shouting and trying to wave them off. Suddenly, he raised the pistol in the air and fired it twice. The gunshots echoed off the cliffs with a dull boom.

"Get out of here!" he screamed.

The ski boat driver wheeled the boat around and shoved the throttle to full. The boat shot forward and they sped away.

"Not a wise move, El Cobra," Grandpère said, half to himself.

I saw instantly what he meant. The combination of a hard turn and the application of full power from the ski boat had created a huge wake. Waves were rippling outward in all directions, including toward the sandbar and El Cobra's boat.

Armando and Eileen saw it too. She screamed. He shouted something. They grabbed each other's hands and leaped over the side just before the wave hit the boat.

The boat rocked violently, once, twice. We could see the water pouring over the gunwales. There was a gurgling sound, and a moment later, the boat slipped beneath the surface, taking untold millions of dollars with it.

Grandpère and I stood together on the sandbar, watching the two figures in orange life jackets bob past us about a hundred yards away. They were swimming hard, but they were in the current, which was moving them downstream faster than they could swim toward us.

"Help us," El Cobra shouted. "Help."

I cupped my hands and shouted back. "It would probably be better if you didn't show your pistol to someone who stops to help." I had the biggest grin of my whole life on my face. It was over. Well, not fully. Someone had to find us and go after the gang and get Clay and Mom and Dad and Cody. But it was over with El Cobra.

I sat down with Grandpère and slipped my arm through his. After a moment, Grandpère reached in his pants pocket and brought out a cell phone.

"They left you your cell phone?" I cried.

"Of course. You heard the man. He said he had to keep track of us."

My mouth opened but nothing came out.

With an exaggerated flourish, he hit the button to turn on the screen.

"It won't work. Not after it's been in water."

"Oh? That's not what the man at the store said. I asked him if I were ever to accidentally fall into Lake Powell if it would continue to work. He said he thought it would."

"You did not," I exclaimed. "You're making that up."

But just then, his phone lit up and the picture of me and Cody he kept as his screen saver came up. He touched the text message button and began to type with his thumbs. He was very fast at it.

I was flabbergasted. "Who are you texting, Grandpère?"

"The FBI command center at Bullfrog." There was the tiniest

smile on his face. "Clay forgot to mention that one over the radio. Thought I'd better catch them up on things. Clay's going to be getting very anxious right about now."

I stared at him as he continued texting with what was pretty impressive dexterity. I couldn't text that fast, and his skill was totally, seriously cool in my book. I laid my head against his shoulder and hugged myself. "I'm sorry I lost the pouch, Grandpère."

"You mean the nanny pouch?"

I pulled a face. "I don't call it that anymore, Grandpère. I'm sorry I ever did."

"It's an honorable title. Or was, until Hollywood got their hands on it."

"I like *Le Gardien* much better."

"Well, then you got to that point much sooner than I did. I didn't start calling it that until I was in my midtwenties."

I pulled back to look at him. "Really? Or are you just saying that to make me feel better?"

"It's not my job to make you feel better," he chided.

"What did you call it?"

There was the slightest hint of a smile behind his eyes. "The DI."

"DI? What's that?"

"Drill instructor. That's the guy in the army who turns raw recruits into soldiers. It wasn't a term of great affection."

Well, well. So Grandpère had had his own problems with the gift. "I'm just so sorry that I lost it, Grandpère. It's been in the family for generations, and I'm the one to lose it."

"Ah, it may turn up. Maybe we should leave a notice on the bulletin board at Bullfrog or post it on Craig's Head."

"You mean craigslist?"

"Yeah, that's it. Or we could do some Twittering on your Facebooks."

I laughed, realizing he was pulling my chain again. I was such a sponge, believing everything he said. "I love you, Grandpère. Thank you for coming with me. I'll never forget it."

He sent his text, then put his phone away. His arm came up around my shoulder. "I'd give you my jacket," he said, "but I think it's colder than you are."

"I'm fine now. How soon do you think someone will be here?"

He pulled the phone out again, and, half closing one eye, peered at it. "Says here their ETA is about fifteen minutes."

I laughed again—I was doing that a lot—then kissed him on the cheek. "You are a wonder, Grandpère. An absolute wonder."

"That's what my mother always said too." He chuckled. "But she didn't mean it as a compliment."

CHAPTER 79

Grandpère was right. The FBI arrived fifteen minutes later—a team of three men in a speedboat. They waved as a similar boat raced past us going downstream; a helicopter passed overhead a few moments later. They had brought blankets, sandwiches, and bottled water. Soon we were both warm and comfortable.

Since we were closer to Iceberg Canyon than we were to Bullfrog, they wanted to wait until they heard from the others before moving out. In another ten minutes, the reports started coming in. The first one was that El Cobra and his wife were in custody. They had been picked up by a couple of bass fishermen who were now making their way back upstream. The two had surrendered without a fight; Armando had dropped the pistol when he and Eileen had jumped out of the boat.

Evidently, El Cobra had sent some kind of coded "all clear" signal for the helicopter pilot. When the pilot approached the airport at Hall's Crossing, he suddenly veered away and disappeared. The FBI still got the registration number and were following up to see where it had come from. Next came the news that Dad was free. Agents had been waiting at the marina and swarmed in before the bad guys knew what hit them. The other boat had been taken a short time later.

Finally, and best of all, about an hour after that, the other FBI team returned. The boat turned out of the main channel and joined us on the sandbar. Clay, Mom, and Cody were in it. It was a warm and sweet reunion. Clay reported that the helicopter had taken Rick to the Lake Powell Medical Center in Page, Arizona, where he would have the bullet removed from his leg. Once we got back to Bullfrog, Clay had another chopper coming in to fly me, Mom, Cody, and Grandpère to Page to see Rick. They were also flying down Charlie Ramirez and Rick's two sisters.

Since Dad, under duress, had already called his Canadian associates and moved up the signing to Monday afternoon, he decided it would be more complicated to revert back to Tuesday than to just go ahead with it. So he left with the first boat headed to Salt Lake. The rest of us planned to fly up later. What Dad will do with twenty million dollars is yet to be determined, but I'm pretty sure Rick and I will have some say in it.

That left only one group unaccounted for. The other boat with three men on it had not yet been found. Clay speculated they had turned downstream and were headed for Wahweap, down by the dam. That or Hite, which was upstream. Either way, someone would be waiting for them.

Obviously, we were all generous in our praise of Clay and his team, and I was quick to apologize for the lingering doubts I had harbored about them. In return, he promised to have our family over for dinner where we could meet his family.

As we wrapped things up and the FBI started loading things into the boats, I went to fetch Grandpère. He had walked to the west end of the sandbar and was gazing out across the water. Though the sun wouldn't go down for a few more hours, the cliffs were so high that we were in shadow. As I approached, I saw him look down, then bend over at the water's edge and retrieve something, but the light was such that I couldn't see what it was.

He started a little when I came up to him and spoke. "Did you find something, Grandpère?"

"Uh . . . no. Nothing much."

I grabbed him by the shoulders and spun him around. He still had a blanket around him, but I could see that the whole front of his shirt was wet beneath it. My eyes grew wide. "Did you find *Le Gardien,* Grandpère?"

"The pouch?" he scoffed. "It's too heavy to float, and besides, it would drift with the current. There's no way it would be clear over here."

"Then why is your shirt wet? What do you have under there?"

He seemed surprised. He turned around, looking down at where he had bent over, as if trying to figure out what I was talking about. When he turned back to face me, his shirt front was totally dry. Which only accentuated the fact that there was something beneath it, something fairly large and bulky.

"Grandpère," I chided.

He put an arm around me. "You have a vivid imagination, Danni. I think you have had way too much excitement for a girl from Hanksville. I mean, seriously, totally, way too much excitement."

And with that, he gave me a nudge forward, and we started back for the boats.

CHAPTER 80

Page, Arizona, came into existence in 1956. The town was created to support the construction of the Glen Canyon Dam, not far below the Arizona and Utah border. Now it's a modern, bustling town of about seven thousand people. It sits on the bluffs overlooking Lake Powell from the south.

The Lake Powell Medical Center in Page is a small but modern clinic serving local and regional populations, as well as any of the tens of thousands of visitors to Lake Powell who end up needing medical attention.

We arrived at the Page airport about seven thirty and found a car waiting to whisk us to the clinic. We had learned from Clay that the clinic did not have a surgical center, but the doctor was able to remove the bullet from Rick's leg without performing any major surgery. They had used only a local anesthetic, and so he was awake and in good spirits when we came trooping in. About an hour later, his father arrived with Kaylynn and Raye.

It was a small and relatively quiet group. I told Rick that he better appreciate it while he could. When word hit Hanksville tomorrow that one of their native sons had been shot by an international kidnapping ring, he was going to be inundated with calls and visitors. Frowning, he begged his Dad to let him go with us to Salt Lake. But the doctor had already nixed that. Rick had to be careful with his leg for at least two weeks; they even issued him crutches.

We all teased him about walking about town with his new "badge of honor." Kaylynn told him that they would help him look more mature, which he desperately needed. Raye said they would make him look silly.

A little before nine, a girl brought in a huge floral spray that surely must have cost several hundred dollars. She explained that the owner of the floral shop had received a call from the FBI saying this was an unusual situation and they would do whatever they could, the cost being no object. The girl handed Rick a large get-well card, then left.

"Who's it from?" Raye asked. She was sitting on the bed beside his good leg.

"All his girlfriends in Wayne County?" Grandpère suggested.

"No, only about half of them," he said with an impish grin. "There'll be more flowers coming tomorrow."

"Not!" I cried. "You are so full of yourself. I'm going to ask the doctors to put that bullet back in again."

He ignored me and opened the card. As he read it, a smile spread over his face. "It's signed Clay Pigeon."

I gave a hoot. "Really?" I walked over beside the bed. He was laughing softly to himself as he read. "What?" I said.

He looked up, then read the card out loud. "'Rick. Sorry about the flowers, but when I told my wife what had happened, she said I was to send the biggest bouquet I could find. I'm sure Danni is envious—'"

"Not!" I cried again.

He continued. "'But tell her that none of the florists we contacted could produce anything nearly as large as we needed for her on such short notice. Tell her several semitrucks will be coming to Hanksville tomorrow afternoon.'"

"Yeah, right," I said. I felt my cheeks getting warm.

My family and the Ramirez family broke into applause, which only turned my face a brilliant pink. Even Rick joined in. Then Raye and Kaylynn insisted on kissing me on the cheeks as everyone snapped pictures with their cell phones.

Finally, Rick lifted the card again. "'My wife asked if your family and the McAllisters would join us for dinner next week. We'll send a limousine so you can travel in the style to which you have grown accustomed. Then we'd like to go through a full debriefing with all of you. BTW, the Deputy Director of the FBI in Washington, DC, will be flying out to meet the both of you. Thanks for making me look so good.'"

"What's BTW mean?" Raye asked.

"It stands for 'by the way,'" Grandpère volunteered with a smile. "I think Clay must have grandchildren who text."

Rick read on, then laughed. "Listen to this. 'I've asked the doctor on call to save the bullet. Since Danni has her beat-up capris and a couple of nylon handcuffs, the bullet will give you something to show when you tell your own grandchildren about this day. With warmest thanks and much respect, Clay Zabriskie, Special Agent in Charge, Salt Lake City Field Office.'"

I turned away and looked out the window.

"Danni?" Rick asked softly. "What is it?"

I shrugged. "I was just thinking about how close I came to refusing to talk to him. Then someone came along and told me I was being stupid."

"You said that?" Charlie Ramirez said, scowling at his son.

Rick's face went red. "Well, not exactly in those words."

"I'm glad someone did," Grandpère said, giving me a look of reproof.

I touched Rick's arm. "Thank you. Thank you for being that kind of friend."

"And with that," Charlie said, looking up at the clock, "I think it's time we got two young girls to bed."

"And a boy and his mother," Grandpère said, nodding. "Let's go, Cody."

To my surprise, he didn't object. He came over and stood beside me. Then he extended his hand to Rick. "Danni's right, Rick. You're the best ever."

"And so are you, Code," he said, his voice suddenly husky. "I mean that." Then he laughed. "Us guys with only sisters—we have to stick together."

They bumped fists. "Amen to that," Cody said happily.

Mom took him by the hand. Then she looked at me. "Call me when you're ready, and I'll come get you."

"You don't have a car."

"I know. But the motel's only a couple of blocks from here."

"Okay, I would like that."

Suddenly her eyes were glistening, and she had to wipe at them with the back of her hand. Then she bent down and gave Rick a kiss on the forehead. "Thank you, Ricardo Ramirez. We are forever in your debt."

She and Cody hurried out.

"I won't be long," I called after her. "Rick needs some rest. Before all those girls show up tomorrow."

———————

After everyone was gone, I pulled up a chair alongside his bed. As I sat down, he reached out and took my hand. I smiled at him, interlocking my fingers with his. For the next several minutes, neither of us said anything. We were content just to be safe together after what seemed like months of tension and danger.

"You tired?" I finally asked.

"Getting there," he admitted, his eyes drooping a little. "The pain pills are kicking in."

"I'll get out of here and let you sleep."

"Not yet."

"I'll be back in the morning, I promise." I nudged his arm. "Before the hordes arrive."

I squeezed his hand, then stood up.

His eyes popped wide open. He wouldn't let go of my hand. "Danni, I . . ."

I raised my other hand and shook a finger in his face. "No, Rick," I said fiercely. "No apologies. Not now. Not ever."

"I . . . What makes you think I was going to apologize?"

"Because I know you," I managed to say through a choked voice.

"Okay, on one condition."

"Which is?"

"No more beating yourself up for mistakes made. Not now. Not ever. Deal?"

"You drive a hard bargain."

He laughed. "You're a hard person to bargain with."

"How did we ever get to be friends?" I asked softly.

His eyes filled with wonder. "I've asked myself that same question a dozen times this last week. I've come to one conclusion. It's not possible."

"A week? It's only been a week?"

"Yeah, can you believe that? Seems like a month."

"Or a decade." I withdrew my hand from his. "You sleep now. I'll be here first thing tomorrow."

"Okay," he murmured.

I leaned over and kissed him on the forehead, like Mom had done. As I pulled away, he smiled up at me. "You missed," he said.

"I know." I touched his cheek for a moment, then turned and walked out. "See you tomorrow."

———

I am so tired, I can barely keep my eyes open. I'll write more tomorrow, but I have to say this much tonight.

There is purpose to my life.

I am unique.

I am free to choose.

I am not alone.

Carruthers (Danni) Monique McAllister

Sunday, June 19, 2011. Page, Arizona.

ACKNOWLEDGMENTS

When I was a young boy growing up, television had just been invented, and no one I knew owned one. We had radios and phonographs, but not CDs, DVDs, iPhones, iPads, iTouches, MP3 players, Droids, laptops, desktops, flash drives, or any of the other miraculous technological marvels of today.

What we had were books.

Books came in two basic formats back then—print and audio. Only in our case, the audio formats were not performed by professional voice talent and recorded for anyone else to hear. They were performed live, usually just before bedtime, or on a day when winter blizzards kept us inside. The readers were typically parents, grandparents, or older siblings. In spite of their amateur status as readers, the experience was magical and totally enchanting.

It was my father who most frequently read to me, my brothers, and my sister at night. My love of books came as much from those countless hours of listening to his voice as it did from going to the library (nearly a two-mile walk each way) and coming back with an armload of books. As I have never taken a formal writing class, I must attribute any skills I acquired as a writer to the thousands of books I read or heard in my childhood.

———

When my wife and I married and began a family of our own, we continued the tradition of reading in our home. She often read to the children during the daytime, but bedtime stories were my responsibility, and one I warmly welcomed. It was a favorite time of day for me.

Then, about forty years ago, something happened to alter the pattern. I can't remember exactly what triggered it, but one night, I decided that rather than reading a story to them, I would make one up. The kids thought that sounded immensely fun and agreed to the plan instantly.

For some time, I had had this character in my head. It was a girl in her midteens—spunky, lively, a touch feisty—whose name was Carruthers Thompson. It was a name she detested, so she insisted on being called Carrie. I cannot for the life of me remember how I came up with that name, but it intrigued me, and she became the main character of the story.

I gave her a family, a background, and a conflict—a gang of criminals who tried to kidnap her and her younger brother and hold them for ransom. To give a touch of mystery to it all, just before the crisis hit, Carruthers came into possession of a magical pouch that did marvelous things, but was completely unpredictable.

That is the genesis of this book.

I never finished the story for my children. We were living in Southern California and my work with the Church Educational System often took me away at night. Eventually, the story just faded away. From time to time over the years, my children would bring up Carruthers, and we'd return to it briefly, but it never went much further than that. Finally, because I still liked the idea, I wrote a brief synopsis of the concept and put it in my "idea" file. And there it languished for the next thirty-five or so years while I wrote eighteen other novels.

Then, one night in November 2011, while I was in the midst of doing research on another possible historical novel, Carruthers's name popped into my mind almost like the proverbial bolt out of the blue. "Popped" is probably too weak a word. It came with such forcefulness that I could not put it from my mind.

I hadn't seriously considered her story for years, so this was a surprise to me. But even though I was engaged in something else, I found my old affection for her and her story stronger than ever. After a day or two, I decided it was time to finally bring Carruthers back to life. Carruthers Thompson became Carruthers McAllister, and her nickname became Danni rather than Carrie.

Once I committed to give Carruthers a full voice and life, I recognized immediately that I had a unique challenge. Danni is in her teens, and I am in my seventies. I had to rely heavily on those who are closer to the real life and language of today's modern teens than I am. Those included a couple of trusted friends, several of my daughters and daughters-in-law, and more than half a dozen of my grandchildren, who are experiencing all of the joy, frustration, angst, and wonder of being teenagers. Their input was invaluable in giving Carruthers life and validity. Learning "teen speak" was a growing and fun experience for me as well.

To them I express my love, my thanks, and my amazement at what they are and who they are in a world that grows increasingly more challenging for their generation.

It has taken four long decades, but now at long last I have finally fulfilled my promise to tell Carruthers's story. Happily, I can now introduce Carruthers to my children's children, and to their children's children's children.

ACKNOWLEDGMENTS

There are so many people who contribute their support, time, effort, and talents to a work as complex as a novel. I acknowledge with gratitude those whose influence will be seen and felt—if not recognized—in the novel. Their help has greatly strengthened the story and added to the quality of the finished book.

The staff at Deseret Book has been in partnership with me in writing and publishing for more than forty years now. We have not only developed a strong professional bond filled with mutual respect for each other, but we have become great friends and valued associates.